PRAISE FOR THE NOVELS OF JOE WEBER

DEFCON One

"Chilling and credible . . . An ominous, nightmarish scenario of how World War III could happen."
—STEPHEN COONTS

"A thriller not for the faint of heart. If military thrillers are for you, then *DEFCON One* is a must-read."
—*Atlantic City Press*

Primary Target

"A chilling scenario of global warfare . . . The suspense never stops."
—W.E.B. GRIFFIN

"Weber weaves a frighteningly real story of international terrorism in America . . . His knowledge of weapons, military aircraft, and terrorist tactics is superior."
—*Publishers Weekly*

Targets of Opportunity

"Some writers get better with age; Weber is among them."
—*Library Journal*

JOE WEBER

DANCING with the DRAGON

A Novel

PRESIDIO

BALLANTINE BOOKS • NEW YORK

A Presidio Press Book
Published by The Ballantine Publishing Group
Copyright © 2002 by Joe Weber

www.ballantinebooks.com

ISBN 0-89141-799-0

Manufactured in the United States of America

First Mass Market Edition: January 2003

10 9 8 7 6 5 4 3 2 1

In memory of
Joyce A. Flaherty
Literary Agent

Joyce was a wonderful friend who guided my writing career
with patience, humor, and devotion.
I will miss her.

Twenty years from now you will be more disappointed by the things you didn't do than by the ones you did.

So throw off the bowline, sail away from safe harbor, catch the trade winds in your sails. Explore. Dream.

—MARK TWAIN

Acknowledgments

I wish to thank those who assisted with the development of this book. I send a special salute to Jeannie, my wife, friend, editor, and business manager. Thank you for your contributions to every phase of my efforts.

A heartfelt thanks goes to Bob Kane and my friends at Presidio Press for their Herculean work preparing the book for release.

Other contributors include Lt. Col. Ray Ruetsch, USAF (Ret.), Lt. Comdr. Rich "Snake" Jackson, USCG, and Todd Keithley.

Prologue

The People's Republic of China poses the most dangerous as well as *least* manageable military threat the United States faces early in the twenty-first century. During the year 2000, China's leaders proclaimed in a white paper, "The One-China Principle," that if the Taiwan authorities do not agree on a peaceful settlement of reunification through negotiations, Beijing would be compelled to use military force to bring Taipei into compliance.

The Taiwan Relations Act, public law 96-8, April 10, 1979, stipulates that an assault on the island of Taiwan will be countered by the armed forces of the United States of America. Invading Taiwan is tantamount to invading the United States.

In a confrontation between the United States and China, Beijing would need only local military superiority in the narrow confines of the Taiwan Strait to counterbalance American capability. Short of striking the Chinese mainland, there is no guarantee that U.S. forces would prevail in such a scenario.

The years since the Tiananmen Square massacre have been very tenuous for Chinese-American relations. Every time Beijing and Washington seem to be making positive diplomatic progress, disaster strikes. The accidental bombing of the Chinese Embassy in Belgrade in May of 1999 caused a crisis from which Chinese-U.S. relations have never fully recovered. The tragic incident left a gnawing sense of uncertainty in Beijing and deepened nationalistic, anti-American sentiment in many Chinese citizens.

The diplomatic abyss widened on March 22, 2001, when

Singapore allowed, for the first time, a U.S. Navy aircraft carrier to make a port call in the Republic of Singapore. The USS *Kitty Hawk*'s visit to the new Changi Naval Base had a significant impact on Beijing. Chinese leaders viewed the port call as an official announcement of yet another U.S. naval base in the region, one with direct access to the South China Sea. Senior Chinese military officers considered the de facto U.S. base a frontline port in the escalating confrontation between China and the United States.

On March 31, 2001, nine days after *Kitty Hawk* arrived in Singapore, the uneasiness between Washington and Beijing snowballed into a quasi crisis when a Chinese fighter plane collided with a U.S. reconnaissance aircraft. Following the midair collision, which destroyed the jet fighter and killed its pilot, the navy EP-3E Aries II had to make an emergency landing on the Chinese island of Hainan. The crew of twenty-four men and women were detained until April 12, 2001. Relations between the two countries took a dangerous nosedive before both sides stepped back from the brink.

The spy-plane affair reminded the world that China is an authoritarian, one-party state, resistant to political change, and dependent on its military, the ultimate power broker. The generals of the People's Liberation Army exploit emotional issues like the damaged reconnaissance plane to rally the citizenry against the United States and to legitimize their regime.

Faced with a new U.S. administration, China timed its belligerence to make a point. The United States is the only barrier to Chinese ambitions in Southeast Asia, particularly in the South China Sea. The military and civilian leaders in Beijing, believing the United States to be fundamentally lazy and corrupt, were not sure whether the newly elected U.S. president would stand up to a resurgent China, or whether he would expose the softness of Washington's willpower.

The standoff with China prompted the United States to revise its defense strategy to focus primarily on Asia rather than on Europe as the next potential battle theater. From the "think tanks" to the White House it was clear that China wanted nothing less than to replace the United States as the dominant force in Southeast Asia, if not the world.

On June 1, 2001, two months after the dustup over the U.S. Navy reconnaissance aircraft, Beijing state media announced large-scale Chinese war games that would include a practice invasion of an island near Taiwan. Code-named "Liberation One," the exercises included nearly ten thousand troops, amphibious tanks, missile units, submarines, warships, marine units, and Russian-manufactured Sukhoi Su-27 fighter aircraft.

The extensive war games also included a mock attack on an aircraft carrier. The drill was designed with a U.S. carrier battle group in mind. The announcement ended with a warning not to underestimate Beijing's determination to use force to rein in Taiwan.

With a combination of favorable economic conditions, open ambitions in the region, and a growing military, Beijing was increasing tensions with Taiwan and other Asian neighbors. The long-range plans of the expansionist dictatorship guaranteed more confrontations with the United States, and more questions from Beijing. Would Washington continue its delicate dance with the dragon, and possibly trade Los Angeles for Taipei in a face-off with China, or would the United States quietly leave the South China Sea?

Many of Beijing's questions were answered when the Islamic extremists attacked the United States on September 11, 2001. In the aftermath of the destruction of the World Trade Center, the damage to the Pentagon, the crashed airliners, and the thousands of dead and injured U.S. citizens, the American people had galvanized behind their president. Not since Pearl Harbor had their resolve been as strong and resilient. The message: "Assault the United States of America and we will rise up to vanquish you and your ilk."

Would Beijing view America's commitment to a long-term war on terrorism as an inherent U.S. weakness in the South China Sea and Asia? Would they miscalculate Washington's resolve to defend the democratic island nation of Taiwan and attempt to settle the issue on Beijing's terms by using force?

1

Knifing through the calm seas off the coast of southern California, USS *Abraham Lincoln* and her battle group turned into the wind for the last aircraft launch of the evening. High above the *Nimitz*-class supercarrier, a luminous commander's moon dominated a black canvas splashed with millions of twinkling stars. Except for a few isolated thunderstorms in the southern California operating area, the balmy night was perfect for carrier training exercises.

The slippery flight deck, dangerous enough during the day, but extremely hazardous during night operations, was alive with airplanes, tow tractors, yellow-shirted aircraft directors, and green-shirted aviation boatswain's mates prepping the two forward catapults. Bathed in a soft haze of red floodlights, shadowy figures with yellow flashlight-wands carefully guided pilots around the crowded maze of airplanes waiting to taxi to the catapults.

From bow to stern, the 4.5-acre flight deck of *Abraham Lincoln* was a genuinely hostile environment of screaming jet engines, blazing exhaust gases, whirling propeller blades, guillotine-like arresting gear cables, and foul-smelling catapult steam mixed with jet fuel and salt spray.

Listening to the low whine of his two jet engines, Lt. Comdr. Sammy Bonello saw two wands of light suddenly flash on in front of his plane. The time had arrived—no turning back now.

Following the taxi director, Bonello released the Super Hornet's brakes and taxied his sleek two-seat F/A-18F across the jet-blast deflector behind the starboard bow catapult. *De-*

spite all my years as a fighter pilot, these night carrier operations still give me the creeps, he thought.

Unlike day operations, when pilots can visually and viscerally tell if a catapult shot is good, night operations rob aviators of critical visual cues. When the catapult fires, the pilot accelerates under heavy G-forces straight into a seemingly endless black hole. The sensation is an eerie feeling of being completely at the mercy of fate. To say the least, night catapult shots and landings (traps) on the boat are character-building exercises.

Manning the backseat of the supersonic, twin-engine strike fighter, Lt. Comdr. Clarence "Chick" Fossett went through his checklist and then gazed across the busy flight deck.

Even with the additional anxiety of night operations, Bonello and Fossett could wring the best from the Super Hornet's combination of performance and firepower. The single-seat F/A-18E and two-seat F/A-18F are evolutionary upgrades of the combat-proven F/A-18C/D Hornets. The newest night-strike fighters are able to conduct unescorted missions against highly defended targets early in a conflict.

This evening Bonello and Fossett would be flying a routine training mission with a more junior crew from the VFA-113 Stingers of Carrier Air Wing Fourteen.

Fossett, the weapons-systems officer, adjusted his oxygen mask and then looked down at a sailor holding a lighted weight board. Noting their total weight for the catapult shot was correct, he gave the teenager an okay signal with his flashlight.

"There's a confirmation on sixty thousand pounds." Chick glanced at his kneeboard. "Lookin' close this evening."

"Yeah, we'll be a little tight on gas." Feeling the normal amount of oxygen escaping from his mask, Sammy completed his takeoff checks and set the trim for takeoff. He glanced at the full moon and then looked at his instruments. "If we run short on gas, we'll hit the tanker."

"We're always short." Fossett glanced at the catapult officer. "That's what makes this so damn much fun."

Sammy adjusted his helmet visor. "If we lose an engine, I'm gonna concentrate on the HUD—you back me up."

The head-up display could easily spell the difference between a deadly crash and a successful single-engine landing back aboard the ship. Projected at eye level on the windscreen, the HUD provided the pilot with his plane's angle of attack, airspeed, attitude, and rate of climb.

"Roger that." Fossett checked the status of their wingman. "Ham's gone into tension—looks like a go."

Casting off a momentary feeling of claustrophobia, Sammy glanced at the other Stinger F/A-18F; it belched long, jagged white/orange flames from its powerful General Electric turbofans, each producing twenty-two thousand pounds of thrust. He turned his flashlight on in case of an electrical failure—*nothing like a dark cockpit when the grits hit the fan.*

Shortly after Bonello saw the Hornet's exterior lights flash on, the all-weather, Mach 1.8 fighter squatted on the catapult, then blasted up the flight deck and thundered into the inky darkness.

Sammy watched the twin yellowish-orange streaks as the pilot made a shallow clearing turn and started climbing. *Okay, God, it's our turn.*

"I'll counter any roll or yaw with rudder and stick," Sammy said. Swirls of hazy, reddish superheated steam drifted out of the port catapult track, but Bonello's practiced routine was taking over and shoving his anxiety attack aside. "Throttles will remain at military or min burner. I'll snap the rollers up and jettison the luggage if we have a problem."

"Roger."

On cue Sammy followed the yellow-shirted taxi director as he positioned the airplane in the catapult shuttle. Following a signal from the taxi director, Bonello eased off the brakes. The catapult fires with such force that brakes would be useless in trying to stop the launch. The tires would simply explode, sending deadly shrapnel flying down the cat track.

Deck crewmen scurried beneath the powerful aircraft as they prepared the jet to be launched. Bonello and Fossett felt the Hornet squat, then, at the command of the yellow-shirt, Bonello raised the launch bar. Out of habit, he reached for the ejection handle between his thighs to make sure he wasn't sitting on it—split seconds count in the carrier business.

Seconds later, the catapult officer, known as the shooter, began rapidly rotating his lighted wand.

"It's show time." Sammy inched the throttles forward into the detent, locking his left hand on the throttle grip. The engines spooled up to an earsplitting howl as the blast deflector took a beating from the tremendous heat of the white-hot flames. The airplane shook and vibrated while Sammy completed his final cockpit checks and did a wipeout on the flight controls.

"Stick forward, aft, left, right, rudders right and left," Bonello said, verifying the movements of the major flight control surfaces.

"Lookin' good, Burner."

"Hydraulics, oil, rpm, and EGT are normal," Sammy said, monitoring the exhaust gas temperature and the master caution panel. "Everything looks clean—I like it." He braced his helmet against the back of the ejection seat. "You ready?"

"Ready."

"Here we go." Bonello took a breath of cool oxygen and snapped on his external lights, indicating that he and his jet were ready to fly. Sammy reached forward with his right hand and grabbed the catapult handle to brace for the launch.

With their pulse rates increasing, Sammy and Chick anticipated the crushing G-forces that would hurl them into the dark void beyond the bow. Their destiny, whatever it was going to be, would be out of their hands for the next few seconds.

The catapult officer made one final safety check of the flight deck and then dropped to one knee. He pointed his flashlight wand toward the bow, giving the signal to launch the Super Hornet.

After a short pause the catapult fired, hurling the strike fighter from zero to 152 knots (175 mph) in 2.1 seconds. Sammy's helmet was pinned to the ejection-seat headrest as his eyeballs flattened, causing momentary tunnel vision during the impressive shot. He uttered a guttural sound as the airplane raced toward the black emptiness—the dark void waiting to trick him into taking a one-way trip to the bottom of the ocean.

Off the end of the flight deck and finally climbing, they filled the cockpit with a mutual sigh of relief.

"Good airspeed, good shot," Sammy said. His adrenaline-induced sensory overload was becoming more manageable. *Thank you, God.*

He snapped the landing gear handle up and immediately made a clearing turn. "How you doin'?"

"Couldn't be better—let's see how quickly Ham can get aboard."

"I'd bet about forty-five seconds," Bonello said.

While they continued to accelerate, Sammy cleaned up the Super Hornet. Trimming for a normal climb profile, he reduced power a small amount while they intercepted an arc around *Lincoln.* Bonello and Fossett checked in with the departure controller and contacted the strike controller while they waited for their wingman to rendezvous with them.

Less than two minutes later, Lieutenant "Ham" Hamilton guided Stinger 303 into a loose parade position. "Dash Two's aboard."

"Okay, Ham." Bonello smoothly advanced the throttles to continue his climb. "Let's switch to Black Eagle and go upstairs."

"Roger, switchin'."

Sammy keyed his radio. "Black Eagle, Hornet Three-Oh-Seven, flight of two, state thirteen-point-eight."

"Roger, Hornet Three-Zero-Seven." The mission systems operator in the E-2C Hawkeye airborne-early-warning aircraft closely watched the two strike fighters.

The latest version of the venerable Hawkeye incorporated a mission computer upgrade for the nerve center of the weapons systems, an advanced control-indicator set that revolutionized operator interface in the combat information center, and a sophisticated navigation suite with state-of-the-art laser technology.

The Hawkeye systems operator keyed his radio. "Three-Zero-Seven, for weather avoidance recommend heading one-niner-zero."

"Okay, that's one-ninety on the heading, Three-Oh-Seven," Sammy said as the flight climbed through seventeen thousand feet. He eased into a shallow bank and scanned his instruments at the same moment the isolated thunderstorms to their right were silhouetted by a bright flash of cloud-to-cloud lightning.

"Black Eagle, Hornet Three-Oh-Seven has a request."

"What the hell is that?" Lt. Lou Emerson, Ham's weapons systems officer, interrupted from the backseat of Dash Two. "Sammy, we have a strange-looking bogey at nine o'clock high! See it?"

All eyes turned to the left.

"That's the moon—the one they landed on in '69," Chick radioed. "Did you forget your glasses again?"

"No—off to the right," Emerson said. "Just below the moon."

"Yeah, I see it," Sammy said. A warning signal flashed in the small reptilian section of his brain. He felt a cold chill run down his spine, a sensation caused by fear and adrenaline. "Black Eagle, what are you painting at our nine to ten o'clock, let's see, about twenty-five to thirty thousand feet?"

A long pause followed.

"I'm not showing anything in that area."

Sammy stared at the object for a few seconds. "Well, I'm telling you that we have a bogey at our nine o'clock high."

"Stand by, Three-Zero-Seven. I'll check with Mother and *Chancellorsville*—see what they have."

"Copy," Sammy said, smoothly altering course to intercept the unknown bogey. *Okay, settle down.*

The Hawkeye systems operator contacted the carrier and then the *Ticonderoga*-class Aegis cruiser.

Fossett adjusted his air-to-air radar and studied the screen. "I don't show a thing—there isn't anything there."

"Lou, do you have anything on your scope?" Sammy asked.

"Negative, but whatever it is, it's moving to the left."

"He's right," Hamilton said. "It's passing under the moon, looks like it's movin' at about four to five hundred knots."

"Hornet Three-Zero-Seven, Black Eagle."

"Go."

"The boats don't have anything."

"Copy," Sammy said, watching the object. "We're gonna get a visual ID on our bogey."

"Keep us informed."

"Three-Oh-Seven."

Bonello studied the round, bright, bluish-white object. It appeared to be a ring of lights with a large dark center. It decelerated for a few seconds and then rapidly accelerated in a steep climbing turn. "Holy shit!" he swore to himself.

"Sammy, did you see that?" Hamilton asked.

"Yeah, I saw it." Bonello was trying his best to sound calm and collected. "I've *never* seen that kind of action."

Cotton mouthed, Hamilton was transfixed by the apparition. "That was a *real* bat-turn—unbelievable."

"We can't match that," Sammy said.

"What the hell is it?"

"I don't know, but the Gs would scramble your plumbing."

"Maybe it's a drone," Lou Emerson said. "An experimental UAV or UCAV, something without a pilot."

"I seriously doubt it," Bonello said, breathing more rapidly.

The radios were quiet for a few moments while the crews considered their next move.

"Ease back into cruise," Sammy said. "Let's go for knots and see what we have here."

Hamilton clicked the radio button twice, acknowledging Sammy's call, then advanced the throttles to stay in cruise formation.

"Burners," Sammy said, shoving the throttles all the way forward. "Let's see if we can catch this thing."

"We're hangin' in there," Hamilton reassured him.

Climbing through twenty-three thousand feet, Bonello banked the Super Hornet in order to rendezvous on a constant bearing line with the object. Seconds later, the bogey leveled off above the jets and rapidly reversed direction to the left. Feeling warm perspiration on his forehead, Sammy snapped the straining fighter into a tight port turn and then leveled the wings.

Bonello tensed as his reflexes went into survival mode. "Ham, drop back in trail and give me some maneuvering room—a little space to operate."

"How about if I drop back to Texas?" Hamilton inched the throttles aft a notch. "Be careful."

Fossett keyed his radio. "Hey, relax."

"Yeah, right."

"Burner, you think it's a stealth?" Lou Emerson asked.

Breathing hard, Sammy gulped oxygen as he reefed the Hornet into a face-sagging climb. "Have you ever seen a round stealth?"

"Well, not exactly," Emerson said, chiding himself for having asked such a stupid question.

"Watch your speed, Burner," Fossett said urgently. "We're gettin' way too slow."

"We're okay," he said a split second before the elusive bogey started a rapid descent. Sammy felt his heart pound as the adrenaline once again kicked in. Still in full afterburner, he rolled the fighter inverted and pulled the nose through the horizon, then boresighted the bright object. "We're closin' on it—whatever it is."

"Take it easy," Fossett said. "Let's not do anything crazy."

Without warning, the bogey appeared to be expanding in size. A midair collision seemed imminent.

"Idle and boards!" Sammy slammed the throttles back, popped the speed brake out, and yanked the airplane into a punishing evasive turn. *Oh, shit!* He could literally smell the fear.

"Son of a *bitch!*" Fossett gasped for oxygen. "Let's knock it off! Now! Knock it off!"

"I'll buy that," Emerson groaned from the backseat as Hamilton pulled six Gs to follow Bonello. "Let's back off."

"Stay with me!"

"I'm trying to hang tight," Hamilton radioed.

With his heart in his throat, Sammy snapped his head around and simultaneously closed the speed brake and slammed the throttles forward.

"It's turning, going away from us," Bonello said, hauling the Hornet around and pointing it straight at the mysterious bogey. "Black Eagle, Black Eagle, Hornet Three-Oh-Seven requests permission to—"

Startled by a brilliant streak of light, Hamilton and Emerson saw a blinding flash and then stared in horror as their flight leader's plane exploded before their eyes. The stunned aviators watched the bluish-white bogey accelerate out of sight in less than ten seconds. Their pulse rates spiked to near-aneurysm levels.

Hamilton's mind recoiled in horror and disbelief. *Oh, Mother of God, what are we dealing with?* Ham banked into a steep turn to stay over the general area and then keyed the radio. "Black Eagle, Three-Oh-Seven just exploded—just blew to smithereens! We need SAR out here *now!*"

"Say again," the systems operator asked.

"They're gone," Hamilton exclaimed in shock. "Three-Oh-Seven exploded and we need SAR ASAP!"

A suffocating stillness followed.

Ham keyed the radio. "Hornet Three-Zero-Seven has gone down!"

"Stand by."

"Stand by, hell! Do you have any other targets out here—besides us?"

"Negative."

Swallowing hard, Lou Emerson keyed his radio. "The bogey fried 'em, blew 'em to hell!"

"Sweet Jesus," the E-2C operator said.

2

The Mediterranean Sea

Watching the shimmering sun peek above the horizon, former Marine Corps Harrier pilot Scott Dalton sipped coffee while he relaxed on the private teak veranda outside his luxurious cabin atop *Silver Cloud,* a yacht-like cruise ship. He felt the balmy sea breeze rustle his hair and then closed his eyes and leaned back in his deck chair. For Scott, nirvana came after a pot of freshly brewed Kona coffee and breakfast alfresco.

The descendant of a Confederate general, and son of a retired Marine Corps brigadier general, Scott Johnston Dalton was a native of Nashville, Tennessee. A three-year varsity quarterback for the "Commodores" of Vanderbilt University, Scott was six feet even, ruggedly handsome, and had blue eyes that exuded charm and wit.

After his military obligation was complete, Scott joined the Central Intelligence Agency. There he established an excellent reputation for successfully completing complex and hazardous assignments. Scott's daring and courageous feats, following his qualification as a counter-terrorism-strike-force team leader, made him an instant legend in the Agency. As his reputation spread, the White House began calling on his expertise to conduct special covert operations in various hot spots around the world.

Tired of the political infighting within the Agency, Scott finally decided to resign and start his own consulting firm. The news of his impending departure did not go unnoticed at

1600 Pennsylvania Avenue. Because of his excellent performance during several covert operations, his parachuting experience, his outstanding flying skills, and his Marine Corps training, Scott received a surprising and flattering offer from the White House.

He would conduct special operations on behalf of the national security adviser, completely outside the boundaries of congressional-oversight requirements that encumber CIA-directed covert operations. In his role as a private citizen and aviation safety auditor for U.S. and international corporate flight departments, Scott could circumvent certain obstacles that might prove politically embarrassing to the president of the United States, the Justice Department, the State Department, the Central Intelligence Agency, or to the Pentagon. His primary objective was to leave no fingerprints, no ties to any division or branch of the U.S. government, and no headlines.

Under an assumed identity and rank, Scott attended the army's High Altitude, Low Opening School (HALO) to learn how to infiltrate enemy positions, or land on ships or other moving objects, by falling from high altitude and opening his parachute at low level to avoid being detected by radar or guards.

Shortly thereafter he traveled to Hereford, England, for training with the Special Air Service Regiment, considered by many military organizations to be the most elite special-forces unit in the world. Originally founded during World War II by British captain David Stirling, the SAS has mastered the art of anti/counterterrorism and operating behind enemy lines on covert missions.

Dalton's training had concentrated on handling special weapons, insertion skills, anti-interrogation tactics, close-target reconnaissance, free-fall parachuting, secrecy and stealth, close-quarter battle skills, and survival, escape, and evasion techniques.

When he heard the cabin door open, Scott glanced at Jackie Sullivan, his new partner in their consulting business. Breathing hard, the former air force F-16 pilot was attired in jogging shorts and a Jimmy Buffett T-shirt that highlighted her slim, athletic figure.

Jackie and Scott had originally met by chance at an elegant restaurant in Georgetown. He had invited her to go sailing with him on Chesapeake Bay and she had graciously accepted. However, Scott left the following day for Buenos Aires, and during his unsuccessful attempt to capture an international terrorist, he misplaced Jackie's name and phone number. After returning to Washington, he went back to the restaurant on a number of occasions but never saw her again.

A year later they were miraculously reunited to work as a team to rescue one of Jackie's colleagues. Maritza Gunzelman, a "civilian" consultant like Jackie, had infiltrated a major terrorist training compound in the Bekaa Valley. The CIA, the Brits, and Mossad had been desperate to debrief her, but the terrorists had become more suspicious of Maritza by the day. She was under close surveillance and essentially trapped in the compound.

When Hartwell Prost, the president's national security adviser, brought Scott and Jackie together for a second encounter, Scott did not immediately recognize her. Finally, it had dawned on him like a load of bricks falling on his head. When they first met, her hair had been longer and she had been wearing a stunning black cocktail dress instead of a flight suit.

Scott had not been aware that she was a clandestine officer with the Defense Human Intelligence Service. Likewise she had no idea that Scott had been a former CIA agent turned troubleshooter for the White House.

After their mission in the Bekaa Valley, Jackie and Scott decided to join forces. Having worked closely with them during the dangerous operation, Hartwell Prost fully endorsed the merger. Although the proposition was inherently dangerous—they would be considered mercenaries if anything went wrong—the upside of the arrangement for Dalton and Sullivan was collecting a veritable fortune in fees. Payment for their extraordinary services was simply deposited in their account at an offshore bank.

The Agency had fully expunged their records. Except for their military jackets, every trace of their involvement with the U.S. government mysteriously vanished, including any information contained on computer hard drives at the Agency. The Dalton & Sullivan Group maintained a nice office in Washington, had a full-time secretary, and conducted actual safety audits between sensitive assignments and special operations.

The most difficult aspect of their new role was getting used to reporting directly to Hartwell Prost.

"How was your workout?" Scott asked.

"Great." She was still trying to catch her breath after lifting weights in the fitness center and enjoying an invigorating jog around the top deck. She glanced at the silver urn on the cocktail cabinet. "Any coffee left?"

"I think so."

She reached for a cup and saucer and picked up the urn. "How about a massage later this morning?"

"Sure."

The phone rang. Jackie answered it and exchanged pleasantries with their secretary, then motioned for Scott to step inside the suite. "It's Mary Beth."

He nodded and grabbed the phone.

Jackie winked at him. "I'm going to take a quick shower."

Scott barely heard Jackie's parting words—he was already focused on Mary Beth's terrible news. He took the news calmly, asked a few questions, and said good-bye.

He stared blankly at the horizon for a minute and then placed a call to San Diego. A quick glance at his wristwatch told him it was almost 9:00 P.M. in southern California. When Tracy Bonello answered the phone, Scott's heart sank and a wave of grief swept over him. His voice cracked once, but he managed to maintain his composure.

The gut-wrenching conversation was just coming to an end when Jackie walked out of the marbled bath and approached the veranda. She saw his downcast appearance and her smile disappeared.

"Scott, are you okay?"

"I've been better."

"What's wrong?"

"Sammy Bonello was involved in a strange accident during carrier ops off the coast of southern California."

"Is he okay?"

"No, he isn't." Scott's voice caught in his throat. "He's missing at sea and presumed dead."

"Oh, no."

For a few seconds she was at a loss for words.

"I know the two of you became close friends at Kingsville," Jackie said, placing a comforting hand on his shoulder. "Weren't you his best man after you received your wings?"

"Yes, I was."

Scott paused as fond memories of Sammy flashed through his mind. "He was flying an F/A-18F. His backseater didn't make it either."

She gently squeezed his shoulder. "I'm so sorry."

"Sammy was a model husband and father—they have three kids."

Scott lowered his head. "Tracy called our office and Mary Beth thought I should know about the accident and the memorial service."

Jackie sat down on the sofa. "Of course you'll attend."

"Yeah. I'll get off the ship in Gibraltar and fly to San Diego. If you want to continue the cruise, we can meet when the ship reaches Barcelona."

"No," she quietly protested. "I want to go with you"—she paused—"if that's okay?"

"Sure, I'd appreciate it." Scott remained quiet for a moment and then met her eyes. "There's something *very* strange going on."

"Strange—what do you mean?"

"Tracy wants me to talk to a reporter from the *San Jose Mercury News,* a guy named Cliff Earlywine."

"Why?"

"Earlywine was on board the ship when the accident happened. He was doing a piece about carrier flight operations. The navy was giving him the grand tour, the usual show-'n'-tell stuff."

"What does he know about the accident?"

"I'm not sure."

Scott took a moment to review what Earlywine had told Tracy Bonello. "During Earlywine's visit to the combat direction center, he overheard the radio conversations between the ship, the Hawkeye, and Sammy's flight. According to Tracy, Earlywine has some interesting—disturbing—information."

"Disturbing?"

"Yes. He knew the names of the people in the two Hornets. He said something weird happened during a night intercept of an unknown bogey, and Sammy's plane went down during the encounter."

"Could it have been a midair?"

"It doesn't sound like it. When Sammy's wingman returned to the boat, the navy wouldn't allow Earlywine to interview the flight crew. In fact, the navy hustled Earlywine back to San Diego right after Sammy's wingman returned to the ship."

"Well, I can understand the navy's concern about investigating the accident before someone starts speculating about what happened."

Scott took a breath and slowly let it out. "The navy doesn't know that Earlywine was taping his tour of the ship."

"Aha."

"A few seconds after the accident, Sammy's wingman and the backseater can be heard yelling over the radio, and I quote, 'The bogey fried 'em, blew 'em to hell.' End of quote."

"What were they chasing?"

"I don't know, but Earlywine thinks he has the answer. He hasn't gone public with the story yet, but he told Tracy that it sounded like they were trying to intercept something that no one could see on radar."

Jackie rolled her eyes. "A UFO?"

"That's what she thinks."

"O-*kay,* but why would it destroy an airplane?"

"I don't know, but Earlywine played the tape for her. Tracy told me she could hear panic in their voices—that it was very evident."

"Pardon my skepticism, but have they found any wreckage, any debris in the water?"

"If they have, they're keeping it quiet. According to the Associated Press, both the navy and the Pentagon reported that the jet disappeared during a routine training exercise. The search effort has been called off, and the names of the crew members are being withheld pending notification of their relatives."

"Obviously, your friend's family and his wife have been notified. What about the other guy's relatives?"

"Both families have been notified."

Jackie paused a moment. "Let's see if I have this straight. We have an unexplained loss of a Hornet and its crew. Then, not aware that Earlywine taped the radio conversations, the Pentagon has thrown a blanket over the accident, calling it a mishap during routine training exercises."

"That's about it."

Jackie gazed at the sea. "I think the Pentagon is engaged in a cover-up because they don't know what they're dealing with."

"Looks that way." He suppressed a sudden feeling of grief and anger. "Tracy was upset and skeptical when Earlywine first contacted her, but he convinced her that he can find out what's behind the stonewalling."

"Let me guess. That's when she mentioned you to Earlywine—does she know about the Agency?"

"No, she and Sammy didn't know I was with the CIA, and she believes our consulting firm is as advertised."

"That's good."

"Tracy told him I was a former naval aviator who had been carrier qualified, and he wants to meet me after the memorial service."

They sat in silence for a couple of minutes, each contemplating the sudden, awful changes wrought in the life of a young woman and her three children. Scott could visualize Tracy sitting on the divan, her teeth clamped on her lower lip, tears cascading down her cheeks, while she attempted to explain to Sally, Paul, and Sam junior why Daddy wasn't coming home again.

"Well," Jackie said, "we're due to arrive in Gibraltar at one, so we'd better start packing."

"Yeah." Scott stared at the tranquil sea and then reached for the telephone. "I'll make some reservations."

Victoria, Canada

As early morning sunlight began to embrace the radiant city, Dr. Dixon Owens, a celebrated physicist, walked unsteadily to the large window in his suite at the Ocean Pointe Resort. The towers and turrets of the unique hotel made it look like a modern version of Camelot.

Nursing a king-size hangover from quaffing three bottles of Dom Perignon champagne the previous evening, he surveyed the regal Empress Hotel and the boat traffic in the picturesque Inner Harbor. A grossly overweight man of elaborate taste and expensive habits, Owens had always lived well beyond his means.

Now, much to his satisfaction, he could ditch his nagging wife and demanding job. No more endless meetings. No more working on weekends. No more compromises. His future would include chartered jets to exotic locations, lounging in the best hotel suites, drinking fifty-year-old Scotch, clothes tailor-made by famous designers, and only the finest wines.

Owens followed the slow progress of a small whale-watching cruise ship until it sailed out of view beyond the harbor entrance. He smiled to himself as he continued to examine the mixed collection of colorful sailboats and graceful yachts.

A few moments later, a bright yellow-and-blue Cessna 185 floatplane swooped low across the harbor and gently splashed down on the mirror-smooth water. Owens checked his wristwatch and realized that he would be pushing the envelope to drive to Ogden Point in time to catch the 7:30 ferry to Seattle.

Deciding it was too late to brush his teeth and shave,

Owens quickly threw on his rumpled clothes, packed his bag, and then called the front desk.

"This is Dr. Owens in three-twelve," he said brusquely. "I'm checking out and I need you to get my car from valet parking—immediately," he said, and hung up. He grabbed his luggage and rushed out of the room.

Reaching the elegant lobby of the resort, he walked past the woman at the checkout counter.

"Owens, three-twelve—send me the statement, sweetheart." He tossed his key on the counter.

"Sir, if you would—"

"I don't have time," he said with a dismissive wave.

He hurried outside and handed a single U.S. dollar to the young man holding his car keys.

"Thank you, sir."

Ignoring the lad, Owens tossed his bag in the front seat of the Rolls-Royce Silver Seraph and awkwardly slid behind the wheel. He started the V-12 engine and raced out of the hotel driveway, narrowly missing a horse and carriage.

Mashing the accelerator to the floor, Owens roared across the Johnson Street Bridge and flew down Government Street, passing the Empress Hotel at a high rate of speed. Braking heavily, he turned west on Belleville in front of the Parliament Buildings and followed the waterfront route toward Dallas Road. Pushing the car hard, he had to lock the brakes to make the entrance to the ferry terminal.

Having driven the Rolls to the limits of its performance capabilities, Owens arrived at the *Princess Marguerite III* less than a minute before the last vehicle was allowed to board the two-hundred-car ferry.

As he parked the luxury automobile on the ship, he caught the glance of a middle-aged man in a crisp nautical uniform with epaulets on his shoulders. Their eyes met briefly, and the man with the pencil-thin mustache gave Owens an impish grin before he turned and made his way to the spacious upper decks.

Relieved to have made it to the ferry on time, Owens removed his keys, heaved himself out of the car, locked the doors, and went topside to tour the well-appointed ship.

While the pristine 1,070-passenger *Princess Marguerite III* got under way, Dr. Owens followed a cheerful crowd of commuters and vacationers to the bountiful buffet. Relaxing and reading the *Seattle Times,* he drank orange juice, steaming coffee, and devoured a hearty breakfast large enough to feed three average-sized men.

Afterward he wandered into the large, glassed lounge area to take in the beautiful scenery of Admiralty Inlet and Mystery Bay. He found a comfortable chair and sat down with a broad smile on his face. Most of his share of the $42 million payoff was safely stashed in a bank on Grand Cayman Island.

A few minutes later, Owens noticed the first remnants of fog beginning to appear on Puget Sound. The cloudlike mass of water droplets soon became as thick as pea soup. At regular intervals, the ship's foghorn sounded its mournful warning. Owens hoped the thick fog would burn off by noon, their expected time of arrival at Pier 48, Port of Seattle.

He was about to doze off when the same middle-aged gentleman with the impish grin and pencil-thin mustache approached him. The man's nautical uniform and epaulets were immaculate. Owens looked him up and down. *What does this stooge want?*

"Excuse me, sir," the man said with a clipped British accent. "I'm First Mate Peterson, and I couldn't 'elp notice the splendid vehicle you brought aboard this morning."

Owens wasn't quite sure how to respond. "Is there something wrong with the car?"

"Not with your vehicle, sir."

Owens's eyes narrowed.

"On the other 'and, it seems as if we 'ave a bit of a sticky problem."

A scowl formed on Owens's face. "What kind of a problem?"

"Our chief engineer needs to gain access to a machinery space, and your elegant vehicle is obstructing the opening."

"Well, I can damn sure fix that for you." Owens reached into his jacket pocket for the car keys and offered them to the officer. "Do whatever you need to do; I'll be right here."

"Thank you, sir. 'Owever, our insurance company does not permit crew members to drive vehicles that belong to passengers—particularly the likes of a Rolls-Royce." He smiled his impish smile. "Liability concerns, you understand."

"What next?" Owens rose from his chair and dropped his keys in his jacket pocket. "Lead the way."

"We appreciate your kind consideration, sir."

"Okay, let's just get it done," Owens said with a disinterested sniff.

"Yes, sir."

The two men went belowdecks and made their way aft to the area where the Silver Seraph was parked. Owens was surprised to find not a single person in the cavernous parking area.

Then again, he asked himself, *why would anyone be down here with so many things to see and do topside? After all, no one is going to steal a car and drive off.*

They walked to the last three cars on the starboard side of the ship. Nearing the rear of the Rolls, Owens retrieved the keys and turned to ask which way he should move the car. "Do you want me to back up a few feet?"

Owens saw the blur of the tire iron too late. The staggering blow to the side of his head was the last feeling Dr. Dixon Owens would ever have. He slumped forward, striking his head on the car as he collapsed in a heap. His body twitched with a slight but rapid motion for a few seconds before the final death rattle sounded in his lungs and air passages.

With his skull crushed and his head bleeding profusely, the physicist was unceremoniously stuffed inside the trunk of the Rolls. The man in the sharply creased uniform carefully cleaned Owens's blood off the ship's deck and the exterior of the car, then tossed the soaked rag into the trunk with the body.

When the *Princess Marguerite III* reached port in Seattle, a middle-aged man dressed in khaki slacks and a green-and-white sweater carefully drove Owens's Silver Seraph off the ferry and away from Pier 48. The dangerous part of the mission was over. Now, following explicit orders from his employer, he had to make Owens's death look like an accident.

3

San Diego, California

The mild and refreshing weather was perfect for the outdoor memorial service. The officers and sailors, each with a fresh haircut, were resplendent in their eye-catching dress whites with their colorful military ribbons. Conspicuously absent from the commemorative service were Lieutenants "Ham" Hamilton and Lou Emerson.

At Tracy Bonello's request Jackie and Scott sat beside her. Sammy's father and mother sat on the other side of their tearful grandchildren. Sammy's brother, Tony, tried to comfort his inconsolable mother, but his efforts were in vain. The other members of the family grieved in stony silence while a lone sailor played taps as four F/A-18s flew low over the chapel grounds and executed the traditional missing-man formation.

Tracy's eyes brimmed with tears. Trembling with emotion, she began to softly cry. Scott comforted her and tried with all the self-control he could muster to maintain his own composure. He had attended many other services for fellow aviators over the years, and there was never a dry eye when taps sounded.

After the service everyone went to Tracy's home for a lunch provided by Sammy's squadron mates. By early afternoon the mourners began to thin. The pilots and naval flight officers quietly paid their respects to Tracy and her family, then left to attend the memorial service for Chick Fossett. Later, after spending time with Fossett's grieving wife, and a baby boy who would never know his father, the fliers would rendezvous at the officers' club to get properly inebriated and salute their fallen comrades.

Scott and Jackie waited until Tracy was finally alone with her immediate family before they left for their meeting with Cliff Earlywine at the U. S. Grant Hotel, their residence while in San Diego. Arriving promptly, Jackie and Scott were surprised to see Earlywine waiting for them. Looking more like a muscular college linebacker than a newspaper reporter, Earlywine rose to greet them.

Introductions were quickly made while Scott and Jackie seated themselves. There was an air of expectancy that increased the tension hanging over their table.

While they waited for their drinks to be served, Jackie and Scott set the ground rules about confidentiality. The entire conversation would be off the record, no recorders.

"Cliff," Scott said after their drinks arrived, "tell us exactly what happened after the accident, after you heard the shouts over the radio."

"Well, I could see that everyone was basically in shock for a few seconds, then they all looked at me."

"What did they say?" Jackie asked.

"Nothing at first. Someone, I can't remember who, ordered the lieutenant who was my handler to escort me to that big structure on the right side of the flight deck."

"The island," Scott said.

"Yeah, that's where they took me when I flew out on the COD, so I figured my visit was over."

"Did the lieutenant say anything to you?" Jackie asked.

"Not really. He was a PR type and polite, but he was all business after the accident happened."

Scott lowered his voice. "Did you still have your recorder on?"

"Yes. It's real small—fits in a cigarette pack in my shirt pocket."

"Will you give us a copy of the tape?"

"Yeah, I already made you a copy." He reached into his pocket and handed a miniature Sony tape to Scott. "I have another copy in a safety deposit box."

"What happened next?"

"The other airplane, the wingman, landed and people surrounded the airplane. A few minutes later, here comes the pilot and the guy in back. When they came through the door, I stepped forward to ask them some questions and all hell broke loose."

"Go ahead," Scott said.

"There was a lot of commotion, and the next thing I knew two guys had me by the arms and took me straight to the COD. I was confined there for about twenty-five minutes before they flew me back here."

"Have you tried to contact the flight crew?" Jackie asked.

"At least a half-dozen times. The backseat guy has apparently been transferred to the Pentagon and the pilot, who is now stationed in Pensacola, won't return my phone calls."

Earlywine looked at Dalton. "After I talked with Mrs. Bonello, I figured that you, with your background and all, might be able to get the pilot to talk to you."

"Do you have a name and phone number?"

"Right here," Earlywine said proudly. He handed Scott a slip of paper with Lieutenant Hamilton's phone number. "I have a friend, a lieutenant commander, who owed me a favor."

Scott glanced at the Florida area code before handing the piece of paper to Jackie. "This should be interesting."

"No doubt."

Dalton looked at Earlywine. "If I can get any information, it has to be from an anonymous source. I don't want any names used—not ours or anyone we talk to."

"I give you my word." He presented each of them a business card. "I don't reveal my sources unless I have permission. I just want to know what *really* happened before I take this to my editor."

Scott nodded. "So do we."

"All I know is something mighty strange happened that night, and I think—no, I'm positive—that whatever happened is being covered up."

"We'll see what we can find out," Scott said, pocketing the tape.

"I appreciate it."

When they finished their drinks, Earlywine paid the tab and excused himself. Afterward Jackie and Scott walked into the Grant Grill and were seated at a cozy booth.

Scott waited until they were alone, then leaned closer to Jackie. "Can't wait to play this tape."

"Same here. Maybe we should contact Hartwell and see what he can tell us about the accident."

Scott looked at his wristwatch. "Good idea. We should give him a heads-up about Earlywine's story and the tape."

"Yeah. Besides, we'll be better off if we have as much information as possible before we contact the pilot."

"True, but I don't want to have that conversation over the phone. I want to go there, in person, unannounced."

He smiled. "How do you feel about spending a few days in Florida?"

"You call Hartwell," she said without hesitation. "I'll book us on a morning flight to Pensacola."

"Let's do it."

The Winslow Estate, Maryland

Hartwell Prost sat down in his study to read the first draft of a speech he intended to give at his alma mater. The only child of a wealthy father who oversaw their family-owned investment empire, Prost had surprised his parents by joining the Central Intelligence Agency after graduating with honors from Harvard Law. He became a rising star at the CIA and, in his ensuing years there, an astute power broker and political wizard.

Now retired from his position as director of operations, Prost was the president's closest aide and confidant. On the surface, his soft voice and ever-present tweed tam-o'-shanter cap could lull people into underestimating him, a costly mistake many opponents had made.

On the inside, however, Prost was clinically analytical.

Known by many as a Renaissance man, he had little tolerance for the whiz kids who made up the Beltway crowd. He considered most of them to be educated beyond their intelligence.

Although he was the consummate gentleman, Hartwell Prost would not hesitate to cashier someone he judged unsuitable for the task at hand. Scott Dalton had never been in that category, not even close. Scott was the kind of person Hartwell Prost showcased, even to the commander in chief, President Cord Macklin.

When the phone rang, he removed his glasses and reached for the receiver. "Prost."

After a short conversation with Scott, Prost had a firm set to his jaw. "Let me check into this first thing in the morning."

"Yes, sir."

"I sense a smoke screen coming from the Pentagon. In the meantime, go ahead and see what you can find out from the other pilot—the one in Pensacola."

"Okay."

"Oh, one other thing. Keep that tape in your possession until you can give it to me in person."

"Will do, sir."

When Scott returned to their booth, Jackie had their travel itinerary neatly detailed on a small notepad.

"What did he say?"

"He knew about the accident but was unaware of the circumstances. He didn't know that a civilian reporter had been on board the ship and taped the radio transmissions."

"Well, no one else knew either."

Scott paused while a well-dressed gentleman was seated near their table. "It's probably going to land on the president's desk."

"That's going to get his attention."

"You bet it is. Hartwell thinks someone is trying to throw a blanket over the details of what happened."

"He'll jump on that," she said.

"Yeah, he seemed to be miffed that he hadn't been briefed on the details surrounding the crash, especially under the circumstances."

"What did he say about contacting the pilot?"

"He thinks it's fine, but he cautioned me to be careful. He doesn't want us setting off any alarms with the navy."

"We're *always* careful," she said with mock seriousness. "You've had a really tough day."

He nodded and opened his menu. "After dinner we'll find a recorder and listen to the tape."

Jackie reached for his hand. "How about a martini before dinner?"

"You're on."

Eagle Rock One-One

High above the Bay of Bengal a U.S. Air Force RC-135S reconnaissance plane was preparing to observe a missile test that intelligence reports expected to take place hundreds of miles inside India. Data from the secret test would be transmitted directly from the Boeing Cobra Ball aircraft to the White House and the State Department. The ongoing conflict over Kashmir was again ratcheting up the tension between Pakistan and India. With no buffer zone between the rival nations, the possibility for a nuclear confrontation was nearing certainty.

Deployed from the secretive 55th Wing at Offutt Air Force Base, Nebraska, the sophisticated four-engine Cobra Ball spy plane, call sign Eagle Rock One-One, could instantly detect a missile launch, track the object into space, mark the missile engine's cutoff, then quickly calculate its trajectory and point of impact.

The airplane was equipped with an upgraded sensor suite and sported four large windows on the right side of the fuselage. Made of optical-quality glass, the windows were designed to enhance the capabilities of the Cobra Ball's primary sensor systems. The package included a medium-wave infrared array, a real-time optical system that recorded visible light using a combination of thirteen sensors, and a large-aperture tracking system, which was an optical telescope that provided a clear resolution to small targets.

Long surrounded by secrecy, Cobra Ball's capabilities were well known and feared by the Soviet Union during the Cold War. In order to observe missile testing on Kamchatka Peninsula on Russia's east coast, the RC-135s from the "low-density, high-demand" 6th Strategic Wing at Eielson Air Force Base, Alaska, routinely flew established patterns in international airspace.

A disastrous incident was triggered in 1983 when senior commanders in the Soviet military attempted to shoot down an unarmed Cobra Ball. Instead of destroying the secret reconnaissance aircraft, the Russian fighter pilot mistakenly downed Korean Airlines Flight 007 with a missile, killing all 269 on board. The lone RC-135 was hundreds of miles east of the accident site.

Although night had fallen over the Bay of Bengal, the Cobra Ball crew would be making visual observations and spectral analyses of the fireballs that surround intercontinental ballistic missiles when they reenter the earth's atmosphere. Working with the CIA and the Big Safari reconnaissance program at Wright-Patterson Air Force Base, Ohio, the Cobra Ball crewmen were expecting India to test a new long-range ICBM in approximately twelve minutes.

Major Dale Kirby, the aircraft commander of the complex spy plane, glanced at the pale crescent moon highlighted in the dark sky and then did a double take. *What the hell is that?*

"Hey, Gregg, take a look—one o'clock high." Kirby motioned toward a bright, circular, bluish-white object slightly above the moon.

"At what?" Capt. Gregg Tyndall asked.

"The bright object passing over the top of the moon."

Moving at high speed in the opposite direction, the strange aberration appeared to be a bright ring of light with a large dark center. The object slowed, then reversed course and began ascending at an astonishing rate of climb. It then abruptly leveled and hovered in place.

Kirby stared in disbelief. "Do you see it?"

"Oh, yeah," Tyndall said, staring intently at the light. "How could I miss it?" He studied the object for a few seconds and let out a slow whistle. "I've never seen anything like that."

"I haven't either." Kirby craned his neck to watch. The eerie object climbed, then began a shallow descent. "It's there, we can see it, and it's being maneuvered by some form of intelligence."

"No question about it." Tyndall turned and glanced aft on the flight deck. Unaware of the strange light, both navigators were working on last-minute preparations for the missile test.

"Hey." Tyndall motioned for the navigators to come forward. "Take a look at this thing."

The captains joined the pilots and quietly stared at the highly maneuverable object.

"We'd better alert the crew," Kirby said. He pressed the intercom switch to inform the mission commander and turned to his copilot. "I'm going to take pictures."

"Maybe it's an advanced UAV," Tyndall said.

Kirby reached for his Minolta. "I don't think we have anything with that kind of performance."

"What about Area Fifty-one and all those black programs?"

"Yeah, but we're over the Bay of Bengal."

"True, but I guess it could've come from anywhere."

"Look at that thing move," Kirby said. "I remember when we were off the coast of China and our mission commander said—" Kirby froze in midsentence, then stared wide-eyed as the bluish-white object rapidly slowed to a halt and descended. Without warning, it changed direction and crossed the flight path of the Ball.

"Holy shit!" Kirby reached for the control yoke. "I don't like this—someone is screwin' with us!"

"It's coming straight at us!"

The object shot past the cockpit, causing the four men to duck.

"Son of a *bitch*," Kirby said.

The light disappeared behind them for a few seconds and then reappeared a few hundred feet off the right wing.

Fascinated and clearly frightened, Tyndall spoke in a halting voice. "It's huge—easily the size of a 747."

Shocked by the close call, the navigators quickly returned to their crew station and strapped themselves into their seats.

The mission commander and the other crewmen in the back of the airplane went into shock. The intercom became a party line when everyone began talking at the same time.

"Get a camera on it!" the mission commander ordered as he initiated voice contact with the State Department and the White House. "We gotta have this on film—hustle!"

"We're getting it," a technician said.

Seconds later, the object accelerated straight ahead and climbed at a sixty-degree angle, then appeared to be coming straight at the Ball. It shot past, made a sweeping right turn, and flashed over the cockpit.

"We need to get the hell out of here," Kirby announced.

The object climbed straight up, appeared to stop in midair, and then turned toward the airplane.

Kirby felt his blood chill. "Oh, shit . . ." He trailed off.

"We better take evasive action," Tyndall said.

Suddenly a bright flash startled the pilots and crew. Seconds later the RC-135S exploded into millions of fragments, lighting the night sky with a mushrooming fireball that arced toward the Bay of Bengal.

4

Pensacola, Florida

Scott lowered the Mustang's convertible top, shifted into gear, and drove away from the regional airport.

"You're right," Jackie said.

"Right about what?"

"The climate here really *is* ideal." The soft southern breeze was tousling her hair and she seemed to be enjoying it. "I didn't realize what a paradise this place is."

"Yeah, it's hard to beat—once you've become acclimated to the humidity. That's why I've planned to retire here."

"Really? You never told me that."

"You never asked."

"I figured you'd be the type who would have a rustic cabin in the Smoky Mountains, maybe on a picturesque lake."

Scott winked. "There are lots of things I haven't told you."

"Well, now's a good time to fess up."

"First things first," Scott said. He turned north on Tippin Avenue.

"We're going the wrong direction, aren't we?"

"Just a short detour."

Scott jockeyed the Mustang into the flow of traffic. "I thought we'd take the postcard route to the air station."

"No complaints here."

Turning right on Langley Avenue, Scott tightly gripped the steering wheel and thrust his head above the windshield. His short hair blew wildly until he plopped into the seat. "This *is* paradise, no doubt about it."

"The Redneck Riviera."

Scott laughed out loud. "Exactly, and I love it this way."

Jackie was making every attempt to keep Scott's spirits up. After listening to the tape recording of Sammy Bonello's last flight, Scott had been unusually quiet and reserved. Around nine o'clock, he had left the U. S. Grant and gone for a long walk alone. When he returned, it was as if nothing had happened.

His normal effervescent personality remained the same until they landed in Pensacola. Then the memories of Sammy and flight school came pouring out, causing Scott a few minutes of uneasiness.

"We have to come back here for a real vacation," Jackie said, basking in the warm sunshine.

"Count on it."

"I'm going to hold you to that."

"I won't forget." He put on his sunglasses. "We'll get a sweeping view of Escambia Bay from Scenic Highway. It'll only take a couple of minutes longer to get to the air station."

Jackie closed her eyes, allowing the sun to warm her eyelids. "You're the tour director."

They drove in silence until Scott turned south on Scenic Highway. He glanced in the rearview mirror. "Don't turn around."

"What's wrong?"

"I think we're being followed."

"What?" Jackie fought the instinct to look behind her.

"There's a white car with two men in it about a quarter of a mile behind us. They're maintaining a constant position."

"Are you sure they're following us?"

"I'm pretty sure."

Scott glanced in the side mirror. "That car—I think it's a Mazda—was parked just outside the airport. The driver pulled in behind us."

"Maybe you're becoming paranoid?"

"Well, I'll tell you what—ninety-nine out of a hundred people wouldn't have taken the route I chose."

He increased his speed and headed south toward Summit Park and Mallory Heights. "They're still with us."

The Mazda quickly matched their pace.

"What do you think?" he asked.

"It may be a coincidence, but I don't think so."

"I agree."

"Why would someone be following us?"

He darted a look at her. "I haven't the foggiest idea."

"Maybe they're the prize patrol."

Jackie let her gaze roam until the Mazda came into her periphery. "You're the sweepstakes winner and don't know it."

He glanced at her and then checked the mirror again. "Yeah, I think that's definitely the answer."

"What do they want with us?"

"I don't know, but I have a hunch we're about to find out."

After reaching Cordova Bluffs, Scott was forced to slow down for traffic on the two-lane highway. He checked the rearview mirror. The Mazda remained in formation.

He felt the first spike of pain in his chest. "We need to lose these guys and concentrate on finding Hamilton."

"I'm with you."

"Uh-oh," Scott said.

The white Mazda was rapidly closing on them.

"They're making their move."

"Great—why are you always driving when we get ourselves into one of these situations?"

"Just lucky, I guess." Scott unbuckled his seat belt. "You're the high-speed driving instructor—do your stuff."

He kept one hand on the steering wheel and crawled into the cramped backseat. "It's all yours."

"Get a grip," Jackie said. She quickly slid over the console and into the driver's seat. "This is going to be tricky with all this traffic."

Scott reached for his 9mm Sig Sauer P226. Carrying both FBI *and* CIA "smart-card" identification supplied to them by Hartwell Prost, Scott and Jackie could carry a weapon on board any domestic airliner.

Alternately glancing in the mirror and checking the road

ahead, Jackie was becoming more concerned about being able to escape their pursuers. "We're getting pinned in by traffic in front of us."

"You have to do something."

"I'm doing the best I can."

"Okay, stay with it," Scott said, bracing his six-foot frame. He aimed his Sig Sauer and then lowered it. There were too many vehicles and too many innocent people in the line of fire. "Hang on—they're going to ram us!"

Jackie checked the rearview mirror. "They're crazy!"

With a high closure rate, the Mazda pulled out to the left, then sharply swerved into the left rear of the Mustang. With reckless abandon, the driver of the Mazda kept the throttle to the floor as Jackie mashed her accelerator to shoot out in front and correct the slide.

The kinetic energy generated from the desperate maneuver caused the Mustang to brush the rear bumper of a Nissan Sentra. The driver of the Nissan ran off the road and frantically locked her brakes, sliding sideways to a safe stop.

Recovering from the jarring impact, Scott fired three rounds at the Mazda's right front tire. Jackie braked hard and slammed the Mustang into the right side of the Mazda, forcing the car into oncoming traffic.

The passenger in the Mazda leaned out the window and fired a handgun as the driver swerved to the left to avoid a head-on collision with a Volvo station wagon.

Two rounds punctured the side of the Mustang near Jackie's left knee. Scott returned fire as the Mazda ran off the opposite side of the road and spun out of control, then almost sideswiped an Astro passenger van.

"Pull over," Scott shouted.

Jackie braked hard and swung to the right side of the road.

"We need to stop these maniacs!" Scott said.

"They're headed straight at us!"

Jackie swung the driver's door open and started to get out.

"Get in the car!" Scott said.

The Mazda was accelerating across the road toward them when Jackie dived into the front passenger seat.

Scott raised the Sig Sauer and held his fire until he saw an arm extend from the passenger's window.

"Okay, we'll play hardball," Scott said to himself. He methodically fired three rounds at the windshield and then ducked and waited for the impact. At fifty-five miles an hour and still gaining speed, the Mazda sideswiped the left side of the Mustang, tearing the open driver's door completely off its hinges.

In stunned silence, Jackie and Scott watched as the heavily damaged Mazda bounced off another car and raced out of sight near East Pensacola Heights. A few seconds later, the angry driver of the Nissan Sentra honked her horn and gave Scott and Jackie the middle-finger-salute as she drove past the Mustang.

"Welcome back to paradise," Scott deadpanned, following Jackie through the gaping hole where the driver's door had been.

"Are you still in one piece?" she asked.

"Yeah, I'm fine." He headed for the crushed door. "Let's get this off the road before someone gets hurt."

"Look." Jackie pointed to a handgun lying in the road thirty yards in front of the Mustang.

They placed the driver's door in the backseat of the car and hurried toward the 9mm Beretta.

"Jackie, look at this," he said, pointing to the fresh splatters of blood on the road. "The shooter is going to need some medical attention."

"You nailed him." Jackie turned to get her satellite phone out of the car. "I'd better call nine-one-one and get this scene secured."

Both of them involuntarily had a flashback to the terrorist attack on September 11, 2001. The image of the hijacked airliners plunging through the twin towers of the World Trade Center would never fade from memory.

"Ah, that won't be necessary." Scott walked to the edge of the highway to flag down an approaching patrol car from the Escambia County Sheriff's Office.

As the car slowed to a stop, Jackie turned to Scott. "What are we going to tell the friendly folks at Hertz?"

Scott shrugged. "We're sorry we broke your car, but we need another Mustang, preferably one with two doors and no bullet holes."

Jackie shook her head. "I can just picture the smiles on their faces."

"Oh, yeah."

Before the sheriff's deputy stepped out of her car, Scott turned to Jackie. "Did you get a look at the shooter?"

"No. I was—how should I say this?—a bit preoccupied at the time. How about you?"

"I got a good enough look to know he's Oriental."

Naval Air Station Pensacola

After their statements were taken and the paperwork was completed at the sheriff's office, a deputy contacted the Hertz manager to inform him that the damage to the rented Mustang had been reported to the authorities. Jackie and Scott drove the battered Mustang back to the airport.

The Hertz manager, who observed the driver's door in the backseat of the car, politely suggested that Jackie and Scott see a competitor for their transportation needs.

Thirty minutes later, they were again on their way to the Pensacola Naval Air Station. However, this time they were in a shiny new Mitsubishi Eclipse convertible from Alamo.

The damaged Mazda, which had been stolen from long-term parking at the Pensacola Regional Airport, was found abandoned near McGuire's Irish Pub and Brewery on East Gregory Street.

Inside the car, detectives found a state-of-the-art walkie-talkie with blood on it and on the seat. A trail of blood splatters ended about nine feet from the Mazda, leading police to believe the men had an accomplice in a getaway car.

Checks of area hospitals and health-care centers were negative for gunshot wounds. The Beretta was registered to a Chicago Laundromat owner who had reported the weapon missing seventeen months before it had been dropped on Scenic Highway.

Scott completed his call to Prost and placed the phone down as he neared the entrance to the interstate. "Hartwell was as shocked as we were. He doesn't have any idea why anyone would bushwhack us in Pensacola—in broad daylight, no less."

"Well, someone was desperate enough to attack us on a busy highway."

Scott accelerated as he smoothly entered traffic. "The question is *why* were we attacked, and *who* the hell are they?"

"Maybe it's something about your personal life, like the stuff you haven't told me about."

Scott grinned. "Is it what we know about the downed Hornet, the mysterious bogey?"

"I don't know, but I want some answers from the Pentagon. Someone, somewhere, knows why we were attacked."

Scott shifted lanes. "Hartwell is going to see SecDef this evening and he'll get back to us as soon as he can."

Concerned about their attackers returning, Jackie took a quick look behind them. "Who do *you* think they were—any ideas?"

"I don't have a clue, but I think we're in the middle of something that's more than a bureaucratic cover-up by the guys at the Puzzle Palace."

"And?"

"The navy, more likely the Pentagon, is afraid of something. I can just feel it when these kinds of things happen."

"That makes sense, but the last time I checked, the navy and the Pentagon weren't into assassinating people."

"True, as far as we know," Scott said. "Which means we're missing a major piece of the hypothesis."

"Stellar observation, Sherlock."

Scott exited the freeway at Garden Street. "The Pentagon may be trying to sanitize something they can't explain, but the goons who customized our Mustang are clearly not affiliated with the Pentagon."

"I'd say that's a safe bet."

"After our chat with Lieutenant Hamilton, we need to re-group and take a look at this from all sides."

"You're right," she said. "I think we need to tap into the resources that Hartwell can provide—like getting the straight story from the Pentagon."

"I'll second that."

"Like you mentioned, we're not seeing the big picture."

"Obviously not," he said. "We didn't anticipate being run off the road and having our car riddled by bullets."

"How did they know we would be here?" Jackie paused a moment and thought about the strange happenings in the last couple of days. "Where's the common thread between us and the jokers who tried to run us down?"

"My best guess would be Cliff Earlywine."

There was a moment of silence.

"You're probably right," she said. "Someone is watching him *and* watching us. Someone who has a vested interest in not having this incident revealed."

"I'd like to add one *minor* correction," Scott said with a pronounced emphasis. "They may be watching him, but they're trying to *kill* us."

"You make a good point."

"Actually, I'd bet our boys know you and I solve *difficult* problems for the U.S. government."

"They're efficient, no doubt about it," she said. "They had us pegged in record time—right on top of us."

"Like I said earlier, they were waiting for us at the airport."

"We have to assume that Earlywine doesn't know he's being tailed."

"We didn't know either," Scott said with an embarrassed look. "And we're supposed to be trained observers."

"Emotionally, our guard was down."

"A major mistake," he admitted.

After checking at the bachelor officers' quarters, Scott and Jackie located Lt. Merrick Hamilton at the almost vacant of-

ficers' club bar. Hamilton had a pleasant smile, high cheek-
bones, and piercing hazel eyes. Dark haired and trim, Ham
looked like a typical young fighter pilot, except for one obvious difference: Merrick Hamilton was female.

Sitting at the bar in a stylish dress, the Texas-bred Hamilton was quietly conversing with a male officer in uniform.
She glanced at Jackie and Scott as they approached, then
turned a wary eye toward them.

"Lieutenant Hamilton?" Scott asked.

"Yes."

"I apologize for interrupting you. My name is Scott Dalton, and this is my colleague, Jackie Sullivan."

Hamilton eyed them suspiciously. "How did you know my
name?"

"A friend gave it to us."

"What do you want, Mr. Dalton?"

He gave her a friendly smile. "If you could spare a few
minutes to visit with us, we'd sure appreciate it."

"Are you selling something?"

"No, absolutely not," he said with a quiet chuckle. "Please
allow us a couple of minutes to explain. It's very important."

When Hamilton hesitated, Jackie smoothly intervened.
"Scott and Sammy were friends—they went through flight
school together."

Hamilton's eyes reflected her pain. She studied Scott for a
moment and then softened her stance. "You're a navy pilot?"

"Both of us are pilots," he said. "We're civilians now, but
I flew Harriers in the Marines. Jackie was an air force pilot—
F-16s—and she learned to fly helicopters as a civilian."

Merrick nodded in open respect and turned to her com-
panion. "Bob, I'll be back in a few minutes."

"Sure, take your time."

"So, what do you do now, Mr. Dalton?" Merrick asked,
walking away from the lifeless bar.

"We're FBI," Scott said in a monotone as he and Jackie
flashed their personal identification. "But we aren't here in an
official capacity."

Hamilton grew cautious again. "I'm sorry, but I don't understand. Why *are* you here?"

Scott turned his head away a moment, and then looked Merrick in the eye. "Sammy was my best friend during advanced flight training. Since his accident things have transpired that have been, let's say, intriguing and suspicious. I promised his widow that we would look into it for her."

Merrick took a deep breath and then let it out. "I'm not sure I should be talking with you. I'm not at liberty to say anything about Sammy or the accident—that has been made very clear to me."

Scott nodded. "As I said, we're not here as part of an official investigation team. Anything you discuss with us stays with us. Your name won't be revealed, I give you my word."

Hamilton glanced at Jackie.

"You can trust him."

"Besides," Scott continued, "it may be helpful for you to know what has happened since the accident."

"What do you mean?"

"Let's take a ride and we'll explain."

Once they were in the car and leaving the parking lot, Hamilton unexpectedly opened up. "I feel like I'm being watched—I can't prove it, but I sense it."

"By the navy?" Scott asked.

"I don't know, but I was read the riot act before I left the carrier."

"The riot act?" Jackie asked.

"Yes. I'm not supposed to discuss the accident with anyone. Not even with my immediate family. The admiral made it *very* clear."

Scott glanced at her. "Lieutenant Hamilton, I can assure you—"

"Please call me Merrick."

"Merrick, regardless of what develops, we'll keep your name out of it. I just want to know firsthand what happened."

Jackie turned to her. "Just take your time and tell us what happened that night. Everything you can remember."

Hamilton unfolded the story up to the point of arriving back on the carrier. "When we went to the ready room, it was almost vacant. Our skipper, who was alone, looked very grim. In fact, I'd never seen him look like that—completely down and wouldn't make eye contact."

"What did he say?" Scott asked.

"He asked us if we were okay or something to that effect. He talked to Lou and me for a couple of minutes, then said CAG and the admiral wanted to talk with us."

"That's always good for the blood pressure," Jackie said.

"Lou and I were still in shock when the admiral, CAG, and the skipper of the ship entered the ready room. They asked how we were feeling, then got down to business."

"Down to business?" Scott asked.

"Yes. They were pleasant, but the admiral made it crystal clear that we were not to discuss the accident with anyone, including each other. It came out as an order without the admiral actually having to say it was an order."

"One of those 'Do you understand?' kind of orders," Jackie suggested.

"Exactly."

Scott drove past the National Museum of Naval Aviation. "I'm interested in knowing why the admiral acted the way he did."

"At first I thought it was an overreaction. Many people who have encounters with 'strange things' are labeled crackpots. It can ruin careers, as I'm sure you know."

"A bubble off center," Scott said.

"That's all it takes. In retrospect, I still don't know what precipitated the events that happened next."

"What happened next?" Jackie asked.

"After Lou and I saw the flight surgeon, we had some medicinal brandy and went to our staterooms. About ten minutes later, our squadron skipper called us back to the ready room. That's when Lou and I found out we were being transferred, immediately, to separate commands. No explanation, no questions allowed. Pack your trash and keep your mouth shut."

She leaned back in the seat. "That's all I know. I'm waiting for orders to become a flight instructor at VT-6. Any chance of becoming the first female Blue Angel pilot has gone straight down the toilet."

Scott and Jackie remained quiet, sensing the anxiety and animosity Merrick was experiencing.

"What do you think it was, the object you chased?" Jackie asked.

"I honestly don't know what to think. It happened so quickly—it's like a horrible, chilling nightmare that haunts me day and night. Whatever it was, I can assure you there weren't any humans in it."

"How do you know?" Jackie asked.

"They'd be dead from the G-forces."

Without exchanging a word, Scott and Jackie contemplated what Hamilton had revealed. Scott politely changed the subject. "Merrick, you mentioned being watched—feeling that someone was tailing you."

"Yes. From the day I arrived here, I've had this, call it intuition, that someone was watching me. Sometimes close by, sometimes at a distance. I keep trying to shake it, but I can't."

Scott turned toward the officers' club. "After our experience today, you may be right."

Caution flashed in Hamilton's eyes.

"Let me explain how Jackie and I got involved in this and what happened to us this afternoon."

Scott related the story, including the evidence Cliff Earlywine had gathered on board the carrier. He explained how they had met Earlywine and what had happened after they left the Pensacola airport.

When Scott was finished, Merrick sat in silence for a moment. "Now I'm really confused. What's going on?"

"We're not sure ourselves," Jackie admitted.

Merrick's unshakable demeanor began to crack. "Is my life in jeopardy—is that what you're trying to tell me?"

There was a pause before Scott answered. "Merrick, we don't know any more than you do. We came down here to listen to your version of what happened the night of the accident, and that's all. We had no idea we would be ambushed, and we don't want you to be caught off guard."

Merrick remained silent, void of any expression.

Jackie turned to her. "My advice would be to take some leave and don't tell *anyone* where you're going, not even the navy."

"I'll have to give them an address and phone contact, but I could be camping in the wilds of Alaska."

Jackie handed Merrick a slip of paper with a telephone number written on it. "That's my satellite phone number. If you want to contact us, we'll keep you informed about our investigation."

"Yes, I do want to stay in touch with you. I have about three weeks on the books and I could use some time off. I'm almost certain I can leave in the morning—hopefully."

"Good," Jackie said.

"I'll let you know where I can be reached."

"Please do," Scott said, approaching the club. "Stay alert and stay with friends until you go on leave. If you notice anything strange, call security."

"I will, and thanks."

5

The Taiwan Strait

Returning from the Persian Gulf and war-at-sea exercises in the South China Sea, the USS *Kitty Hawk* and her battle group were transiting the Taiwan Strait en route to their homeport at Yokosuka, Japan. The night was coal black with calm seas and a humongous line of thunderstorms between the carrier and Taipei, Taiwan.

Ninety-five nautical miles northeast of the carrier, Lt. Comdr. Wade "Tex" Denton and his wingman, Lt. Todd Justice, were returning from a simulated long-range air strike in the Ryukyu Islands.

Caught off guard by the size and intensity of the storms, they didn't have enough fuel to go over or around them. Their tanker, an S-3B Viking, was waiting on the other side. Rather than diverting to Taipei, Denton was determined to reduce speed and punch through the teeth of the raging thunderstorm.

With Justice welded to Denton's right wing, the single-seat F/A-18Cs penetrated the line and immediately flew into heavy rain and severe turbulence. Todd tried to hang on to his flight leader as they lost and then gained hundreds of feet of altitude, bouncing and bucking wildly.

Tossed from side to side and up and down, the pilots fought to control their planes while hail pounded the fighters and lightning flashed around them. Moments later, St. Elmo's fire caused a blue web of sparks to form on their canopies. The sensation was like going over Niagara Falls in a kettle-drum while strobe lights flashed in your face.

As hard as he struggled, Justice lost sight of Denton's recognition lights in the dark haze and blinding rain. Fearing a midair collision, Todd banked his F/A-18 away from Denton's fighter and flew an offset heading nearly parallel to his section leader. With his heart stuck in his throat, he eased his throttles back and began nursing his plane lower. Seconds later, after being struck by lightning, the two fighters blasted through the line of storms and found themselves in clear skies and calm air.

Denton keyed his radio. "Todd, I have you at three o'clock low. Close it up and we'll hit the tanker."

"Roger that." Justice forced himself to take slow, deep breaths. *Well, that was an experience I don't care to repeat.*

As they began their rendezvous with the Viking, Denton and Justice noticed a large, round, bluish-white object streak out of the western sky, flash by their fighters, and climb almost vertically directly over them.

"Tex, what the hell was that thing?" Todd asked.

"I don't know, but it scared the bejesus out of me."

"Oh, shit, here it comes again." He drifted away from his flight leader as he craned his neck to follow the course of the strange object.

While Denton attempted to call *Kitty Hawk*'s carrier air traffic control center, the bluish-white object slashed downward and stabilized about a hundred yards off the port side of the formation.

"It's huge," Todd said. *It looks like a big Frisbee flying at a thirty-degree angle to the horizon.*

Denton was talking to a CATCC controller when the object accelerated, climbed skyward, paused a few seconds, then came hurtling straight at them. Todd saw a bright flash at the same instant Denton's plane exploded like an aerial fireworks display. The bright, bluish-white object slashed by Todd's Hornet, made a tight 180-degree turn, and accelerated out of sight in a matter of seconds.

Todd instinctively turned on his master armament switch. He frantically radioed the carrier. In shock and suffering from visceral fear, he reported what had happened. Todd began searching for unidentified targets using his air-to-air radar and the heat-seeking head of an AIM-9 Sidewinder air-to-air missile. Nothing registered on the scope, and the missile remained inert.

Trying to calm himself, Justice gave the CATCC controllers the coordinates of the downed Hornet and then managed a shaky rendezvous with the tanker. Because of the overwhelming adrenaline rush he had experienced, it took five attempts to ease the fighter's refueling probe into the Viking's basket.

After he finished taking on fuel, Todd turned toward the carrier and replayed over and over what had happened only minutes before. Nothing made sense. He was certain that whatever it was that had destroyed Denton's plane was under the control of some form of intelligence, artificial or human. He quietly talked to himself until he began his approach to the carrier and then relied on the LSO to coach him in the groove.

Following normal procedures, Todd went to full power when his plane slammed into the flight deck. Thrown forward against his straps when the Hornet snared the fourth wire, he was still pushing on the throttles seconds after the plane had come to a violent halt. Finally, when his situational awareness caught up with the jet, Todd yanked the throttles back, raised his tailhook, and extinguished his exterior lights.

His landing, although it made everyone on Vulture's Row cringe, was reasonable considering the emotional state he was in.

After he taxied clear of the landing area, Justice realized his legs were shaking uncontrollably. He shut down the engines and leaned his helmet back against the ejection-seat headrest. His heart was pounding and his breathing was ragged. Expecting his teenaged plane captain to greet him, Justice was surprised to see his squadron commanding officer appear next to the cockpit.

"Are you okay?"

"Yes, sir."

"Did you see a chute?"

"No, sir. He didn't get out."

"What happened?"

"Skipper, something, I don't know what it was, jumped us and blew Wade's plane out of the air. The whole thing happened in a matter of seconds, literally. Whatever it was disappeared at a speed that had to have been at least eight maybe Mach ten or more."

"It?"

"Yes, sir."

"Could you see what kind of shape it was, you know, what kind of wings it had?"

"Sir, this thing, whatever it was, it wasn't an airplane."

A long silence ensued.

"What are you saying?"

"I'm saying . . ." Justice trailed off. "Sir, it, whatever *it* was, made turns at warp speed. It looked like a gigantic Frisbee, and it could accelerate faster than anything I've ever seen."

The CO stared at Justice for a long moment and then patted him on the shoulder. "Let's go see the fighter doc, then we'll have a chat while everything is fresh in your mind."

"Sir, I'm not crazy."

"Todd, no one is accusing you of anything."

There was a sudden tension between them.

"I just want the doc to see you before we talk to anyone."

"Skipper, I'm telling you the truth. Something shot him down, something unlike I've ever seen before."

Another awkward silence followed until a synapse finally took place in the recesses of Todd's brain. "Skipper, as God is my witness, I didn't accidentally shoot him down. You can check it out, sir. I still have all my ordnance—nothing's missing."

Pensacola, Florida

Flounders Chowder House on Pensacola Beach was crowded with tourists when Jackie and Scott were seated at an outdoor table. The bright, warm sun was high in the clear blue sky and tiny waves gently lapped the shoreline of Santa Rosa Sound.

Scott unfolded his *Pensacola News Journal,* glanced at the
headlines, then turned the page and froze.

1 MISSING IN NAVY JET CRASH

Pilot lost during routine flight
Associated Press

YOKOSUKA, JAPAN—A U.S. Navy F/A-18C jet
crashed into the Strait of Taiwan during carrier exercises Monday night, Pentagon sources said. The pilot
was missing and the cause of the crash was not known.
The name of the pilot is being withheld pending notification of next of kin.

The Hornet disappeared at 10:48 P.M. local time
while conducting routine flight operations from the
USS *Kitty Hawk* approximately 45 miles southwest of
Taipei, Taiwan. An extensive search is currently under
way, said Comdr. Audrey Satterwhite, spokeswoman
for commander, naval air force, U.S. Pacific Fleet.

The armed fighter plane was taking part in joint exercises when it went down 60 miles from the carrier.
The pilot was a member of Strike Fighter Squadron
195, based at Naval Air Field Atsugi, Japan.

The crash came seven days after another F/A-18
Hornet was lost off the southern coast of California,
killing its two crew members. Anonymous sources close
to the Pentagon admit both accidents were similar in na-
ture and happened under very unusual circumstances.
Five members of Congress plan to hold hearings early
next week in an effort to unravel the mystery surrounding both crashes.

Absorbed in the article, Scott was startled when his satellite
phone rang. He shoved the paper toward Jackie. While he took
the call, she ordered lunch for them. Jackie carefully studied
the people in their immediate vicinity and around the perimeter of Flounders's outdoor seating area. Satisfied that no threat

existed, she divided her attention between the employees, the other patrons, and the article about the F/A-18 crash.

"That was Hartwell." Scott placed the phone on the table. "We're officially on the case."

"Interesting. What's the latest news?"

"He wants us to meet him in D.C.—actually at his home."

"When?"

"As soon as we can get reservations."

"I'll take care of the tickets."

"Hartwell will give us a complete brief tomorrow afternoon."

"Has he met with Secretary Adair?"

"He just left a meeting with the president and SecDef. They're giving this—Hartwell's euphemism was 'mystery'—the highest of priorities."

"It must be getting warm in the White House and at the Pentagon."

"According to Hartwell, the president considers these unexplained crashes a definite threat to national security."

"Did Hartwell say anything about the crashes?"

"Yes. He said they're trying to keep a lid on the 'events' until they have some firm answers. They don't want to create mass panic."

He leaned closer. "Besides the two Hornets that have gone down, the air force lost a Cobra Ball over the Bay of Bengal."

"How?"

"Apparently to the same thing, or kind of thing, that brought down Sammy—it's really eerie."

"You're kidding."

"That's what he said. The Cobra Ball's mission commander was in direct communication with the White House and the State Department when they lost all communications and data links from the airplane."

Scott glanced around the immediate area. "But not before the mission commander described the same kind of object that Merrick Hamilton talked about, right down to the bluish-white color and the same kind of high-speed, abrupt maneuvers."

"That's really hard to comprehend. It doesn't make sense. This whole thing—from southern California, to the Taiwan Strait, to the Bay of Bengal—is beginning to sound like something from the science fiction channel."

"I think you're right," Scott said. "When the Cobra Ball crashed, the mission commander was describing the object and the crew was taking photos. Then, all communication with the Ball ceased."

Jackie waited until the waitress had served their lunch. "Did you discuss the details of our conversation with Merrick Hamilton?"

"No, I didn't. I'm going to stick by my word. Her back-seater—what's his name, at the Pentagon?"

"Lou Emerson."

He's shuffling papers in the Puzzle Palace, and I'm sure they have the whole story straight from him."

"Ah, yes. The female pilot obviously would've been too hysterical to remember all the details accurately."

"Easy," he said, allowing the word to roll off his tongue. "I'm just reporting what I think the facts are, ma'am—nothing more."

"Sorry. It's another one of those gender spikes I warned you about."

"No problem. Just put the bayonet away."

Jackie tapped her finger on the F-18 article in the newspaper. "Coincidence? I don't think so."

"Yeah, sounds suspicious to me."

After lunch they went to their room at the Hampton Inn to pack and book a flight to Washington, D.C. With their bags ready to go, they started for the door and both stopped at the same time. They were looking down at a note card that had been slipped under the door. To preserve any fingerprints, Scott picked it up by the edges, read it, then silently handed it to Jackie.

You were lucky yesterday. Very lucky. Perhaps not
so lucky next time. P.S. The lady is a good driver.
ZY

"Well, we're dealing with someone who likes the challenge of playing cat-and-mouse," Scott suggested.

She studied the card. "Someone with very precise, neat penmanship. I don't know about you, but I think it looks feminine."

"I'd say that's a fifty-fifty shot."

"Then again, it could be a red herring." Jackie handed him the card. "'Perhaps not so lucky next time.'"

"We may be reaching, but it does have an Oriental ring to it."

"I think so."

Scott studied the card. "Z Y?"

"Who knows?"

Dalton placed the note card in his shirt pocket. "We'll get this to the FBI—see if they can trace our joker."

"Somehow, I don't believe they'll find any prints."

"I doubt it," he said.

"He, if it is a he, likes to taunt his victims, make them jumpy and nervous so they'll make mistakes."

Scott looked around the room. "Well, he or she made a gross miscalculation this time."

"Yeah, but they don't know it yet."

"Let's not underestimate them."

Holding an index finger to his lips, Scott motioned for Jackie to remain quiet. He walked to the phone, picked up the receiver, and unscrewed the mouthpiece. They saw the bug and Scott reacted immediately.

"Well, let's go to the airport." He checked his Sig Sauer. "We don't want to miss our flight and get stuck here."

"I'm right behind you."

After checking out of the Hampton Inn, they left the rental car in the hotel parking lot and walked toward Flounders Chowder House.

Scott talked in a hushed voice. "These people are real pros."

"Yeah, but they're reckless."

"First thing we do is contact the police and get a bomb squad out here to isolate the area and check our car."

"Good idea."

With a heightened sense of awareness they continued toward the restaurant, while Scott kept his eyes moving. "As usual, Hartwell made it clear that we have carte blanche for whatever we need."

"Well, we better send a distress signal."

Scott reached for Flounder's front door and opened it. "Think I'll have Hartwell arrange for us to be flown to D.C."

"From the regional airport?"

"I don't think that would be in our best interest. We've already been ambushed. We'll take a cab to the air station and the navy can fly us to Washington."

"You're right. They have several Sabreliners and Beechjets here that they use for training."

"Bingo."

Jackie suddenly stopped, causing Scott to inadvertently bump into her. "It just came to me—we weren't paying attention."

"What are you talking about?"

"The other night at the Grant Grill—in San Diego—the dapper Oriental man who was sitting across from our table?"

Dalton paused, searching his mind. "You're right." He recalled the small, well-dressed man who had examined his menu for an extended period of time. "He was Chinese, if my memory serves me correctly."

"That's right, and he must have been reading our lips."

"I'll be damned."

"Remember, he was in the lounge too. He probably read Earlywine's lips and knows the whole story."

"We should've noticed." Scott's satellite phone rang. He answered it as they sat down at an empty table.

Jackie cautiously looked around the crowded patio. She listened to Scott, noticing his face take on a troubled expression. Seconds later, he absently placed the phone on the table.

"Hartwell."

"What is it?"

"Lou Emerson supposedly committed suicide in his apartment."

"No."

"There's only one problem. Actually, there are two prob
lems. No suicide note has been found."

"And?"

"He was found in his bedroom, weapon in hand, but there
were small drops of his blood in the hallway and in the
kitchen—which happens to be thirty-seven feet away."

Scott rested his chin in the crook of his thumb and fore
finger. "That's a helluva long way to walk with part of your
head missing."

"Why would someone move him to the bedroom?"

"I have no idea."

"Was there any tissue, any evidence, in the kitchen?"

"Nothing but a few minuscule blood drops leading to the
hallway. The entire kitchen had been sanitized. JAG is inves
tigating, but I don't think they'll find any evidence leading to
the murderer."

"We don't know how to contact Merrick," Jackie said.

"Let's find out if she's gone on leave yet."

"Do you think Emerson's death is related to the first
crash?"

"Absolutely. According to Hartwell, Emerson was consid
ered to be a stable guy who didn't have an enemy in the
world."

"Well, he had at least one."

6

New Orleans, Louisiana

With her yellow voile dress blowing softly in the warm Louisiana breeze, Adriana Douville leaned against the ivy-covered balcony railing of her magnificent antebellum home. The pale moonlight accentuated her aqua-blue eyes and creamy smooth complexion. A native of Oxford, Mississippi, Mrs. Douville didn't look like a newly minted grandmother. Trim and soft spoken, she looked like the quintessential southern belle and cheerleader she had been at Ole Miss.

Mrs. Douville took in a deep breath of the humid night air and let her shoulders relax, then gazed down at the lighted fountain and gaily decorated courtyard. Their festive anniversary celebration had been a rollicking success, and she was glad that the last of the dinner guests had finally left.

She sipped her cordial and admired the lush green liriope that bordered brightly colored petunias and magenta impatiens planted around the old-fashioned gas streetlamps. Beyond the towering, moss-draped oak trees and the ivory magnolias, a classic garden gazebo added the final touch to the vintage courtyard of their distinctive New Orleans residence.

Her quietude was interrupted when her husband, Dr. Lavon Douville, a preeminent theoretical physicist, ascended the softly lighted spiral staircase and transferred his fresh mint julep to his left hand. Tall and chunky, he was the son of a New Orleans cop who had drunk himself to death after his wife ran away with another man. Raised by his fundamental-

ist grandmother, Douville had been a brilliant student who
won a full scholarship to the Georgia Institute of Technology
and subsequently received his doctorate at MIT.

"Happy anniversary, Addy," Douville said. He leaned
against the wall and raised his glass.

"And happy retirement to you." She extended her manicured hand in a toast. "The party was a huge success, especially the musicians."

"I'm glad you enjoyed them."

"They were so pleasant and professional, not like those
ragtag hooligans we had last year."

"Now, Addy, I've apologized for that." Douville downed
half his drink. "These fellows are some of the best in New Orleans, the very best you can find in this part of the country."

"They were certainly an improvement." Adriana looked at
the small boat floating in the large, round fountain. The can-
dle inside the cabin cruiser had finally gone out. "I can't wait
to start decorating our yacht."

"You'll get your chance." Douville swirled the ice in his
glass and tossed back the last of his mint julep. "We have to
find a permanent captain too."

"What about a cook?"

"Whatever you want, dear. This is going to be our magic
carpet. We aren't going to spare any expense."

Mrs. Douville never questioned her husband's financial affairs, but his unexpected retirement and the new motor yacht
were certainly puzzling to her. Steeped in southern culture,
Mrs. Douville was a traditional wife and mother. Money was
none of her concern. Men made the money and women raised
the children and, with the help of maids, butlers, nannies, and
gardeners, maintained their homes.

"Are you sure our new boat can make it to the Bahamas?"

"*Boat?* It's a seagoing *yacht.* We can go anywhere—as
long as they have water."

"You know I trust you."

"After thirty-one years of marriage, I certainly hope so."

"It's just that so much has happened so quickly, so many
changes we have to make in our lives."

"You'll get used to them." A chorus of katydids serenaded them from the far corner of the yard. "I'm going to fix another drink."

"Here, I'll get it. I'm going to freshen mine too."

"Thanks," Douville said, then looked at the moon. "We're going to see the world and watch beautiful sunsets. We'll do anything we want to do." His last few words were slurred.

She kept her thoughts to herself. For the past eight months, her husband had been drinking heavily during his infrequent trips home. Lost in her thoughts, she walked downstairs to the kitchen.

Dr. Douville shoved himself upright and unsteadily approached the balcony railing. He stopped and placed his hands on it, breathed in the night air, and then turned around and leaned against the railing. There was a sudden snap, followed by a desperate gasp. Dr. Douville plunged backward into the fountain, striking his head on the brick border. A huge wave of water sank the toy boat.

With his head cradled in Adriana's lap, Lavon Douville died four minutes before the ambulance arrived.

The Winslow Estate, Maryland

Jackie glanced at the groundskeepers as Scott drove up the private avenue leading to Hartwell Prost's sprawling European-style residence. Canopied by stately trees, the approach to the mansion was immaculately manicured. Serenely situated on thirty-seven acres of beautiful hunt country outside Baltimore, the prestigious home featured six fireplaces, a guest lodge, caretakers' cottages, swimming pool, tennis court, and a putting green. In addition, the estate included two stables and landscaped grounds extending to a wide footbridge that spanned a stream leading to a large pond.

"This is incredible," Jackie said. "Truly incredible by anyone's standard—like a movie location."

"I had the same reaction the first time I came out here."

"It reminds me of the gardens of Versailles."

"That it does, especially the flair of Italian Renaissance blended into the theme of Versailles."

He slowed his rare Ferrari 275 GTB Spider to a stop at the center of the huge circular driveway and then checked his watch.

"One minute to three," he said, noticing a white car parked on the far side of the driveway. The driver, a young navy seaman in dress whites, was contentedly reading a magazine.

"It looks like we have company," Scott said, opening his door.

"SecDef?"

"I doubt it." Scott climbed out of the handsomely restored car and carefully shut the door. "He'd be in his limo."

One of the oversized doors opened before they reached the top of the steps. They were greeted by a tall, distinguished looking gentleman.

"Good afternoon, Mr. Dalton."

"Hello, Zachary."

"And this must be Miss Sullivan," the butler said.

"Yes." She smiled.

"Welcome. Mr. Prost will be with you in a moment." He motioned down the hallway and escorted them to a spacious library. "Please make yourselves comfortable."

"Thank you," Scott said.

"You're quite welcome." Zachary quietly closed the door.

They were about to take a seat when Hartwell Prost entered the room through a different door and removed his cap. A young navy lieutenant wearing dress whites followed Prost into the darkly paneled library.

Introductions were made and Hartwell asked everyone to be seated around a large polished conference table. Prost explained to the lieutenant that Scott and Jackie were former military aviators who now handled special investigations for the government.

"Lieutenant Justice was the wingman of the pilot who was lost in the Strait of Taiwan. He was kind enough to fly from the carrier to Tokyo, then catch a commercial flight in order to give the president and SecDef a firsthand account of the event."

Surprised, Scott and Jackie glanced at each other. In his gentlemanly way, Prost was attempting to make the young lieutenant feel at ease. Pilots don't normally report directly to the White House after witnessing an unusual incident.

Hartwell looked at the lieutenant. "Todd, why don't you tell us exactly what happened that night."

Visibly nervous, Justice recounted the entire incident. It was a mirror image of Merrick Hamilton's experience.

"Lieutenant, what do you *really* think you saw?" Scott asked.

"I'm not sure, sir."

"Was there any similarity to other objects you've seen at other times?"

Justice glanced at Prost.

"It's okay, son. You're free to speak your mind."

The lieutenant remained silent for a moment and then looked directly at Dalton. "Sir, what we saw was not like anything I've ever encountered. I would be speculating if I attempted to answer your question."

"I understand. What do you think caused your flight leader's plane to explode—any idea?"

"I've thought about it over and over." He paused, physically and mentally tired. "I have a master's degree in aeronautical engineering, and the only thing that comes to mind is a laser, a very powerful deuterium fluoride laser with pinpoint accuracy."

Justice stopped for a second. "But that still doesn't explain the circle of lights and the abrupt, high-G maneuvers."

"You mentioned a bright flash."

"Yes, sir."

"Deuterium fluoride lasers are invisible to the naked eye."

"I'm aware of that, sir, but there *was* a bright flash."

"You're sure?"

"I'm absolutely positive. I just don't know where it came from—the surface or the sky."

"Why do you believe it was a laser?" Jackie asked.

"I don't know of anything else that could blow an airplane out of the sky—destroy it completely—other than a missile."

"Did you have any kind of warning?" Scott asked. "A missile lock, or anything suspicious prior to the encounter?"

"No, not a thing."

"And nothing on radar?"

"Not on mine, and as far as I know, no one else was tracking the bogey, whatever it was."

Prost rose from his chair. "Todd, why don't you get some rest and visit with your family and friends. I've arranged ten days of basket leave for you, so relax and enjoy yourself."

"Thank you, sir." He energetically shook Prost's hand and then politely excused himself. Zachary had the front door open before Lieutenant Justice cleared the library.

Hartwell motioned for Jackie and Scott to sit down. "Well, the two of you made a wise decision in Pensacola. One that undoubtedly saved your lives."

"Beg pardon, sir?" Scott said.

"Your rental car, the Mitsubishi convertible, had an explosive charge attached to the underside of the frame. It was fused to detonate when the drive shaft rotated."

Wide eyed, Jackie and Scott glanced at each other.

"The bomb disposal people said it would've blown the car into the Gulf of Mexico—they called it a Wile E. Coyote bomb."

Scott and Jackie remained quiet, contemplating their fortuitous escape from almost certain death.

Hartwell reached for his pipe. "There's a definite correlation between your awareness of these crashes and the attempts on your lives. The driving force behind these attacks knows that the incidents are being officially denied for the time being, but they also know the two of you are conducting an *unofficial* investigation."

Scott had a question. "Are these events the result of some black program gone askew, some kind of skunk works project so supersecret that an investigation invites murder?"

"I honestly don't have any idea. I had a long session with SecDef and he's as befuddled as everyone else."

"Befuddled?" Jackie asked.

"Yes. The White House, the Pentagon, the FBI, the CIA, the National Reconnaissance Office, the National Security Agency, our entire intelligence community, and the spooks who head the black programs that operate outside the checks and balances of oversight had a coming to Jesus."

Hartwell lit his pipe. "The president thinks we could soon be facing a fire storm of antigovernment paranoia. He pulled no punches during the meeting. He praised everyone for their hard work and achievements, then told everyone to come clean or face possible criminal charges and dismissal."

Prost reached into his shirt pocket to retrieve his notes. "There weren't any surprises, so the spooks quietly went back to their bunkers and secret hangars while the Pentagon—actually, the navy—temporarily went into a state of paralysis."

"Paralysis?" Scott asked.

"For the time being, the navy is going to stand down from night flying operations from their carriers, with one exception. The Hawkeyes will continue to cover the battle groups, while manned and armed fighters will be standing by on the catapults."

Scott slowly shook his head. *That's a mistake.*

"Secretary Adair is deeply concerned about the strange objects. He doesn't want to take any chances until we know what we're dealing with, unless, of course, we're forced to conduct actual combat operations."

Jackie frowned. "Sir, it won't take long for those who oppose the U.S. to realize that our carrier planes are grounded at night."

"I know. The president wants to keep this, ah, *situation* as quiet as possible for as long as we can. In order to solve this mystery, we're going to use every resource we have, including your assistance."

"How about launching some satellites with teeth?" Scott suggested. "We need an overview of the carrier battle groups and reconnaissance aircraft like Cobra Ball."

"The president and the National Reconnaissance Office happen to agree with your way of thinking. The air force is going to launch two Orion SIGINT spacecraft into geosynchronous orbit—one over the Eastern Pacific and one over the Western Pacific."

Hartwell looked at his briefing notes. "After the satellites are safely parked, they will monitor communications from the Sea of Okhotsk, Japan, North Korea, China, Indonesia, the west coast of Canada, the U.S., Mexico, and the western fringes of Central America. They will operate in harmony with our other spacecraft to provide continuous eavesdropping over most of the Pacific Ocean."

Hartwell folded his notes. "Scott, I've arranged for you and Jackie to have access to the FBI, CIA, NRO, and NSA. If there is anything you need, including military assets, they will be at your disposal."

Prost handed each of them a piece of paper. "These are the names and private telephone numbers of the contacts at the various agencies."

Scott and Jackie immediately recognized the names of the directors of each of the government bureaus listed.

"If you have any problems, don't hesitate to contact me. The president wants answers, and as usual, he wants them yesterday. Whatever it takes, find out what we're up against."

"Yes, sir," Scott said.

Zachary tapped on the door and hurried into the library. The perpetual smile was missing.

"Mr. Prost, Secretary Adair is on your secure line."

"Thank you."

Hartwell rose and walked to the desk phone as Zachary left the room and closed the door. Jackie and Scott sat quietly while Prost took the call. He mostly listened, then swore softly as he placed the receiver down and turned to his visitors.

"The air force lost a B-2 near Guam. According to the crew of a KC-10 tanker, the bomber was maneuvering into position to refuel when a bright, bluish-white object flashed into view and circled the planes. According to the boom operator, fifteen to twenty seconds later he saw a bright flash and the *Spirit of Mississippi* blew up, completely disintegrated in a huge fireball. The tanker pilots said the object streaked out of sight in a matter of seconds."

"Does the press know about this?" Jackie asked with some alarm.

"Not yet, as far as we can tell, but they'll know very shortly. It's hard to hide the loss of a two-and-a-half-billion-dollar stealth bomber, especially when foreign intelligence teams keep track of the whereabouts of each one of our B-2s. Later this evening, the Air Combat Command at Langley is going to confirm that a B-2 was lost during a show-of-force training mission to Guam."

Prost cast his gaze at the floor. "According to SecDef, why it went down is going to be left to official investigators. The tanker crew, which has been confined to their quarters at Andersen, has been ordered not to say anything about the crash to anyone."

Hartwell's voice was barely audible. "We have to resolve this crisis before we have a worldwide panic envelop us."

Scott remembered Cliff Earlywine's tape and reached into his jacket pocket. "Sir, sorry to interrupt, but this is the tape I was telling you about."

"Yes," Hartwell said as he eagerly reached for the miniature tape. "Yes, indeed."

"Sir, I'd appreciate it if we could keep Mr. Earlywine, the reporter who made the tape, out of the loop for his sake."

"As far as anyone is concerned, I received it in the mail— anonymously."

"Thank you, sir."

Hartwell rose from his chair.

Jackie and Scott followed his lead.

"We'll be in touch soon," Scott said.

He and Jackie shook hands with Prost and walked toward the door.

"Be careful."

"Yes, sir," Scott said. He reached for the door handle and then hesitated. "By the way, sir, I do have one special request."

7

En Route to Georgetown

After leaving Prost's estate, Scott skillfully negotiated the heavy traffic on Interstate 95 as they drove south toward Washington, D.C. Glancing at a line of dark thunderstorms, he was anxious to get his glossy red Ferrari back in his garage in Georgetown. An uncommon car, Scott's GTB Spider had made its first public appearance in the original movie version of *The Thomas Crown Affair.*

With two phone calls, one of which was to President Macklin, Hartwell Prost had set in motion the ingredients to fulfill Scott's special request. It was the foundation for a daring plan to solve the mystery behind the series of deadly crashes.

Scott couldn't wait to return to the Marine Corps Air Station at Cherry Point, North Carolina. Cheerless Point, as it was referred to by many of those individuals stationed there, was the home of VMAT-203, the AV-8B Harrier readiness-transition training squadron. The U.S. Marine Corps had been instructed to requalify former Capt. Scott Dalton in their two-seat TAV-8B Harrier trainers.

Pleasantly surprised by Dalton's bold initiative, the president and Prost endorsed the scheme and imposed two conditions. Only a small coterie of people would know about the operation, and if anything happened to Scott and Jackie, they would be remembered as having disappeared while conducting personal business in South America. To authenticate the cover story for the White House, the Agency would leave a trail leading from Scott and Jackie's home to Venezuela.

As always, regardless of the type of operation, Jackie and Scott would go in sterile. No form of identification or identifying jewelry or clothing. In addition, all articles of clothing and footwear had to be free of identifiable tags or logos. As far as the White House and U.S. government were concerned, Dalton and Sullivan were aviation consultants.

While Scott was requalifying in the TAV-8B, Jackie would be receiving a thorough indoctrination to prepare her to fly in the backseat of the unique attack aircraft. Also known as the Jump Jet, the Harrier is designed to land and take off vertically like a conventional helicopter, then fly at speeds in excess of six hundred miles per hour.

"I'm having a problem with your plan," Jackie said.

"Would that be the *expendable* part of the operation?"

"Lucky guess."

"That's why we get anything we want, any support we need, plus a huge infusion to our retirement portfolios."

"*If* we pull this off without being incinerated."

"We're going to be just fine, trust me."

"Let's see, where have I heard that expression before? Oh, yes, our last operation—when we were involved in two helicopter crashes and an aircraft ditching, in the space of one week."

"Hey, everyone has things go sour now and then."

"*Sour?* That's your definition of an ongoing disaster?"

Scott braced for the inevitable backlash.

"Why didn't you discuss this harebrained idea with me before announcing your plan to Hartwell?"

"It just came to me as we were about to leave."

"Oh, no, no, *nooo*. That didn't just fly out extemporaneously. You had thought it through and decided not to discuss it with me. Why?"

"That's not true."

"I've been laboring under the illusion that we're a team."

"We are a team—a good one. I *had* thought about the idea, but it didn't really gel until Todd Justice told us he thought his flight leader could have been struck by a laser."

"Come on."

"Jackie, if you'll take the time to think about this, it isn't crazy. The Pentagon and the CIA are convinced that the Red Chinese, with the help of Soviet scientists, have developed an antisatellite laser that could cripple the U.S. military's orbiting reconnaissance spacecraft."

She nodded. "It's probably like the MIRACL chemical laser—the vintage mid-infrared advanced chemical laser."

"That's right, but the Chicoms may have come up with something much more powerful. Something that can fire a laser beam hundreds of miles into space and obliterate our spies in the sky, the space station, or even a space shuttle—who knows?"

Jackie glanced at him. "If they can do that, it seems like hitting a rocket or an airplane would be relatively easy."

"Sure—look at our breakthrough in directed-energy weapons. The future belongs to DEW, and they're making great strides at the Air Force Research Laboratory at Wright-Patterson and at Lockheed Martin."

"But that's a system using an airborne laser in a radar-like function to foil SAMs and air-to-air missiles—send them off course."

"I'm just looking at the concept," Scott said. "A laser can be pointed down to jam or destroy something as easily as it can be directed upward. If the Chinese do have the capability to hit our recon satellites and space shuttles, we're facing an eventual war in the heavens. The same with our desire to control the ultimate high ground. When we deploy a whiz-bang weapon to protect our interests in orbit, it will trigger an arms race in space and eventually lead to a war with somebody."

"Just like the seventeen hundreds."

He looked at her. "What?"

"We had to form a navy to protect our interests on the high seas. And that led to a number of famous sea battles over the years."

"Yeah, and space *will* be the battle zone of the future."

"Well, that's the future. At the present time we don't know what the Chinese really have or what they plan to do."

"Correct. That's why we're going to have spacecraft and

reconnaissance planes eyeballing everything within a five-hundred-mile radius of our carrier. If there's an airborne laser or surface laser out there, we want evidence of the platform—the mother ship or whatever we find."

"I still don't like the idea."

"Jackie, we're going to be using an unmanned, brightly lighted Fox-4 as a drone—piece of cake."

"*That's* the upside?"

"What better target than a remotely piloted Phantom to draw fire from whatever it is we're up against?"

Jackie slowly shook her head. "What if *it,* whatever *it* is we're trolling for, targets us instead of the drone—blows us out of the sky?"

"Our Harrier is going to be blacked out and offset about two hundred yards. We won't be visible."

"Let me try this again. What if *it* targets us?"

"That should be obvious. We jump out—jettison the airplane."

"And if we don't have time?"

"Everyone who has witnessed these encounters says the same thing. The 'bogey' plays with the target before any—"

"Before it turns them into crispy critters."

"Jackie, there are a lot of tools of manipulation and deception that make potential enemies hear, see, and believe things that don't actually exist. Our job is to find out what's going on and who's behind it."

He glanced at the dark clouds and turned to her. "I get the distinct impression that you're not *uninhibitedly enthusiastic* about the Phantom mission."

"What gave you that idea?"

"You know"—he paused and then gave her a sidelong glance—"you don't have to do this with me."

"Don't be ridiculous. Who else could you get to operate the camera and video equipment?"

"Well, that could be a problem."

She ignored him. "Besides, after the other dumb things I've seen you get away with, I'm convinced God isn't going to let anything happen to you."

Scott laughed and then maneuvered the Ferrari into traffic on the notorious Capital Beltway. "New subject?"

"Sure."

"Are we positive the man we saw at the Grant Hotel was Chinese?"

"I can't swear he was, but that was my impression."

Scott reflected on the encounter. *I glanced at him only once or twice.*

"You mentioned the passenger," Jackie said quietly. "The Oriental man in the white Mazda."

"Yes."

"Was he Chinese?"

"I don't know," Scott said, trying to remember the details. "He could've been Japanese for all I know."

"What was your first thought?"

"Chinese, but I saw his face for only a split second." They locked eyes momentarily before Scott spoke. "Where are you going with this?"

"I'm just thinking about all these strange encounters. A Hornet goes down off southern California, a Cobra Ball down in the Bay of Bengal, another Hornet down in the Strait of Taiwan, and a B-2 downed near Guam."

"Do you think the Chicoms or Japanese are behind these encounters?" Scott asked.

"That's always a possibility. Except for the incident off the coast of California, the other planes were lost—attacked is a better description—in an area of the world with a lot of chilly relationships."

"True." A flash of lightning caught his eye. "The steady growth of the Chinese military is an ongoing crisis for Washington—the jitters over the eventual clash between China and Taiwan."

"Yeah, and the prowling dragon isn't going to ask Washington for permission."

"Not on your life."

She hesitated a few seconds. "Do you think China's burgeoning economy might keep Beijing from invading Taiwan?"

"No, unless China breaks out in a flurry of democracy—about as likely as an orangutan piloting the space shuttle."

Scott exited the beltway and turned toward their home in Georgetown. "In the last twelve years, China has increased military spending by more than three hundred percent. That buys a lot, including three Russian-made *Sovremmennyy*-class destroyers equipped with nuclear-tipped cruise missiles—anti-ship missiles that travel at twice the speed of sound. That's raising the stakes very high in the Taiwan Strait."

Scott glanced at Jackie. "Wait until Taiwan takes delivery of our Aegis-class destroyers. They could defend the island against China's medium-range missiles."

"Yeah, that could trigger a harsh response."

The entire sky had turned black as Scott watched the first few drops of rain splatter on the Ferrari's freshly waxed hood. "Beijing may think we're too involved in our war against terrorism to respond to a Chinese attack on Taiwan."

A brilliant flash of lightning and a booming clap of thunder signaled the beginning of a downpour.

Jackie watched the rain stream across the window. "Yeah, that's the big one. Under the Taiwan Relations Act, an assault on the island would be tantamount to the Chinese attacking the United States."

She thought about the scenario. "Do you think Beijing would *really* be crazy enough to test us over a renegade province?"

"Who knows? America and China are at another crossroads in history. In 1992, China's National People's Congress passed a law asserting ownership of the Spratlys, the Senkakus, the Paracels, and Taiwan. The Chicoms may feel like it's time to recover the territories lost during the *bainiande ciru.*"

"The what?"

"The century of shame."

Her voice became flatter. "When I think about it, Beijing has shown an increased willingness to take risks."

"Well, we've been treating the regime with kid gloves, and Beijing just keeps slapping us in the face—like holding twenty-four of our military personnel eleven days after the Chinese pilot slammed into our recon plane. Accommodating the Chinese leaders isn't going to prevent a military clash."

"Bull's-eye." She half turned in her seat to face Scott. "After our past policy of appeasement, I'm afraid we're going to have an armed conflict with China at some point. It just seems inevitable."

"That's the way I view it. Appeasement is not what you want to do with the People's Republic of China. Beijing is trying to convince Japan, South Korea, Taiwan, and the Philippines that we're a declining power that can no longer protect them."

Scott turned onto their street. "They're making steady progress in the Western hemisphere too. From Canada, to Cuba, to Panama, to South America, Beijing is working on eroding U.S. ties to our allies. It's insidious and reaches into every segment of society, whether it's defense contractors, scientists, politicians, or whoever.

"The PLA and the Chinese government have penetrated U.S. capital markets. They're methodically sucking billions of dollars from unsuspecting Americans, and we're letting them get away with it—billions of American dollars to help Beijing build a powerful military to confront us. Incredible— while our politicians just waddle along, blissfully dancing with the dragon."

His jaw became rigid. "Here's the real problem for the Chicoms in Beijing. Time is not on their side."

"In what way?"

"One of these days the boys in Beijing will look around and see the rise of the Chinese middle class, the growing social unrest, America's ever-expanding technological edge, the U.S. military becoming stronger, Taiwan's increasing assertiveness, and conclude that they have to do something drastic. That's what makes the situation so dangerous."

Jackie's satellite phone rang and she answered it.

Scott drove into their driveway.

"Okay, have fun, enjoy yourself, and we'll keep you informed."

"Merrick?"

"Yes. We missed her at the base by ten minutes."

"Where is she?"

"In a hotel near Santa Barbara."

Scott eased the dripping Ferrari inside the garage. "You didn't tell her about Lou Emerson?"

"No, for a reason."

"At this stage, that was probably the right thing to do." Scott got out of the car and double-locked the garage door from the inside. "At least she's in a safe place."

"Let's hope so."

Georgetown

The early morning sky was showing a hint of daylight as Jackie brewed a pot of mint tea and poured fresh orange juice into their glasses. While she fixed breakfast, Scott brought in the *Washington Post* and *USA Today*. He checked the weather for the flight to Marine Corps Air Station Cherry Point, North Carolina, filed an instrument flight plan, and called Signature Flight Support at Washington Dulles International Airport.

He instructed the customer service representative to have the fuel tanks on his Beech A36 Bonanza topped off, then sat down to have a light breakfast with Jackie. He was about to pepper his scrambled eggs when he turned to the third page of *USA Today* and fixed his eyes on the leading headline.

"Here we go again."

"What?" Jackie asked while she poured tea.

"Another mysterious crash."

"Where?"

"The Sea of Japan—a Japanese AWACS." He scanned the article and handed the paper to her. "All military aircraft so far—no civilian airplanes in these crashes."

She folded the paper to look at the headline. "An AWACS isn't a fighter plane or bomber—it isn't a direct threat, so why was it downed?"

"Who knows?"

She studied the article.

No Survivors in Japanese AWACS Crash

By Thad K. Marlow
USA TODAY

NAGOYA, JAPAN—A Japanese Air Force Boeing 767 AWACS reconnaissance plane crashed into the Sea of Japan approximately 125 miles northwest of Kanazawa, Japanese Air Force sources have confirmed. There were no survivors, and the cause of the crash is being investigated.

Operating from the Hamamatsu Air Base near Nagoya, the $450-million aircraft, the most expensive in the Japanese inventory, went down at 11:37 P.M. local time while conducting a routine patrol flight. The remaining fleet of Japanese 767 AWACS planes will be grounded pending the outcome of the initial accident investigation, said Lt. Comdr. Yoshio Okura, spokesperson for the Japanese Air Force.

A senior official at the Air Traffic Flow Management Center in Fukuoka, Japan, who spoke on condition of anonymity, said the AWACS reported being harassed by an unidentified object moments before communications were lost with the early-warning airplane.

The crew of a trawler operating in the Sea of Japan reported seeing a strange, fast moving bluish-white light in the night sky prior to observing a bright, loud explosion high over their position. The trawler crew, who reported no survivors from the AWACS plane, recovered two bodies and several small pieces of debris from the crash site.

"Well," Scott said, "I guess we can eliminate the Japanese from the likely list of suspects."

Finished with the article, she looked up. "I wouldn't be too sure."

"Why not?"

"It could be a ruse to cast doubt elsewhere."

"You have to be kidding."

"No, I'm not kidding—they're very clever people."

Scott chuckled as he reached for his juice. "Almost a half-million dollars to create a smokescreen?"

"What better way to develop an illusion?"

"How about downing three or four less expensive airplanes?"

"That would look like—"

From the window ledge, Jackie's satellite phone interrupted their conversation. She answered while Scott downed his glass of juice and reached for the *Post*.

"No, it's perfectly okay," she said to the caller. "I've been up for nearly an hour and a half."

She listened intently.

When he saw Jackie frown, Scott stopped eating and placed his fork on his plate. While he listened to the one-sided conversation, Jackie reached for a pen and a scratch pad. She wrote the name *Merrick* and shoved the note toward Scott. He glanced at it and then addressed his eggs.

"I understand. Please listen carefully to me. Don't go near your car. Leave it where it is. Go to the hotel lobby and stay there until we can make arrangements to have the FBI pick you up and take you to a safe place."

Jackie switched the phone to her other ear. "Yes, we have the authority—trust me. In fact, I'll be talking to the director of the FBI as soon as we hang up. The closest field office is in Los Angeles, so it may take a while. Pack your belongings and head for the lobby—call us when you're settled in."

After she hung up, Jackie stared at the phone.

"What's going on?"

"Cliff Earlywine is dead."

Scott was stunned. "What?"

"He's been killed."

"How did he die?"

"Merrick saw a report on television about Earlywine dying in a traffic accident last evening near Oceanside, Cali-

fornia. The commentator said Cliff was a well-known news
paper reporter who had broken a number of big stories and
was apparently working on a major story at the time of his
death."

"Where is she, and what's with the FBI?"

"She's at the Rancho Santa Barbara Marriott. After we
talked to her yesterday, she met some people who invited her
to join them for an afternoon tour of the wineries in the re
gion."

"Were they Orientals?"

"I didn't ask—damn," she said, reaching for Scott's phone
directory. "I'll call information."

"Yeah, we need to find out."

"At any rate, when they got back from the tour, they went
out for a late dinner. Afterward her friends brought her back
to the hotel and she went to bed. She couldn't go to sleep, so
around three o'clock she switched on the television to get a
news update. When she heard Cliff's name, she sat up in
shock, then called us."

"What's her frame of mind now?"

"From the sound of her voice, she seems pretty con
cerned."

"Good—she needs to stay alert."

Jackie gave him a stern look. "She can take care of her
self."

"Okay, okay." He extended his palms toward Jackie.
"Lighten up; try relaxing for a change."

"I *am* relaxed."

"Good," he said with a smile. "How about calling Mer
rick's hotel, and I'll use my home phone to call Jim Eber
sole?"

"Will do."

The director of the FBI answered on the third ring. The ur
gent request was quickly forwarded to the senior agent in Los
Angeles. Scott gave Jackie the high sign and she told Merrick
that help was on the way.

"Her friends were *not* Oriental," Jackie said, placing the
satellite phone on the table.

"That's a relief."

"Earlywine didn't have an accident." She pushed her plate aside. "He was killed and we both know it."

"Yes, we'd better ask the FBI to investigate."

"I'll take care of it."

He could see the sadness in her eyes. "I don't know about you, but I've lost my appetite."

"Same here."

Scott folded his napkin and caught her eye. "Let's load the dishwasher and head for the airport."

She rose from her chair. "There's something very wrong with this picture, something sinister."

"Why don't you fly this morning—concentrate on other things."

"Yeah, good therapy."

8

Rancho Santa Barbara Marriott

Entering the empty lobby of the hotel, Merrick felt a gnawing sense of uneasiness as she walked to the counter to check out. Glancing at her wristwatch, she was surprised to see it was almost 4:00 A.M.

"Is there something wrong, Miss Hamilton?" the desk clerk asked.

"No, there's nothing wrong. I've thoroughly enjoyed my stay, but my plans have changed."

"Well, we hope you'll visit us again."

"I'm looking forward to it."

Nervously alert, Merrick checked the accuracy of her hotel account. Satisfied, she folded the statement and slid it into a side pocket of one of her bags. A sudden flash of headlights caught her attention when a maroon Mercury Grand Marquis pulled into the drive.

The car stopped a few yards past the entrance to the lobby and two men got out. Assuming they were FBI agents, Merrick picked up her luggage and walked outside to greet them. As they approached, Merrick had a sudden feeling that something was wrong.

"Are you Miss 'amilton?" the man with the pencil-thin mustache and impish grin asked.

"Yes."

The middle-aged man and his partner, an Oriental man, flashed their official-looking badges.

"Chauncey 'arrington, FBI. We 'ave been instructed to escort you to our district 'eadquarters."

This doesn't feel right, Merrick told herself. The revelation dawned with gut-wrenching clarity when she glanced at their Mercury and noticed the rental-car sticker on the back bumper. *Don't panic, for God's sake. These guys are imposters, probably the same ones who caused Earlywine's death. Think before you do anything.*

"May we 'elp with your luggage, ma'am?" The mischievous smile remained the same—cheesy and insincere.

Merrick could feel the palms of her hands turning sweaty. *Who are these people?* "That's okay," she said, remembering that Jackie had specifically told her not to go near her car. *Well, I have to take a chance.* "I'll just throw them in my car and follow you to your, ah, office."

"I'm sorry, ma'am, but we 'ave strict orders to drive you to our 'eadquarters. It's standard policy, you understand."

Merrick was afraid to make a move. *How did they know? There must have been a wiretap, a bug in my room.* "I can't leave my car here."

The Oriental opened his suit jacket just enough to expose the handgun in his shoulder holster. There was no way out. The hotel parking lot was completely deserted.

I have to do something, but I have to pick the right time. With her heart in her throat, she silently prayed. *Dear God, I need some help.* "Would one of you gentlemen be kind enough to drive my car?"

"Of course." Harrington looked at his partner and nodded. "If you'll 'and us the keys, we'll be on our merry way."

If I try to run, they could easily shoot me.

"Ma'am, the keys," Harrington said.

With a great sense of trepidation, Merrick fished her keys out of her handbag. She handed them to the silent man and then picked up her two leather bags. With Harrington on one side of her and the other man slightly behind her, Merrick waited for an opportunity to draw attention. Harrington opened the back door of the Mercury and

stepped aside as Merrick tossed her bags in the backseat
and got in.

"Don't you want to know which car is mine?" Merrick
asked, feeling a surge of adrenaline stab her heart.

Harrington's smile faded but quickly reappeared. "Indeed,
that would be quite 'elpful, now, wouldn' it?"

"The gray Chevy Cavalier next to the end of the first row."

With a wave of his hand, Harrington directed his partner
toward Merrick's rental car.

She knew what to do, but it would take some luck. *They
knew which car was mine.*

Harrington got in and started the Mercury. The other man
retrieved Merrick's car and drew up behind the Grand Marquis. Leading the way down Highway 101 toward the Santa
Ynez Mountains, Harrington remained quiet while Merrick
nervously looked for a police car. She had to cause a commotion, anything to draw attention to her plight.

Nearing Santa Barbara, Merrick felt a pain in her chest.
She reached inside one of her bags beside her on the backseat. A weight lifter and marathon runner, she would have to
use her physical conditioning to escape. "What do you think
of your new director of the FBI—what's his name?"

"Don't know—'aven't 'ad the opportunity to meet the
gentleman."

Merrick began to ease her hand out of her bag. *Wait for the
right opportunity. You need to draw attention, not get yourself
killed.*

The Mercury rounded the curve northwest of the Amtrak
train station. Out of the dark, a California Highway Patrol
cruiser appeared from behind and accelerated past the two
cars. It was time to act. She tightly gripped each end of a
sturdy braided belt and flipped it over Harrington's head, then
yanked as hard as she could.

He gasped and struggled like a man who knew he was
about to die. His feet alternately mashed the accelerator and
the brake, resulting in a lurching and swaying ride. Releasing
the steering wheel to use both hands to claw at the belt, Harrington choked and gagged. Merrick pulled as hard as she

could. Without warning, she felt something snap and he went limp. The Grand Marquis ran off the right side of the highway, dangerously swerving and swaying.

Merrick shoved Harrington toward the passenger side, at the same time desperately grabbing the steering wheel to get the car under control. The Mercury careened back on the highway and lurched to the right again. Merrick struggled to climb over the seat and Harrington's tangled legs. *Take control!*

An instant later, the cruiser's flashing lights came on. The officer began slowing the car and easing toward the shoulder of the highway. Afraid that he might be rear-ended, he kept moving while the Mercury driver was steering in such an erratic manner.

With one leg twisted behind her, Merrick swerved to miss the cruiser and smashed into her smaller rental car. The Oriental driver made an attempt to pass her and they collided again. Both cars sprayed glass and twisted parts on the highway as the drivers fought for control. The man floorboarded the Cavalier and continued driving, passing the Mercury and the CHP cruiser.

Shocked by the collisions, Merrick stomped on the brakes. She brought the Grand Marquis to a screeching, smoking stop on the right side of the highway. The patrol car pulled in behind the battered Mercury and stopped. The officer radioed a description of the gray Chevy to headquarters, while he kept an eye on the driver of the Grand Marquis.

Feeling the effects of the adrenaline boost, Merrick finally opened the door and stumbled out. Her knees were shaking as she turned toward the patrolman. *He must think I'm falling-down drunk.*

In the process of running the Grand Marquis's license plate, the officer opened his door. He stepped out of the cruiser and put his hand on his weapon. "Ma'am, step to the back of your vehicle and place your hands on the trunk."

Merrick complied and turned her head toward the patrolman. "Officer, the car I collided with is *my* rental car."

"*Your* rental car?"

"That's right."

"Well, after eighteen years on the job, that's a new one."

She looked straight ahead. "It might be a good idea to radio a description of the *stolen* vehicle—this isn't it."

More curious than concerned for his safety, the patrolman ignored her suggestion. "Ma'am, do you have any weapons on you?"

"No, but the FBI impostor lying in the front seat has a handgun."

"FBI impostor, huh?"

"That's right."

"Well, that's another first."

The trooper cautiously walked toward the driver's door. "Ma'am, have you been drinking?"

"Yes, I have, if you count one glass of wine with dinner about nine-thirty last night."

The officer shone his flashlight on Harrington for a long moment. "Has your passenger been drinking?"

"He was the driver until I saw you, and then I overpowered him. I think he may be dead."

"Overpowered him?"

"Pardon me, but do we have to go over everything twice?"

The patrolman slowly shook his head and cautiously walked to the front passenger door. He kept his light on Harrington while he checked his vital signs, then stepped back.

"You're right about that," he said without taking his eyes off Merrick. "He certainly is dead—looks like he was strangled."

"He was, with one of my belts."

More cautious now, the trooper returned to the back of the Mercury and shone his light in Merrick's face. "Let's start over. Do you have any identification with you?"

"Yes." She squinted at the light. "It's in my handbag in the car."

"Would you mind getting it for me?"

"I'd be happy to," Merrick said, and opened the rear door. She grabbed her purse and then gave the trooper her driver's license and her navy identification card.

He carefully inspected the IDs and handed them to her. "Well, Lieutenant Hamilton, what do you do in the navy?"

With the rush wearing off, Merrick chuckled. "I'm a fighter pilot."

The officer again shook his head. "Why does that not surprise me?"

Cape Canaveral, Florida

The sun was barely above the horizon when a U.S. Air Force Titan 4B Centaur booster, carrying an advanced six-ton NRO Orion signal intelligence spacecraft, gracefully lifted off from Complex 40. Launched by Lockheed Martin and the 5th Space Launch Squadron of the 45th Space Wing, the intelligence-gathering spacecraft would be maneuvered into geosynchronous orbit over the equator north of the Solomon Islands.

Once safely in orbit, Orion, with its antenna spanning more than a hundred feet, would be released and parked at approximately twenty-three thousand miles above the earth to monitor communications from most of the Western Pacific.

Two days later, another Orion spacecraft would be parked on the equator north of French Polynesia in the Eastern Pacific. Working in concert with older KH-11 optical-imaging spacecraft and Lacrosse imaging radars, the latest evolution of sky spies would provide wide-area coverage and greatly bolster U.S. intelligence assessments.

The National Security Agency would be the primary user of the Orion spacecraft, with the CIA and State Department aiding in the interpretation of communication intercepts.

Washington Dulles International Airport

With Jackie in the left seat of the Beech A-36 Bonanza, she and Scott listened to the automatic terminal information service. The latest ATIS provided the ceilings, visibility, obstructions to visibility, current temperature, dew point, wind direction, wind speed, altimeter setting, remarks about the airport, instrument approaches, and the runways in use.

Next Scott called clearance delivery and copied his instrument clearance to MCAS Cherry Point, then read it back to the controller. Even though the weather was good, Scott preferred the safety of an IFR flight plan and the accompanying radar coverage. He called ground control and received permission to taxi to runway one-nine-left as Jackie smoothly added power and turned toward the taxiway.

Scott glanced at a sleek new Citation X that was about to land. "Sure beats the airlines."

"Yeah, no comparison."

"Going where you want, when you want." Scott watched the corporate jet touch down. "If everything goes smoothly this year, I'm hoping to move up to a King Air."

"Need a partner—in an airplane?"

"I'd have to think about that."

After reaching the departure end of the runway, Jackie gently braked to a halt. She completed a thorough engine run-up, checked the flight controls for proper response, glanced at the GPS unit, rechecked the trim and fuel selector valve, then looked at Scott. "I'm ready when you are."

"Dulles tower," Scott radioed, "Bonanza Seven-Seven Hotel Delta is ready to go."

"Bonanza Seven-Seven Hotel Delta, wind is one-six-zero at eight, runway one-nine-left, cleared for takeoff."

"Seven Hotel Delta is rolling."

Jackie turned the strobe lights on, then visually checked for approaching air traffic and taxied onto the active runway. Smoothly adding power, she glanced at the engine instruments while the Bonanza rapidly accelerated straight down the centerline of the runway. Approaching sixty-five knots, Jackie began easing back on the yoke and the airplane gently lifted off the ground.

"It looks like you've done this a time or two."

"Actually, I feel a little rusty," Jackie admitted, raising the landing gear. "I need to fly more often."

After the tower handed them off to departure control, Scott checked in with the controller while Jackie enjoyed hand-flying the Bonanza. Once they had been switched to the Washington Air Route Traffic Control Center, Jackie continued the climb to seven thousand feet before engaging the autopilot.

"What a beautiful morning," she said, surveying the countryside. "This is the best time of day to fly."

"We'll have to do this more often."

"Let's plan on it." Jackie scanned the sky for other aircraft. "When are you going to take me flying in your Great Lakes?"

"As soon as we have time."

"Promise?"

"You have my word."

"Seriously, *Mr.* Dalton, would you consider a partnership in one of your planes—fifty-fifty?"

"That's how guys get into trouble."

"What do you mean?"

"A fifty-fifty partnership with a woman means the woman's in charge. That's how things work on this planet."

"You're incorrigible."

"Wake me when we get there."

"Aye, aye, *Captain.*"

Scott napped while Jackie monitored the instruments, radios, and the GPS moving map. One hour and thirty-two minutes after takeoff, Jackie looked down at the Pamlico River and then studied the Neuse River. A few moments later, she was given permission to begin a descent and contact Cherry Point approach control.

Scott raised his head when Jackie eased the nose down. "When you talk to the tower, see if they'll clear us for a military break."

"Great idea."

"It's smooth this morning," he said. "You can make a shallow descent at cruise power and break at the bottom."

"Are you sure you don't want to fly?"

"You can do it as well as I can."

"Okay, but I don't think we'll get any vapes out of the break."

"If you pull that hard, we'll be landing without any wings."

Jackie keyed the radio. "Cherry Point approach, Bonanza Seven-Seven Hotel Delta is with you out of five point five for three thousand, negative ATIS."

While Scott surveyed the familiar terrain, Jackie was handed off to the tower controller. He gave her permission for a right downwind to runway three-two-left and a break over the middle of the runway. Keeping the power on, she flew downwind, turned base, then final.

She keyed the radio. "Cherry Point tower, Bonanza Seven-Seven Hotel Delta numbers for the break."

"Bonanza Seven-Seven Hotel Delta cleared for the break midfield."

"Seven-Seven Hotel Delta."

Still descending, Jackie crossed the runway numbers at six hundred feet. She waited until midfield and snapped the airplane into knife-edge flight at four hundred feet. After 180 degrees of turn, nailed exactly on four hundred feet, Jackie eased the power back and simultaneously rolled wings level.

"Very nice."

"Thanks."

Slowing, Jackie lowered the flaps and reached for the landing gear handle. She paused and then lowered the wheels. A split second later, a deafening explosion from under the engine cowl horrified them.

"What the hell," Scott exclaimed.

The engine suddenly shook and clattered, threatening to tear itself from the engine mounts.

"Pull the power back!"

"I've got it at idle!" Jackie said, steeply banking the plane toward the runway. "Tower, Seven Hotel Delta has an emergency!"

"Hotel Delta is cleared to land on any runway. You have fire—there's fire coming from under your engine!"

Scott pulled the mixture knob to idle-cutoff while Jackie turned the fuel and ignition off. The engine shook a couple of times and then quit running, as the propeller froze in place.

"It looks like your nosewheel fell off," the controller said, hitting the alarm to roll the crash trucks.

Jackie kept the turn going while Scott scanned the twisted engine cowling. It was shaking and vibrating from the wind whipping it back and forth.

"Keep the speed up!"

"I'm trying to."

The controller keyed his radio. "You have flames and black smoke pouring out of your lower cowling."

"Copy," Jackie snapped.

"You're lookin' good," Scott said, and glanced at the landing gear handle. There was no indication that the main wheels were down. "Tower, are our mains down?"

"They're down, but I can't tell if they're locked."

"Hotel Delta."

Jackie was desperately trying to stretch the glide, but the parasitic drag caused by the canted engine and mangled cowling was forcing her to keep the nose unusually low.

"It's going to be close," she said. "Real close."

"You're doing great—you're a test pilot now."

"Yeah, what a way to start."

Nursing the Bonanza toward the runway, Jackie was still banking the plane with only a few feet of altitude left.

Scott cinched his seat belt tight. "Hang in there."

"Uh-huh—this is going to be an attention getter."

The left wingtip scraped the runway. She made a play for the centerline. Without warning, the blazing engine ripped loose when the main wheels thudded onto the runway.

Scott braced himself for a sudden stop.

Tumbling under the left wing, the engine tore the left landing gear off. There was a wrenching, agonizing screech of metal as the airplane skidded on the twisted wing.

Jackie tried using right brake and right rudder to keep the Bonanza on the centerline, but the drag of the left wing swung the airplane perpendicular to the runway.

"We made it! You did it!"

"Yeah"—she sighed—"terrific."

Yellow flames licked around the leading edge of the lef
wing, then erupted in a searing conflagration. The heat wa
intense. Jackie and Scott clawed at the buckles to free them
selves from their restraining harnesses.

"Let's get outta here!" Jackie said.

Scott wrestled the door open and they scrambled out of the
wreckage. Seconds later, the first crash truck arrived.

They sprinted to the right side of the runway.

"How're you doing?" Scott asked.

"Okay, all things considered."

They stopped to watch the crash crew extinguish the blaz
ing inferno in a matter of seconds.

"Scott?"

"I know what you're gonna say."

"That was a bomb," she said angrily. "It was rigged to gc
off when the landing gear was lowered."

Scott stared at the charred, smoking remains of his prized
A-36 Bonanza. He swore under his breath and then looked a
Jackie. "Hey, partner, at least we're okay."

"Thank God." Her emotions had changed from basic sur
vival mode to open hostility. "Playtime is over for these bas
tards."

"Yeah, we're going to have to get our environment under
control—like today at the latest."

Two firefighters began walking toward them.

"We'll charter one of Greg's Lears," Scott continued,
"minus the pilots, and continue to march."

A fellow Marine Harrier pilot and best friend since Desert
Shield and Desert Storm, Greg O'Donnell was now a civilian
who owned a thriving jet charter company. The growing busi
ness featured two pristine Learjet 35As and a single Lear
36A.

"Great idea, one of your best. Just one minor question."

"What would that be?"

"Are you type rated in Lears?"

"Typed and current." Scott glanced at his destroyed plane. "Greg gave me my latest check last month."

"What are we going to do about security?" Jackie asked. "At this rate, our luck is going to run out if we don't get aggressive—like right now."

Before replying, Scott thought about the blanket offer Hartwell Prost had made to them. *If the president and his national security adviser want results, we have to use some of Uncle Sam's finest assets.*

"We're going to get *fangs-out* aggressive. I'll call Hartwell and we'll have some SEALs assigned to guard the Lear 'round the clock."

She smiled approvingly. "I'd say that should do it, and you need to tell him what has happened here—don't need the Feds snooping around."

"If you'll entertain our reception committee," Scott said, then activated his satellite phone, "I'll contact Hartwell and Greg."

"Yeah, what a grand entrance."

Scott managed a smile. "Look at it this way—we're legends in our own time, at least at Cherry Point."

"Oh, for sure. This will be a great story for the cocktail circuit."

9

Marine Corps Air Station Cherry Point, North Carolina

After dealing with the postaccident reports, including the unpleasant task of notifying his insurance company, Scott received a return call from Hartwell Prost. Scott had barely finished his conversation when he and Jackie were ushered into Maj. Gen. Byrd Grunewald's office.

Grunewald, an unsmiling man with facial scars and a crew cut, was the commanding general of Marine Corps Air Bases Eastern Area/MCAS Cherry Point. His manner and rugged features belied a dry sense of humor and an absolute devotion to the Marines under his command.

"Come in," Grunewald said, walking around his desk and shaking hands with Scott, then Jackie.

"Have a seat." He motioned toward two chairs in front of his desk. "I have to tell you, that was quite an arrival."

Grunewald returned to his chair and sat down.

"Yes, sir," Scott said in a subdued voice. "Most of our landings aren't quite that spectacular."

The general pointed to a long table behind them. "I believe that piece of airplane belongs to you."

Jackie and Scott turned to see the Bonanza's blackened and mangled nosewheel and strut lying on a blanket on the table.

"My ordnance diposal unit tells me a bomb did that."

"Well, sir," Scott said, "we were as surprised as everyone else—believe me, it wasn't pleasant."

"I have no doubt."

Scott focused on the general's eyes. "I'm just going to have to be a lot more careful during my preflights."

Grunewald shifted his gaze to Jackie, then back to Scott. "I don't know who or what you're involved with and I don't want to know. My orders came straight from SecDef, which, I don't need to tell you, is extremely rare. However, after watching your spectacular arrival, I have to know if I need to increase base security while you're here for training."

"That might be a good idea, sir," Scott said.

The general mulled over the advice. "Captain Dalton, you know the threat facing you better than I. What do you suggest?"

"Increased gate security, including checking all vehicles for stowaways and bombs. Also, the entire perimeter of the base should be patrolled around the clock."

"Anything else?"

"Your Marines should be heavily armed. The people who put the bomb on my airplane are well equipped and ruthless."

"Terrorists?"

"We aren't sure yet. I'd say they're more like hired killers."

Grunewald's expression remained unchanged. "As I understand this, after you requalify in the Harrier, we need to send two of our trainers, along with a support team, to Miramar. Is that your understanding?"

"Yes, sir."

"Do you have any idea how long my jets will be there?"

"No, sir."

"How about a guesstimate?"

"I'd say fifteen days, maybe less."

"Well, good luck to you," Grunewald said, rising from his chair to hand Scott a set of car keys. "We have transportation for you. It's the white four-door Chrysler directly in front of the building."

"Thank you, sir."

"Our pleasure. If you want to check into the BOQ, and then go over to 203, I'll call the CO and let him know you'll be there in about what—thirty to forty minutes?"

"That sounds great, sir. Who's the CO?"

"Lieutenant Colonel Reggie Warrington."

"Reggae Reggie?" Scott asked, and then stopped himself. "I apologize, sir, but he was one of my flight instructors when I transitioned into the Harrier."

"No apology needed. Everyone calls him Reggae—one of our best."

Grunewald shook hands with both of them. "Be careful."

"Thank you, sir," Scott said. "I'll try to take better care of *your* planes than I did of mine."

A slow smile crossed the general's weathered face. "Make damn sure you do, captain."

"Yes, sir."

Grunewald pointed at the table. "And take that wreckage with you."

Scott grabbed the twisted nosewheel and strut while Jackie picked up their singed, foam-stained luggage. Once they were outside, Scott loaded the nose gear in the trunk of the Chrysler and turned to Jackie. "Since you flew us here, I'll see if I can get us safely to our quarters."

"Is that a slam?"

"No. Besides, Hartwell gave me quite a bit of information, and I need your undivided attention."

"There you go again."

"What?"

"I can drive and listen at the same time."

Scott tossed her the keys.

When they drove away from the general's headquarters, Scott gave Jackie directions to the BOQ.

"First off, you were right," he began.

"About what?"

"There weren't any fingerprints on the note card from Z Y."

"Did you really think there would be?"

"No, but you always have to check. New subject?"

"Go."

"Our friend Merrick Hamilton was kidnapped by two guys masquerading as FBI agents."

"Kidnapped?"

"Yes, and one of them was Oriental."

"Do they still have her? Is she okay?"

"No, they don't have her, and, yes, she's fine. The real agents arrived at the hotel about thirty minutes after Merrick walked out of the lobby."

"The bogus agents must have been monitoring her calls."

"That's right. The FBI found two bugs in her room, one on the phone and one in the bathroom. When she was talking to us, the bad guys were listening to every word."

"Was she injured?"

"No—in fact, she's in better shape than one of her abductors."

"What do you mean?"

"She strangled him."

"Killed him?"

"That's right—graveyard dead."

Scott filled her in on the details leading to the encounter with the California highway patrolman.

"Where's she now?"

"Under the protection of the FBI. Her parents live in Denver and the FBI has stashed her in a top-notch hotel there."

"Good," Jackie said, genuinely concerned about her fellow aviator. "She needs protection until we can figure out what's going on."

Scott nodded. "We'll stop and visit her on our way to California—get the story directly from her. Maybe she has some information or minor detail that we wouldn't get otherwise."

"What about her obligation to the navy?"

"Hartwell has made arrangements for her to be placed in a temporary reserve status for the time being."

"Does she know about Lou Emerson?"

"Yes. The whole story was revealed when the FBI interviewed her in California. She didn't take it well."

"She's had a rough time."

"Let's hope it's over," Scott said. "She's been through enough."

"Anything else?"

"Well, not surprisingly, the FBI found evidence of foul play in the death of Cliff Earlywine. According to the coroner, and the FBI investigators, Earlywine was killed by blunt trauma to the back of his head. The medical examiner believes the injury that killed him was inconsistent with the type of accident he had."

"How did he arrive at that conclusion?"

"Earlywine's car ran off the road and plowed into a ravine. It never turned over and the damage wasn't severe enough to kill anyone, plus the airbags worked as advertised."

"Scott, why do I have a feeling Hartwell Prost isn't telling us everything he knows?"

"Because he *hasn't* been telling us everything."

Jackie turned into the BOQ parking area and abruptly stopped. "This had better be good, especially after surviving an explosion and a crash landing. Start talking and don't leave anything out—not one little tiny item."

"Hartwell convinced the president that we needed to know *everything*, including the classified information."

"Well, let's have it. I've trusted you to tell me *everything* you know about every operation we've worked together—no secrets."

"There aren't any secrets. Hartwell told me what he could over the phone before we went into General Grunewald's office. He wants to meet us in Denver and give us an up-to-the-minute brief on the whole picture. After our chat in Denver, he's going to Seattle, then he'll join us in San Diego for the Phantom operation."

"Yeah, that'll be a circus."

Scott glanced at a small group of Marines jogging along the road. "I'll tell you exactly what Hartwell told me. The Japanese AWACS that crashed, the article in *USA Today* . . ."

"Yes."

"Besides the flight-crew report of being harassed by an unidentified object, and the eyewitnesses on the trawler, our recon spacecraft have photographic and radar images of a blacked-out, stationary ship near the crash site."

"At night?"

"Yeah, they caught the ship in the flash of the explosion."

"Very interesting."

"I thought so."

"Where's the ship now?"

"It's headed toward the Strait of Korea. It's a Chinese cargo ship named *Chiang Hai-ch'eng*."

"Chinese," Jackie said with a thin smile. "That *is* interesting."

"It sure is—after what we've experienced."

"Are the Japanese going to get involved?"

"They're going to protest, as usual, but that's about it."

"What about the response from the White House? Are we going to pressure the Chinese for an explanation?"

"Well, from what Hartwell said, one of our frigates or destroyers is going to intercept the ship and request the master stop his vessel for consensual boarding. If the captain declines, I don't know what's going to happen next, if anything."

"Maybe we've caught a break." Jackie glanced at her watch. "We'd better pick up the pace and get out to Miramar."

"One other thing. Our Learjet will be here at fifteen-thirty, and the SEALs will be here at seventeen hundred."

"Super—I feel better already."

"The SEALs are from the Naval Special Warfare Development Group."

"You're kidding."

"Nope. DEVGRU is the SEALs' top-of-the-line counter-terrorist unit. They used to be known as SEAL Team Six."

"How did we rate the avant-garde?"

"You know Hartwell."

"Yeah, everything is going to be first cabin with built-in redundancy."

Jackie opened her door. "Well, things are finally looking up."

"That's the way I see it."

"What are we going to do with the nose gear?"

"Well, unless you want to bronze that little beauty," Scott said with a sly grin, "I don't have any use for it."

"It might make a nice yard ornament for your retirement

home in Pensacola," Jackie suggested. "You know, mount it
between a couple of pink flamingos."

"Yeah, what a wonderful reminder."

Beijing, China

A bright yellow moon was beginning to rise when the China Xinjiang Airlines ATR-72 twin turboprop climbed away from Beijing
Capital International Airport. It turned on course to Shanghai, a
major seaport situated on the coast of the East China Sea.

All sixty-six seats aboard the airplane were occupied, with
seven extra passengers sitting in the aisle. Although it vio-
lated the airline's safety regulations, powers on high had au-
thorized the carrying of the seven men at the last moment
before boarding.

Captain Zhou Chan smoothly adjusted the power and settled in for the flight to one of China's burgeoning airports.

Once the regional airliner was at cruising altitude, Captain
Zhou and his first officer, Ts'ao Yat-sen, enjoyed snacks they
had brought on board with them. They discussed the recent
changes in company management and the anticipated addition of five new airliners in the next four months. That would
mean promotions and better pay for some pilots.

Approaching the city of Lianyungang, located on the coast
of the Yellow Sea, copilot Ts'ao made a radio call to the air
traffic controllers.

Zhou studied the darkness of the sea. He could pick out a
few lights on the water, but most of the sea was inky black.

Ts'ao excused himself to use the lavatory while Zhou
studied the flight plan for the next leg of their trip. He was
about to return it to his chart case when suddenly the cockpit
was flooded with a bright, bluish-white light.

At the same instant, shrieks of anguish and terror could be
heard coming from the passenger cabin. He looked toward
the left wing and froze. A huge object with brilliant bluish-
white lights was flying in close formation with the turboprop.

Ts'ao scrambled back into the cockpit and slammed the

door. Zhou banked sharply to the right; at the same time he frantically called the air traffic controllers. The screams coming from the passenger cabin continued as Zhou completed a course reversal and rolled wings level. Ts'ao was strapping into his seat when the bright object joined them on their right wing.

Terrified, Zhou overreacted and banked so steeply to the left that the turboprop rolled over on its back and the nose fell through in a shallow, high-speed dive.

"I have it!" Ts'ao said, grabbing the controls. Using the primary flight instruments, the former aerobatic instructor continued the roll to the left until the airplane was once again wings-level and upright. With Zhou's encouragement, Ts'ao applied smooth G-forces to slowly bring the nose up level with the horizon.

Ts'ao was surrendering the flight controls to Zhou when the object slashed past the cockpit, then pulled straight up and disappeared in a sea of brilliant stars. Frightened and astounded by the encounter, Ts'ao was talking with the air traffic controllers when the object reappeared and made a steep, head-on dive at the airliner.

"No radar," Ts'ao yelled above the screams coming from the cabin. "Nothing on radar! They show nothing!"

"Turn off the lights!" Zhou ordered. "Exterior and interior!"

Ts'ao snapped the switches off. "Dive and make a steep left turn!"

Five seconds later, the pilots and passengers were blinded by a bright bluish-white flash a moment before the ATR-72 exploded, then rolled to the left and exploded again. For more than six minutes, debris continued to impact the Yellow Sea four miles northeast of Lianyungang, China.

MCAS Cherry Point, North Carolina

Lieutenant Colonel Reggie "Reggae" Warrington, commanding officer of Marine Attack Training Squadron 203, the only

Harrier training squadron in the United States, walked into
his office and handed Scott a mug of steaming coffee.

Reggie and his wife had entertained Jackie and Scott
the previous evening. The dinner party had been filled with the
revelry of countless war stories from the early days in the Harrier community.

For Scott, the biggest surprise of the evening was Reggie's
announcement that he, not a squadron instructor, would be requalifying Dalton in the two-seat TAV-8B.

During the next few days, Scott would attend a concentrated and accelerated version of ground school from early
morning until noon, break for lunch, then brief, fly, and debrief two instructional flights with Reggie in the afternoon.
The third day would culminate with a trip to the boat to
carrier-qualify, followed by a night-flying exercise, including
refueling from a KC-130 Hercules.

While Scott was going through the abbreviated requalifying syllabus, Jackie would complete a specialized Harrier
ground school, then receive a thorough checkout in the backseat of the attack plane. After a comprehensive review of all
emergency procedures, she would be scheduled for three
FAM (familiarization) flights and a ride to the boat.

The third and final day of Scott's requalification in the
Harrier, two TAV-8Bs, flown by VMAT-203 instructors,
would depart at 0600 for Marine Corps Air Station Miramar,
California. They would pre-position the jets for Scott and
Jackie, then catch the next available military flight back to
Cherry Point.

The base was beginning to stir as Warrington sat down behind his desk and blew steam from the top of his coffee mug.
"I'm sure you remember what I told you about the Harrier."

"Well, most of it," Scott said.

Reggie took an exploratory sip of coffee. "If you don't
want to bust your ass in a Harrier, you *must* obey the laws of
aerodynamics of V/STOL flight. Like conventional airplanes,
if you disregard what the flying machine is trying to tell you,
things generally go south rather quickly."

A slow grin creased the corners of Scott's mouth. "Yeah, I've been there a time or two—maybe six times."

"In a Harrier it's all over, guar*own*teed, if you don't obey the basic physics of flight. You can have Sky King 'seat-of-the-pants' flying skills, along with the reflexes of a gunfighter, but the Harrier will nail your ass if you let it draw first."

Scott nodded, reflecting on the close calls he'd experienced in the unique attack aircraft. It could be a handful if you let your guard down.

"We'll start with vertical takeoffs, then work on slow-landing touch-and-go's, followed by rolling-vertical landings to a full stop. After that we'll depart the pattern for some air work."

"Sounds good."

Having flown the AV-8B, Dalton didn't anticipate any problems with his refresher training. However, he knew Warrington was dead right. One moment of inattention, one misstep, and the outcome could ruin your day.

Warrington looked at his wristwatch. "You'd better head for the school yard. I'll see you after lunch."

"Lookin' forward to it, sir."

At precisely 1300, Scott reported to Warrington's office. Dalton had changed into his flight gear and was carrying his helmet. Scott and Reggie briefed airfield operating procedures, FAM-one expectations and maneuvers, and all emergency procedures. Finally, after a lengthy question-and-answer session, they were ready to walk. They checked the aircraft's maintenance records, gave the airplane a thorough preflight, and then strapped in for Scott's first sortie.

Start-up, taxi, and takeoff went very well and Scott rapidly felt at home in the plane again. After a half hour it was as if he had never stopped flying the Harrier.

10

The Strait of Korea

At the first hint of daylight on the horizon, the USS *John S. McCain,* an *Arleigh Burke*–class guided missile destroyer, slowly closed on the port side of the Chinese-flagged cargo ship *Chiang Hai-ch'eng.* An SH-60B Seahawk LAMPS Mark III helicopter rose from the aft helo deck of Big Bad John and banked into a shallow 360-degree turn to the right before taking up station on the port side of the destroyer.

Slightly astern of *McCain* and on the starboard side of the rust-covered Chinese vessel, the USS *Vandergrift,* an *Oliver Hazard Perry*–class guided missile frigate, launched one of its SH-60Bs. The Seahawk helos provided all-weather capability for the detection and interdiction of surface ships and submarines. For close encounters of the worst kind, the helicopters were equipped with Mark-46/50 torpedoes, Hellfire and Penguin air-to-surface missiles, and .50-caliber machine guns.

Two *Kitty Hawk*–based F-14 Tomcats from the famous Black Nights of VF-154 loitered overhead the *Chiang Hai-ch'eng* at five thousand feet. Above the sleek fighter planes, two VFA-27 Royal Maces F/A-18 Hornets orbited at seven thousand feet. The four aircraft had refueled from a Marine Corps KC-130 Hercules prior to taking up station over the suspicious cargo ship.

On the bridge of *McCain,* Comdr. Antonio Lavancia raised his binoculars and carefully studied the Chinese ship. Off to the side, Lieutenant Erik Pomeroy, the ship's damage-control officer, quietly cleared his throat.

"What is it?" Lavancia asked without taking his eyes off the cargo ship.

A stickler for regulations and minutiae, Pomeroy stepped forward to address his commanding officer. "Sir, according to the Convention of the High Seas adopted at Geneva, except where acts of interference are derived from powers conferred by treaty, a warship which encounters a foreign merchant ship on the high seas is not justified in boarding her unless there is reasonable ground for—"

"Erik," Lavancia interrupted, "I am fully aware of the rules of international law relating to boarding vessels on the high seas."

Tall and stooped, Pomeroy started to speak, then decided against it when he saw the muscles in Lavancia's neck and face beginning to tighten.

"Our orders are unambiguous. We have been directed to request *permission* to board the ship. That, Mr. Pomeroy, is not a violation of international law. If we are denied permission, that will be the end of our responsibility. No shots across the bow, no further action required, no broken laws."

"Yes, sir," Pomeroy said, and stepped back.

Lavancia felt a twinge of guilt. Ill suited for a career in the military, Erik Bretton Pomeroy was the only son of a highly respected retired navy captain. A graduate of the U.S. Naval Academy, albeit near the bottom of his class, Pomeroy was expected to continue the family tradition. Alas, due primarily to Pomeroy's lack of ad rem reasoning power, the tradition was destined to become a memory at the conclusion of his current sea-duty obligation.

After many attempts to contact the *Chiang Hai-ch'eng*, the ship's master finally responded to the request to stop for consensual boarding. The Chinese captain was pleasant but made it very clear that he could not stop his vessel without permission from his parent company.

When asked about the name and address of the company, the master replied, "Wang Zhaoxing Limited, based in Hong Kong."

Commander Lavancia immediately transmitted the infor-

mation to Washington, D.C. While *McCain* and *Vandegrift*
continued to follow the Chinese ship, U.S. State Department
officials attempted to contact its parent company. After
twelve hours of delays, and with reluctant assistance from
Chinese government officials, the facts finally emerged.
Wang Zhaoxing Limited did not exist, not in Hong Kong or
any other Chinese city or province.

Camp David

Nestled in Maryland's Catoctin Mountain Park, the presidential retreat was established in 1942 by President Franklin
Delano Roosevelt, who named it Shangri-La. President
Dwight David "Ike" Eisenhower renamed the mountain hideaway Camp David after his grandson.

The retreat, a half-hour helicopter ride from the White
House, included ten comfortable cabins, a dining lodge, a
movie auditorium, two bowling lanes, clay tennis courts,
horse stables, a trout stream, two swimming pools, and a one-
hole golf course.

The hideaway afforded a solitary atmosphere where no reporters were allowed. Only the first family, cabinet members,
and a select group of invited guests and foreign dignitaries
had ever been allowed at the retreat. Camp David's attraction
was casual attire, simple cuisine, and straight talk. President
Cord Macklin preferred the solitude when dealing with difficult situations.

Wearing a golf shirt with the logo of his alma mater, a
navy-blue sweater, pleated khaki slacks, and shined cordovan
loafers, the commander in chief walked into the dining lodge
and entered the president's private office. Inside, Macklin's attractive wife, Maria Eden-Macklin, was having coffee while
she waited for him.

"Good morning," she said with a warm smile.

"And good morning to you." He gave her a light kiss on the
cheek while she checked his busy schedule to make sure there
were no obvious glitches.

He reached for a glass of tomato juice and glanced at the set of clocks on the wall. "Well, they should be here in a few minutes."

"They're on time."

Tall and trim, the chief executive looked the part of the consummate, highly confident Washington politician. Boisterous and stubborn-natured at times, Cord Macklin had an infectious smile, silver-gray hair, and deeply set blue eyes.

An air force F-105 Thunderchief pilot during the Vietnam War, he was a no-nonsense straight talker who did not tolerate laziness or indecisiveness. A graduate of the Air Force Academy, Macklin had played football there with his lifelong friend, air force general Les Chalmers, the current chairman of the Joint Chiefs of Staff.

Hearing the familiar sound of a Marine VH-60 VIP helicopter, Macklin placed his copy of the *President's Daily Brief* on his desk. Considered to be the most expensive and least distributed newspaper in the world, the *PDB* had been personally delivered to Macklin at 0610 hours by a senior analyst from the CIA.

The brief was a thorough, up-to-the-minute summary of world events and the latest analysis of problematic areas and thorny global situations. The analyst and Macklin had discussed a number of plausible what-if scenarios, plotting what courses of action the White House might pursue if the events developed.

After finishing his juice the president and Maria rose and walked outside to greet their guests.

A retired foreign correspondent, the gracious first lady was an intelligent, shapely brunette a decade younger than her husband. At the tender age of eleven, Maria had traveled with her father to live in British East Africa. She had been schooled by a private tutor until returning to the United States to attend college.

Stately and friendly, self-disciplined to project the proper image of a first lady, Maria *almost* always displayed a sense of serenity. She and her husband worked well as a team. His aides and advisers notwithstanding, Cord Macklin relied heavily on Maria's instincts and common sense—traits missing in many beltway circles.

After a pleasant greeting, Macklin and the first lady escorted Hartwell Prost, Secretary of Defense Pete Adair, and Gen. Les Chalmers inside.

Although Chalmers and the president had gone their separate ways after Vietnam, they had remained close friends and often fished or hunted together when their busy schedules would allow. Still muscular and athletic, Chalmers was the embodiment of a four-star officer. He was an even-tempered man who had a reputation for being a mentor to less senior officers. The general had a wide forehead and thin lines etched down his cheeks. A slow smile added to his handsome features, not to mention the twinkling hazel eyes that squinted through narrow slits.

Surrounded by Secret Service agents, the group entered the dining lodge and then settled in Macklin's private office, which doubled as a conference room. Fresh coffee, orange juice, tomato juice, and warm pastries awaited the men and Maria while they made themselves comfortable for the early morning meeting.

A former Green Beret captain, Pete Adair had been born on a small farm in the Oklahoma Panhandle. Adair's boundless enthusiasm was contagious at the White House and at the Pentagon. His folksy personality was appealing to military personnel, but that wasn't all they liked about him; they considered him a man of integrity and honesty. He was extremely knowledgeable about military affairs, and they knew he fought hard to provide the very best in pay and equipment for the soldiers, sailors, airmen, and Marines. He even pounded home the need to keep the U.S. Coast Guard on par with the other services, even though they were officially outside his area of responsibility.

"Well, gentlemen, what can you tell me about this Chinese cargo ship, the . . ." Macklin paused.

"*Chiang Hai-ch'eng,*" Hartwell Prost offered, then continued as he opened his briefcase and methodically spread papers before him on the table. "Mr. President, we've had some very interesting developments in the last few hours."

Macklin reached for his coffee. "As I've been told."

"The *Chiang Hai-ch'eng* departed from Long Beach en route to Fuzhou, People's Republic of China, on the same day we lost the F-18 Hornet from *Abe Lincoln*."

The president sat upright, almost spilling his coffee on his khaki slacks. "The same day? Are you sure?"

"Yes, sir," Prost said. "Seven hours and ten minutes prior to the incident—it's a matter of record."

"Do we know where it was when the other planes went down?"

"We aren't sure, but we know the *Chiang Hai-ch'eng* changed destinations en route to Fuzhou and sailed to Niigata, Japan." Prost adjusted his new reading glasses. "Niigata, which is located at the mouth of the Shinano River, is the leading port on the Sea of Japan."

"When did it leave Niigata?"

"Late in the morning the same day the Japanese AWACS went down in the Sea of Japan—at night."

"Are you positive—absolutely positive?"

"Yes, sir. We have computer records from the port authority, tapes of radio conversations with the *Chiang Hai-ch'eng,* and more than a dozen eyewitnesses who watched the ship get under way."

"I'll be damned. What do we know about the Cobra Ball crash?"

"We have unimpeachable evidence that the Chinese cargo ship *Xiamen Express* left Singapore for Madras, India, four days prior to the downing of the Cobra Ball, Eagle Rock One-One."

"And?"

"The *Xiamen Express* arrived in Madras early in the afternoon on the day following the crash of Eagle Rock One-One."

"The speed-distance equation," General Chalmers quietly interjected, "suggests that the Chinese ship would have been in the immediate vicinity of the Cobra Ball when the flight crew reported the suspicious object."

"What about our B-2 bomber?"

"Our people are working on it," Prost said. "The tanker crew is being debriefed as we speak."

"Any possible Chinese connection—anything suspicious about the crash of the bomber?"

"We don't know at this point. However, we believe that another Chinese ship may have been involved in the F/A-18 crash in the Strait of Taiwan, and the Chinese airliner that—"

"China Xinjiang Airlines," Adair volunteered.

"—that crashed into the Yellow Sea near Lianyungang, China. The *Deng Ju-shan,* a new state-of-the-art freighter, sailed from Ho Chi Minh City to Qingdao, about a week before the F/A-18 went down. It would have been in the general area of the *Kitty Hawk* battle group at the time the Hornet was lost, *and* it arrived in Qingdao the day after the Chinese airliner went down seventy-five miles south of Qingdao."

The president hunched his shoulders and absently set his coffee cup on his desk. "Let me make sure I understand what you're telling me."

"Yes, sir."

"Are you saying we can forget about these mysterious sightings and concentrate on the Chinese ships?"

"At this stage I wouldn't rule out anything. The information we have was generated by analyzing thousands of voyage itineraries of ships from all nations and from every region on the planet. It looks very suspicious to me, but we can't be certain."

Macklin sat back and rubbed his chin. "But the preponderance of evidence points toward the Chinese, right?"

"On the surface, yes. However, we could be chasing coincidences, anomalies, the supernatural, who knows?"

The president turned his attention to Adair and Chalmers. "What about our military options? What's the easiest and fastest way to find out for sure what's on those Chinese cargo ships?"

General Chalmers deferred to the secretary of defense.

"There isn't any *easy* way," Pete Adair admitted. "Considering the growing tension between Beijing and Taipei, and Beijing and Washington, we're on the verge of open hostilities in the Taiwan Strait, not to mention the fact that the Red Chinese are the gatekeepers of the Panama Canal."

Adair paused and faced the president. "The last thing we want to do is forcefully stop and search a Chinese ship in international waters."

"What about the CIA?" Macklin asked. "Couldn't we somehow manage to infiltrate, to smuggle someone on board one of those ships while it's in port? Is that a possibility?"

Everyone turned to Prost. "Gentlemen, from what our operatives are telling us, these particular ships are very heavily guarded."

"Which makes my point," the president said.

Prost continued. "According to my sources, the ships are carrying their own specialized security teams. We wouldn't stand a chance of boarding one, unless we came up with an invisible agent."

Irritated and frustrated, Macklin waved his hand. "Let's go back to the Chinese airliner. Why would they down one of their own planes on a domestic flight? It doesn't make sense to me."

Hartwell was about to offer a hypothetical opinion when an aide stepped into the office.

"Mr. Prost, you have an urgent call on the secure line."

MCAS Cherry Point, North Carolina

After an early breakfast with Major General Grunewald and Lieutenant Colonel Warrington, Jackie and Scott thanked the colonel for his hospitality and returned with the general to his office. They retrieved their luggage, flight gear, and helmets, and then headed to the flight line to load their belongings into one of Greg O'Donnell's Learjet 35As.

While Scott completed a detailed preflight of the exterior of the jet, Jackie entered the cockpit and settled into the right seat. A squad of four SEALs boarded next, followed by Scott.

A few minutes later the jet was wheels-in-the-well and climbing to its assigned altitude. Out of Flight Level 270, Lear N960BL was cleared direct to Centennial Airport, Denver, Colorado. The well-equipped Learjet was a delight to fly, and Scott felt very comfortable in the snug cockpit.

After ascending to Flight Level 350, Scott leveled the jet and Jackie assumed control of the Lear. Scott briefed MCPO D. R. Slocum, the leader of the SEALs. Together comprising one-half of a normal eight-man squad, each SEAL was armed with either a Heckler & Koch P9S 9mm automatic pistol or a Smith & Wesson .357 revolver. The latter provided an immediate stopping punch to a determined assailant.

Six Heckler & Koch MP5 compact submachine guns were on board for additional firepower in close-quarters combat. Two of the submachine guns were for Scott and Jackie. As a last resort, the SEALs had a handheld M60 machine gun for platoon-level fire support.

Scott gave Master Chief Slocum an overview of their situation, and then described the ambush and gunfight in Pensacola and the bomb-induced crash landing at Cherry Point. While Dalton and Slocum had coffee and discussed security details for the Lear, Jackie requested Flight Level 390 and then eased the corporate jet up to its cruising altitude. Once the power was set and everything was stabilized, she used the cockpit-mounted Global Flitefone to call Merrick Hamilton at her hotel to reaffirm their morning meeting in Denver.

Passing north of Cape Girardeau, Missouri, Jackie looked to her right and studied the bustling city of St. Louis. The stainless steel Gateway Arch was easily visible in the bright morning sunshine. She responded to a radio frequency change for Kansas City Center and then turned to Scott when Slocum returned to his seat.

"You haven't said much about the refresher course in that—what do you call it—a pogo jet?" she teased.

He quietly laughed. "There isn't much to say."

"Did everything go okay?"

"It went great—no problem."

"Seriously."

"It's like riding a bicycle and all the other clichés that—"

"Except if you fall over in a Harrier, you're roasted in a giant fireball."

"Well," Scott said as he turned to her and peered over the top rim of his sunglasses, "you certainly have a way with words."

"Since I have to fly in the back, I'd like to know if you're comfortable in the front. Yes or no?"

"Very comfortable. How about you?"

"Truthfully?"

"Of course."

"It scared the hell out of me."

"If it's any consolation, I felt the same way my first couple of flights in it—the intimidation factor."

"The refresher flights?"

"No." Scott smiled broadly. "When I first transitioned into the beast, back in my other life."

Camp David

When Hartwell Prost reentered the president's office, conversation ceased and all eyes turned to him. He calmly sat down and placed a sheet of paper on the table.

President Macklin turned to his most trusted adviser. "Bad news?"

"Actually, it's breaking news on two fronts."

"Let's have it."

"Our sources in China, both U.S. agents and our Chinese operatives, have irrefutable evidence that the China Xinjiang Airlines plane that went down in the Yellow Sea was full of political activists and prominent members of dissident groups."

Everyone in the room seemed to freeze momentarily.

"Beijing's increasingly insecure leadership is taking a severe toll on all of the opposition groups and the individual critics of Liu Fan-ding's regime. Others out of favor include nine former leaders in the Chinese Democracy Party and more than a dozen members of the Falun Gong Buddhist spiritual movement. They died in the crash, along with many other human-rights critics. Our people in Beijing say the situation hasn't been this bad since Tiananmen Square."

"It may well be the beginning of a new crackdown," Pete Adair suggested. "Sounds like the Party could be returning to its old ways."

"He's right," Les Chalmers said. "As we know, the Chinese have no desire to think or act like Western society. They have long been governed by absolutist rule. Their contempt for Western contact and influence dates back to the nineteenth century."

Prost nodded in agreement.

Chalmers shifted in his chair. "If Liu Fan-ding is concerned—paranoid—about the stability of his regime, he may have given the order to terminate the rapidly expanding free-enterprise system in China. We've already seen many Chinese entrepreneurs leave the country while it's still possible. They fear that at some point Liu Fan-ding will lump them together with the activists and dissidents."

Prost acknowledged the general. "True, and the historical record of China and her dictators doesn't indicate a yearning for a free-market society. What we're seeing may be a plan to end the enterprise experiment with a concerted effort to combine enforced political loyalty with military expansionism—always a recipe for disaster."

Prost scribbled a note to himself. *The two pilots and the flight attendants were sacrificial lambs for the good of the masses.*

The president had a question. "How can they be certain about the passengers aboard the Chinese airliner that crashed—their identities?"

"Many of the bodies were recovered and positively identified. Some of China's most notorious and vocal political dissidents and activists were on the airliner. A number of the recovered bodies were in handcuffs—the ones who had been in the *laogai* slave labor camps."

"What about the manifest?" Adair asked. "Were the passengers listed by their real names?"

"Every one of them. Beijing claims the political prisoners were being sent to a new government facility when the airliner was attacked by an unidentified weapon."

"Incredible," Adair said. "They're very creative."

Prost fixed his gaze on the president. "To make the accident scenario even more convincing to the general public, Beijing has repeatedly broadcast the tapes of the frantic pilots talking with the air traffic controllers."

Maria couldn't resist. "Hartwell, what do you think?"

"Quite frankly, this was a typical Chinese ruse to divert attention from their questionable activities."

"Their probable ties to the other crashes?" she suggested.

Prost nodded. "In one smooth operation, Beijing muddled their involvement in the mysterious-crashes question, *and* the powers that be eliminated some well-known voices of opposition. It's a chill wind of repression known as 'killing the chicken to scare the monkey.'"

Before anyone could react, Prost announced the second piece of breaking news. "On another subject, the FBI has discovered a secret skunk-works laboratory near San Clemente, California. The research facility has recently been abandoned, but Jim Ebersole thinks he has evidence that ties the Red Chinese directly to the laboratory and the people who worked there."

The president looked bewildered. "Chinese—what kind of lab?"

"According to Ebersole, they were working on a prototype high-energy laser weapon system."

"They? Whom are you talking about?"

"From what the FBI has discovered, the Chinese recruited seven of our best and brightest scientists and engineers, plus a Russian engineer. All of them but the Russian, Dr. Vasiliy Kalenkov, have been associated with Boeing or its airborne laser team of Lockheed Martin and TRW. In fact, their secret research laboratory is not far from the TRW Capistrano Test Site."

Hartwell slid his papers into his briefcase and closed it. "Two of the recruits had previously been involved in developing high-power microwave and laser-based weapons at the Air Force Research Laboratory's Directed Energy Directorate at the Eden Research Site."

The president slowly removed his glasses. "I assume these people are tied to the string of crashes?"

"It would appear so. Six of the treasonous recruits have died mysterious deaths in the past two weeks and the other two are missing."

Hearing the Black Hawk VIP helicopter come to life, Hartwell reached for his cap. "Sir, I must excuse myself. Ebersole is waiting to give me a thorough briefing at the FBI Crisis Center."

"Get back to me as soon as you can," Macklin said.

"Yes, sir. Mr. President, I think it would be prudent to have our secretary of state fly to Beijing ASAP and personally visit with President Liu Fan-ding. In my opinion, he's on the edge of the precipice, and I think Secretary Shannon needs to visit with him in person."

"That would add some leverage," Macklin said, and looked at the world map on the wall. "We have to make damn sure Liu Fan-ding and his cronies understand the consequences of their actions."

Pete Adair spoke in a clear voice. "The tougher we are on China, the more quickly they get into compliance."

"I know, but we have to be very careful. We're already spread thin with the goings on in the campaign on terrorism."

Prost picked up his briefcase. "Mr. President, it's also time to start discussing issues with Beijing about China's military buildup near the Panama Canal."

"Let me think about that," Macklin said, then turned to his close friend, General Chalmers. "It's time for a summit, Les. How fast can we get two aircraft carriers into the waters of Southeastern Asia?"

He cast his gaze down and then looked at the president. "It's going to take a while—I'll let you know in a few minutes."

11

Three hours and sixteen minutes," Scott said as the Lear-jet 35A touched down on runway one-seven-left.

Jackie removed her sunglasses and placed them in their case. "Not bad for a jarhead—you're a minute early."

"Better than being a minute late."

"Dinner at the Grant Grill says you can't hit a one-minute-window to San Diego—to Miramar—this afternoon."

"You're on. However, you're flying the leg to California, so I'm challenging you—can you handle it?"

"Piece of cake, hotshot."

After rolling out, Scott turned off the runway, and Jackie contacted ground control for permission to taxi to the Denver Jet Center, a local fixed-base operator.

When Scott brought the shiny Lear to a smooth stop in front of the FBO, her satellite phone rang. Jackie removed her headset and answered the phone while Scott shut down the engines, then joined the SEALs on the parking apron.

Dressed in nondescript business suits, the SEALs could have passed for typical corporate executives, even with their ultrashort haircuts. With their weapons concealed under their coats, Slocum and another SEAL stayed close to the Learjet, while the other two men surveyed the automobile parking areas and approaches to the aircraft apron.

While Scott was overseeing the fueling for the trip to MCAS Miramar, California, Jackie exited the aircraft and spoke to him in a hushed voice.

"That was Hartwell on the phone. I don't know what's going on, but he's canceled his trip to Seattle."

"Is he still going to meet us here?"

"Yes. He wants us to meet him at Denver International at thirteen hundred local. We'll meet him at Signature Flight Support, and then he's headed to Los Angeles. From what I gather, he'll join us at Miramar as soon as he can finish his business in Los Angeles."

"Wonder what's up?"

"We'll know soon enough. Hartwell was in a hurry, but he said it's imperative that he talk to us in person."

"Uh-oh," Scott said. He looked at the fuel truck and then hurried over to the young man who was servicing the jet. "Whoa, partner, stop the fueling—shut it down."

The lineman quickly shut off the fuel and gave Scott a questioning look. "Is there something wrong?"

"Our destination has changed. We're going *nonstop* to Denver International."

The lineman gave him an understanding look and went about rewinding the fueling hose.

"Well," Scott said, "I suppose we had better meet Merrick, then see if we can manage to navigate all the way to International without getting lost."

"Are you sure we have enough fuel?"

"Just barely."

FBI Crisis Center, Washington, D.C.

Nearly as large as a football field and capable of tracking many crises at the same time, the $20 million FBI Crisis Center complex houses the new Strategic Information and Operations Center. Covering more than forty thousand square feet on the fifth floor of the FBI headquarters, the supersecret SIOC (pronounced "sighock") facility has no windows.

Heavily shielded to prevent detection of electronic emissions, the state-of-the-art crisis center is packed with high-resolution five-by-fifteen-foot video screens and computers that can gather information instantaneously from around the world. The last seventy-two hours had been a madhouse, with analysts and agents working overtime to sort through one crisis after another.

Smart in dress and demeanor, FBI director Jim Ebersole was a small, wiry man with a large nose and an even larger ego. The oldest son of a washed-up, punch-drunk boxer from Hackensack, New Jersey, Ebersole had put himself through law school by driving dump trucks during the day and taking classes at night.

Cautious and crafty, Ebersole spent an inordinate amount of time buffing his image in front of television cameras and user-friendly reporters.

After Hartwell was ushered into Ebersole's antiseptically clean high-tech office, the director and another man rose to greet Prost. Ebersole handled the introductions in his usual unctuous manner.

Before the elderly stranger offered his big paw, Hartwell could tell that Dr. Filo Neubauer was an eccentric man. The yellow bow tie adorned with a dozen smiling faces of Mickey Mouse was an obvious sartorial statement. Sporting a thick pompadour of snow-white hair and a neatly trimmed beard that was variegated in color, much like the fur of a calico cat, Neubauer looked morose.

Ebersole turned his attention to Prost. "Hartwell, as you know, Dr. Neubauer is an acclaimed physicist who is an expert in the field of lasers."

Hartwell politely nodded.

On the edge of his chair, Ebersole sat upright and cleared his throat. "He has an interesting story to tell you, one I think you will find quite intriguing and frightening."

"I'm sure I will."

"Dr. Neubauer," Ebersole prompted.

The Brown Palace Hotel, Denver

When Scott and Jackie joined Lt. Merrick Hamilton in her suite, the threesome settled in the living area. Merrick's two FBI escorts sat down across the room and tried to appear relaxed and inattentive to Hamilton and her visitors. Told by their superiors that Jackie and Scott were also FBI, the agents were not concerned.

Outside, a team of FBI agents guarded the entrances to the grand hotel while two special agents surveyed the surrounding area from the roof of the triangular landmark.

"How are you doing?" Jackie asked.

"I'm fine, really—just tired of being isolated in this hotel room."

"I know what you mean."

"Hopefully," Scott interjected, "you won't have to be here much longer."

Merrick smiled. "At least I'm catching up on my reading."

"Can you tell us what happened in Santa Barbara?" Jackie asked. "It's important that we know every detail."

For the next twenty minutes, Merrick gave them a precise and full account of the incident with the kidnappers, including a description of her abductors and the encounter with the highway patrolman.

"Were there any distinguishing characteristics, anything that was odd about either one of them?" Scott asked.

"The Caucasian had a thin mustache and a clipped English accent, and the Oriental man had his forearm and hand wrapped in a dressing."

"Do you remember which hand?"

"Yes, it was his right hand."

Scott and Jackie exchanged knowing glances.

"What about names?" Scott asked.

"The British guy introduced himself as Chauncey Harrington and referred to his partner as Zing or Zheng, something like that."

"Anything else?"

"Yes, now that I think about it. Although Harrington did

all the talking, I had the distinct impression that Zheng was in charge."

"Why's that?"

"I saw Harrington catch Zheng's eye a couple of times, as if to seek his approval, and Zheng would discreetly nod his head."

Jackie looked at Scott. "Zheng Y-something with an injured arm and hand—could be our man."

"I think he's our guy," Scott said, and turned to Merrick. "You've been a great help. Any chance we can take you to lunch?"

"That, I'm sorry to say, is strictly verboten." She handed him a menu. "But we can call room service and pamper ourselves."

Scott smiled. "Ah . . . an *actual* free meal."

Andrews Air Force Base, Maryland

After the Marine Corps VH-60 Black Hawk helicopter landed on the apron, Hartwell Prost and his three assistants quickly boarded one of the air force C-32A VIP transports. A specially configured derivative of the twin-engine Boeing 757-200 airliner, the gleaming executive transport was part of the 89th Airlift Wing of the Air Mobility Command. Replacing the aging fleet of four-engine Boeing VC-137s (Boeing 707s), the new planes were used by the vice president, members of the cabinet and Congress, and various government officials.

While the jet taxied for takeoff, Hartwell settled into his seat, kicked his shoes off, and began devouring the neatly organized notes compiled by Dr. Filo Neubauer. Once he was finished with Neubauer's report, there was an intriguing stack of files Jim Ebersole had given him.

Immersed in his research material, Hartwell was impervious to the deep-throated thunder of the powerful engines. The sleek jet accelerated to rotation speed and gently lifted off the runway. After a quick stop at Denver International, Prost would continue to Los Angeles to inspect the secret laboratory near San Clemente, and then proceed to Miramar.

12

Denver International Airport

Scott slowly taxied the Learjet to Signature Flight Support and shut down the engines when a fuel truck approached. While Master Chief Slocum and his men reconnoitered the area around the Lear and the FBO, Scott monitored the fueling for the trip to California. Jackie went inside to check the weather and file an instrument flight plan to MCAS Miramar.

Fifteen minutes later, a pristine air force C-32A transport smoothly touched down at Denver International and taxied to Signature Flight Support.

After the big Boeing came to an imperceptible stop on the parking apron, Jackie casually checked her wristwatch. "Exactly thirteen hundred."

"Yep, they're almost as good as we are."

"No one's that talented."

With the engines winding down, Hartwell Prost met Jackie and Scott at the forward entrance to the spacious VIP plane. He escorted them to a conference area, where the trio could converse in private. Once they were comfortably seated, Hartwell loosened his tie, then opened his briefcase and placed a briefing booklet on one of the foldout tables.

"We have a lot to cover. You may want to take notes."

They reached for the government pens and writing pads conveniently placed by their seats.

Prost cleared his throat. "We have reason to believe that Beijing may, and I emphasize *may,* be connected to the rash of strange accidents. Let me lay this out for you, then I'll answer questions and we'll discuss our options, okay?"

Scott and Jackie nodded.

Prost explained in detail about the voyage itineraries and movements of the various Chinese-flagged cargo ships and the related aircraft disasters, including the Chinese airliner full of dissidents and political activists. He continued the briefing with the latest information concerning the secret laboratory near the TRW Capistrano Test Site.

Hartwell concluded the summary with a report about eight engineers and scientists who had been the nucleus of the laser experiments at the laboratory.

"What was the focus of their work?" Scott asked.

"From what we understand, they were refining a prototype high-energy laser-based weapon system."

"Like the laser in the Team ABL 747s?"

"Yes, but they weren't concentrating their efforts on a system to destroy missiles in the initial stage of flight. The primary role of *their* system is to destroy aircraft and spacecraft. CIA analysts believe the weapon system could be deployed in cargo planes, railroad cars, truck trailers, cargo ships, possibly submarines, or adapted for use as a satellite killer."

Uncertain about a point in the FBI report, Prost reached for a briefing note. "According to Jim Ebersole, they believe the scientists and engineers were recruited by the same person, a Chinese national."

"Do you know his name?" Jackie asked.

Hartwell consulted his point paper and the photograph of the recruiter. "Let's see, his name is Zheng Yen-Tsung, and he is the—"

"That's our man," Jackie suddenly declared as Hartwell handed them the picture. "Sorry to interrupt."

"No problem."

"What do we know about him?" Scott asked before he and Jackie studied the photograph of the man.

"Zheng is a self-proclaimed aide to a former Chinese prime minister who now chairs the National People's Congress. Zheng reports directly to General Wang Zedong, the deputy chief of staff of intelligence for the People's Liberation Army. As China's chief military spymaster Wang oversees all of the espionage efforts in the United States and around the world. He is very powerful and extremely ruthless."

Hartwell paused to reclaim the photograph of Zheng. "General Wang is the man who in the mid-nineties threatened to incinerate Los Angeles with nuclear weapons if the United States supported Taiwan. Through the People's Liberation Army, Wang again threatened L.A. with a nuclear strike in February of 2000."

"If I recall correctly," Scott said, "wasn't General Wang the puppet master at Tiananmen Square?"

"He certainly was. As a matter of fact, he personally directed the crackdown on the demonstrators—killing hundreds of supporters and injuring more than ten thousand students and workers."

Jackie remembered the horrible scenes. "Politically, Tiananmen ranks right up there with Pearl Harbor, Hiroshima, and the World Trade Center."

"No kidding." Scott thought about a photograph that had been widely circulated inside the walls of the CIA. "Didn't the former SecDef host and toast him at the Pentagon in early 2000?"

"Yes, I'm afraid that's true."

Sensing the embarrassment Hartwell felt, no one commented.

"Zheng and his associates have ties to the 'Four Seas' Triad gang, and he has been implicated in espionage at Los Alamos, Oak Ridge, Sandia, Lawrence Livermore, and two or three other national U.S. laboratories."

He reached for a copy of a recent article in *Xinhua News Service*. "Zheng is mentioned twice in this piece about how China's national defense technology and weaponry have closed with the United States in a very short period of time." He handed the article to Jackie.

"Zheng and other operatives in his gang have been given credit for purloining sensitive data on a variety of state-of-the-art weapons systems and atomic secrets related to our modern nuclear weapons."

Hartwell waited for her to share it with Scott before he went on. "They don't even try to camouflage their stealing and bribery. In fact, Zheng is applauded for his highly successful record of recruiting foreign engineers and scientists to assist the People's Liberation Army."

"Anything else on Zheng?" Jackie asked.

"Just the usual narcotics trafficking, prostitution, gun smuggling, extortion, money laundering, and contract murders."

"An all-around prince of a guy," Scott said.

"Oh, yes, a real peach."

Jackie handed the copy of the news article to Prost. "How did they—the FBI—find out about the secret laboratory and the scientists and engineers?"

"From an informant."

"One of the traitors?"

"Let me explain. They were initially contacted by Dr. Filo Neubauer, a prominent physicist who was a close friend of Dr. Lavon Douville and his wife."

"Didn't Douville die in an accident?" Scott asked.

"Yes. Dr. Douville, also a highly regarded physicist, had a deadly accident at his home in New Orleans. It seems as if someone used a hacksaw with a fine-tooth blade to cut most of the way through a balcony railing that Dr. Douville regularly leaned against."

"Any suspects?"

"One obvious one. The Douvilles' Chinese gardener of five months, a Mr. Chu-ko 'Benny' Kuang, who hasn't been seen since Dr. Douville's unfortunate plunge into his fountain."

"Were they, Neubauer and Douville, involved in the lab?" Scott asked.

"Douville was a key player, but Neubauer had turned down three offers from Zheng in the past two years."

"Smart decision."

"Neubauer suspected the lab was located somewhere in

the vicinity of the TRW test site. He also knew some of the members on the research team, but he was out of the loop until Douville's wife contacted him."

Jackie started to ask a question.

"Let's finish first," Prost suggested. "Then I'll take questions and explain our options, *if* you agree with my thinking."

"Fair enough," she said evenly.

"Mrs. Douville, who was celebrating their anniversary and her husband's retirement the night he died, became suspicious when a homicide detective discovered that the balcony railing had been sabotaged in two places. When the detectives questioned her, Mrs. Douville told them everything she knew, including what little she knew about her husband's secretive work."

Prost paused. "She also told them about Dr. Douville's new three-million-dollar motor yacht. Douville's previous craft was a well-worn forty-two-foot houseboat."

"Yeah, keep it low key," Scott said.

"Neubauer, who feared for his life after Mrs. Douville located him, immediately contacted the FBI, and the investigation has been interesting, to say the least."

"I'll bet," Jackie said.

"Dr. Dixon Owens, one of the eight recruits, was found dead in Mount Rainier National Park. A casual observer might have concluded that Owens crushed his skull when he fell off his mountain bike while negotiating a steep trail."

Jackie caught Hartwell's eye. "Was he wearing a helmet?"

"No. Also, he was overweight and out of shape, not exactly the type to be riding a mountain bike."

Prost poked a finger at one of his notes. "The local coroner explained that it would have been impossible for Owens to ride a bike *after* the onset of rigor mortis."

"That makes sense," Scott said.

Hartwell glanced out the window as a Bombardier Challenger 604 corporate jet taxied past the air force transport. "Not long after Dr. Owens's demise, Dr. Clyde Aycock, another member of the secret dream team, accepted a complimentary dinner at one of San Francisco's finest Chinese restaurants. Afterward he got into his car and promptly had a massive heart attack."

Prost's eyes narrowed. "As in the Owens case, the coroner found a problem with the cause of death."

"The heart attack was induced," Jackie surmised.

"That's right. The needle mark behind Aycock's ear and the lab reports were a dead giveaway."

Prost cupped his chin in his hand. "In addition, three other members of the dream team have recently died under suspicious circumstances."

Hartwell sighed. "While vacationing in Hawaii, Dr. Hugh Fitzpatrick fell from his sixth-floor lanai and did a belly flop on Waikiki Beach, inches from a sunning honeymoon couple."

"Any sign of foul play?" Jackie asked.

"Perhaps, if you consider the fact that he had 'consumed' a fifth of bourbon by early afternoon. After getting him falling-down drunk, someone tossed him off the lanai."

Prost looked at the police report. "His wife had lunch with him about thirty minutes before he died and he was completely sober. After they finished lunch, she went shopping and he went to their room to write some postcards and take a nap."

Prost fell silent. "I almost forgot. Fitzpatrick never drank bourbon, couldn't stand the stuff."

"Any signs of a struggle?" Scott asked.

"None. Another unfortunate traveler, Dr. Victoria Mills-Morrison, apparently fell from her veranda suite on a steamboat cruise somewhere north of Vicksburg."

Jackie's glance fell on her neatly written notes. "I assume that's where her body washed ashore?"

"That would be correct."

Prost turned another page. "A CIA operative in Russia noted the death of another team member, Dr. Vasiliy Kalenkov, in the newspaper *Nezavisimaya Gazeta*. According to the paper, Kalenkov was the victim of a hit-and-run accident."

Hartwell placed his lengthy notes on the foldout table. "Suffice it to say, we have a pattern of premature deaths associated with the secret Chinese lab—which *appears* to be connected to the mysterious crashes. And there are other strange deaths tied to having possible knowledge of the cause of the accidents."

"Don't forget Cliff Earlywine and the attacks on us," Jackie said, and looked at Prost. "All of this in a matter of weeks."

Hartwell gave her a slight nod. "Besides the deaths and attacks, we're still missing two of the team members: Dr. Guy Nash and Dr. Richard Cheung, a Chinese-American who is the big kahuna in the conspiracy."

Dalton leaned back and closed his eyes. "Now that the Chinese scientists have pumped the team for every scintilla of weapons technology they possess, it's time to close shop, pay off the brain trust, then eliminate them."

"You're close."

"Why would the Chicoms pay?" Scott asked. "Once they have the gouge, why wouldn't they call an off-site meeting, kill the entire team, and dispose of them?"

Jackie had a quick answer. "If the word got out, it would put a damper on further recruiting. The money was to entice more engineers and scientists, but the recent incidents drew too much attention. Someone decided to eliminate the laser team and anyone who was getting too close to the truth about the secret project."

"That's possible," Hartwell said. "According to the FBI, about fifteen or sixteen months ago the Chinese scientists and engineers had the pertinent knowledge and a full-scale operational weapon. They moved part of the laser project to a research, development, and production complex in the heart of China."

Hartwell grabbed Jim Ebersole's meticulously handwritten summary of the secret operation. "Approximately two months ago, the remaining Chinese engineers began the process of closing the lab in California and moving the last of the Chinese team members to their homeland."

"Do you suppose Cheung and Nash went with them?" Scott asked.

"We don't know anything about Nash. The FBI is convinced the Chinese forced Richard Cheung to go to the laser-weapons fabrication complex."

"Do you know where it's located?"

"Mianyang," Prost confided with a hint of satisfaction. "The CIA is convinced that the laser complex is an integral part of the Mianyang facility—they have firsthand knowledge from a reliable informant."

A small frown entered Scott's expression. "How can they be sure Dr. Cheung is there?"

"They can't—the informant has disappeared."

Prost reached for a glass of water. "However, Cheung's wife contacted the FBI. She told them her husband mailed some coordinates to her before he disappeared, no written word, just the latitude and longitude. That's Mianyang, so we have to assume he's there—perhaps under house arrest."

"Nice play," Scott said.

"The CIA believes China may have as many as eighteen to twenty laser weapons deployed on cargo ships. I think Cheung is being held in Mianyang to work out any bugs in the system while the weapons are being evaluated."

"Isn't Mianyang near Chengdu, in western China?" Scott asked.

"Yes. It's about seventy-five to eighty miles north-northeast of Chengdu. The buildings in the production facilities are strung along narrow valleys and blend in with the local terrain features and agricultural patterns. They did a great job of camouflaging the place."

"What about a covert operation to rescue Cheung and interrogate him?" Jackie quietly asked.

"That's being discussed, and that's all I can say at this time."

Prost anxiously checked his watch. "Earlier, I mentioned options. The president has made it very clear that he considers these suspicious crashes to be a threat to national security. He wants answers and he *isn't* a patient man, as you well know."

Hartwell lowered his eyes and took a few seconds to form

his words. "We're going to pursue the drone operation first. If we aren't successful in uncovering the truth about this phenomenon—whatever it is—then I have another suggestion. Actually, it's the president's idea."

"Would you care to share it with us?" Jackie asked.

Prost looked at Sullivan without meeting her eyes. "I really don't want to get into it until we've completed the drone operation."

She suppressed a response.

"What's the status on the op?" Dalton prompted.

"Three of the Phantoms are on San Nicolas Island, and the carrier is operating off the southern California coast."

"Are they flying at night?"

"Not yet—only the Hawkeye will be launched at night until we see what happens with the drone."

"What about the Harriers and recon assets?" Jackie asked.

"The Harriers have arrived at Miramar. Our intel spacecraft and recon planes are ready, and we're sitting on *go* for tomorrow night."

Hartwell had an afterthought. "We're also tracking a number of Chinese ships due to arrive or depart Los Angeles, Long Beach, and Oakland."

Jackie looked through her collection of notes. "Are any of them the ones you mentioned before?"

"No, but we're closely watching two cargo ships that have had some strange itineraries, including one Russian ship, the *Kapitan Zhirnovsky,* which is crewed entirely by Chinese sailors. The other ship in question is the *Chen Ziyang.*"

"Interesting," Scott said. "Where are the ships?"

"The *Kapitan Zhirnovsky* is in Los Angeles and the *Chen Ziyang* is docked in Long Beach."

Scott wrote a note. "When are they scheduled to sail?"

"According to the voyage itineraries, both ships are departing tomorrow—within an hour of each other."

"Do you know their destinations?"

Hartwell nodded and read the itineraries. "*Chen Ziyang* is going to Papeete and the *Kapitan Zhirnovsky* is bound for Rarotonga."

Jackie raised an eyebrow. "If my calculations are right, that would place them on a course near the carrier."

"That's why we're watching them very closely. We can't prove that Beijing is getting classified information, but it seems too coincidental that the ships are scheduled to leave the day we plan to conduct flight operations near the carrier."

Scott and Jackie eyed each other.

"Well, duty calls." Hartwell rose, signaling the end of the brief. "Sorry to rush, but I have a full day ahead. I'll see you in Miramar tomorrow afternoon for a complete update before you launch."

"Yes, sir," Scott said, and shook hands.

He and Jackie gathered their notes and retraced their route to the forward exit of the VIP aircraft.

The SEAL squad waited until Jackie and Scott boarded the Lear, then climbed into the jet and secured the door.

Now in the left seat, Jackie started the engines while Scott listened to the ATIS and contacted clearance delivery. They watched Prost's air force transport taxi for takeoff while Scott copied and read back their instrument clearance to Miramar.

After Scott received permission from DEN ground control, Jackie added power to taxi the Learjet from Signature Flight Support to the active runway. As she maneuvered the airplane onto the taxiway, Master Chief Slocum looked out the window and did a double take.

"Stop the plane," Slocum shouted as he sprang toward the door. "Stop the friggin' plane, now!"

Jackie immediately applied the brakes while Scott swung around to face the frowning SEAL leader. Slocum tossed Dalton a compact submachine gun and turned back to the window.

"Skipper, we got us a big-time problem."

"What's up?"

Scott quickly climbed out of the cockpit.

"Lookit." Slocum was aggressively pointing to the window. "See that pearl-colored van over there?"

"Yes."

"The same van was at the other airport, and the side door has been removed from that bugger."

Scott studied the suspicious van for a few seconds. "Yeah, something doesn't look right—it's out of place."

"Oh, shit!" Slocum barked, reaching for the door. "Let's go! Move it! Move out! Go-go-go!"

Following Slocum, the SEAL squad vaulted out of the airplane and sprawled on the taxiway. A Ford Econoline van rapidly accelerated toward the tail of the stopped Learjet.

Scott turned to Jackie. "Get the plane out of here! Go—firewall it!"

"Get out," she shouted. Fueled by a sense of danger, Jackie shoved the throttles forward. "Jump!"

Scott leapt out of the plane and dropped to a prone position on the hot taxiway. The searing jet blast almost lifted Dalton and the SEAL squad off the ground as they scrambled to take their positions.

As the van rapidly gained speed, a man who was braced against the seat by the door opened fire with an automatic weapon. The SEALs and Scott poured a steady stream of fire into the front of the van, shattering the windshield and headlights, and riddling the hood and engine compartment. Dense black smoke poured out of the engine. The van continued to accelerate toward the SEALs and the tail of the taxiing Learjet.

"Move out," Slocum yelled at the top of his lungs.

Scott and one of the SEALs jumped to their feet and ran toward the right side of the taxiway, while Slocum and the other two SEALs ran to the left. They continued to pour fire into the van. The man in the open door went limp, dropped his weapon, and then fell out headfirst.

"Got him," someone yelled above the earsplitting clamor of gunfire.

Scott and the SEALs stopped shooting as the van passed between the opposing fire teams, then they opened up again. The van swerved to the right, then back to the left. Although the windows of the van were blown out and the vehicle was trailing thick black smoke, it was still accelerating.

Horrified to see the van catching the Learjet, Scott took careful aim and squeezed off three rounds at the back of the driver's head.

The van swerved to the left side of the taxiway, abruptly lurched to the right, missed the tail of the jet by inches, then departed the taxiway and flipped over on its left side. Less than two seconds later, the demolished van exploded in a huge, thunderous fireball that shot a hundred feet into the air.

Slocum and Dalton raced toward the burning van. The SEALs quickly checked the immediate area for other threats.

"Lear November Niner-Six-Zero Bravo Lima," the tower controller said, "you can slow down—you can stop now—it's over."

"Sixty Bravo Lima." Jackie's voice was two octaves higher than normal. "What the hell is going on?" she asked, bringing the Learjet to a smooth stop in the middle of the taxiway.

"Perhaps you can tell us, ma'am," the controller said in a flat, stiff voice. "We're rolling the emergency equipment at this time."

Jackie keyed the radio and paused. "Sixty Bravo Lima, request permission to shut down here."

"That would be just fine with us—perfect."

"Bravo Lima."

Slocum ran toward the van while Scott covered him.

"I'll be a son of a bitch!" Slocum cautiously approached the burning vehicle and noticed some of the spilled contents. "This was a damn four-wheeled Molotov cocktail, big time."

"I noticed." Dalton slowed to a walk when he heard sirens in the distance. "A suicide bomber."

"This friggin' thing is plum full of gas cans." Slocum kicked one of the burning containers out of the way. "This here was your basic rolling bomb—a thousand-pounder with wheels."

Feeling the intense heat from the blazing van, Scott stopped to catch his breath. He turned to the SEAL leader. "From all the black smoke, it looked more like a Scud missile."

A slight smile crossed Slocum's rugged face. "Well, this here Scudmobile ain't gonna be makin' no more trips under its own power."

The other SEALs, one of whom had a minor flesh wound,

ran to the burning hulk and surrounded Slocum while he checked the van more closely. A few seconds later, the SEAL leader approached Scott.

"The dead gunner looks to be Chinese," he announced, jerking a thumb in the direction of the van. "The other guy ain't gonna be recognizable."

Dalton nodded as the crash trucks raced toward the burning van. "That's a sure bet."

"I don't know who it is you're messin' with, but you may need more than half a SEAL squad."

"Well, I don't have any complaints," Scott said firmly. "You guys are incredible, no doubt about it."

Scott turned and ran toward Jackie, meeting her halfway to the Learjet.

"What a mess," she said loudly as a crash truck thundered past. "Thank God for the SEALs."

"Yeah, no kidding." Scott watched a crowd gather near the burning van. "Is the plane okay?"

"Not a scratch."

"Good. In case you're wondering, this was the work of Zheng Yen-Tsung and his Chinese thugs."

"The thought *had* crossed my mind," she said, catching her breath. "Do you think either one of them was Zheng?"

"I don't know, but I do know this: They sat right there and watched us meet with the president's national security adviser."

Jackie observed the crash crew. "If Chief Slocum is right, they were at Centennial earlier."

"And they didn't have the maneuvering room to ram us."

Jackie shook her head. "How did they know we were going to be at Centennial, or here, for that matter?"

"I think I know, but we'll discuss it later."

"Yeah, this isn't the time or place."

Scott watched the crash crew quickly douse the raging fire. "We'd better get on the sat phone, or we could find ourselves stranded in the middle of an FBI-FAA power grab."

"Since you've already talked with Mr. Ebersole, why don't

you contact the FBI, and I'll call Hartwell—he needs to keep this out of the headlines."

"You got it."

Jackie glanced at the Learjet. "My phone is in the cockpit."

"Here they come." Scott watched the stunned airport security officials approach them. "I'll bet they don't see too many heavily armed SEAL squads around here."

"Well, we've made their day." With her hands on her hips, Jackie cast a look at the security personnel. "It might be a good time to use our FBI credentials."

"Yeah, that thought occurred to me about the time the van exploded."

13

CIA Headquarters, Langley, Virginia

Located on the sixth floor of the building, the Global Response Center resembled a modern military command post complete with video monitors and high-tech workstations. The antiterrorism center was buzzing with a different kind of activity. Within hours, warnings had been triggered by agents in Panama, Cuba, North Korea, China, and by spy satellites monitoring North Korea, Taiwan, the South China Sea, and the eastern half of China.

The amount of intelligence collection and counterintelligence investigations had increased dramatically since the Islamic radicals destroyed the World Trade Center, damaged the Pentagon, and crashed an airliner in Pennsylvania. China alone was having sixteen territorial disputes with ten different countries. The Middle East was bubbling again and Russia was having an internal hemorrhage.

Secure phones rang as dedicated analysts studied spacecraft photographs of activity at the Chinese-controlled entrances to the Panama Canal. After the giveaway of one of America's most strategic footholds, China, the remaining communist superpower, was now the gatekeeper of the canal. Other specialists monitored a continuous flow of highly classified information about Chinese activities in Cuba.

Computer screens flashed warnings and dispatches as more information surfaced about a forward deployment of Chinese and North Korean forces, suggesting possible attacks on Taiwan and South Korea.

The president of Taiwan had again set off a huge uproar by insisting that Beijing have a dialogue with Taiwan on a state-to-state basis and not as part of China. The Taiwanese president went on to say that China was playing the terror card and that Taipei would not be intimidated.

Beijing's fighting words raised deep concerns in Washington. The *South China Morning Post* of Hong Kong reported President Liu Fan-ding's warning to Taiwan that the Chinese people would spill their blood and lives to maintain the motherland's territory and sovereignty. The Chinese president had gone on to threaten drastic measures if Taiwan continued to defy Beijing.

The sudden destabilization in Southeast Asia had an adverse effect on stock markets around the world. The markets took a big dive when President Liu Fan-ding threatened to use missiles to virtually close Taiwan's military airfields, civilian airports, shipping ports, power plants, and waterworks.

Shortly after that announcement Liu Fan-ding used blackmail by threatening to launch medium-range missiles to strike the countries that hosted America's forward-deployed bases.

President Macklin had dispatched his secretary of state, Brett Shannon, to have a face-to-face meeting with Liu Fan-ding in Beijing. In the meantime, Macklin and senior members of the State Department had implored the Taiwanese president to offer room for concessions, but he steadfastly refused to back away from his comment.

Macklin promptly dispatched a top State Department envoy and members of his staff to meet with senior Taiwanese government officials to discuss the crisis. The message from the White House was clear and straightforward: Resolve the issue before Taiwan is blown back to the Neolithic Age.

In Beijing a Chinese Foreign Ministry spokeswoman said that Taiwan was taking extremely dangerous steps and that China was prepared to use deadly force. The ruling Chinese Communist Party's flagship newspaper, *People's Daily,* warned Taipei and the Taiwanese people that a formal declaration of independence would automatically provoke a military attack.

The newspaper went on to say that the president of Taiwan was doomed to failure, and those who followed him should realize they were heading into a blind alley from which there would be no escape.

The *China Youth Daily* published a front-page report on exercises by the People's Liberation Army in the northern waters of the Taiwan Strait. Another front-page article warned Washington against interfering in China's internal affairs.

Using vitriolic language, Beijing warned the United States and her allies not to interfere in the Taiwan-China dispute. In Washington, the State Department was put on notice by Beijing that America was playing with fire, and any intervention by the U.S. in Chinese-Taiwanese relations would be considered an act of war.

With the Western Pacific unguarded by an aircraft carrier, tensions were mounting at the Pentagon and the White House.

The USS *Kitty Hawk* and her battle group had been ordered to return to the Strait of Taiwan, the USS *Theodore Roosevelt* was en route from the Adriatic Sea to the northern region of the South China Sea, and the USS *John C. Stennis* was hurriedly making preparations to get under way from San Diego, California. *Stennis* would take up station in the southern area of the Yellow Sea to act as a deterrent to North Korea and China.

Marine Corps Air Station Miramar, California

Located ten miles north of San Diego and five miles from the Pacific Ocean, Miramar is home to approximately 225 aircraft, including KC-130 Hercules, F/A-18 Hornets, CH-53 Stallions, and CH-46 Sea Knights.

The late afternoon sun was casting long shadows across the air station when Jackie greased the Lear 35A onto the runway.

"Twenty seconds early," she noted with satisfaction.

"Make the reservations at the Grant Grill for seven-thirty *and* bring plenty of money—it's going to be the meal of the millennium."

"Actually, I have another plan."

She lowered her head and looked at him suspiciously. "You're not going to try to weasel out, are you?"

"No way."

"What's your plan? And it had better be good."

"Let's discuss it after we put the plane to bed."

"Don't have a memory-fade on me, hotshot."

"I don't think you'll be disappointed, trust me."

"Don't say *trust me*," Jackie warned, taxiing off the runway and heading toward a pair of two-seat TAV-8B Harrier trainers. "It always makes me nervous when you say that."

A dozen Marines were working on the attack planes. When Jackie brought the jet to a stop, a young member of Hartwell Prost's staff appeared at the cabin door.

Low key and quiet, Juanita Trujillo greeted Scott and Jackie, then gave them the keys to a rental car. Rooms had been reserved at the bachelor officer' quarters and Mr. Prost had requested their presence for lunch at the officers' club at 1200 the following day.

While Jackie and Scott were unloading their luggage and flight gear, Master Chief D. R. Slocum and his men were relieved by a four-man squad from SEAL Team Three based at Coronado Naval Amphibious Base, San Diego. Slocum gave the SEAL leader a thorough briefing about security for the Harriers and the Lear, then approached Dalton and snapped a crisp salute.

Although he was not wearing a cover, Scott returned the courtesy. He warmly thanked Slocum and his SEALs. They chatted with the leader of the new arrivals for a few minutes. Scott exchanged satellite phone numbers with the new chief. While the SEALs went about their duties, Jackie and Scott walked to their car and loaded their gear.

"Where's Ms. Trujillo?" Scott asked, expecting to give her a lift.

"She had a ride waiting."

"Okay," Scott said with a grin. "If you don't mind, I'll be the ground captain, since I know where we're going."

"And just where would that be?"

"We're not staying in the BOQ."

"Is that right?"

"Yep."

"Well, out with it."

"I have a friend who has a knockout home overlooking the ocean. Stan's a captain with Continental. He's on a trip, so he has graciously offered us the use of his home."

"No argument from me. However, *Captain,* we'd better find a supermarket and buy some provisions."

"I've started a list."

"Excellent—be sure to note that you still owe me dinner at the Grant Grill, and I have a very long memory."

"You're unmerciful."

"This is absolutely beautiful, stunning," Jackie said, entering the home's outdoor kitchen overlooking the tranquil Pacific Ocean. "It's like a postcard from paradise."

Complete with a large built-in barbecue and buffet table, refrigerator and ice maker, double sink, fireplace, soft lighting, concealed stereo speakers, and abundant seating, the combination kitchen/shaded patio was designed for entertaining.

"Yeah, you can't beat the view," Scott said, shading his eyes while he looked out to sea. "It's like a setting from some epic movie."

"It's incredible," she went on. "Soft, warm breezes and a view of the ocean and sky. What else could you want?"

"Nothing I can think of at the moment."

"Be sure to thank your friend."

"I already have."

Jackie took in the brightly colored flowers and plants, then inhaled the fresh air. A freestanding trellis next to a fountain and reflecting pool caught her attention. "I always enjoy the sound of burbling water."

"Then I'm sure you'll enjoy the spa." He opened a bottle of wine and partially filled two glasses.

They walked out to the built-in spa on the wooden deck and watched the last spectacular rays of sunlight slide beneath the shimmering Pacific. The soft, diffused twilight painted the sea in subdued pastels.

Jackie turned to Scott. "I'm curious about something."

"And what would that be?"

"You."

Scott chuckled. "What do you want to know—if I'm some kind of weirdo-wacko-psycho trying to masquerade as a normal person?"

"Seriously, after everything we've been through, I realize I don't know much about you. You never say anything about your background or your family—you do have a family, right?"

He quietly laughed. "Yeah, I have a family—a very nice one."

"All I know is that Scott Dalton flew Harriers in the Marine Corps and then went to the CIA."

Scott smiled and looked her in the eye. "Ms. Sullivan, would you like a résumé?" he asked good-naturedly.

She ignored him. "I don't even know where you were born."

"Okay, take notes," he said with a smile. "I was born in Nashville, Tennessee, where my family kept a permanent home. I graduated from Vanderbilt. My father is a retired Marine Corps brigadier general—we get along great. My mother was a navy lieutenant who resigned her commission after they got married, and she's the best of the best. I have one younger sister, and she is completing her internship at Johns Hopkins."

"Impressive. Maybe I'll get to meet your family one day."

"Perhaps."

"Did your sister go to Vanderbilt too?"

"Yeah, she graduated a couple of years ago."

"Interesting—I feel like I'm really getting to know you."

"Okay, that's it for this session."

Jackie eyed him for a moment. "Before we get too cozy, I have to ask you another question."

"I hope this is still personal and not business."

"Sorry, it's business."

"Oh, well," he said with a wink, "I didn't want to get too serious about our personal lives anyway."

"Just humor me for a few minutes, okay?"

"You have the floor." Scott stretched out on a thickly padded chaise lounge and inspected his wineglass.

"How do you think the Chinese are tracking us? You mentioned it in Denver, and I haven't been able to get it off my mind."

"Well, a bright red warning light flashed in my head after the smoke cleared in Denver. That's why I was hogging the Flitefone during the trip out here. I contacted the NCIS and then called a close friend of mine, a counterintelligence ace at the Agency."

"Would that be the Naval Criminal Investigative Service?"

"Yes, indeed."

"And?"

"Do you recall the gunny outside General Grunewald's office?"

"The gunnery sergeant? The Chinese-American sitting at the desk?"

"Yes. His name is Roger Wong, and I'm having him checked out from stem to stern—something just didn't feel right."

"What prompted the feeling?"

Scott slowly sat up and swung his legs over the side of the lounge. "After everyone calmed down in Denver, I thoroughly searched the Lear, every piece of our luggage, all of our flight gear, the SEALs' equipment, and their gear."

"Looking for a tracking device?"

"Right, and I didn't find anything."

"So you figure Sergeant Wong may be associated with the people who tried to take us out?"

"It's a possibility. If he's tied to the Chinese espionage faction, he could've passed our flight information to someone who ordered or directed the attack on us."

"You're talking about a network of Chinese secret agents, an alliance of spies, right?"

"Not just Chinese. It's bigger than that. There are other people involved in the espionage, including nationals from Russia, Israel, India, *and* U.S. military personnel and private citizens."

"After 'Lost' Alamos, I thought the Energy Department and the CIA had cleaned house and everything was sailing along smoothly."

"Not exactly. The Chicoms have more than three thousand seven hundred front companies, from the contiguous United States and Alaska and Hawaii to the far corners of the earth. They attempt to buy or pilfer every conceivable piece of advanced technology the United States has developed."

Scott lifted his wineglass. "This whole thing goes back to the Persian Gulf War. The Chinese were stunned by the enormous gap between U.S. military technology and weapons systems and their meager military capabilities. They realized that our military technology was anywhere from twenty to forty years ahead of their best systems."

Dalton swirled the wine. "Then we began imposing our value systems on other countries, like Kosovo. Beijing became more convinced than ever that we were going to do the same thing to Taiwan."

"I can understand their concerns."

"Because of Beijing's feelings of powerlessness in a world they perceive as ruled by the U.S., their appetite for information and technology has become so enormous that the PRC has been actively recruiting spies. They have openly targeted U.S. sailors and civilian tech reps when their ships make port calls in Hong Kong."

"What?"

"Beijing doesn't rely on the old-fashioned cloak-and-dagger spies. As we discussed before, the Chicoms use subtle espionage methods to gather seemingly innocuous information. They identify certain employees at U.S. labs, invite them to China, and then ask them for assistance with a wide variety of technologies. If the employee has ethnic ties, the recruiters use that to their advantage."

"Just a second," Jackie said. "Go back to the port calls in Hong Kong, the sailors and tech reps."

"The Chinese especially like U.S. military technicians and civilian tech reps who are assigned to ships that have the Aegis weapons system."

Scott paused and glanced at the running lights of a distant sailboat. "You know that the Aegis combat system can simultaneously handle a hundred enemy targets, airplanes, submarines, ships, whatever, while it synchronizes guns, missiles, and the electronic umbrella to protect the fleet."

"Yes, I'm familiar with it."

"Knowing how to defeat the Aegis system, and its ability to track baseball-size targets over a wide range, would come in mighty handy if the People's Republic of China launched a massive invasion to recapture Taiwan—which we know is not farfetched."

Jackie tilted her head. "The way things are going, that could happen at any moment. This recruiting effort in Hong Kong, do you know that to be a fact, or are you speculating?"

"It's true. The Agency, the FBI, and the NCIS have documented proof from several sources in the U.S. and Hong Kong. In fact, special agents from the NCIS even have one of the Chicom's high-dollar prostitutes feeding them information from the Peninsula Hotel in Kowloon. She's a spy recruiter working both sides for big paydays."

"Why hasn't any of this corruption made the mainstream print media or cable news networks?"

"They're keeping a lid on the Hong Kong crew until the Agency and the FBI are ready to launch a sting operation to nab the top dogs."

"How? We don't have any authority in Hong Kong."

"The kingpins in the operation get together in California once a year to check on the operation from that end. The money going to the U.S. informers is funneled through a central clearinghouse in San Francisco and distributed by

Chinese-Americans to bank safety deposit boxes in California, Arizona, and Nevada."

Jackie sat down beside Scott. "How deep does this go, the recruiting efforts in Hong Kong?"

"No one knows for sure. It's part of Beijing's new rules of unrestricted warfare on all fronts."

"War with no boundaries," Jackie suggested. "Terrorism, thievery, threats, bribery, illicit campaign financing, whatever it takes, right?"

"That's right. Anything goes, and I mean *anything*. The PRC is currently engaged in recruiting spies at the Pentagon and at installations like NORAD and the Air Force Space Command at Peterson Air Force Base."

"The Pentagon?"

"On a daily basis. They're also recruiting a large number of moles, well-educated Chinese-Americans, to join the U.S. military and infiltrate our most sensitive weapons systems and command sites."

Jackie shook her head. "If they're caught, they should be executed—hanged in public."

"I couldn't agree more." He took a sip of wine. "Unfortunately, our country is so focused on terrorism and the Middle East that most people are chasing the nits and lice while the elephants are running loose."

"Don't get me started."

"The Chicoms pay top dollar for information about our most advanced weapons systems. When you're in the service and trying to raise a family on fifteen thousand, say, seventeen thousand a year, two hundred thousand dollars in cash can be *very* attractive."

"No doubt. And you think Sergeant Wang—"

"Wong."

"—Wong is working with the Chinese?"

"Well, he *is* in a position to hear and know a great deal of information."

"That's true."

"I expect to have some news by tomorrow afternoon."

Jackie leaned next to him and Scott put his arm around her. "Let's take the pack off and enjoy the evening," he said. "No more business tonight."

"I second the motion."

They sat quietly and watched the vessels that dotted the Pacific. On the horizon the stars blended with the lights of the larger ships.

"Do you know what causes the stars to twinkle?" Scott asked.

"It's caused by atmospheric turbulence."

"Very good—that's why you're an academic whiz." Scott rose from the lounge. "C'mon, you can help me fix dinner."

"Yeah, I think you could use some direct supervision, especially in a kitchen full of sharp utensils."

"Hey, I'm a guy."

After a dinner of salmon sushi salad and minced chicken satay, Jackie and Scott changed into bathing suits, charged their wineglasses, and entered the warm, bubbling spa. They relaxed and watched the bright moon rise high in the clear California sky. Their view of the earth's natural satellite was highlighted by a quartet of traditional Hawaiian torches.

"I could get attached to living like this," Scott said, listening to the soft, melodic music coming from the array of concealed outdoor speakers.

She leaned her head against his shoulder and sighed. "Yeah, let's enjoy it while we can."

He embraced her. "Then again, in my humble opinion, there isn't anything like a full moon over Waikiki."

"Don't tempt me."

"I'm serious—give it some thought."

"I don't need to think about it." She looked up and gave him a beguiling smile. "I can be packed and ready to go in three minutes—maybe less if we don't take anything formal."

"Jackie," Scott said, and then froze, sensing a presence moving toward them. Perhaps it was a sixth sense, a natural intuition, but it was definitely real. Someone, or some thing, had entered the outdoor kitchen and was invading a specific

.rea of Scott's cerebral cortex. He rose on one elbow and fo-
used his attention on the kitchen and garden area. The hair
tood up on the back of his neck.

"Scott," she whispered, "what is it?"

He placed a finger to her lips at the same moment he de-
ected movement behind the wide vine-covered lattice screen
ext to the spa.

"Scott?"

Instinctively, Dalton leapt out of the spa and plunged
traight through the screen, slamming headlong into a lean
nd sinewy man. The violent impact knocked the assailant's
'mm Smith & Wesson to the floor and sent both men sprawl-
ng across the wooden deck.

With his heart pounding, Scott repeatedly smashed the
maller man's face and upper torso, missing twice and strik-
ng the deck with his knuckles. The searing pain was nullified
y rage.

During the struggle, Jackie scrambled out of the spa and
printed toward the home to get her 9mm Glock.

The horrendous fight on the deck continued as both men
anded one devastating blow after another. Scott was gaining
he advantage until the small-but-powerful attacker kicked
im in the groin.

Reeling in excruciating pain, Scott savagely smashed his
ists against both sides of the man's face. A resounding
RACK accompanied the severely broken jaw and teeth.

Desperate and writhing in agony, the wiry gunman fought
ike a trapped animal and finally broke free.

Bent over in mind-numbing pain, Scott allowed the in-
ruder to flee through the backyard gate and escape down the
ircle driveway. Searching for the assailant's weapon, Scott
vas startled when Jackie turned on the bright outdoor flood-
ights.

"No!" he protested, realizing it was too late. His night vi-
ion was gone for the next few minutes.

"Where is he?"

"He's gone." Scott could feel the blood vessels throbbing
n his head. "Turn off the lights."

Jackie flipped the light switch off and backed toward Scott with her weapon locked in both hands. "Are you okay?"

"Yeah," he answered, still breathing hard. "I've been in worse shape."

Spying the intruder's firearm at the edge of the deck, Dalton cautiously picked it up to preserve any fingerprints.

Still charged with fear, Jackie looked at Scott. "Should we notify the police or sheriff's department?"

"No, absolutely not. We don't want to get the locals involved." He took a break to catch his breath. "That's the last thing we need."

"Yeah, you're right. That could jeopardize the whole operation."

They walked to the outdoor kitchen and Scott opened a beer while his pulse rate continued to drop. "Would you care for a beer?"

"Sure."

He opened another bottle and handed it to her. After taking a long pull from the cold bottle, he looked at Jackie. "Our attacker . . . was Oriental."

"You're sure?"

"I'm positive." He took another swig. "There was just enough light from the torches to see his face—definitely from a Far Eastern origin."

"What a day," Jackie said, and sipped her beer. "Maybe I should check into that librarian correspondence course."

"Yeah, see if they have a slot for me." Scott set his bottle down. "Our latest attacker has been well trained in the martial arts—probably under the influence of Taoism and Zen."

She stared at him for a moment. "How do you know that?"

"Because he was in a mental and spiritual state that I think suspends certain functions of the mind."

"Come again?"

"His mind and body were acting as one unit—a unit that was blocking the pain until I crushed his jaw."

Jackie tilted her head and studied his face. "Ah . . . pardon me, but that sounds like psychobabble."

He shrugged and reached for his beer. "Perhaps so, but 've seen it demonstrated and it made a believer out of me."

"Whatever you say."

Scott surveyed the mangled lattice-covered screen. "From ow on we'll have our weapons on us or within easy reach wenty-four hours a day."

"You have my vote. I wonder if the Chinese know that ve're going to be flying near the carrier tomorrow night?"

"That has crossed my mind." Scott gently massaged his hrobbing right hand. "You may want to reconsider and stay n the ground."

"No way," she said without expression. "We're a team, re-nember?"

"Yes," Scott said with a smile. "I'm going to contact Iartwell and let him know the latest news. We have a major eak someplace."

"That'll make his night."

"I'm sure."

Astonished by the news of the ambush, Hartwell Prost juickly mobilized the proper authorities. Minutes later, FBI gents and members of the CIA were zeroing in on southern California and in particular the beautiful home overlooking he Pacific.

Scott placed his satellite phone on the table. "Well, I sup-ose we should change into something more appropriate for ntertaining."

"True, but we'll at least have security."

"What a way to ruin a perfect evening with a—"

"The night isn't over."

14

MCAS Miramar

During a leisurely lunch at the officers' club, Jackie and Scott recounted the events of the previous evening to Prost. After their meal, the trio left the club and drove to a hangar to meet with the pilot who would be remotely controlling the supersonic drone, a converted F-4S Phantom II.

Wyatt Craine, a laconic former navy fighter pilot, was a friendly man with a quick smile and an acute sense of humor. Prost had briefed Craine about the operation and the need for absolute secrecy. Regardless of the outcome of the mission, Craine could not mention it to anyone, ever.

"Since we're doing this at night," Craine said, "I'm going to have to rely on you to guide me into position near the ships."

"I'll do the best I can. I think we should keep the drone between the ships and our aircraft."

Craine tilted the back of his chair against the wall. "Are you going to fly directly over the ships or set up a pattern around them?"

Scott considered the options. "I want to approach from the stern at eight thousand feet about a mile or so from the target."

"Are you going to be on the left or right side of me?"

"We'll be at your four to five o'clock position."

"So you'll want to come up the starboard side of the ships?"

"That's right."

Craine mentally constructed a three-dimensional world of situational awareness that allowed him to project himself into the drone.

"When we're abeam," Scott explained, "I'll call for a shallow left turn to set up a left-hand orbit around the ships."

"How close will you be to my Phantom?"

"About two hundred yards."

"Good. I don't want to midair you if something goes . . ." He paused, innocent eyed.

"Tits up," Jackie offered with a friendly smile.

"Yeah, when we fly these things NOLO, no live operator, there's a ten percent chance that it will be the last flight for that particular Fox-4."

"How many have you lost?" Prost asked.

"Just one."

"Well, you're considered to be the best, so it sounds like you've been doing something right."

"I just hope my luck holds."

They continued the brief, deciding on a time and place to rendezvous in the Whiskey-289 Warning Area in the special-use airspace over the Pacific. When Dalton and Craine were comfortable with their plan of action, the flight crew of an E-2C Hawkeye airborne early warning aircraft joined the meeting.

Like Wyatt Craine, the commanding officer and his crew from the VAW-113 Black Eagles had taken an oath of secrecy about the mission. The carrier-based Hawkeye crew would guide Scott and Jackie to the suspicious cargo ships and provide airborne and surface surveillance. Everyone copied the radio frequencies and call signs they would use and then covered emergency procedures. The final item in the brief included contingencies if an aircraft went into the water.

When the briefing adjourned, Jackie, Scott, and Hartwell sat down alone to discuss what their course of action would be if one of the ships blew the Phantom out of the sky.

Scott finally asked the question that had been on his mind since lunch. "If that happens, how is the president going to respond?"

Prost was caught off guard.

"I don't mean any disrespect, sir," Scott said politely, "bu is he going to take an aggressive stance toward Beijing, o will he take the appeasement approach?"

Prost had a troubled look on his face. "To tell you th truth, I don't know yet, and I don't think he knows yet. He' talked to me, the chairman of the Joint Chiefs, SecDef, and the secretary of state. The military side wants to immediatel' stop the ship and seize it."

Prost paused and contemplated how much information h should divulge. "On the other hand, the State Departmen doesn't want to confront the Chinese right now, especiall' with Secretary Shannon on his way to Beijing to assuag President Liu Fan-ding's fragile ego."

"They can't just ignore it," Jackie said. "If the plane is sho down, I mean, that's a blatant attack on the United States."

Prost seemed ill at ease. "Let me bring you up to date. Th media people aren't aware of it yet, not even CNN or Fox, bu we have some major problems brewing with China."

Scott and Jackie hung on each word.

"Currently, we have no contact with the Chinese military no engagement at all, and China-U.S. relations are unde siege in Beijing. Actually, in the last few hours, our relation with China have become more tenuous than they've been in long time."

"Worse"—Scott paused—"than they were after we bombe the Chinese Embassy in Belgrade, or the spy-plane flap o Hainan Island?"

"A lot worse." Hartwell removed his glasses. "They'v been increasing the number of military troops and equipmer at both entrances to the Panama Canal, and they're forward deploying troops, weapons, and warships in southeastern Fu jian Province."

"Directly across from Taiwan," Scott noted.

"Yes. And the Chinese navy is currently conducting mis sile exercises near Taiwanese waters north of the Strait c Taiwan."

"Do we have any carriers in the Strait?" Jackie asked.

"Not yet, but the *Kitty Hawk* and *Roosevelt* battle groups are en route. The *Vincennes* has departed Yokosuka for the Strait and *Seawolf* is in the area. Two other attack submarines have left Pearl Harbor for the waters surrounding Taiwan."

"What about Panama?" Scott asked.

"The president is sending a carrier battle group and two amphibious carriers chockful of Marines into the Colombian Basin. He's made it clear to Beijing that we won't tolerate any interruption of traffic in the canal. No debates, no stalling for time, no ambassadors gabbing away, absolutely nothing will be tolerated."

"If the Chinese try something," Jackie asked, "do you think President Macklin will use military force?"

Prost spoke with conviction. "You can bet on it."

A hint of a smile crossed Dalton's face.

"We *will* retake the canal if the Chinese cause *any* problems or try to intimidate anyone. Secretary Shannon is going to personally reiterate that message directly to Liu Fan-ding."

"That could be a problem," Scott said. "Especially with the Chinese working so closely with Cuba."

"That's why we've been sending a lot of military assets to bases in the southeast, including Key West. In fact, we've been advertising the move to Cuba and the Chinese."

Prost seemed to derive a sense of pleasure from Macklin's aggressive position. "The president wants the Cubans and the Chinese to think about what's sitting on their doorstep. He would relish an opportunity to turn every military airfield and military installation in Cuba into rubble—it's one of his fondest desires."

"Do we have any ships or subs in the Gulf of Mexico?" Jackie asked.

"They're moving into place as we speak."

"It sounds as if we're spread fairly thin," Scott said.

"Oh, it gets better by the minute," Prost said dryly. "Now that we've removed all of our military personnel from Panama, drug traffickers, Colombian guerrillas, and rightist paramilitary forces have been conducting incursions deep into Panama. They've overpowered most of Panama's meager

security forces, and the Chinese are bringing in thousands o
ground troops to squelch the invasions."

Jackie looked at Hartwell. "It appears that Beijing has a
perfect cover to surround the canal with Chinese forces while
claiming their innocence."

"That's why the *Washington* battle group and the Marines
are en route to the Colombian Basin."

Prost shook his head. "On top of everything else, North
and South Korea are at it again."

"More clashes on the high seas?" Jackie guessed.

"I'm afraid so. One of our cruisers, *Mobile Bay,* departed
Yokosuka this morning, and the *Stennis* battle group is headed
toward the Yellow Sea. In the meantime, we've sent more AC
130 gunships to southern Korea to patrol the waters off North
and South Korea. We've also sent more B-1Bs to Osan as a
show of force—same with F-117s and F-15Es to Kunsan."

"Ambiguity," Scott said. "Too many flash points."

"What?" Hartwell asked.

"We haven't been standing firm with these countries.
think this drone operation has the potential to escalate into a
military clash with the Chinese—we have all the ingredi
ents."

"It's very much on the president's mind." Hartwell remem
bered Macklin's exact words. "But he's absolutely committed
to the operation. He wants tangible evidence so he can con
front Beijing and take action to destroy the weapons."

Scott glanced at Jackie before he continued. "Beijing may
be attempting to remind the world that it remains a powerful
global military menace in an effort to gain leverage and sta
tus."

"Then again," she suggested, "the PRC may have
weapon that they believe can render our military impotent."

"And we're the tip of the spear," Scott said. "Again, what
if one of the ships downs the drone?"

"Or us," Jackie interjected.

"And we don't have any proof of what happened?" Scott
added.

"Well, the president and I have talked about another op

tion, if one of the Chinese ships attacks the drone, or you, and we don't have proof."

Scott and Jackie patiently waited.

"*If* the drone is hit or downed, we'll explore the president's idea."

"That's it?" Dalton asked.

"That's it," Prost said in a voice that didn't invite any questions. "One step at a time."

"Okay."

"Try to get some rest." Prost got up and shoved his chair against the table. "I'll be out at the island with Craine."

Prost started for the door, and then turned around and smiled. "By the way, Jim Ebersole is personally overseeing the investigation into the terrorist attack on your Learjet."

His smile grew larger. "As you know, one cannot discuss the details of an ongoing FBI investigation—especially with the media. Jim will sit on this until everyone forgets about it."

"Good," Jackie said with a smile. "We don't need any ink."

"Be careful—don't take any unnecessary risks."

"Oh, we *never* do that," Jackie said with a smile.

MCAS Miramar

Earlier in the day, after a carpenter had built and erected a new lattice screen at Scott's friend's home, Jackie and Scott had checked into the Miramar bachelor officers' quarters.

The warm afternoon was fading into a pleasant California evening when Jackie donned her flight suit. She picked up the rest of her gear, including a Canon 35mm camera and a Sony camcorder, then left her BOQ room. She walked to Scott's room and quietly knocked on the open door. "Anybody home?"

"Come in."

"Hey, hotshot, ready for the Phantom gig?"

"Just about."

He zipped his flight suit and reached for his boots, then sat down in a chair. "I had a call from my connection at the Agency."

"The counterintelligence guru?"

"Mr. Counterintel," Scott said, slipping his feet into the flight boots. "For the past two years, he's been working on Chinese espionage cases with special agents from the NCIS."

"Did they have anything on Sergeant Wong?"

"They sure did. They'd been keeping an eye on him for about a year and a half. Wong was originally involved in the intel community—I think he was an oh-two-thirty-one intelligence specialist. At any rate, while he was stationed in Okinawa, he made two trips to Hong Kong and one to Beijing."

"I take it they weren't sightseeing trips."

"Hardly."

"Did they have a shadow on him?"

"Yep, but they never caught him in a compromising situation. His PRC recruiters, a man and a woman posing as a husband and wife, were very careful and conducted their business with Wong in a residence with guards at the entrance."

"Military guards?"

"They may have been, but they were wearing business suits."

"So they just continued to keep him under surveillance?"

"That's right, until he finally made a mistake."

"What mistake?"

"When he received orders to report to Camp Pendleton, Wong and his wife bought a very expensive home near Mission Viejo. They paid a hundred thirty thousand dollars down on the home and then paid cash for a new Chevy Tahoe."

Scott chuckled. "This, of course, after living in apartments and rental homes and driving used cars since he joined the Corps."

"They must've had a terrific run in the stock market."

"Or, they were *very* thrifty with their cash. After his wife was observed leaving one of three California banks known to have safety deposit boxes to distribute money to spies, the NCIS folks arranged to have Wong transferred to Cherry Point."

"Did his wife go with him?"

"No way. She had to stay where the cash was flowing."

Scott rose from the chair. "When Wong arrived in Cherry Point, he was very cautious for a while. He didn't know that an NCIS agent, a former Marine lieutenant disguised as a sergeant, was working with him in the general's office."

"Did the general know?"

"No one knew."

"So, what are they going to do, if anything?"

"They've already taken him into custody. They bluffed him and he started breaking down. When they asked him if he could spell *court-martial* and *Leavenworth,* he started singing like a roadhouse honky-tonk band. He gave them the details of the call he made to the Chinese coordinator in San Francisco who arranged the attempt on our lives. The man, who answered directly to Zheng Yen-Tsung, is currently being interrogated along with two of his senior assistants."

Scott reached for his flight gloves. "As you might have guessed, Zheng has obviously placed our names at the top of his hit list."

"Somehow that doesn't come as a surprise. Your friend at the Agency had a very productive day."

"That, he did." Scott reached for his helmet. "I hope we have a productive night."

"I'm sure it'll be memorable."

"Excuse me. Did I just detect a cutting remark—a slam?"

"Let's go, before I come to my senses."

USS *Abraham Lincoln*

The hundred-thousand-ton supercarrier was steaming slowly 135 nautical miles southwest of San Diego when the ship's skipper received word that the highly classified operation was about to get under way. Only a handful of *Lincoln*'s senior officers knew about the drone mission.

Below the flight deck, the majority of officers and sailors had

had dinner and were relaxing or taking care of personal business. After being away from their home port at Everett, Washington, for nearly three weeks, the crew was looking forward to making a port call in San Diego the following morning.

Above the flight deck, in the island containing the navigation bridge, admiral's bridge, flight-deck control, chart room, and primary flight control, planning sessions were being conducted. Proving Chinese involvement in the mysterious plane crashes was paramount in the minds of the senior officers who were aware of the drone mission.

Escorted by the Aegis cruiser USS *Princeton* and the Aegis destroyer USS *Benfold*, the *Lincoln*'s air wing was continuing to stand down from night air operations. However, two SH-60B Seahawk helicopters from the HS-4 Black Knights were manned and standing by to launch on short notice. The escort ships also had SH-60Bs ready to assist in a possible search-and-rescue mission.

After flying their Grumman E-2C back from MCAS Miramar, the Hawkeye flight crew had a quiet dinner and manned their aircraft for a pinkie launch just before the sun went to sleep. As the pilots started the turboprop engines and began completing their checklists, there was a sense of uneasiness among the mission systems operators. Not dread or obvious fear, just a definite feeling of concern.

Following hand signals from the yellow-shirted taxi director, the pilot deftly guided the airborne early warning aircraft toward the port catapult at the bow of the ship. In the back of the E-2C a naval flight officer had removed and stowed the ditching hatch in case they went into the water.

The Hawkeye, having been upgraded by the radar modernization program, could track smaller targets and air and surface targets simultaneously. The sensory perception of the E-2C is capable of searching more than three million cubic miles of airspace, plus tracking objects on the surface of the ocean or land.

Once the E-2C was in position on the catapult and the wings were unfolded and locked, the pilot came up on the power. "Engines look good, hydraulics check good, circuit breakers are in; I like what I see."

He turned to the copilot. "How about you?"

"Looks like a winner."

"Are you ready in the back?" the pilot asked over the intercom.

"We're ready to go."

The pilot scanned the instruments one more time and then signaled the shooter that Prime Time 602 was ready to fly.

The catapult officer completed his checks, then knelt down on one knee and touched the deck with two of his outstretched fingers. Seconds later, the Hawkeye blasted up the deck in a swirling cloud of steam vapor and began climbing to altitude.

The E-2C would fly a wide pattern around the carrier and coordinate with other reconnaissance aircraft, including an RC-135S Cobra Ball spy plane and three innocent-looking civilian surface vessels. The two reconditioned motor yachts and the trawler were packed with cleverly camouflaged surveillance gear.

One yacht and the trawler were positioned south of the cargo ships *Kapitan Zhirnovsky* and *Chen Ziyang*, while the other yacht was trailing twelve miles astern of the *Kapitan Zhirnovsky*. As soon as the Hawkeye crew pinpointed the cargo ships, they would guide the Harrier and the F-4 drone to the targets.

In geosynchronous orbit twenty-three thousand miles above the earth, an advanced NRO Orion signal intelligence spacecraft would be eavesdropping on communications in the Eastern Pacific. KH-11 and Lacrosse intelligence-gathering spacecraft would work in concert with the Orion to unravel the mystery behind the elusive and deadly unidentified flying objects.

15

Scott completed a thorough preflight of the Harrier while Jackie stowed her camera and camcorder in the backseat of the plane. The handpicked ground crew, who had no idea what kind of mission the two pilots were flying, helped Jackie and Scott get settled into their ejection seats. Although the aviators were pleasant and seemed to be relaxed, the Marines found it strange that neither pilot wore anything displaying their name or rank.

Scott started the engine and completed his checklists, then keyed his radio to receive his instrument clearance. He copied his clearance to the rendezvous point with the Phantom, then read back his instructions and called for taxi to the duty runway.

Keying the intercom, Scott spoke to Jackie as he began taxiing for takeoff. "Everything okay back there?"

"Couldn't be better."

"Excellent."

"Do I get an in-flight movie?"

"Naw, the movies are reserved for the pilot."

Jackie glanced at two F/A-18s taking off in formation. "How are things in the wheelhouse?"

"Well, all the bells and whistles are quiet."

"That's always a good sign."

Scott completed his takeoff checklist as they approached the end of the runway. "Ready to go?"

Jackie keyed her ICS. "Yeah, I just hope everyone is on time."

"They will be."

"You're such an optimist."

He laughed under his oxygen mask. "It's contagious, you know."

"Well, I haven't caught it yet."

Just before reaching the runway, Scott called the tower for permission to take off. The response was immediate.

Dalton keyed his radio. "Spooky Four-Fourteen is on the roll."

He added power and made a normal short takeoff. Seconds after leaving the runway, Scott raised the landing gear and flaps and began accelerating to his climb profile.

"Spooky Four-One-Four, contact departure control."

"Spooky Four-Fourteen switchin' to departure."

After Scott checked in with departure control, he established radio contact on a common frequency with the E-2C Hawkeye and with Wyatt Craine, call sign Rocky Nineteen. Less than two minutes later Dalton leveled off at ten thousand feet and looked at the moon. "At least we'll have some light this evening."

"And so will the Chinese."

San Nicolas Island, Southwest of Los Angeles

Sitting at a universal console, Craine studied his remote control cockpit. It was equipped with a control stick, rudder pedals, wheel brakes, throttle control, and instruments to fly and navigate without reference to any outside stimulus. The integrated target control system employed a nose-mounted television camera on the QF-4S Phantom that allowed the operator to make remote takeoffs and landings.

The drone's capability was the same as that of a regular McDonnell Douglas F-4. The powerful fighter was capable of Mach 2.2 and had a service ceiling of sixty thousand feet. Other specifics of the QF-4S were classified, but the 82d Aerial Targets Squadron (ATRS) from Tyndall Air Force Base, Florida, and Craine's unit had developed proven techniques for safely flying and maneuvering four airplanes in close formation.

Craine keyed his radio. "Spooky Four-Fourteen, say your posit."

"We're seventeen southeast at base plus four." Scott checked his instrument panel. "Ah, lookin' for a turkey."

"You have a bird on the way."

"Copy, Rocky Nineteen."

With Hartwell Prost sitting close to him, Craine taxied the QF-4S onto the runway and carefully aligned the aircraft for takeoff. He held the brakes and turned on the normal exterior lights, then checked his wristwatch for the umpteenth time and keyed his mike. "Prime Time Six-Oh-Two, do you copy Rocky One-Nine?"

"Rocky," the systems operator in the E-2C Hawkeye radioed, "Prime Time Six-Oh-Two has you and Spooky five-by."

"Copy." Craine mentally prepared himself to fly the drone. "Rocky Nineteen is launching a bird."

"We're standing by," the Hawkeye systems operator said, as he watched the Harrier on his radar screen.

Prost adjusted his radio headset and closely watched the former fighter pilot. Craine continued to hold the Phantom's brakes and eased the throttles forward. With the powerful engines winding up to full song, he released the brakes.

The drone rapidly accelerated. Craine waited, correcting for a slight left drift, then eased back on the control stick. Once the console instruments indicated that the F-4 had a positive rate of climb, Craine raised the landing gear and flaps.

The fighter plane thundered across the water and began a steep climb in the Whiskey-289 Warning Area. Out of ten thousand feet, Craine eased the power back and leveled the Phantom at twelve thousand feet and three hundred knots. He gently banked the aircraft to head toward the appointed rendezvous holding pattern and then began a wide circle to the left.

Spooky 414

With only a thin trace of daylight left Scott turned the Harrier's external lights off and began searching for the Phantom. Seen from ten thousand feet, the brightest stars were twinkling like faceted diamonds. Dalton's eyes rapidly adjusted to the dark. The moonscape had slowly changed from pale yellow to diaphanous silver.

Scott keyed his intercom. "It should be at about our one to two o'clock in a wide left orbit."

"I'm looking," Jackie said, rigging her camera and camcorder for instant use. "I don't see anything."

"Spooky Four-One-Four, Prime Time."

"Spooky Four-Fourteen," Scott replied.

The Hawkeye systems operator studied his radar screen. "Come starboard about fifteen degrees."

"Fifteen right."

"Your playmate is level at base plus six, two o'clock high."

"Copy." Scott had a request for Craine. "Rocky, how about the fireworks? We need some light."

"Stand by."

Three seconds later the F-4 came alive with flashing white strobe lights on each wingtip and the tail. Like the midday sun a bright, reddish-orange glow emanated from the empty cockpit.

"That would get anyone's attention," Jackie said in awe.

"Yeah, it certainly *is* different."

She snapped a couple of quick photos and reached for the camcorder.

Scott keyed his radio. "Rocky, your boys have certainly outdone themselves."

"Pretty impressive, huh?"

"Oh, by all means."

"Rocky Nineteen," the E-2C operator said, "our pilots want to know how much of California you could power with that system—help them out with their energy problem."

Craine ignored the remark and clicked his transmit button. "Spooky, do you think you'll be able to fly form on it?"

"Can you regulate the intensity or turn off part of the package—tone it down some?"

"I'm afraid not. They fabricated the system in record time, and it's all or nothing—sorry about that."

"Okay, no problem. If you'll just turn it off until we rendezvous and position ourselves."

"Lights out. Tell me when you want 'em on."

"We'll do it," Scott said, watching the Phantom momentarily disappear in the sea of flickering stars. "What's the drone's speed?"

"Three hundred even at twelve thousand. I'll keep it in a shallow left bank until you get aboard."

"Thanks." Scott reversed to the left and began climbing and turning inside the Phantom to follow a constant bearing line to the F-4. The radios remained quiet while Scott searched for the drone.

"Do you have it?" Jackie anxiously asked.

"Yeah, barely."

"Well, I'm not in the mood for a midair."

"Don't worry, I can't afford the payments on a new Harrier."

"Yeah, the general would have your ass . . . ets."

Scott adjusted the Harrier's speed to 315 knots and closed on the left side of the F-4. As Dalton got closer, he eased the power back until he was stabilized in a loose parade position. He smoothly added a touch of power and crossed under the Phantom, then drifted out to a relaxed location at the drone's four o'clock position.

"Lights."

"Comin' on."

Scott studied the glowing empty cockpit of the F-4 and keyed the intercom. "Look, Ma, no pilot."

"That doesn't give me any warm fuzzies. It just isn't natural to see a plane flying around with no one at the controls."

"I feel the same way."

Scott radioed Craine. "Rocky Nineteen, we're finally aboard and ready to head for the carrier."

"Prime Time," Craine said, "what's a good heading for *Lincoln*?"

"One-eight-zero."

"Copy."

Dalton and Craine remained silent while the formation turned south toward the carrier and the cargo ships.

Scott called the Hawkeye. "Okay, Prime Time, Spooky Four-Fourteen is ready for our first look-see."

"We have one ship, the *Kapitan Zhirnovsky,* at Mother's seven o'clock for fifty-five miles. The other ship is at Mother's three for thirty-seven. Your choice, Spooky."

"We're closer to the *Chen Ziyang,*" Jackie suggested.

"Let's take the target at Mom's three for thirty-seven." Scott mentally figured a heading of 205 degrees to the cargo ship.

"Steer two-zero-zero," the systems operator said.

"Two hundred on the heading. We'd like to pick up the speed and descend to eight thousand."

"Spooky is cleared as requested," the Hawkeye operator radioed, then added, "the area is clear of traffic, maneuver at your own discretion."

"Copy, Spooky Four-Fourteen." Scott keyed the ICS. "Okay, Jackie, are you ready to make the first pass?"

"As ready as I'll ever get. Let's take it down and see what we find."

"Rocky, we're ready to descend to eight thousand and pick it up to five hundred knots."

Wearing his own headset and microphone, Hartwell Prost nervously chewed on an unlit cigar while he listened to the action.

Craine keyed his radio. "Starting down and coming up on the power."

Hartwell's assistant, Juanita Trujillo, was monitoring a secure link to President Macklin and Secretary of Defense Pete Adair at the White House.

"Prime Time, Spooky."

"Go."

"Do we have all the recon players on line?"

"That's affirm, Spooky. We're good to go—you're the star of the show."

Scott checked again to make sure his exterior lights were turned off. "Jackie, I have an idea."

"Shoot."

"Let's keep the camcorder on the ship and continuously record until we break off and depart."

"You don't want any still photos?"

"If we're dealing with a laser-based weapon, we'd probably miss it with a regular camera, even if you were snapping pictures as fast as possible."

"Makes sense—I've got the camcorder ready."

"Good."

Scott moved farther away from the Phantom while his eyes darted around the cockpit. Convinced that everything was normal, he glanced at the altimeter. They were descending through 8,400 feet. Dalton continued to move away from the drone. Leveling at 8,000 feet and 505 knots, Scott judged his distance from the F-4 at 200 yards.

"Spooky," the controller radioed, "Prime Time."

"Go."

"Come right five degrees, your target is at twelve o'clock, ten miles."

"We're looking."

"Spooky, we have confirmation that the ship is slowing and that it isn't showing any lights."

"Copy." Scott looked for any sign of a ship's wake. "They're probably monitoring all of our frequencies."

"Yeah, for sure," the Hawkeye operator said. "They obviously know something is up."

"But the question is," Scott said to Jackie, "will they show their hand?"

"We won't know until we try."

"Rocky," Scott radioed, "I can't see much from here. Let's take it down to four thousand."

"Down to four." Craine eased the drone's nose down and tweaked the throttles. "Still want five hundred knots?"

"You can leave the power where it is, uh, and come back left a few degrees—need to be in a little closer."

"Rocky Nineteen."

"Six miles," the Hawkeye operator warned.

"Do you have anything yet?" Jackie asked, trying to sound calm.

"Not yet."

Seconds later Scott caught a telltale glimpse of a ship's wake. "There, down to the left—see it?"

Jackie surveyed the ocean, and then saw the slowly vanishing wake. "I have it—the video is running."

"Great," Dalton said, then switched to the radio. "Rocky, let's ease it out to the right a little bit, about five degrees of bank."

"Coming right." Craine expertly maneuvered the F-4 Phantom away from the ship.

Hartwell Prost chewed his cigar and watched the remote control panel.

"Three miles," the systems operator said.

"Okay, Rocky, level the wings," Scott said calmly. "I have a tally on the ship, looks like it's almost dead in the water and completely blacked out."

Craine concentrated on flying the Phantom as smoothly as humanly possible. "Just let me know when you want to come left."

"Will do."

Scott concentrated his attention on the *Chen Ziyang* and leveled off at 4,000 feet. Abeam the ship and a mile away, Dalton keyed the mike. "Okay, Rocky, let's start a shallow, climbing turn to the left."

"Coming up on the power." Craine banked the F-4 to the left.

Flying in very loose formation, Scott glanced at the ship and keyed the ICS. "Keep your eyes open."

"Open? I haven't blinked in three minutes."

Passing through ninety degrees of the turn and 9,300 feet, Jackie sharply sucked in her breath. "Nine to ten o'clock high."

"I see it!" Scott focused on the brilliant bluish-white object. It streaked down from high above the jets and made an astonishing turn, then shot directly over the Phantom.

"Prime Time, we have a visitor! Do you have anything on radar?"

"Negative, but our recon folks have the bogey visually."

"Keep the camcorder on the ship."

"I'm trying." Jackie twisted around in her ejection seat. "Tighten the turn to give me a better angle."

Scott glanced at the darkened ship. "Rocky, tighten the turn and bring your nose up about five degrees."

"Copy, what does the object look like?"

"A circular, bluish-white light that's being manipulated by someone. It made a sharp turn and flew over the Phantom, then quickly disappeared, going straight up."

"Here it comes again," Jackie said.

The eerie-looking bogey reappeared and flashed under the drone.

"Rocky, could you give us a nice, lazy barrel roll to the left?"

"Yeah, here goes." He added power and brought the nose up. "Are you out of the way?"

"Affirm, low and to the right."

"Copy."

The F-4 began a roll to the left and completed a revolution about the longitudinal axis while the direction of flight was approximately maintained.

"Nice, very nice," Scott said, moving another fifty yards away from the drone. "How about giving us a five-G loop?"

"Comin' up."

Suddenly the bright object streaked across the star-studded sky and made a slashing move at the Phantom as it was passing the vertical.

"I'll be damned," Scott said over the ICS. "This thing is all over the place. It's coming back."

The F-4 was on its back in afterburner with the nose falling through the horizon when the bluish-white bogey made a sharp turn and headed straight at the Phantom.

"Uh—too close," Dalton said when the frightening object barely missed the drone. "Turn out the lights and come out of burner!"

"Roger."

In an instant, the F-4 was almost invisible.

"I'm going to ease out to the right," Scott said to Jackie. "It'll give us a little extra room if the Phantom gets out of shape."

"Sounds like a *great* plan."

In the blink of an eye, a bright flash startled Jackie and Scott.

"I saw it—I got it!" she said. "A laser beam! It came from the ship!"

"Are you sure?" Scott asked as the bogey shot straight up and disappeared in a mass of stars.

"Yes! It was maybe a half second to a second in duration, but it was definitely a laser beam! We've got it on video!"

Scott was curious. "Rocky, is the Phantom okay?"

"Yeah, I'm just recovering from the loop, level at three thousand."

"Okay, give me the lights for a few seconds so I can join on you."

"You got it."

The drone's lights flashed on.

Scott keyed the radio and tried to sound calm and professional. "The ship, the *Chen Ziyang,* fired a laser at the drone."

"Did you get it on video?" Hartwell asked.

"We're pretty sure we did."

"Good work."

"Spooky, Prime Time."

"Go."

The Hawkeye systems operator was talking more rapidly than before. "The Ball and the satellites got it."

"Super."

"Spooky, Rocky Nineteen."

"Spooks up."

"Stand by one."

"Copy," Scott said, moving closer to the F-4. "Lights out."

The Phantom became a phantom, an illusory form barely visible against the backdrop of stars.

"Ready to break it off and return to base?" Scott asked.

"Negative RTB," Craine said in a hushed voice. "Mr. Prost is on the horn—go ahead, sir."

"Scott, the president and SecDef would like for you to check the other ship, if you have the fuel."

"Jackie?" Scott asked, surveying the fuel.

"As long as we're up here, we might as well."

"Roger that," Scott said to Prost. He instantly calculated the heading to intercept the *Kapitan Zhirnovsky*. "Rocky, let's come right, say about zero-six-zero, I'm aboard."

"Zero-six-zero."

"Prime Time, how's the heading?" Scott asked.

"Close enough, and your target is sixty-three out."

"Spooky, copy."

Jackie keyed the ICS. "What do you think the odds are that the other ship is equipped with a laser weapon?"

"Given what we've seen, both ships departing around the same time, I'd say they probably have the same technology."

"I'll bet you're right."

"We'll find out in a few minutes."

"What was that thing?" Jackie asked.

"I don't know, but I can assure you that extraterrestrials are not working in unison with the Red Chinese."

Jackie glanced at the Phantom. "Could it have been some kind of advanced holography? A continuous-wave holographic image, or something like that?"

"Yep, that's what it looked like." Scott thought about the bogey's ability to maneuver and accelerate. "I think what we have is a three-dimensional holographic image—an optical illusion."

"You're positive, huh?"

"As positive as deductive logic can be," Scott answered, rechecking the fuel. "In my mind, what we saw was an object that appeared to be solid, but it was a hoax—an illusion. It's like pointing a flashlight beam on a wall and making the beam stop, start, reverse course, climb, dive, and disappear in a matter of seconds."

"But it looked so real. It's like watching an old-fashioned searchlight scan the night sky over a drive-in movie."

"I know, but think about the physics, the energy, and the impossible-to-believe maneuvering. The bogey aspect of the weapon is simply an illusion to camouflage the laser—distract people and keep them guessing."

"Yeah, chasing something that doesn't exist."

Scott paused and then keyed the ICS. "That's what Sammy was doing."

"I know," she said painfully.

"Spooky, come left five degrees," the Hawkeye lieutenant said.

"Left five degrees. Rocky, let's start an easy climb to four thousand and turn on your lights."

"Roger," Craine said a second before the F-4's strobes and cockpit glow lighted the night.

The Hawkeye operator studied his radar screen while listening to the crewman in the RC-135S Cobra Ball spy plane. "Spooky, the ship is slowing and has gone black."

"Copy."

"Your target is at your twelve, uh, for fifteen."

Scott clicked the mike twice and keyed the ICS. "This time let's see if we can capture the bogey on video."

"I'll do my best."

"Scott," Hartwell said, "the president wants the F-4 to be a sitting duck. He suggests two-fifty on the speed at five thousand feet in a wide circle around the ship."

"That's fine with us," Scott said, and then talked to Jackie. "I think we'll stay farther away this time."

She raised the camcorder. "No argument from this gallery."

"Let's go to five thousand," Scott radioed.

"Going to five. We'll slow after we level off."

The radio remained strangely silent until the Hawkeye called. "Target's at twelve, three miles."

"Back to two-fifty," Scott said, spotting the *Kapitan Zhirnovsky*. "I have the ship in sight."

Dalton called for a slight heading change to bring the flight up the starboard side of the ship. He matched the speed of the Phantom and descended two hundred feet below it. Scott glanced at the cargo ship as they passed abeam. He waited a few seconds and keyed the mike. "Okay, a shallow turn to the left for a three-sixty—see what we have."

"Coming left."

As the wide turn slowly progressed, nothing was happening, not even a radio call from anyone.

Scott keyed his ICS. "This is like trolling for the 'Creature from the Black Lagoon.'"

Jackie was intently searching the sky. "Yeah, but what do you do when you catch it?"

"There it is!" Scott said. "It's at seven—"

"I got it, I got it." Jackie worked hard to keep the bright bluish-white object in her viewfinder.

"Rocky," Scott said excitedly, "we have another bogey, an exact duplicate of the last one, making erratic passes."

The radios came alive while the Phantom completed two full circles around the ship. The bright, mysterious object made several passes at the Phantom, always appearing to narrowly miss the fighter, then shot straight up and disappeared.

At the beginning of the third circle, Scott keyed the radio. "Rocky, I don't know about the Phantom, but we're getting tight on gas."

"Scott," Hartwell Prost said, "the president has requested that you make a high-speed low pass over the ship. Would that be a problem?"

"Stand by, sir."

"Jackie, you have a vote here."

"Well, they've fired a weapon at the Phantom and he's trying to intimidate them, trying to get them to take a swing. I'm game, but one pass and we're out of here."

Scott switched to the radio. "We have enough fuel for one pass."

"That's all he wants," Prost said.

"Rocky, lights out, take up a heading of two-three-zero and descend to five hundred feet."

Craine immediately extinguished the lights and read back the instructions. Descending more rapidly than normal, the F-4 and the Harrier quickly accelerated to 420 knots and leveled off at five hundred feet.

"Okay, let's have a nice thirty-degree bank to the right and we'll roll out on a heading of zero-five-zero."

"Here we go," Craine said, totally absorbed in flying the drone. "Looking for zero-five-zero and five hundred feet."

"Three miles," the Hawkeye systems operator prompted.

After rolling wings level, Scott hurriedly called for a minor course correction and an easy descent to two hundred feet. "Come up on the power, we're looking for five hundred knots."

"Copy five hundred."

At a mile and a half from the ship, the jets were screaming across the water at 250 feet, still descending at 490 knots. When they were one mile from the *Kapitan Zhirnovsky*, the planes were level at 200 feet and the dark bridge of the ship was centered in Scott's windscreen.

At three quarters of a mile from the ship, Scott keyed his radio. "Lights on and afterburners—now!"

The Phantom belched twin yellowish-orange flames from the burner cans while the brilliant strobes lit the surface of the water and reflected off the windows on the bridge of the *Kapitan Zhirnovsky*.

Approaching the ship at 515 knots, Scott called for a gradual climb. "Ease it up, nice and easy on the pull."

"Oh, shit!" Craine said in mind-numbing shock. "I lost it—I lost the plane—too low!"

Scott frantically pulled up as the QF-4S crashed into the ship's bridge with the force of tons of TNT. The thunderous explosion shook the Harrier and temporarily blinded Jackie and Scott. In stunned silence, Dalton keyed his mike. "Rocky, I just put the Phantom through the ship's bridge."

"What? Say again."

"The Phantom just bull's-eyed the ship's bridge. It's my fault—I took us in too low."

"Spooky, it's just one of those deals," Craine said.

"Yeah," Scott said, rolling into a tight turn over the burning *Kapitan Zhirnovsky*. "I just made a *big* mistake."

"How bad is it?" Prost asked.

"The bridge is gone, completely wiped out, and the ship is on fire."

The radios became unreadable as everyone tried to talk at once.

Scott interrupted the chaos. "Prime Time, the ship just exploded in a huge fireball. We'd better get help to them quickly."

"Roger, we're on it."

"Rocky, we're at bingo fuel and headed toward Miramar."

"Copy," Craine said.

Prost informed the president of what had happened.

Jackie keyed the ICS. "Well, do you think we might be able to find positions as mercenary fighter pilots with some banana republic?"

"That'd be too much to hope for." Scott pulled the throttle aft to save fuel. "We're probably looking at something along the lines of the Pakistani Civil Air Patrol."

16

The *Kapitan Zhirnovsky*

Fourteen minutes after the Phantom blasted through the lower section of the bridge, the *Kapitan Zhirnovsky* exploded a second time and rapidly started taking on water. The devastating impact of the F-4 started numerous fires, ripped jagged holes in the hull, twisted bulkheads, and compromised watertight compartments.

The nine surviving Chinese crew members desperately tried to extinguish the spreading fires, then backed away when the cargo vessel began listing to port. They turned their attention to launching a lifeboat on the starboard side of the ship but gave up when the angle of the deck became too steep.

A few seconds later, another deafening explosion rocked the ship and knocked the crew to their knees. Suffering from shock, the crew moved to the port side and struggled with another lifeboat. They stopped when they heard the first sounds of helicopters approaching the ship.

Two SH-60B Seahawks arrived overhead *Kapitan Zhirnovsky*. The cruiser USS *Princeton* and the destroyer USS *Benfold* raced at flank speed to reach the stricken vessel.

As the helicopters slowed to a hover, both navy rescue swimmers motioned for the crewmen to abandon the badly listing ship and swim clear. Panicked, the men again tried to launch a lifeboat. They stopped when seawater began sloshing over the main deck.

The cargo ship was in the final throes of dying when a third Seahawk helicopter arrived. With little warning, the

Kapitan Zhirnovsky commenced a very slow roll to port and began to slip below the waves. A minute later, the bow dipped beneath the ocean and the stern rose out of the water.

The crew, with no other option, jumped into the water and swam as hard as they could to get away from their ship. One at a time, the three helos dropped down to rescue survivors, until there was only one man left. When the SH-60B moved in closer to the crewman, the *Kapitan Zhirnovsky* exploded a final time as the trapped air and gases blew the stern open.

The huge concussion rocked the helicopter and forced the pilot to make another approach. The ship disappeared under the ocean while the helo hoisted the sailor aboard. With all the survivors safely in the helicopters, the Seahawks set course for USS *Abraham Lincoln*.

MCAS Miramar

When Scott cleared the taxiway and brought the Harrier to a smooth halt next to their spare TAV-8B, he and Jackie noticed Juanita Trujillo patiently waiting for them. The slight woman appeared to be relaxed and unaffected by the tragic confrontation with the Chinese.

Scott keyed the ICS. "You think she's my escort to the firing squad?"

"Well, she isn't armed."

Scott began shutting down the jet. "Getting into hot water is always a lot easier than getting out."

She unfastened her kneeboard. "Let's close the shop and find out how much trouble we're in."

"You're not in any trouble."

"Both of us were up there. And both of us know that *we* brought the Phantom in too low."

After securing the Harrier, Jackie and Scott climbed down and greeted Juanita. She quickly assured them that President Macklin and Hartwell Prost were very pleased with the operation, notwithstanding the sinking of the cargo ship.

"According to the president," Juanita said, "the loss of

control over the Phantom was an accident caused by *his* excessive enthusiasm. He made it very clear that you and Mr. Craine are not at fault."

Nothing else was said after they drove away from the flight line. When they reached the hangar, Hartwell's navy Huron utility transport was just arriving. Prost stepped off the military version of the popular turboprop and explained that Wyatt Craine was staying on San Nicolas Island to complete the accident report. Prost talked with Juanita for a few minutes, then joined Jackie and Scott in a private office in the hangar.

"Well," Hartwell began as the threesome sat down at a conference table, "it's good that we now have two Washington-Moscow hot lines to try to avoid misunderstandings and surprises."

Scott and Jackie looked perplexed.

"The State Department is using one of the lines to read from our Official Apology Manual while the president is on a secure line trying to calm Beijing and Moscow. The ship sank, and we're pretty sure the Russians are in bed with the Red Chinese on this laser weapon system."

"How many casualties?" Scott asked.

"We don't know." Hartwell removed the new brown leather flight jacket the Marines had given him. "Three navy helos rescued nine survivors. However, before they could get them to the carrier, the Chinese ambassador, the Chinese foreign minister, the Russian foreign minister, and the Russian prime minister were screaming bloody murder. They wanted the survivors flown directly to Long Beach and turned over to Chinese authorities. The word *immediately* was used often and loudly, along with a constant reminder that no one was to attempt to interrogate the crewmen."

Scott's head sagged and then he looked up. "Well, I made a mess of things—don't know if we can keep our role secret."

"Let us deal with it," Hartwell said. "No doubt the Phantom did extensive damage to the ship; however, we believe there were explosive charges placed at strategic locations to make sure the ship would sink before prying eyes could see what was inside."

"I don't doubt it," Jackie said.

"Beijing sent a strongly worded message to the White House and the State Department to inform us that a Chinese salvage vessel would soon be over the site of the sinking. Their foreign minister has made it clear that Beijing will not tolerate any interference."

"It may be a diplomatic mess," Jackie said, "but we now have proof that the Chinese are using some type of laser-based weapon to bring down airplanes—U.S. warplanes."

Hartwell's sour expression gave him away. "Unfortunately, we don't have a recorded event. We need a video or a series of pictures, where a laser beam actually strikes an aircraft and destroys it."

Jackie sensed something was wrong. "Are you saying we risked our lives for nothing? We have video."

"No, that's not what I'm saying. We *wanted* them to shoot down the drone, but the aerobatic maneuvers seemed to cause a problem with the laser locking on to the plane."

Scott caught Hartwell's attention. "You think it's manually aimed and not radar locked?"

"Maybe, at this stage of development, but it won't be too long before they adapt to using radar. Then we'll have a bigger problem."

"So, where do we go from here?" Jackie asked.

Hartwell seemed to perk up. "Let me set the stage, then we'll discuss our options. As I've told you, we have a lot of geostrategic problems bubbling to the surface. Over the past two days, we quietly extracted our ambassador to China, his immediate staff, and his security detail. The Chinese discovered it about two hours before you took off this evening."

Hartwell poured himself a glass of ice water. "Our spacecraft detected heavy message traffic between the Chinese ships and Beijing, and between Beijing and Moscow. After the encounter with the *Chen Ziyang,* headquarters in Beijing forbade the master of the *Kapitan Zhirnovsky* to fire his laser. It was okay to use the decoy, whatever it is, but the order was clear about not firing the laser."

Prost drank half the glass of water. "We have a dangerous

dance going on with the China-Taiwan situation, and the Koreas are on the brink of open warfare. Either situation could trigger a reaction from the other powder keg and cause open warfare in the region."

"Are any of our carriers in the area yet?" Scott asked.

"The *Kitty Hawk* will be on station shortly in the Taiwan Strait, and *Roosevelt* will be in the South China Sea before too long."

Hartwell fell silent for a moment, the strain of his responsibility showing in his eyes. "The president is calling for an emergency meeting in Bangkok. He wants to work with the Association of Southeast Asian Nations and its Asian and Pacific partners to try to mend fences with China and Russia. He knows this is going to be tantamount to playing football in a minefield, but he is determined to try this approach."

A smile touched Hartwell's mouth. "Although President Macklin wants to mend the rift with China, he has no intention of giving Beijing an inch of ground. In fact, he wants to go to Bangkok with overwhelming evidence to show all the ASEAN partners that Beijing is fielding a very destabilizing laser-based weapon system. He also wants the world to know how China gained the knowledge and expertise to develop the weapon system."

"Why do I suddenly feel uncomfortable?" Scott asked.

Hartwell's expression turned serious. "We don't have much time. The president needs an answer by tomorrow morning."

"To what?" Scott asked. "Sir, it isn't like you to be evasive."

Prost sat upright. "Would you consider parachuting onto the *Chen Ziyang* at night and documenting what's on board?"

Scott and Jackie were astonished.

Hartwell turned to Jackie. "We want your help too."

Dalton at first stifled a laugh but allowed a small grin to spread across his lips. "You're kidding . . . of course," he said, and locked Prost in his gaze. "Aren't you?"

"No, I'm not kidding," he said with a straight face. "As you know, all of your records since the military—along with Jackie's records—have been completely sanitized."

Scott glanced at Jackie and saw the concern in her eyes.

"We can't have any fingerprints leading to anyone in the administration, or pointing to any agency in the government. Scott, this is exactly the kind of operation we had in mind when we asked you to leave the Agency. This has to be a stealth operation, clean and neat with no congressional questions until after the president confronts Liu Fan-ding in front of the world."

Taken aback, Scott was calculating the odds of a successful jump and a safe means of escaping.

"You can write your own ticket, buy a new jet, whatever you want," Hartwell said, and looked at Sullivan. "The same for you, Jackie. Just let me know what equipment you'll need."

"Mr. Prost, would you mind if I discuss this with Jackie before we give you an answer?"

"I insist that you do." Hartwell rose from his chair. "However, I'll need an answer bright and early in the morning, before I fly back to Washington."

"Yes, sir."

Hartwell donned his cap and adjusted it. "How about breakfast at the club, say seven sharp."

"That'd be great," Jackie said.

After Hartwell left the office, Jackie and Scott stared at each other for a long moment and then laughed at the same time.

"We can move up from a Bonanza to a jet," Scott said with the parachute jump still playing on his mind. "What do you think?"

"We?"

"As in the two of us—you and me."

"How about taking me to dinner?"

"Let's go," Scott said with a grin.

"I think I need a Manhattan."

"You got it," he said with excitement in his voice. "We have a tough decision to make."

Jackie rose from her chair and pulled Scott to his feet. "*You* have a tough decision, my friend. I'm not the one who has to parachute onto a Chinese ship in the middle of the night."

The Panama Canal

After the strategic waterway was returned to Panamanian control at noon on December 31, 1999, another December day that will live in infamy, the Red Chinese military became the de facto gatekeepers of the ports at the Atlantic and Pacific ends of the big ditch.

Hutchison Whampoa Limited, of Hong Kong, a powerful conglomerate with strong ties to the Chinese government and the People's Liberation Army, won underhanded contracts to operate the critical ports of Cristóbal and Balboa. The deceitful and lucrative twenty-five-year lease, along with the optional twenty-five-year extension, were a cause of great concern in many circles, including the Pentagon.

The unorthodox bidding, along with shiploads of money from China to Panamanian government officials, provided a means for the Red Chinese to delay or stop expedited treatment normally reserved for U.S. warships.

One of the most strategic choke points on the globe was transferred from the most powerful nation on earth to a small Third World country with a population of 2.8 million people. This major international asset was now controlled by a corrupt communist power.

Because Panama no longer had a military, Beijing quietly began moving thousands of Chinese soldiers into the Panama Canal Zone. They did this on the pretext of protecting Hutchison Whampoa civilian employees from roving bands of Colombian insurgents, drug traffickers, and the guerrillas of the Marxist Revolutionary Armed Forces of Colombia.

With more than 83,000 Chinese nationals and 12,800 Chinese troops dispersed in the ten-mile-wide swath across the Isthmus of Panama, Beijing was using the former Howard Air Force Base and the Rodman Naval Station to base warplanes, missiles, bombs, submarines, and warships only nine hundred miles from U.S. soil.

Under the vacuous and controversial Panama Canal Neutrality Treaty signed in 1977, the United States reserved the right to intervene militarily if the canal was threatened or invaded. President Macklin, Hartwell Prost, the secretary of defense, and the joint chiefs were secretly making contingency plans to deal with the growing Chinese military force in Panama.

Over the Gulf of Panama

Based at Biggs Army Airfield, Fort Bliss, Texas, the de Havilland RC-7 reconnaissance plane was approaching Panama City three hours before dawn. Though ostensibly it was a U.S. counternarcotics aircraft, a National Defense Authorization Act had expanded the charter of Joint Task Force Six to conduct counterinsurgency missions and to keep a watchful eye on Colombian guerrillas and the Red Chinese in the area of the canal.

Packed with sophisticated intelligence equipment for the interception of radio and mobile phone communications, the four-engine turboprop RC-7 could gather burst communications, the latest digital voice encryptions, or low-probability-of-intercept signals and transmit them to the National Security Agency for analysis.

The flight crew also shared information with more than three hundred covert operatives from the Drug Enforcement Administration and the CIA. The mission was the Pentagon's biggest covert operation in Latin America.

Eight miles from Balboa, at an altitude of seven thousand feet, the reconnaissance aircraft made a slight course correction to follow the Panama Canal from Bahía de Panama to Bahía Limón at the entrance to the Caribbean Sea. The winding, slate-black fifty-one-mile lake-and-lock waterway was easy to see in the ivory-and-gold moonlight.

The pilot in command, army captain Barbara Yankovitz, studied the former Howard Air Force Base and turned to her copilot. "Since we pulled out of Panama, the druggies have had a field day."

Captain Ronald Jansen gazed at the sprinkling of lights on the ground. "Yeah, giving up the canal was a gigantic blunder. It left a huge hole in our drug-fighting efforts."

"And it's getting worse."

Jansen looked at the strobe lights of another plane in the distance. "I'm just surprised that the Chinese aren't doing something about it."

"Well," Yankovitz said as she made a minor course correction, "they sure haven't been timid about fortifying their defenses near the ditch."

"Not exactly subtle." Jansen reached for his coffee cup. "I heard that we have a battle group in the Colombian Basin."

"That's what I hear." Yankovitz studied the lights on the ground as they passed over the coastline north of Balboa. "A friend of mine, a pilot stationed at Hurlburt Field, told me the Special Operations Wing has two AC-130 Spooky gunships on standby around the clock."

"I have a feeling something is about to happen, especially with a carrier battle group just off the coast."

Yankovitz chuckled. "And it isn't going to be good."

"Not with the Chinese at our back door."

In the cramped fuselage of the aircraft, three army reconnaissance specialists and two Colombian antidrug officers were gathering a variety of covert information about the Chinese, the Colombian guerrillas, and the bands of Colombian drug traffickers.

The de Havilland flew directly down the center of the canal. Nearing the canal lock east of Gatun Lake, Yankovitz complied with a request from one of her aerial surveillance experts. The pilot flew the plane in a wide 360-degree circle to the right and rolled out over the canal.

Suddenly, as the crew reacted in shocked silence, a man-portable surface-to-air missile slammed into the right inboard turboprop and exploded in a blinding fireball.

"SAMs—we've been hit!" Jansen said, and looked back at the engine. "We're on fire! We have a fire in number three!"

"We're getting out of here," Yankovitz shouted. "Hang on!"

The tremendous explosion had almost ripped the burning engine from the wing. The pilots desperately tried to feather the prop and extinguish the flames. Yankovitz turned sharply to the northeast while Jansen made repeated mayday radio calls.

Once the stricken de Havilland reached the placid waters of the Caribbean Sea there was a collective moment of relief among the crew, but it was short lived.

After following the emergency procedures for an engine fire, Ron Jansen again looked to the right and was shocked to see that the flames were growing more intense. "It's out of control!"

"That's all we need."

Jansen didn't hesitate. "We're going to have to ditch before the fire burns through the wing."

"I know," Yankovitz said, lowering the nose and turning to fly parallel to the beach. "Get the crew ready."

Jansen leapt out of the cockpit while Yankovitz slowed the crippled plane and prepared to ditch the de Havilland in relatively shallow water. She keyed the radio. "Mayday . . . Mayday . . . Mayday . . . Kingfisher Three-Seven is ditching." She repeated the distress call four times and gave the GPS coordinates of their location.

Seconds later the copilot was back. "Everyone's strapped in."

"Good."

Jansen quickly tightened his restraining straps. "Now we know how the crew of the navy EP-3 felt."

"And it isn't a good feeling."

Leaving the landing gear up, Yankovitz lowered the flaps and slowed the airplane until it was floating through the air a few feet above the calm water.

"Brace yourselves, we're going in," Yankovitz said over the ICS as she felt the airplane beginning to shudder. The RC-7 was on the verge of stalling. The de Havilland's belly skipped across the water a few times and then settled into the sea. The aircraft was immediately engulfed in a large spray of water and quickly came to a halt.

17

The Yellow Sea

The sun was low in the hazy sky when the guided-missile cruiser USS *Mobile Bay* rendezvoused with the South Korean flotilla of two destroyers, one frigate, and seven patrol boats. The crew of *Mobile Bay* and the sailors in the South Korean warships were at battle stations.

Three thousand yards away, North Korean warships, patrol boats, and torpedo boats were escorting two dozen fishing boats through a prohibited zone of crab-rich waters demarcated by the United Nations.

The disputed area lay south of a UN-imposed sea border between the North Korean mainland and five South Korean islands located sixty miles northwest of Seoul. This was the third major confrontation in sixteen months between North Korea and South Korea over the disputed fishing waters. The South Korean Defense Ministry had warned Pyongyang not to invade their territorial waters. If they did, the ministry promised to respond swiftly and sternly.

The South Korean frigate *Jeong Nam,* the destroyer *Kwanggaeto,* and three of the patrol boats began approaching the North Korean ships and fishing vessels. The destroyer *Ulchimundo* and the other four patrol boats spread out, while *Mobile Bay* anchored the center of the small armada.

The North Korean warships quickly maneuvered into a defensive position, with the fishing boats retreating slightly behind them.

Tensions mounted as *Jeong Nam, Kwanggaeto,* and the South Korean patrol boats gathered speed.

A Soviet-built Mil Mi-8 helicopter hovered low over the fourteen tightly spaced North Korean warships. Equipped with 128 57mm rockets, the multirole helicopter could definitely prove to be a problem.

Overhead, a single U.S. Air Force AC-130U Spooky gunship named *Midnight Medusa* orbited in a circle. The Herc's primary mission was close air support, air interdiction, and armed reconnaissance. The heavily armed warbird incorporated side-firing weapons, including two 20mm Vulcan cannons with 3,000 rounds, one 40mm Bofors cannon with 256 rounds, and one 105mm howitzer with 100 rounds.

The menacing Spooky could provide surgical firepower or area saturation for extended periods of time. Nothing, not dark nights or inclement weather, stood in the way of the powerful Spooky gunships.

The opposing ships trained their guns on each other as the South Korean frigate, destroyer, and patrol boats stayed their course. When *Jeong Nam* and *Kwanggaeto* reached a point approximately a thousand yards from the intruding warships, the long standoff ended. Every North Korean vessel simultaneously opened fire at the Korean warships and *Mobile Bay.* The Mil Mi-8 helo sprayed rockets at the destroyer *Kwanggaeto* and the smaller patrol boats.

The South Koreans and *Mobile Bay* answered the volley with a steady barrage of gunfire. The deafening explosions and huge geysers of water erupting around both flotillas were exacerbated when the AC-130U Spooky gunship opened up with a staggering amount of firepower.

Sounding remarkably like a Paul Bunyan–sized chain saw, *Midnight Medusa* rained death and destruction over the entire North Korean armada, including the lone helicopter. The Herc's cannons and howitzer shredded the North Korean warships and patrol boats, destroying four of the craft in less than fifty seconds.

Amid the explosions, flames, and billowing clouds of dark smoke, North Korean survivors dived into the sea and swam for their lives. Abandoned by the entire crew, two of the smaller vessels continued on course while flames danced from their decks.

The helicopter lasted only twelve seconds before it was cut in half, literally, dumping the pilot, copilot, and flight engineer into the sea. Alive and suffering only minor injuries, Russian exchange pilot Maj. Nikolai Ivanov was killed when he was run over by a North Korean torpedo patrol boat. The other two men survived the crash.

Mobile Bay and the South Korean warships fired salvo after salvo at the North Koreans, hitting the tightly bunched fleet with devastating results. A number of North Korean sailors who were blown from the decks of their patrol boats landed on other patrol boats.

The armed clash was over in three minutes. Seven North Korean vessels were sinking, including a fishing boat that was hit by an errant shell from *Kwanggaeto*. Two other North Korean warships would have to be towed to their base or to a salvage yard. Seventy-one North Korean sailors would be reported dead, along with eighty-two injured.

The frigate *Jeong Nam* suffered a direct hit on her starboard bow but wasn't in danger of sinking. One of the South Korean patrol boats was headed for a watery grave, and *Mobile Bay* had sustained minor damage to her port hull amidships. Nine South Koreans lost their lives and twenty-two were injured, six seriously. The American cruiser would put in for repairs at South Korea's main naval base, located in a picturesque natural harbor at Chinhae. *Midnight Medusa* would safely return to her base without a scratch.

The Colombian Basin

The supercarrier USS *George Washington* and her escorts, the frigates USS *Boone* and USS *Underwood,* the destroyer USS *John Rodgers,* and the cruiser USS *Normandy* were steaming south-southwest 220 nautical miles due north of the Panama Canal.

Joining the *George Washington* carrier battle group, the *Wasp*-class amphibious assault ship USS *Kearsarge* and the *Tarawa*-class assault ship USS *Nassau* brought the combined air- and ground-combat elements of Marine expeditionary units to the troubled Panama Canal.

Resembling scaled-down aircraft carriers, the assault ships provided sea control and fast-striking power projections on hostile shores. The Marines use air-cushion landing craft, conventional landing craft, and helicopters to move their assault forces ashore.

Normally constructed around a reinforced battalion, the Marine expeditionary unit was a force with the ability to rapidly mobilize for combat operations in virtually any environment at any time. The force consisted of a battalion landing team supported with artillery, amphibious assault vehicles, light armored reconnaissance assets, and other units as needed for a particular operation.

Depending on the mission, the aviation element of the MEU was comprised of a mix of helicopters and fixed-wing aircraft, including AV-8B Harrier attack jets, CH-53 Super Stallions, CH-46 Sea Knights, UH-1N Hueys, and AH-1W Super Cobra helicopters.

After the army de Havilland RC-7 reconnaissance plane was shot down near the Panama Canal, U.S. space-based assets and reconnaissance planes provided undeniable proof that elements of the Chinese military were rapidly developing sites for antiaircraft guns and surface-to-air missiles along the entire length of the fifty-one-mile canal.

In a prime-time press conference, President Macklin cited the section of the Panama Canal treaties clearly invoking the right of the United States of America to intervene militarily if the canal was threatened. In his judgment, the safety and security of the Panama Canal was certainly in jeopardy and required U.S. involvement.

The president had ended the short but ominous press briefing by announcing that he was placing the army's 82d Airborne on alert. He also sternly warned Beijing about the consequences of their actions. Steel jawed and unblinking,

Macklin insisted that Beijing take immediate corrective action in regard to the SAM sites and the triple-A emplacements. Ignoring questions from reporters, he left the press briefing while the buzz in the room grew louder.

On orders from the White House, a no-fly zone was declared and established over the Panama Canal. Fighter planes from *George Washington* routinely patrolled the entire length of the canal and overflew the former Howard Air Force Base. Two AC-130U Spooky gunships, *Terminator II* and *Hell Raiser,* were making their presence known, one flying at night, the other during the day.

An hour after the assault ships arrived in the Colombian Basin, two Marine AV-8B Harriers took off from *Kearsarge* and flew directly over the canal to the Pacific port of Balboa.

On the return leg to their ship, they came under intense Chinese antiaircraft artillery fire three miles southeast of Colón. The flight leader's plane was hit, but both aircraft retaliated by striking the triple-A site with conventional bombs and cannon fire. When the Harriers departed the area, the site was as quiet as a tomb.

In an impromptu and emotional press briefing in the Rose Garden, President Macklin called the attack on the Marine Harriers an act of war and declared that U.S. forces would use whatever means available to defend themselves.

In closing his concise remarks, he reiterated the right of the United States to intervene militarily if the security of the Panama Canal was threatened. Leaving the media with their mouths agape, Macklin turned on his heel and departed to meet with the members of his National Security Council and their statutory advisers.

Hours later, when the night watch AC-130U Spooky arrived on station at 2200, the air force crew gave a vivid and unforgettable firepower display near a triple-A site close to the site the Marines had flattened. Terrified at the surgical destruction inflicted by the Spooky gunship, the Chicom gunners flew out of their emplacements as if they'd seen the Grim Reaper face-to-face. Within minutes, PLA officers chained the frightened soldiers to their guns.

Washington, D.C.

Air force general Les Chalmers skipped a working breakfast at the Pentagon and went straight to Capitol Hill. As Chalmers and one of his aides, army colonel Anthony Sloan, entered the august chamber and took their seats, he steeled himself for his meeting with members of the Senate Committee on Armed Services. They were about to grill him on a wide range of controversial topics regarding the military.

The breaking news on the cable networks was spilling forth with the latest developments in Panama, the Yellow Sea, and the sinking of the Chinese-operated Russian ship that had been kayoed by the flying lighthouse. The Russians, the Chinese, and the North Koreans were alternately protesting and threatening the United States and her allies.

Dante Raines, the cantankerous chairman of the committee, shuffled his papers and looked over the top of his oval wire-framed glasses. "General Chalmers, what can you tell us about the state of our military readiness this morning?" Raines pointed his finger at Chalmers. "I want you to explain to this committee how we managed to get into this much of a mess in such a short period of time."

With his face a mask, showing no emotion, Chalmers forced himself to be calm and respectful.

"Senator Raines, and members of the committee, I know President Macklin and Secretary of Defense Adair are doing everything they can to turn our military around, but it's going to take time, a long time. Especially when we have so many assets assigned to the terrorism problem."

He paused a moment to read the expressions on their faces. "Over a number of years, American naval and air power have been significantly drawn down in the Persian Gulf, the Mediterranean, the Atlantic, and in the Pacific—particularly in Southeast Asia and the Philippines. And as of this moment, American troops are on a heightened state of alert in South Korea."

Chalmers glanced at the other committee members and then focused on Raines. "We are facing several crises at the same time, and we're short on aircraft carriers and many other critical items. Our readiness is at an all-time low, and our military is stretched paper-thin all over the world."

The general cleared his throat. "We're cannibalizing parts at an alarming rate to keep the equipment we have in operating order. Our fighter pilots are losing to foreign pilots in mock aerial combat. Our navy recently had to stand down a day for ship-driving lessons because of inadequate training. In addition, recruiting qualified people and retaining our top performers is a major problem. We simply don't have the necessary logistical support to respond to every crisis or region that faces a—"

"General Chalmers"—Raines rudely cut him off—"are you trying to tell us that you aren't managing your resources properly, is that it?"

"Resources—what resources? Many of our pilots who flew combat in Kosovo and Afghanistan were conducting on-the-job training because we didn't have the money or manpower to properly train them before sending them in harm's way."

Politically astute his entire career, Chalmers allowed a narrow smile to cross his face. *What the hell, I'm close enough to retirement.* Fueled by disgust and contempt for a man who had publicly displayed his disdain for the military and who had referred to military personnel as dumb, stupid animals, Chalmers stared straight into the pinched eyes of the irascible politician.

"Senator," Chalmers said with venom in his voice, "there's no question that we have a hollowed-out military, a military that has been demoralized because of the faddish social experimentations and the quirky policies handed to it by civilians."

Chalmers's voice hardened. "The Asians and the Europeans know our military is stretched to the breaking point, thanks to force reductions that have partially paralyzed many of our frontline assets. If we had to respond simultaneously to North Korea and deal with China in the Taiwan Strait, we couldn't prevail using conventional weapons."

Colonel Sloan visibly cringed and fixed his eyes on the top of the table.

Chalmers spoke more forcibly. "It isn't the management in the military who controls the purse strings, sir. Years of inept *civilian* management of our military has brought us to our knees and undermined our ability to protect our nation and maintain freedom around—"

"General," Raines said loudly, shaking his finger in anger, "I think that'll be enough—not another word!"

Chalmers talked over Raines. "The best solution for our country is for Congress and the administration to start raising defense spending caps and rebuilding our military and I mean ASAP!"

Inflamed with anger and resentment, Raines slammed the gavel down, called a recess, and stormed out of the hearing room.

Prompted by General Chalmers, Colonel Sloan rose and quietly followed his boss out of the United States Capitol. They were then driven to the White House to have an early lunch with Chalmers's old friend from the U.S. Air Force Academy.

18

MCAS Miramar Officers' Club

Hartwell Prost was waiting when Jackie and Scott were ushered into a private dining room. He rose to greet them and then seated Jackie. "I thought we might like some privacy."

Scott unfolded his napkin. "I hope you haven't been waiting long."

"Only a couple of minutes," Prost said, reaching for his coffee.

They ordered breakfast and coffee, and then Hartwell gave them a brief update on the clashes in Panama and in the Yellow Sea. He also told them about the de Havilland RC-7 reconnaissance plane that was shot down.

Hartwell looked at Jackie. "She managed to ditch the airplane without injuring any of her crew. A helicopter from the *Washington* battle group picked them up and flew them to the carrier. They'll be going to the Pentagon for a debriefing."

"What's the situation in the Korean standoff?" Scott asked.

"Not good. We're going to move two more AC-130 Spooky gunships to South Korea, and we have eleven B-52s and a squadron of F-15E Strike Eagles getting ready to deploy to Asia. Fourteen F-15Cs from the 3d Fighter Wing at Elmendorf will also join the buildup."

The conversation continued in the same vein for another couple of minutes before Scott turned to Prost. "We've decided to give your plan a try, but we have some questions."

Hartwell's face reflected his relief. "Good—that's great. First, let me tell you what I know as of fifteen minutes ago.

The *Chen Ziyang* changed course about three hours after the other ship went to the bottom. From what we can tell, and it's an educated guess, the ship is returning to Chinese waters—probably to its home port."

Jackie and Scott didn't reveal how surprised they were. The cargo ship's change in course negated their original plan of action.

"Unfortunately, we don't have a lot of time to set this up—to keep you and the operation in a cocoon."

"We're going to have to use the navy," Scott surmised.

"That's right. I think the best way to do this is to use *Stennis* as the staging point, but that's up to you."

After a brief glance at each other, Scott and Jackie nodded in agreement.

"That sounds like a good platform to operate from," Dalton said. "It gives us lots of options and support."

Hartwell's enthusiasm was growing. "As soon as I pass the word to the president that you're on board, *Stennis* will make a slight course change to close on the Chinese ship."

"We can use the COD to get out to the carrier," Jackie suggested, referring to the twin turboprop Grumman C-2A Greyhound. The "carrier onboard delivery" aircraft was a mainstay for carrier operations.

Scott was thinking ahead. "Since the COD's ramp can be opened in flight, we can also use it to make the drop."

"That's perfect," Jackie said. "And we can use one of the carrier's Seahawks to pick you up after the operation."

"I've already made the arrangements," Hartwell said, pleased with his plan. "The COD is being fitted with a ferry tank."

"You're way ahead of us," Scott said. "What about a cover?"

"Standard boilerplate. Jackie will be on the manifest as a navy lieutenant commander—you as a Marine major. Your uniforms will be ready by late this afternoon."

Hartwell unfolded his napkin on his lap. "The crew of the COD will be thoroughly briefed before you leave the carrier.

They won't know why you're jumping out in the middle of the night in the middle of the Pacific, and they'll be told to forget any questions they might have."

"And me?" Jackie asked feeling left out of the equation. "Is there anything I can do after we get to the carrier?"

"Besides flying jets, you also fly helicopters, correct?"

"Yes, sir."

"Have you ever flown a Seahawk?"

"No, sir."

"Well, this morning is probably a good time to get checked out as a copilot. I'll set it up and you can fly all day if you want to. You can get copilot qualified and be aboard the extraction helicopter."

"Sounds great."

"Both of you think about it. If you have any other ideas, let me know."

"When do we go to the carrier?" Scott asked.

"Tomorrow morning, oh-two-hundred. The COD will have enough fuel to reach the carrier or divert to Hawaii if the plane has a problem or can't land on the ship for some reason."

"Ah, there's just one small hitch," Scott said.

Hartwell's smile disappeared. "And what would that be?"

"My custom-built chutes, wet suit, and other items are in our spare bedroom at home."

"Not a problem," Prost said with a smile. "I'll have one of the guys at the Agency let himself into your place, and then I'll have it all flown out to you by this evening. Okay?"

"Let's do it," Scott said, and then chuckled. "No doubt about it, you have the magic touch."

"Call me, the sooner the better, when you work out the logistics. I want whatever you need flown out to the carrier, then we'll get you out there as soon as we can."

Scott was already reformulating his plan to parachute onto the deck of *Chen Ziyang*. "We'll call you on your way back to Washington."

"I look forward to it," Hartwell said, falling silent when

their breakfast was brought into the room. He waited until they were alone, then looked at Scott. "The president will be *very* appreciative."

"Let's just hope we can pull this off."

MCAS Miramar BOQ

Scott was mentally rehearsing the drop. He was carefully analyzing all the possible problems that might arise when a loud knock on the door startled him. He checked his watch and walked to the door. He was surprised to see that it was almost 1900.

Scott was greeted by a straight-faced second lieutenant of Marines who had two huge nylon bags containing everything that had been in Dalton's spare bedroom. Everything, that is, except the furniture.

"Thanks, Lieutenant," Scott said, taking custody of the heavy, bulky green bags.

"You're welcome, sir," the squared-away officer replied, and returned to his car.

Scott was in the process of sorting through the second bag when Jackie showed up with her SH-60F Seahawk flight instructor, navy lieutenant David Finchly. They were still in their flight suits.

The muscular lieutenant commander–select was a rugged-looking former college wrestler. Introductions were made while Scott worked on his gear and invited everyone to have a seat.

"Dave is going with us," Jackie said. "He'll be piloting the Seahawk."

"Welcome aboard, Lieutenant."

"Thank you, sir."

"Dave's a NATOPS check pilot, and he has two carrier cruises under his belt, so we're in good shape."

"We can use all of the experience we can get," Scott said, tossing one of his parachutes on the couch. "Is Hartwell in the loop on this?"

"Sure, he's the one who arranged it."

"Good." Scott turned to Finchly. "Dave, how much do you know about this operation?"

"Only that Jackie and I will be plucking you from the water at night. Other than that I don't care to know anything else."

"That's a good answer. Have the two of you had dinner?"

"We had a snack," Jackie said. "We're going to get in some night flying, then pack our gear. We'll see you around one-thirty."

"I'll be there."

"Would you like to ride along this evening?" Finchly politely asked.

"I'd like to," Scott said, and motioned toward his parachutes and assorted gear, "but I'm going to have to sort through some things."

Finchly could tell by the parachutes, small portable oxygen tanks and masks, wet suits, and assorted gear that Scott and Jackie were involved in some type of covert special-operations mission.

"Okay, we'll see you later."

After Jackie and Dave left, Scott inspected his custom-designed black parachute. The special rectangular ramair canopy allowed him to maintain a high degree of control and accuracy after a precision free fall.

When he had everything neatly organized, Scott placed the rest of his equipment and various other items in one of the nylon bags. He would leave it in the Learjet that was being guarded by the navy SEALs. Satisfied that he was prepared for the difficult operation, he went to the officers' club for dinner and a cold beer.

Naval Air Station North Island, California

After a short delay for a mechanical problem to be corrected, the C-2A Greyhound lifted off the runway at 0226 and banked toward the Pacific Ocean. The VRC-30 Provider's lo-

gistics support COD contained a ferry fuel tank, miscella-
neous aircraft parts, snail mail, and six passengers, including
Jackie, Scott, David Finchly, two sailors, and a navy commander.

Wearing the uniform of a navy lieutenant commander,
Jackie made herself as comfortable as possible and closed her
eyes. Exhausted after flying most of the day and part of the
night, she quickly fell into a deep sleep. The sailors opened a
worn deck of cards and the commander relaxed with a paper-
back.

Scott turned to Dave Finchly. "How did you get involved
in aviation?"

"I didn't have an option." He chuckled. "Our family has
had avgas or jet fuel in our veins since my great-grandfather
on my mother's side flew Pan Am flying boats—Clippers—
around the Pacific back in the 1930s."

"No kidding?"

"It's true. He was a captain, but they didn't go by that rank.
They were Masters of Ocean Flying Boats—the Skygods.
Our family has run the gamut from barnstormers to navy car-
rier pilots to crop dusters to airline pilots."

Scott leaned his head back and closed his eyes. "The depth
of our family's aviation history dates back only to Vietnam.
My dad was a Marine fighter pilot who got shot down once,
but he lived through two tours and retired a number of years
ago."

"Jackie told me that you flew in the Marines."

"That's right—Harriers."

A few minutes later Dave and Scott joined Jackie in a
peaceful sleep as the Greyhound leveled off for the long flight
to the USS *Stennis*.

The sunlight awakened Scott when the COD began its
gentle descent to rendezvous with the carrier battle group.
Dave Finchly was already awake and Jackie was stretching
her arms over her head. The rest of the passengers were still
asleep.

"How'd you sleep?" Scott asked Jackie.

"Like I was comatose."

"Same here—it must be the stress."

"Stress—what stress?" She quietly chuckled.

The Greyhound pilots had been given a "Charlie" on arrival (permission to land) and were making a long straight-in approach to *Stennis*. Shortly after the wing flaps and landing gear were lowered, the aircraft commander called the ball—the Fresnel optical landing system that displays visual glide slope information to the pilot—and began the final descent to the flight deck. The C-2A landed with a resounding thud and came to a very sudden stop. The COD would remain on board the carrier for Scott's mission.

After Jackie, Scott, and Dave deplaned, two young officers helped the trio carry their bags to their private staterooms. They stowed their luggage and the threesome went to the wardroom to have breakfast. Later Scott met with the COD pilots to go over every aspect of the hazardous night drop.

When he was finished, Scott joined Dave and Jackie to brief the helicopter extraction. They went over every detail and every contingency, playing devil's advocate about timing, fuel limits, radio calls, and emergencies. Afterward they had a late lunch and retired to their quarters to get some much-needed sleep.

Scott turned off the lights and sprawled on his back. Staring into the darkness, he replayed every move and every second of the jump and the extraction, at least the way it was supposed to happen. The part that bothered him the most was the unknown factor between the jump and the helicopter pickup. He knew that period in time would be a crapshoot.

USS *Stennis*

Surrounded by her escort ships, the supercarrier steamed smoothly on the pleasantly calm ocean. Overhead a pale moon cast a faint shadow of light over the flight deck of *Stennis*. The *Oliver Hazard Perry*–class frigate USS *Ford* had been dispatched earlier to cruise closer to the Chinese cargo ship *Chen*

Ziyang. One of the frigate's two SH-60B Seahawks had been flown to the carrier to make room for Lieutenant Finchly's rescue helicopter if it ran low on fuel or had other problems.

At precisely 0100 Finchly lifted the HH-60H Seahawk from the dark flight deck of the carrier and headed southwest toward the *Chen Ziyang.* The H version of the Seahawk is the navy's combat-search-and-rescue (CSAR) helicopter assigned to carriers.

In the left seat of the HS-8 Eightballers helicopter, copilot Jackie Sullivan worked the radios and kept a running plot on the Chinese cargo ship. Information about the exact location of the *Chen Ziyang* was continuously updated from spacecraft and reconnaissance aircraft and passed to the Seahawk, call sign Black Shadow Six.

In the back of the helicopter the rescue swimmer and the other crewman looked at each other with blank stares. They had never met the mysterious pilots before. According to the aviators they were on a mission to pick up a man who had fallen off a cruise ship.

Both aircrewmen were handpicked senior petty officers. They were seasoned enough to know something strange was going on but smart enough not to ask any questions.

Ten minutes after the Seahawk took off, the C-2A Greyhound taxied to the port bow catapult. Strapped into his rearfacing seat, Scott Dalton braced himself when the twin turboprops came up to full power. The entire aircraft shook, rumbled, and vibrated for what seemed like an eternity, then *kaabooom,* the airplane blasted down the catapult track.

Hanging in his straps, Scott felt the familiar deceleration when the COD went off the bow and began climbing. The landing gear was raised and the flaps were retracted. The boxy Greyhound accelerated and began climbing on a southwesterly course to the jump altitude of twenty-eight thousand feet.

Scott slipped out of his Marine uniform and began getting dressed for his jump. He donned a black wet suit, extra-thick neoprene booties, an assault knife on his lower left leg, and tucked his 9mm Sig Sauer into a compact nylon holster strapped to his right thigh.

Next came two small waterproof cameras in a special pouch attached to his left thigh and two radios in a container on his lower right leg. Finally, Scott wriggled into his black custom-made parachute and black reserve chute. Last came the multi-grip gloves, a black helmet, a wristwatch-sized altimeter, and a small oxygen tank and mask. Due to the buoyancy of the wet suit and the salt water, he wouldn't need a life preserver or life raft.

Scott waddled to the cockpit and conferred with the pilots. Both aviators were friendly, quiet, and nonchalant about the mission, knowing this was a hush-hush operation. The pilots were getting continuous updates on the target's position. The wind was light and they were going to try to be in a position two miles in front of the cargo ship when they gave Scott the signal to jump.

The *Chen Ziyang*

The cargo ship cruised slowly in smooth waters three hundred miles north of Honolulu, Hawaii. Two crewmen stood on the main deck amidships and lighted American-made cigarettes. The balmy sea breeze reminded them of port calls in Hawaii, especially the visits to Zhang Wen-cheng's house and her young, nubile Chinese girls.

Basic seamen in a crew of officers, scientists, and engineers, the two deckhands performed manual duties and stood watches with the armed guards. At thirty-minute intervals, one of the men would walk around the outside of the ship while the other sailor patrolled the interior spaces and cargo areas.

After twenty-five minutes, the two would gather at the same spot on the main deck and have another cigarette break. Like a broken record, they continued their ongoing complaints about their bosses, their meager salaries, and their working conditions. It was their way of life, no different at sea than in port.

Three minutes before his jump, Scott made his way to the back of the Greyhound and sat down near the loading ramp.

The pilots turned off the interior and exterior lights, and then concentrated on following the GPS readouts as precisely as they could. Between the spacecraft and the recon planes, the exact location of *Chen Ziyang* was known within six to nine feet of her actual position.

After Scott and the flight crew went on oxygen, the pilots depressurized the cabin and lowered the cargo ramp. With one minute to go, Scott carefully walked to the open ramp. He pulled his clear goggles down and rechecked all of his parachute fittings. A crewman tapped him on the shoulder, signaling that they had reached the jump coordinates.

Scott bent forward and took two long strides, plummeting from twenty-eight thousand feet into the dark night sky. He could barely discern where the sky met the coal-black water. Once he was stabilized in a facedown, spread-eagle position, he began searching for the running lights of the *Chen Ziyang*. Knowing the basic design of the ship, Scott wanted to land near the open fantail of the bulk cargo carrier. Landing on the bow of the vessel would expose him to the crewmen manning the bridge.

From the information Hartwell Prost had given him, he knew the bridge was slightly aft of midship and that the vessel had two aft holds and two forward holds intended for general cargo. Twin risers resembling king posts served as stacks. The ship had a variety of standard booms and two high-capacity booms, one forward and the other aft.

On board the *Chen Ziyang,* the sailor walking around the exterior of the ship never heard the C-2A Greyhound. He walked slowly, listening to the sounds of the ocean and stopped to look at the luminescent bow wave. Although he and his shipmates constantly complained about their lives at sea, he loved being on the ocean and smelling the fresh breeze.

Passing twelve thousand feet, Scott still hadn't located the running lights of the *Chen Ziyang*. It was an uncomfortable,

xious feeling. He was beginning to think the information
e pilots had received was wrong. He took off his oxygen
ask and tossed it and the portable bottle into the black
ght.

Where is it? Scott thought as he fell through nine thousand
et. The altimeter was unwinding at an alarming rate and he
d to make a decision. If he couldn't locate the ship by five
ousand feet, he needed to pop his chute to give himself
ore time to search for the vessel. *Concentrate. Don't screw
is up.*

Eight thousand feet.

Where is it?

Seven thousand feet.

"Son of a *bitch.*"

Six thousand feet.

Scott gripped the rip cord and started to yank at the same
stant he saw a ship. He hesitated, thinking it was a cruise
ner. *No, a cruise ship wouldn't be three hundred miles north
f Hawaii.*

Five thousand feet.

Scott waited, but there wasn't much time.

Four thousand feet.

It has to be the cargo ship. He spotted a wake and then
nning lights. *Ah, twin risers—got it.*

Three thousand.

Slightly ahead and to the left of *Chen Ziyang,* Scott waited
moment and then pulled the rip cord. The chute opened
ith a soft report and he began his approach to the fantail.
alton could clearly see the name of the ship. He let out a
gh of relief. *I'm almost there.*

The sailor standing on the starboard side of the bow was
artled by the soft, muffled sound. He looked around and
dn't see anything suspicious. More curious than alarmed,
e began walking toward the stern of the ship. The man won-
ered if he'd really heard something or whether his imagina-
on was getting the best of him. He grinned, thinking about

his shipmates. They constantly kidded him about being hard
of hearing whenever there was work to be done.

Playing it cautiously, Scott approached the ship with
plenty of altitude. The last thing he wanted to do was come
up short and land in the water aft of the cargo vessel. At four
hundred feet he could see the details of the deck reasonably
well. He approached from amidships and made a very tight
180-degree turn high and close to the fantail. If he overshot,
he could bleed off altitude quickly and hit the deck from an
almost vertical position.

Scott completed his turn at a hundred fifty feet and focused on the spot where he intended to land. He had a nice
approach going, controlling his descent with judicious use of
his parachute risers. At seventy feet, Scott was about to begin
his flare when he saw a sailor walking onto the fantail.
Stunned, he made a split-second decision.

Keeping up his speed, he brought his knees up and steered
straight at the unsuspecting crewman. As silent as a whisper,
Scott extended his legs in front of him and slammed into the
sailor with the force of four men. The blow knocked the wind
out of the crewman and literally lifted him off his feet. He
staggered backward and fell over the side of the ship, landing
in the churning wake.

Feeling the effects of the collision, Scott quickly got to his
feet and slipped out of his parachute. He threw it and the reserve chute overboard along with his helmet and goggles.

He did a quick check to make sure the cameras and the radios were okay. Scott then began looking for a passageway
leading to the cargo holds. On his third try, he found a ladder
leading to the aft cargo holds. To his surprise he could see, although the light was dim, that the holds contained nothing
more than general cargo and some containers of oil.

Scott retraced his path and went up to the main deck. Quietly and cautiously, he worked his way toward the bow and
found another ladder, leading to the forward cargo holds. As
soon as he saw the giant laser and associated equipment
Scott knew he had hit pay dirt.

He took a moment to study the sophisticated equipment. he two brightly lighted cargo holds had been revamped to low the laser-based weapon and the attached holographic nage-projection apparatus to be hydraulically raised to the ain deck.

The complex mechanism, along with the enclosed control onsole, was well built and mounted to a thick steel plate ith six hydraulic arms. It reminded him of the platforms sed for flight simulators.

Scott quickly removed one of his waterproof cameras om the pouch and began snapping pictures. He moved rap- lly, photographing everything in the combined holds, in- luding the laser with a warning sign in the background. The gn was in Chinese, as were the warning plaques on the con- ol console and on the door.

Dalton was in the process of using the second camera hen a sailor walked out of a passageway and almost stum- led into him. The Chinese crewman was thunderstruck. anic flashed across his face.

19

Black Shadow Six

Dave Finchly flew the Seahawk while Jackie continuously updated their position in relation to the cargo ship. By her calculations, Scott should be aboard the *Chen Ziyang* and about ready to leap overboard. Finchly was slowing Black Shadow Six to maintain a position fifteen nautical miles from the Chinese ship. When Scott came up on the radio, they would quickly move in to hoist him aboard the Seahawk.

The intermediate transmission-oil-temperature light illuminated.

"Uh-oh, trouble," Finchly said. "Ah, we have a major problem."

"Oh, yeah. We need to find a deck ASAP."

"You're right, we gotta get out of here."

"Wouldn't it figure," Jackie quietly said to herself, and stared at the light. *We have to get someone out here to rescue Scott.*

"Watch for any abnormal vibrations," Finchly said. "We're going to have to make a run for the frigate and we're forty miles out."

"Okay, but can we get them to launch a helo to rescue Scott?"

Finchly shrugged his shoulders. "I'll see what I can do."

Jackie reached into the lower leg pocket of her flight suit and grabbed her satellite phone. *We need action from the top.* "Dave, I can take care of this with one phone call."

"Go for it." Finchly prepared Black Shadow Six for a

uto-rotation and ditching. "I'll check NATOPS and call the
igate."

"Okay."

Hartwell Prost was on the phone in a matter of seconds.
ackie quickly explained the situation and told him that Scott
aight be in the water. Prost had her remain on the phone.
/hen he returned, he told her the situation was under control.
or security reasons, he couldn't explain what was being
one, but he told her not to worry about Scott.

"Thank God," Jackie said to herself, returning the satellite
hone to her pocket. "Help is on the way."

"Good deal."

They saw the warning light flick on.

"Oil pressure," Dave said. "What next?"

Jackie watched in silence as the number-two engine's oil
ressure fluctuated up and down on the vertical instrument
isplay system, known as VIDS.

Finchly called the frigate and declared an emergency, then
ad the two aircrewmen prepare for an immediate ditching.
hey strapped into their seats and quietly prayed.

"Hang in there," Finchly said to Jackie and to the petty of-
cers. "The ship is coming our way."

Scott flashed his most disarming smile and stuck his arm
ut to shake hands with the surprised Chinese sailor.

His eyes wide open in fear and confusion, the man became
idecisive and stepped back a pace.

"Do you speak English?" Dalton asked while they awk-
vardly shook hands. "English?"

"I speak little English," the man said, unsure if he should
ee from the strangely dressed man.

"Do you know how much trouble your captain is in?"

The sailor looked totally confused. "Trouble?"

"Yes. We have a security breach. This equipment is sup-
osed to be guarded twenty-four hours a day, and your govrnment in Beijing pays me to inspect security on various
hips. I've been on board since Long Beach."

Frightened, the man looked at Dalton as if he were seeing

an aberration. He became very cautious and evasive. "I kno
nothing. I not in charge—know nothing."

"Well, if you cooperate, you won't get into any troubl
But that's up to you—your decision."

"I copawait—I know nothing."

"Good." Scott motioned toward the laser. "You stand rig
over here by the console while I take your picture."

Bug-eyed, the sailor shook his head. "No pitcher, m
pitcher!"

"No picture, and your name will have to go in my repor
Your days on the ocean will be over."

In silence the man backed against the console.

"Raise your head up and smile." Scott moved back to tal
in the entire laser weapon. He clicked a dozen photos fro
different angles, each with the Chinese sailor in the picture

"Keep smiling." Scott finished the roll of film in his se
ond camera.

The seaman kept the strained smile on his ashen face.

"Okay, good job," Dalton said, and stowed his camera
"You stay down here and guard this equipment until I ser
you a relief in about two hours, okay?"

He nodded his head. "I stay here?"

"That's right." Scott waved his finger at the man. "Don
leave your post for any reason—none."

"I stay here, I copawait."

"That's right."

Scott quietly made his way to the main deck and ca
tiously walked in the direction of the fantail.

"Halt—stop!"

A shot rang out and ricocheted near Dalton's right foot.
"Stop!"

Scott started sprinting toward the stern. More rounds ric
cheted off the steel deck. He knew he wasn't going to mak
it to the fantail. With a mighty leap, Dalton dived over th
side of the ship and swam underwater as far as possible b
fore surfacing. He was tumbled around by the churning wak
while he watched the *Chen Ziyang* continue on course. H
quickly activated one of his radios.

"Black Shadow Six, Garden Party is up and the GPS is
orking."

Nothing.

Scott relaxed on his back and tried again.

Still nothing.

After exchanging radios he tried again.

Silence.

Well, this is great.

Black Shadow Six

ieutenant Finchly went over the NATOPS checklist for "en-
ine oil pressure low" and monitored the pressure and tem-
erature of the number-two engine for secondary indications.
Vhile the minutes ticked off, the fluctuations became more
ronounced.

"Twenty-five miles," Jackie said, checking the distance to
he USS *Ford*. "We have an engine-oil-pressure caution
ght."

Finchly closely scanned the instruments. "If we see any
ther indications, we'll shut it down."

"Okay," she said, calculating time, fuel, and distance. "Do
ou think we should dump some gas?"

"Yeah, good idea." Finchly began dumping fuel.

Jackie glanced at the engine instruments and listened to
he complaining turboshaft. "It's getting worse—really
ounds bad."

"I know."

After three minutes it was obvious that the engine was
bout to pack it in. Finchly secured the fuel dump.

"What do you think?" Jackie asked.

"I'm going to shut it down."

He slowly increased power on the good engine, pulled the
hrottle for the number-two engine to idle, and then turned off
he fuel. They completed the single-engine-failure checklist,
he single-engine-landing checks, and then informed the
rigate of their status.

"Fifteen miles," Jackie reported.

At twelve miles from the ship, the vibrations began in t[h]e intermediate transmission. They were light at first, but the[re] was definitely a pattern of increased intensity. Time w[as] quickly running out.

"You've got it," Finchly said, relinquishing the flight co[n]trols to Jackie.

"I've got it."

She listened to Finchly discuss the situation with the he[li]copter control officer on the frigate. They had already s[et] flight quarters to give the stricken helicopter a green deck.

"Seven miles," Jackie nervously reported.

Finchly took the controls and checked on his two aircre[w]men.

The USS *Ford* was slowing and turning to allow the Se[a]hawk to make a straight-in approach to the fantail.

"Five miles."

The vibrations were rapidly multiplying, and then the[y] slowly developed into a crunching, grinding sound that w[as] increasing by the second.

"Four miles."

No one said a word.

"Three miles."

"There it is!" Finchly said, requesting the relative win[d] from the frigate's landing signal officer.

With his heart racing, Dave kept the speed up and began [a] shallow descent. They were rapidly closing on the ship.

"Come on, don't fail me now," he coaxed under his breat[h]. "Stay together, just a little longer."

He worked hard to fly a perfect single-engine profile whi[le] Jackie called torque and other engine parameters. Th[e] crunching sound was rapidly turning into heavy grindin[g]. The helicopter was beginning to shake itself apart and woul[d] soon be uncontrollable.

Bleeding off airspeed, Finchly decelerated through tran[s]lational lift while the grinding became a high-pitched scree[ch] and the helicopter started bucking and yawing.

The landing was hard but safe. He shut down the remai[n]

ing engine after the frigate's crew secured Black Shadow Six to the deck.

Exhausted by tension and raw fear, Jackie and Dave went limp in their seats. They looked at each other while the two aircrewmen exchanged high fives.

"Another mile and we wouldn't have made it," Jackie said, her voice low and weak.

Dave unbuckled his helmet. "I'd say about a quarter of a mile."

Floating on his back, Scott continued trying to contact someone on the radios. He left both on so the GPS signal would indicate his exact position. Dalton couldn't believe that Jackie would leave him in the middle of the ocean. As the minutes passed, he finally accepted the fact that something had gone wrong. He hoped that Jackie, Dave, and their aircrewmen were okay. His concern for his situation shifted to concern for Jackie.

All thoughts of her evaporated when Scott saw a ship bearing down on him from the same direction the *Chen Ziyang* had gone. A few seconds later, a number of high-powered spotlights on the ship illuminated and began searching the water.

Scott started to reach for his 9mm Sig Sauer and then dismissed his idea. *Yeah, that's going to do a lot of good against an eighteen-thousand-ton cargo ship full of guys with automatic weapons.*

Frantic now that the ship was about a mile away and slowing, Scott racked his brain for a solution, something that made sense. He drew a blank as the vessel closed to within a half mile. This was going to be like a county-fair shooting gallery, and he was the only target.

The first stages of panic were beginning to set in when the *Chen Ziyang* exploded in a huge fireball that shot straight up for hundreds of feet. Astonished, Scott was rattled by the powerful shock wave that slammed into him. *Holy shit!*

Wide eyed, Dalton realized that he was out of immediate danger. He doubted if anyone could have survived an explo-

sion of that magnitude. His greatest fear now was the debris
that was raining down on him. Thousands of small pieces
slapped the water while bigger sections of the ship hit the
ocean with tremendous force.

From what he could tell, the *Chen Ziyang* had blown in half
and was rapidly sinking. Amazed at his good fortune, but wondering what had happened, Scott watched in awe as the cargo
ship burned for fifteen minutes. With an explosive rush of
trapped air, the ship finally slipped under the surface of the sea.

His concern turned to survivors, desperate ones who
might have weapons. He strained to hear a voice or see some
movement. The silence was unnerving after the events of the
past twenty minutes, but it was very comforting for someone
who had come so close to certain death.

Scott slowly backstroked his way out of most of the debris
field, and then rested while he floated on his back. He was
still trying to come to grips with what he had experienced
when the movement of the water around him felt like the first
rise of a rogue wave.

"What the hell?" Scott mumbled in a moment of panic. He
flipped over and was thrashing his legs when he felt movement directly underneath him. Something huge touched him,
lifting him completely out of the water.

Reaching for his assault knife, he was suddenly sliding
back toward the ocean. His heart was pounding so hard that
he was gasping for air. Then he saw it.

"Thank you, God," he yelled in joy when he recognized the
American attack submarine surfacing next to him.

The USS *Pasadena*

Twenty-five minutes after his rescue, Scott was in the officers' wardroom. He was dry and wearing an unadorned khaki
uniform loaned to him by the executive officer of the *Los
Angeles*–class attack submarine. *Pasadena* had submerged
and was under way. Where to, Dalton didn't know. His two
cameras were locked in the commanding officer's safe and a

navy helicopter would pick them up at first light. He was enjoying a cup of coffee when the CO and XO entered the empty wardroom.

The cordial skipper extended his hand. "Well, what's a jarhead doing out in the middle of the ocean at this time of night?"

Scott firmly shook hands. "Trust me, commander, you wouldn't believe me if I told you."

"We probably would," the executive officer said.

He and the skipper poured coffee into their mugs.

"Mr. Dalton," the CO said, motioning for the former Marine aviator to have a seat at the table.

"Sir, Scott would make me feel more comfortable."

"Scott it is. I'm Ron Leinwander and this is my XO, Bill Zakaria, whom you've met."

Dalton nodded.

Commander Leinwander stirred his coffee. "I'll give you a situation report, and then we'll answer any questions you may have, and I'm sure you'll have some."

"Yeah, that's true." Scott softly chuckled. "I can't remember the last time I had a submarine surface under me in the middle of the ocean."

The skipper turned serious. "We've been following the *Chen Ziyang* since it left the coast of California. Our orders called for us to intercept the Chinese ship and follow it until further notice. Well, it didn't make any sense to us, because they can track it with spacecraft and other reconnaissance platforms. But our questions were answered about the time your rescue helicopter ran into trouble."

"How's the flight crew?"

"They're just fine. They had a mechanical problem and had to land on a frigate, but they're safe and sound."

Dalton quietly sighed. *Thank you again, God.*

"We don't know what you were up to, or how you got aboard the ship, but I can tell you this. We received urgent orders while you were on the *Chen Ziyang*. Our job was to rescue you at all costs, including sinking the ship if we could confirm that you were in the water and in jeopardy."

The XO took over. "We rose to periscope depth about three hundred yards dead astern of the ship. We were watching *Chen Ziyang* through our scope when we saw you dive overboard in a hail of gunfire."

"You actually saw me?"

"Like in broad daylight. We were primed for action but figured we'd wait until the ship was gone before we would surface and invite you to join us for breakfast."

The CO took over on cue. "We received confirmation from recon sources that you'd activated a radio and that your GPS position was about seventy yards from us. The recon folks were under orders not to respond to you, but they could clearly hear your calls."

"I wish I'd known that."

"We heard screws returning and stuck our scope up to check on you. You were off to the side of us when their spotlights came on. After we concurred that it was the *Chen Ziyang,* I maneuvered for a better angle and fired a Mark-48 torpedo at the ship."

Scott closed his eyes for a second.

The XO could see that Dalton was beginning to deal with how close he had come to dying. "We have something a little stronger, if you'd like?"

"That would be appreciated."

The skipper set his coffee mug down. "Since the Chinese ship has gone to the bottom, and you're safely on board, we have orders to make a port call in Pearl Harbor."

Scott's eyes lighted up.

"You can ride in with us, or you can go on the helo that's going to pick up your film as soon as the sun's up."

"Uh, skipper," the XO interjected, "we just received a message that a Ms. Jackie Sullivan is going to be in Honolulu to meet him in the morning."

Scott smiled. "No offense, Captain, but the helo sounds good."

"None taken—have a good time."

20

Honolulu International Airport

The morning breeze was gentle and refreshing on this beautiful Hawaiian day, typical of most days in the sun-drenched islands. Jumbo 747s arrived and departed in a continuous stream of activity, while smaller, colorful planes and helicopters flew visitors on sightseeing trips around Oahu and the neighboring islands.

Tired after a stressful, sleepless night, Jackie was waiting at the Air Service Hawaii FBO when Scott's navy SH-60B helicopter landed. The Seahawk helo from the HSL-37 Easy Riders had landed at the Coast Guard air station to turn Dalton's two rolls of film over to special agents from the CIA and two senior navy intelligence officers.

The film would be developed in Hawaii and flown to Washington, along with Scott's sealed after-action report. All of the intelligence information would be made available to President Macklin before he had to leave on his urgent trip to Bangkok.

The emergency meeting of the Association of Southeast Asian Nations Regional Forum and its Asian and Pacific partners was scheduled to begin in four days. The association is an international security structure designed to limit China's ability to pursue its national security objectives while putting other countries at risk.

Still wearing his borrowed khaki uniform, Scott thanked the flight crew and hopped out of the helicopter. Near the main entrance to the FBO, Jackie hugged him tightly and then led him to an empty conference room. She explained what had happened to their helicopter and described the harrowing landing on the frigate.

"Tell me about the operation," she said. "How did it go?"

"Well, first of all, there *was* a laser weapon on board the ship, and our suspicion about a holographic imaging apparatus *is* confirmed—we have the photos to prove it."

"Outstanding."

Dalton quietly replayed the entire adventure, including the ship blowing up and the attack submarine surfacing underneath him. "Other than that, it was a fairly routine, boring evening."

"We felt horrible, but the helicopter would never have made it."

"Don't worry about it. How'd you get to Hawaii?"

"They flew us from the frigate to the carrier, then back here on the COD, the same one you jumped from."

"I thought they were going straight to Barbers Point."

"That was their plan. When the pilots contacted center, they were told to return to the carrier. Dave came with me. He's going back to North Island in the COD."

"Well, what's on our agenda?"

"A lot."

"Have you talked to Hartwell?"

"Oh, yes." She laughed. "I've talked to Hartwell."

"And?"

"He and the president send their best to you. They think you did a spectacular, unbelievable job and both extend their heartfelt thanks."

"Jackie, I know that look."

"What look?"

"The fox-asking-if-it's-okay-to-go-count-the-chickens look."

"I haven't committed us to anything. However, the president wants to thank us in person for getting him the evidence he feels he needs to confront the Chinese in Bangkok."

"Are we supposed to head for Washington?"

"No," she said with a faint smile. "The president is going to stop in Honolulu day after tomorrow."

"Great—we can have some old-fashioned R and R while we wait."

"But there's more," she said excitedly.

He paused for a moment. "I'm afraid to ask."

"We've been asked to accompany the president and Hartwell to Bangkok—to the summit meeting."

"Uh, Jackie, we're supposed to remain at arm's length from the government, not even know anyone in power, let alone be on a plane with the president of the United States."

"It's all arranged," she said with an air of confidence. "We're going as Secret Service special agents being temporarily assigned to the Bangkok duty station at the American Embassy. We will board with other agents from the Honolulu office, and then Hartwell will arrange for us to meet privately with the president."

Scott was puzzled. "Ah, let's see—is there something I've missed, something you've left out?"

"Well, there is one *teeny-tiny* detail that may arouse your curiosity."

"Here we go—I knew it."

"President Macklin wants to talk with us about a plan that he, Prost, and a small group of Hartwell's friends from the Agency have been concocting."

He rolled his eyes upward. "Do you know what it is?"

"No, and Hartwell made it clear that I shouldn't ask."

"I wonder what they're up to this time."

"I really don't know, but whatever it is, I'm sure you'll consider attempting it."

"Don't be so confident," he said with a Cheshire-cat grin.

"Scott," she said in an unusually serious tone, "we don't have to agree to anything, you know that."

"I know," he said, and fell quiet for a few moments. "After last night, I wonder how much is too much."

"You need some rest, then we'll talk about it."

"I'd go for that."

Jackie felt as if she was getting her second wind. "I brought your things from the carrier."

"Thanks."

She leaned back and gave him the once-over. "The first thing we need to do is go shopping and buy you some clothes."

"Yeah, I could use some aloha shirts and baggy shorts."

"I know just the ticket. First we'll find a place to have breakfast, then we'll go to Hilo Hattie's for the very latest in Hawaiian apparel—you can't beat it."

"That sounds good, but I think we need to find a place to stay."

"I've already booked a suite at the Halekulani."

"Music to my ears." Scott chuckled. "A suite on Waikiki sure sounds better than where I spent last night."

"By the way, if we undertake the plan Hartwell mentioned, he said the terms would be the same as the *Chen Ziyang* operation."

"That part appeals to me. I wouldn't mind being able to retire and travel around the world in our own jet."

"Oh, another thing before I forget. We need to call Greg and let him know that he can have his Lear back. You can get the personal gear you left on the plane when we return."

"Yeah, you're right. I also need to give our SEALs back to the navy and check in with Mary Beth. She must think we've left the planet."

"We'll call her after breakfast."

"That's what I'm waiting for."

"Follow me."

They left the conference room and walked toward the entrance to the FBO, then stopped when they heard voices.

Jackie and Scott were surprised to see a group of people huddled around a television set. They could see the bright red "Breaking News" banner beneath the CNN logo.

"We have additional news just in," the man said. "The name of the ship in question is the *Samuel B. Roberts,* and CNN has just been informed that it is a United States navy frigate."

The anchor was handed new information. "According to a Pentagon spokesman, the ship has been stranded in the Panama Canal for approximately five hours. A senior White House aide has told CNN that an unconfirmed report from

Panamanian officials has it that a canal lock malfunctioned, causing the American warship to be trapped in the waterway."

The newsman glanced away for a second and then stared into the television camera. "Tensions between China and the U.S. will likely escalate after the recent clashes in Panama and the sinking of two Chinese cargo ships, one of which we're told went down only hours ago."

He reached for a sheet of paper being slipped onto his counter. "Beijing claims the U.S. is responsible for destroying both ships. Pentagon officials have admitted that military relations between the U.S. and China are extremely strained at this time. We have more from Christine DeSano at the Pentagon. Christine."

"John, senior officers here believe this incident is in retaliation for the attack on a Chinese antiaircraft artillery site in Panama and the alleged sinking of a Chinese cargo vessel by the U.S. Navy. Many worry that Beijing is going to force the issue and cause a significant confrontation between China and the U.S. There was a flurry of activity here about ten minutes ago, and we were told that the canal crisis is about to escalate."

Surprised by the events, Scott and Jackie looked at each other and then focused their attention on the television. When CNN finally broke for a commercial, they left the FBO.

"You're part of the headlines," she said, walking toward her nearby rental car.

"I can think of easier ways to make the news," he said with a frown. "This Panamanian situation could turn into a train wreck, especially after all the bitterness over the treaty."

"Do you know the story behind the story?" Jackie asked. "I've heard two different versions of what happened."

"It depends on which side of the fence you're on."

"What account do you believe is the truth?"

"My version."

"And what version would that be?"

Scott opened the passenger door and got in. "Well, there was a great deal of underhandedness involved in the Panama Canal debacle, including the undeniable fact that Panama never ratified its treaty as required by the Panamanian Constitution."

Jackie started the car, and then lowered the convertible top to drink in the sunshine and fragrant air. She placed the car in gear and headed for the nearby Honolulu Airport Hotel to have breakfast and coffee.

"Furthermore, the treaty was not submitted to the Panamanian people for a plebiscite vote, as required by law. It was illegally pushed through the process—a fraudulent treaty pursued to a successful conclusion by the virtual dictator of Panama."

Scott glanced upward toward the Likelike (lick-e, lick-e) Highway and took in the breathtakingly lush mountains that make up Oahu's Koolau Range.

"At any rate, the Panamanians and the U.S. are now paying a very steep price for our surrender of one of the most important geostrategic maritime choke points in the world."

"Yeah, that treaty was a real soup-sandwich. Inept politicians and corrupt tinhorn dictators—they're mostly interchangeable."

"I can't argue that point," Scott said. "From a national-security interest, turning over control of the canal will prove to be one of the worst mistakes in U.S. history."

Scott glanced at a Falcon 900 corporate jet as it climbed steeply away from Honolulu International. "*La Prensa* says more than sixty percent of Panamanians favor some form of U.S. military presence."

"I can believe it. They've finally figured out how vulnerable they are to outside factions—the ones who would like to take complete control of Panama."

"Someday," he said with a smile, "Panama may invite the Yankees back to stabilize the economy and the environment—same with the Philippines."

"Yeah, they're singing a different tune now," Jackie said. "Two of the Philippine senators who voted to kick the U.S. military out in '92 later reversed themselves—that must have been a humbling experience. Now they want us back to protect their vital interests."

"Another fine example of brilliant decision making by totally incompetent politicians. One of those senators is now the president of the country—a really scary thought—and the other is the secretary of national defense. Think about it."

"I know," Jackie said with a fleeting look. "Unbelievable, but true—the wizards who oversee the Philippines."

He surveyed the lush tropical plants and exotic flowers along the road. "After the Filipinos kicked us out of Subic Bay and Clark Air Force Base, the Chinese moved rapidly to fill the power vacuum in the South China Sea. They claimed part of the Spratly Archipelago that parallels Asia's most important air and shipping lanes."

Jackie slowed and turned into the parking lot at the hotel.

Scott unbuckled his seat belt. "Beijing is becoming more and more belligerent to the Filipinos—to everyone in Southeast Asia—and it wouldn't take much for the entire region to erupt in open warfare."

"Hey, give it a rest," Jackie said. "Aloha, mai tai—and all of that island lingo. You're in Hawaii—safely—and we're going to enjoy every minute we have together."

He broke into a wide grin. "You're damn right—can the problems. Let's get this party under way."

The Taiwan Strait

Also known as the Formosa ("Beautiful") Strait, the Taiwan Strait is about a hundred miles wide at its narrowest point and lies between the coast of China's Fujian Province and the island of Taiwan. Located in a notorious and deadly typhoon zone, the strait extends from the South China Sea northeast to the East China Sea. It reaches a maximum depth of approximately 230 feet and encompasses the Pescadores ("Fishermen") Islands, which are considered a *hsien* (county) under the jurisdiction of the government of the Republic of China on Taiwan.

The drama and tension being played out on and over the strait was rapidly increasing. The sporadic air-traffic-control system over the Taiwan Strait was having an adverse effect on everyone. Foreign pilots and U.S. pilots, both civilian and military, were in agreement about the lack of an ATC capability. It was the proverbial accident waiting to happen. The problem was made even more difficult by the growing number of fighter planes, aerial tankers, helicopters, and surveillance aircraft in the confined area.

Even the notices on the aeronautical Operational Navigation Charts covering the strait were ominous: WARNING— AIRCRAFT INFRINGING UPON NONFREE FLYING TERRITORY MAY BE FIRED ON WITHOUT WARNING. CONSULT NOTAMS AND FLIGHT INFORMATION PUBLICATIONS FOR THE LATEST AIR INFORMATION.

Mainland Chinese jets had buzzed the Ma-kung Naval Base, located on the Taiwanese island of Penghu. Chinese torpedo patrol boats and the destroyer *Luhai* were loitering near the Taiwanese-controlled islands of Matsu and Quemoy.

In addition to the strained relations in the strait, Beijing and Taipei officials had ordered their combat pilots to fly closer to each other's shoreline than had been allowed in the past.

In response to the Chinese pilots' extremely aggressive moves toward a Taiwan C-130H transport, including a head-on pass from a frontline Sukhoi Su-27 fighter-interceptor, the Taiwanese F-5s and F-16s were flying almost over the shoreline of the Chinese province of Fujian.

The USS *Kitty Hawk* and her battle group were northeast of the Taiwan Strait at a point halfway between Taipei, Taiwan, and Naha, Okinawa. Flanked by her escorts *Cowpens, Rodney M. Davis, Fife, Curts,* and the hunter/killer attack submarine USS *Greeneville,* the carrier had four BARCAP (barrier combat air patrol) F-18 Hornets between the flattop and the coast of China.

The Hornets were flying a racetrack pattern outside the Asian Coastal Buffer Zone east of Songcheng and Fuzhou. They would be refueled twice before being relieved on station and returning to the carrier. F-14 Tomcats would take their place as the BARCAP continued around the clock.

Two other Alert Five Hornets were manned and ready for

launch. High above the *Hawk,* an E-2C Hawkeye was airborne and keeping a watchful eye on the Chinese and Taiwanese fighter pilots.

Shortly after 3:00 A.M. a Taiwanese Air Force captain and his wingman flew their F-16s low over Fuzhou, the capital of Fujian Province. Enraged by the aggressive act, the senior PLA officer in charge of eight antiaircraft artillery sites scattered around the perimeter of Fuzhou ordered them to open fire on the encroaching jets.

The wingman's F-16 was hit and went out of control, trailing fire and black smoke. He attempted to eject, but his parachute hadn't fully deployed when he slammed into the Min Chiang River alongside his blazing fighter. The flight leader escaped by flying at rooftop level over the neighboring town of Luozhou and safely returned to his base.

Space-based assets, reconnaissance aircraft, and the E-2C Hawkeye witnessed the episode. The information was immediately sent to the Pentagon, State Department, Central Intelligence Agency, National Security Agency, and the White House.

Less than an hour later *Deng Ju-shan,* a Chinese military ship disguised as a modern freighter, got a radar lock on the Hawkeye. A bright bluish-white object slashed past the E-2C a number of times, made a sweeping turn, and went straight over the Hawkeye a split second before a bright flash startled the pilots.

The starboard engine of the E-2C burst into flames and the wing failed between the engine and the fuselage. The flight crew, pinned into their seats by excessive G-forces, never had a chance to bail out. The aircraft tightly spun into the strait fifty-five miles due west of Taipei, Taiwan.

With both reconnaissance aircraft and spacecraft observing, there was no doubt about the cause of the crash. The laser beam that lasted 1.7 seconds came from the deck of *Deng Ju-shan.* The evidence was undeniable. Beijing would be held responsible for destroying the Hawkeye and killing the entire flight crew.

The Halekulani

Situated on five acres of prime beachfront, the famous resort is a luxurious oasis of tranquility in the heart of Waikiki. With its expansive courtyards and lush tropical gardens the "House Befitting Heaven" embodies the true spirit of Hawaiian hospitality.

An attractive and gracious young lady of Samoan heritage escorted Jackie and Scott to their suite, where registration was completed in privacy. They were impressed with the bowl of fresh fruits and the assorted Halekulani chocolates arranged on a table.

Once the administrative details were completed, they went to the lanai and soaked in the panoramic view of Waikiki Beach and Diamond Head. Many visitors considered the monolith of hardened lava to be the most recognizable symbol of Hawaii. The clear emerald waters along Waikiki were dotted with surfers and outrigger canoes. In the distance a stately cruise ship was barely visible on the horizon.

"This is fantastic—incredible," Scott said, turning to Jackie. "Especially being here with you."

"My sentiments exactly." She looked down at the oceanside swimming pool and the open-air restaurant. "How about a dip in the pool—then a nice quiet lunch?"

He smiled and shook his head. "After last night, I don't know if I'm ready to go back in the water."

"I promise, there are no submarines in the swimming pool."

After a refreshing swim, they toweled themselves and went into the covered open-air restaurant. They ordered seafood and had an unhurried lunch while watching a light rain shower pass.

When he was finished with his meal, Scott leaned back and folded his napkin. "One of the things I like most about Hawaii is the rainbow that accompanies every shower."

"That and the smell of the flowers," Jackie said, pausing as the waitress removed their plates.

They sat quietly for a few minutes, drinking in the scene along the world-famous beach.

"A penny for your thoughts?" Jackie asked.

"Sorry," Scott said, and reached for his iced tea. "I just can't get this situation with the Chinese off my mind."

"What do you think is going to happen with the China and Taiwan standoff—more rhetoric or some military action?"

"Well, this ongoing game is about more than Taiwan moving toward independence. It's about Beijing's belief—and they're firmly convinced by their obsessive distrust of others—that there's a conspiracy among the U.S., Taiwan, South Korea, and Japan to destroy China and force them into a mold that suits the U.S."

"Like bringing the gunboat diplomacy from Kosovo to China. The U.S. will change the cognitive and psychological profiles of the people in China to match our model of what's right and perfect in the world."

"Precisely." Scott glanced at a darkly tanned woman in the smallest bikini he'd ever seen.

"*Heelll*-oh!" Jackie waved her hand in front of Scott's face. "We're having a conversation here, remember?"

"Sorry." Scott chuckled. "The Chinese leaders have always relied on high diplomatic theater, lots of theatrics and huffing and puffing to get their way. They've always expected other nations to send emissaries to the Chinese capital to present tribute, bow a lot, and kowtow to the emperor."

Jackie nodded. "And Liu Fan-ding sees that tradition changing with the rapidly expanding Westernization of China."

"Of course. Reality is setting in and it scares the hell out of him. The U.S. is a powerful country. He knows we move fairly rapidly. Fan-ding's country is very large, twenty percent of the world's population, but at the present time it's a middle power at best—and they move at glacial speed."

Scott leaned back to avoid a collision with one of the many birds scavenging for crumbs. "We, on the other hand, are making the U.S.-China gap grow larger by our quantum leaps in technology, both in the civilian sector and the military. We have long-range sea power and air power, space superiority, and a helluva lot more nukes."

"That could change if we continue to let the Chinese steal us blind, undermine the foundations of our financial markets, and build a military power along the Panama Canal."

"True, but Beijing really had a meltdown when we agreed to cooperate with Japan on research and development for a theater ballistic missile defense program."

Jackie frowned. "What really rankled them was when we announced that the missile defense shield would protect not only Japan but much larger areas of the Asia-Pacific region."

"That's right. The operative word is *Taiwan*."

"I'm sure they had the same reaction in Pyongyang."

"Yeah, I'll bet that caused some tirades."

"I can just hear the North Koreans," she said. "'Japan and the U.S. are going to jack-slap us into the dirt if we don't stop screwing around.'"

"I think you have accurately captured the essence of their reaction." He looked down the beach at the surfers and the colorful outrigger canoes. "Economically, China is way, way overrated, and they have a petroleum deficit of over six hundred thousand barrels a day. Militarily, it's a second-rate regional menace with hopes to evolve into a powerful blue-water navy using the technologies they have purchased or stolen."

"With Taiwan under their control."

"Taiwan, the Spratly Islands, through the Ryuku Islands, across the Philippines, and then sweeping around the South China Sea—a dangerous neighborhood where *trust* is a foreign word."

"It seems to me, if Beijing had a large enough blue-water navy, the dragon could swim out to Japan, down through the Western Pacific, on to Indonesia, Thailand, and Vietnam."

"True," Scott said. "But we're back to China's problems. At the present time they're not a major power and their economy is relatively weak. Politically, Beijing's influence is feeble, and the country is basically backward, isolated from the rest of the world and the technology revolution."

"Not totally isolated from the technology gains."

"Okay, but we're diametrically opposite." Scott caught her eye. "The U.S. is a nuclear superpower that can checkmate Beijing at any given moment."

"I agree with what you've said, but I still believe China is a wild card that could do a lot of damage if they go berserk in Beijing."

He nodded. "I'd have to agree with that assessment. They do have some long-range nukes that are capable of hitting our West Coast."

"And, thanks to you, the White House has confirmation that the Chinese possess some very powerful laser-based weapons cruising the oceans of the world—they could be everywhere."

"That's the problem with China—their tendency to employ military force in all directions."

"And now they have their sights set on reclaiming Taiwan," Jackie said with a trace of scorn.

Scott glanced at a distant yacht. "Let's lighten the conversation and take a nice barefoot stroll down the beach—all the way to Diamond Head."

"Sounds good," Jackie said, gathering her things. "It's time to relax and have some fun."

"Roger that," Scott said, slipping into a colorful Hawaiian shirt that matched his swimming trunks. "Besides, we need to walk this meal off so we'll be ready for the luau."

"Hey, speak for yourself." She laughed. "I didn't eat like some crazed glutton at breakfast."

He smiled as he buttoned his shirt. "Floating around at night in a sea full of sharks, and then getting lifted out of the water by a submarine—well, it tends to increase my appetite for a few days."

21

Oval Office

Pete Adair and Gen. Les Chalmers sat quietly while the president responded to an aide's attempt to contact the Chinese president. From the deep color of Macklin's complexion, Adair and Chalmers knew things were not proceeding well.

Hartwell Prost was ushered into the office at the same time the president placed the phone receiver down. Cord Macklin was not a happy man. The president turned to stare morosely out the window for a moment before swiveling to face his closest and most trusted advisers.

"According to some third-tier spokesperson," the president said, brimming with anger, "Liu Fan-ding says he has nothing to discuss with me until we meet at the summit in Bangkok. He has also shunned our State Department emissaries, including Secretary Shannon."

Prost caught Macklin's attention. "Mr. President, we can't wait for his temper tantrums to subside, or for more political and military skirmishes to occur. We must take action in the Taiwan Strait and the Panama Canal or face the deadly consequences of vacillation."

Macklin looked at his secretary of defense. "Pete, give me the bottom line and don't sugarcoat it."

"Sir, the price of poker just went up. We *have* to call Beijing's bluff and send a very strong message. I recommend sinking the ship that shot down the Hawkeye—for starters."

"Les?"

"Mr. President, we don't have any other choice. The

despots, tyrants, dictators, oligarchs, whatever you want to call them, they're still bullies. Bullies never respond to passiveness, only to brute force. If we do anything less, we'll be backpedaling all over the globe and everyone will start taking potshots at us."

Macklin remained quiet for a few moments. "Les, I want you and the joint chiefs to start drawing up plans for possible military action against China in the Taiwan Strait."

Chalmers showed no emotion. "Mr. President, our plans for China are up to date, along with our plans for North Korea. We also have a contingency plan for the Panama Canal."

"Excellent." Macklin turned to his SecDef. "Pete, in your scenario, do we have all of our military assets in place?"

"We're ninety-five percent ready."

Chalmers quickly spoke up. "Mr. President, we'll be ready in the next few hours—six at most."

The president cast his gaze at the briefing folder on his desk. "Gentlemen, let's go with the concept Pete presented this afternoon. I'll deal with Congress later."

USS *Seawolf*

The most advanced and lethal submarine ever created, *Seawolf* is a 353-foot mechanical marvel designed to be exceptionally quiet, extremely fast, and well armed. An advanced multimission attack submarine, *Seawolf* is capable of rapidly deploying to forward areas of the oceans to destroy enemy submarines and ships, and fire Tomahawk cruise missiles in support of other forces.

Operating as an adjunct to the *Kitty Hawk* battle group, *Seawolf* was quietly waiting in the deeper water of the East China Sea as the Chinese ship *Deng Ju-shan* cleared the Taiwan Strait and set course for the U.S. carrier battle group.

The sun had been up for two hours when the *Seawolf*'s skipper, Capt. Rick Canardi, raised the periscope and scanned the horizon in all directions. The only vessel he saw

was a container ship that his sonar specialist had pointed out
to him.

"Down scope."

Canardi had just received the latest position report on the
Deng Ju-shan, his assigned target. The ship would be visible
on the horizon in seven to eight minutes. The message from
the Pentagon had been short and unambiguous: Identify and
sink the Chinese ship *Deng Ju-shan.*

"Up scope."

Two minutes passed.

"Down scope," Captain Canardi ordered when he recognized the freighter. "Man battle stations."

All hands quietly rushed to their assigned positions. There
was excitement and a twinge of fear in the air. They knew this
was the real thing, no drill.

"Officer of the Deck," Canardi said. "Steady on course
two-three-zero."

The lieutenant read back the instructions while the skipper
checked the time. The minutes passed slowly while the crew
waited in anticipation. Even the salty veterans seemed tense.
This was the first time any *Seawolf* crew member had ever
been on board a submarine about to fire a torpedo with the intention of sinking an enemy ship.

Finally, the captain raised the scope and studied the approaching vessel, and then lowered the periscope. He patiently waited for the ship to pass the submarine so he could
positively identify the freighter by the name on the stern. The
control room/attack center was quiet while the seconds ticked
away.

"Up scope," Canardi said, and then snapped pictures of the
Deng Ju-shan. He and the XO confirmed the name and description of the target vessel. There was no question in their
minds—they had the enemy positively identified.

"My intentions are to engage this contact," the skipper
said out loud, and maneuvered the *Seawolf* into a position he
knew would ensure a kill.

"Shoot on generated bearing."

Canardi watched the ship as two Mark-48 torpedoes raced

toward the *Deng Ju-shan*. The first explosion nearly lifted the seventeen-thousand-ton freighter out of the water. The second torpedo blew the ship in half, leaving the forward third of the vessel pointing up at a thirty-degree angle.

"Down scope," Canardi ordered. He managed to show little emotion, but his adrenaline was pumping.

"Steady course three-three-zero," the skipper ordered. "Chief of Watch, let's stand down from battle stations."

The crew, some with grins plastered on their faces, looked relieved. Others reflected the gravity of the action they had just taken.

"Officer of the Deck, make your depth two hundred fifty feet," Canardi said.

The Panama Canal

The U.S. navy frigate *Samuel B. Roberts* remained stranded in the canal after twenty-two hours. The 3,585-ton man-of-war's skipper, Comdr. LeRoy Gartly, had been awake all night. He and his crew were trying to get what little rest they could while remaining at their battle stations.

Via secure communications, Commander Gartly had learned from signals-intelligence intercepts that Chinese troops were massing in the vicinity of his beleaguered ship. He had also received a message that help was on the way.

The Marines, with the assistance of the air force and navy, were preparing to take command of the canal in a matter of minutes. Gartly passed the word to wake everyone when the first hint of daylight appeared on the eastern horizon.

Whether at sea, or trapped in a narrow canal, a warship flying an American flag is U.S. territory. The skipper had the responsibility to defend his ship and his crew. In this case, Gartly had to rely on a limited number of small-caliber weapons. The single 76mm/.62-caliber gun would be difficult to use in such close quarters.

The Colombian Basin

Cloaked in semidarkness, the amphibious assault carriers USS *Kearsarge* and USS *Nassau* were standing off the coast of Panama near the Caribbean entrance to the Panama Canal. The two ships were in the process of launching air-cushion landing craft and conventional landing craft filled with Marines.

The ships' crowded flight decks were a study in orchestrated chaos as more Marines boarded CH-53 Sea Stallions and CH-46 Sea Knights, the Marine Corps's principal assault helicopters.

Once the flotilla was headed for shore, the assault helicopters took off for their destinations near the entrance to the canal. Overhead, eight Marine AH-1W Super Cobra helicopter gunships, along with seven AV-8B Harrier attack aircraft, were standing by to provide down-in-the-weeds close air support for their grunts.

Backing the Marine expeditionary units and their own mini air wing were two air force AC-130U Spooky gunships, six air force A-10 Warthog tank killers, and the combined firepower of a large group of air force F-15s, F-16s, and the F-14s and F/A-18s from the USS *George Washington* battle group.

After the Marines established a beachhead, they would advance on the lock that was purported to be inoperative. As soon as the lock was under the control of the Marines, two former lock operators would be flown in by helicopter to identify and correct the problem, and then open the lock to free the U.S. warship.

At the same time the Marines were landing on the eastern shore of Panama, an air force E-3 AWACS was vectoring four F-15s and four F-16s toward two separate flights of Soviet-made Sukhoi Su-27 fighter-interceptors. The encounters, twenty-two miles northeast and thirty-seven miles east of the former Howard Air Force Base, were short and devastating.

Three of the seven front-line Chinese fighters had been initially shot down and a fourth had been damaged. The other

Sukhoi pilots had disengaged before the merge and raced southeast toward Colombia.

Hugging the deck in afterburner, one of the Su-27s had plunged into the trees when the quadruplex fly-by-wire flight-control system failed. Seconds later, an F-15 pilot picked off one of the other fighters.

The remaining Sukhoi pilot, flying at Mach 1.3, got away without a scratch—at least for the moment. The AWACS tracked the fighter to an airfield near Chiman, Panama. Shortly after the aircraft landed, two F-15s strafed the fighter before the pilot could get out. He managed to escape with minor injuries, but the aircraft caught fire and exploded.

Unfortunately, one of the air force F-16 Vipers was shot down by a surface-to-air missile. Incapacitated by the blast, the pilot was unable to eject. In retaliation an F-15E dropped an AGM-130 bomb on the SAM site near the canal and blew it off the map.

Minutes after the encounter with the Su-27s a flight of seven Chinese air force Shenyang J-6s (Chinese-made copies of the MiG-19) engaged four U.S. Navy F/A-18 Hornets near the Atlantic entrance to the canal. Three of the outdated MiGs were shot down in a matter of seconds, while two other MiGs had a midair collision and crashed near the north side of the canal. The remaining MiGs separated and streaked toward the former Howard Air Force Base.

After the sky was clear over the Chinese air base south-west of Balboa, one of the two Spooky gunships, *Terminator I,* and two A-10 Warthogs thundered over the base near the western shore of Panama. Overhead, four F-16s were flying cover for the Hercules gunship and the pair of A-10 close-support aircraft.

With an emphasis not on speed but on survivability and lethality against surface targets, the twin-engine Warthog is fitted with one of the most powerful guns ever mounted on an airplane. The beefy 30mm seven-barrel weapon fires milk-bottle-size rounds at a blistering pace of up to 4,200 rounds per minute.

The two attack aircraft also carried almost sixteen thousand pounds of external ordnance, including missiles and bombs spread over eleven hard-points under the wings and the fuselage.

While the Spooky gunship circled the air base, four Chinese antiaircraft artillery sites opened up with a barrage of fire that only slightly damaged the tough Hercules.

Not intimidated by the firepower, *Terminator II* pulverized the gun emplacements with cannon fire while the A-10s strafed two of the four Sukhoi Su-27 fighter-interceptors scrambling toward the runway. The damaged jets slowed and stopped on the side of the taxiway while the other pair of Chinese fighter planes entered the runway and began accelerating down the airstrip.

The Spooky gunship commenced firing with everything it had, cutting a deep furrow across the runway in front of the speeding jets. The flight leader and his wingman never had a chance as the landing gear was ripped from beneath both fighters. One Sukhoi caught fire and exploded while the other fighter slid off the side of the runway and overturned.

Terminator II also hammered a flight of two Shenyang J-7s (MiG-21s) as they scrambled for takeoff. Both aircraft exploded and set fire to another MiG-21 parked near the flight line.

While the Chinese MiGs burned, the air force A-10s moved in, strafing and bombing the rest of the newly delivered fighter planes. The Warthogs then headed east with the F-16s to rendezvous with an air force KC-10 tanker. After they topped their fuel tanks, the A-10 pilots would join their colleagues to fly cover for the Marines while the F-16s went after SAM sites and triple-A emplacements.

Separated at five-minute intervals, *Terminator II* and *Hell Raiser* would patrol the length of the canal. Their mission was to eliminate any missile sites or antiaircraft artillery emplacements that opened fire on anyone. If the Marines got pinned down, the big gunships would be called on to demonstrate their cannons and howitzers to the Chinese forces.

Covered by Super Cobras and AV-8B Harriers, the Marines encountered stiff resistance when they stormed the Panaman-

n shore on both sides of the canal. The Harriers and Super
'obras poured a tremendous stream of fire into the ranks of the
,400 Chinese soldiers on the front line. Antiaircraft artillery
re soon downed two Super Cobras and a Harrier.

One helicopter crew was killed in the crash while the other
uper Cobra crew survived the crash landing of their ship.
'he Harrier pilot ejected low to the ground and his parachute
opped open just in time for him to make one swing before
e hit the ground hard.

Despite a broken ankle, the aviator immediately came up
n his radio and guided a Marine UH-1N Huey to his posi-
on. Covered by two Marine Hornets, the helicopter success-
ully retrieved the F/A-18 pilot, and then plucked the injured
rew of the Super Cobra from the midst of the advancing Chi-
ese soldiers. Low on fuel, one of the Hornets had to strafe
vithin sixty feet of the Huey to keep the PLA troops from
eaching the downed aviators.

When a third Super Cobra was blown out of the sky, the
all went out to the menacing AC-130U Spooky gunships.
'our minutes later *Hell Raiser* and two Marine F/A-18 Hor-
ets jumped into the fray. The firepower erupting from the big
unship was a frightening sight, a show of force not for the
aint of heart.

The PLA forces grudgingly held their ground until *Termi-
ator II* and a flight of four navy F/A-18s joined in the fierce
ighting. The no-holds-barred 105mm howitzers in the
pooky gunships overpowered the Chinese and forced their
taggered lines of defense to break and begin falling back.
'he Marines were quickly enveloping the Chinese on the left
lank and opened a huge hole in the PLA on the right side of
he canal.

Moving very rapidly, the Marines broke through the deci-
nated Chinese ranks at three critical points. The PLA troops
vere being decisively defeated by the fast-moving Marines
nd the devastating and unrelenting close air support.

At the same time air force and navy fighter planes were
unting, and then destroying antiaircraft artillery positions
nd surface-to-air missile sites. Many of the emplacements

were quickly abandoned when the Spooky gunships and the
Warthogs opened fire on nearby sites. Other Chinese soldiers
continued a steady stream of triple-A fire and missile
launches until their sites were turned into smoking holes the
size of swimming pools.

USS *Samuel B. Roberts*

Feeling anxious, Comdr. LeRoy Gartly and his crew watched
with great apprehension as Chinese soldiers cautiously approached his 445-foot ship from both sides of the canal.
Lightly armed with rifles and pistols, the U.S. sailors were
preparing to repel boarders when four navy F-14 Tomcats and
six navy F/A-18 Hornets rolled in on the encroaching PLA
forces. The "Bombcats" and two of the Hornets worked over
the Chinese foot soldiers while the other F/A-18s went after
triple-A emplacements and SAM sites.

A shoulder-fired surface-to-air missile crippled one of the
Hornets and forced the pilot to set a direct course for *George
Washington*. Before the damaged F/A-18 was out of sight, an
F-14 was downed by intense antiaircraft fire. The crew safely
ejected and two orbiting Hornets were vectored to their position to provide air cover until a rescue helicopter could get to
them.

An HH-60H Seahawk from *George Washington* arrived
minutes later. The Tomcat pilot and his radar intercept officer
raced to the helo and dived through the door a second before
the Seahawk lifted off. The helicopter sustained engine damage from a hail of ground fire, but it managed to return safely
to *GW*.

When *Terminator II* could be spared, the Spooky gunship
flew over the trapped frigate and ripped the Chinese positions
wide open with a devastating attack. Soldiers and triple-A
gunners broke ranks and raced in every direction for the nearest cover.

Two CH-46 Sea Knights landed, one on each side of the
canal, and disgorged their load of Marines. By 8:35 A.M. the

each was secure, USS *Samuel B. Roberts* was secure, and he faulty lock was secure.

The Huey helicopter with the former canal-lock operators rrived a few minutes later, and the "problem" at the abanoned lock was found without delay. There was no problem vith the lock. The Red Chinese had deliberately detained the J.S. frigate and her crew.

By noon, the *Samuel B. Roberts* was safely in the waters f the Colombian Basin and her crew was enjoying a steel each picnic with their very relieved commanding officer.

22

Honolulu, Hawaii

Jackie opened her eyes and looked at the alarm clock on the nightstand. She crawled out of bed and gently pulled the curtain open to gaze at Waikiki Beach. The blue sky, clear emerald water, and soft trade winds promised another beautiful day in paradise. Jackie called room service to order coffee and orange juice, and then she turned on the television and selected a cable news station.

Feeling a bit groggy, Scott slowly sat up in bed and turned to look at the clock. "Eight-thirty?" he asked himself, and looked at Jackie. "What happened?"

She quietly chuckled. "We went to a luau at the Royal Hawaiian, made absolute fools of ourselves—at least you did—trying to do the hula, went out dancing until one-thirty, had way too many mai tais, and then walked barefoot on the beach for another hour." She tilted her head and smiled serenely. "That's what happened."

He started to respond and then caught the "Breaking News" logo on the television screen. "Turn up the volume."

The anchor looked up and faced the camera. "This just coming in to CNN—we have breaking news on several fronts—please bear with us. According to a senior White House spokesman, President Macklin is meeting at this hour with key members of his cabinet and high-level national security officials.

"Sources close to the president have told CNN that the purpose of the meeting is to consider the overall U.S. strategy in dealing with the ongoing confrontations with the Red

Chinese military and their communist leaders in Beijing. We hope to have news from the White House in a few minutes."

The anchor shuffled his sheets of paper. "To recap the shocking events of the past few hours, we turn to Barry Pulaski at the Pentagon."

"Randall, we're receiving further reports of casualties from this morning's battle at the Panama Canal."

"Battle?" Scott sat straight up in bed. "What battle?"

"I don't know." Jackie was transfixed on the television screen. "The Panama Canal issue obviously erupted in the last few hours."

Pulaski continued at a rapid pace. "There have been several conflicting accounts on the number of Americans injured, but the latest information we have indicates that at least two hundred Marines have been wounded. The current list of casualties stands at thirty-seven."

Interspersed with live coverage from Panama and scenes videotaped during the intense battle, the reporter recapped the sequence of events during the bloody clash and then tossed it back to the anchor.

For ten minutes, Scott and Jackie quietly absorbed the details of the deadly skirmish with the Chinese.

"We have just been informed that President Macklin will address the country in approximately one hour. Please stay with us for continuing coverage of the crisis with China."

A financial planning commercial flashed on the screen.

"I'm afraid this is only the beginning," Scott said.

The room service waiter knocked on the door.

"Newton's third law of motion," Jackie said, and then walked to the door. "For every action there is an equal and opposite reaction."

"Yeah, it's going to be a hot time in Beijing tonight."

The White House

President Cord Macklin, surrounded by his closest advisers on military matters and foreign policy, listened intently as each person expressed an opinion or suggested options for dealing with the brutal communist regime in Beijing.

The cabinet room was quiet when Macklin finally called a halt to the discussions. Everyone sensed the president was about to take bold initiatives, but no one could have anticipated what the commander in chief was about to say.

Immaculate in a dark gray suit, white shirt, and red tie, Macklin spoke in a steady, even voice. "I would have to agree with most of the views expressed here this afternoon. However, in my judgment, China has committed another act of war and we have responded accordingly."

Although his neck was red from the anger he felt, the president suppressed his emotions. "China has steadily become a more threatening adversary over the last decade, and their military will be a formidable world power in another ten to twelve years, perhaps sooner with the nuclear and laser-weapon technology they have acquired. Knowing their current capability and projecting what their future military capabilities will be, I have decided to deal with them now."

All eyes were riveted on the president.

"After the accidental bombing of the Chinese Embassy in Belgrade, our already fragile relationship with Beijing started over in a deep freeze. Then we had the spy-plane incident that jacked the rhetoric back up. We have tried gradualism, a world of patience, quiet diplomacy—everything in the book—with virtually no success. Even the vaunted trade agreement hasn't thawed our relationship with Beijing."

He paused and then spoke more slowly. "Their denial of human rights and religious freedom isn't going to get any better. We need to be mindful of the literature of the Red Chinese military and the Chinese Communist Party. To this very day, they still refer to the United States of America as 'the main enemy.'"

The expression on Macklin's face was grim. "We know the dictators in Beijing are nothing more than thugs dressed in business suits. It's a foregone conclusion. The communist tyrants aren't going to voluntarily change from a system of brutal, repressive government to a democratic form of govrnment. It just isn't going to happen—they're not going to give away their power."

Macklin looked at each of his advisers. "We no longer have the luxury of time on our side. As each day passes, the Red Chinese are adding to their nuclear capabilities. We have to deal with that fact and stop trying to coddle the bastards in Beijing. The only things they respond to are bluntness and brute force."

He paused a moment to collect his thoughts. "Let's not forget the explosive matter of Taiwan. A Chinese invasion of Taiwan would make Kosovo and the Middle East look like a tea party. The 1979 Taiwan Relations Act commits us to defend Taiwan against an attack from the mainland. I fully intend to honor that commitment and I want Beijing to think long and hard about our obligation—and the absolute power of our armed forces."

Macklin looked at his briefing notes. "Having voiced my opinion on Chinese leadership, the real crux of this matter is Beijing's overt attack on our military aircraft with laser weapons, SAMs, and antiaircraft fire. The weapons experts have no doubt about what happened to the RC-7 reconnaissance plane."

The president reached for his reading glasses. "It was ditched in shallow water and has been raised. According to the experts, the plane was definitely hit by a surface-to-air missile—probably a Soviet-built shoulder-fired weapon."

"You have to wonder what the hell the Chinese were thinking," Pete Adair said lightly.

"You *know* what they were thinking," the president said, slamming his fist on the table. "It couldn't be more crystal clear!"

Silence prevailed while Macklin schooled himself.

"Since Beijing regained control of Hong Kong, almost every aspect of that world-class city has deteriorated or become corrupted. They gained control of the Panama Canal and took what happened. Hell, they're sitting in our backyard, literally nine hundred miles from the U.S. border, with control over a vital choke point between the Atlantic and the Pacific.

"Let me rephrase that statement. The Chinese will no
have control over the canal anymore. We have taken contro
of the canal, and the matter isn't open for discussion. We'l
work with the Panamanian government to reach an agreemen
that works for both our countries. I will give President Li
Fan-ding one month to get the remainder of his communis
storm troops out of Panama."

The other men and women in the cabinet room looked a
each other with wide-eyed expressions.

"For the reasons I have previously mentioned, I'm goin
to take a vigorous approach with China and stop tiptoein
around the elephant in the living room. I'm going to sen
Beijing a very straightforward message. If we are provokec
the United States of America will strike back swiftly and wit
devastating results."

Macklin noted with great pleasure that Hartwell Prost ha
discreetly nodded his head.

"Simply put, ladies and gentlemen, I have chosen this tim
in our history, and this set of circumstances, to take a har
stand against the Red Chinese. If anyone in this room has
problem with my position on China, speak now and don'
hold anything back."

Silence filled the room.

The president turned to Brett Shannon, his Yale-educatec
bespectacled secretary of state. "Brett, I know you just re
turned from Beijing, but I want our remaining State Depart
ment people out of there as quickly as possible."

"Yes, sir."

"And I want all U.S. citizens living in China to be notifiec
immediately that it would be in their best interest to leav
China as soon as possible."

"I will make the arrangements directly after we adjourn.
Dressed as usual in a suit that was a size too large for him
Shannon looked bone tired and somewhat irritable. "I need t
brief our friends and alliance partners in that region to mak
sure we're on the same page."

"Another thing," Hartwell Prost said. "We need bipartisar
support from Congress and the American people. Mr. Presi

dent, you will have to make the case to the citizens of our country. If the people are with you, Congress will follow."

"Let's see if our distinguished congressional leadership will invite me to a special joint session."

Prost shook his head. "In my view, sir, that would be too formal, as if we're looking for a fight or are ready to declare war."

"What do you suggest?"

"The Oval Office. It's the setting most Americans relate to, and you're the only person they'll see. You'll have a captive audience without distractions from cameras panning around a roomful of celebrities—each vying to get their mug on television."

"That makes sense."

"And I recommend a private meeting with key members of Congress, before the telecast, of course. We have to be forthright and *honest* with the American people, and we have to be willing to listen to both sides of the aisle in Congress. That means keeping the leaders of both houses and every American informed about every step we take."

"I concur. If we're pressed into a major military confrontation with China, I'm going to openly request congressional support."

The president looked at the chairman of the joint chiefs. "Les, do you have any recommendations?"

"Yes, sir." He composed his thoughts. "First, I want to say that we've made great strides in the recent past toward rebuilding our military, but we aren't there yet. There's always the danger that we could be backing ourselves into a corner where we would be forced to use our nuclear weapons."

Chalmers kept eye contact with Macklin. "If we engage China, North Korea is sure to see an opportunity to make mischief—we could find ourselves pressed on two fronts and get waylaid in the Middle East."

The president showed no emotion. "I know it's your duty to give me the worst-case scenario, and I appreciate it."

"Yes, sir."

"You mentioned recommendations?"

"Yes—when I recalled the *Roosevelt* battle group to the

South China Sea, I requested joint military exercises with Australia and New Zealand. They have really pitched in for us and joined *Roosevelt*. I strongly suggest we move *Roosevelt* closer to the southern end of the Taiwan Strait and leave *Kitty Hawk* at the northern opening to the strait."

"You want to keep them in deeper water?"

"Yes, sir. We have three submarines in the area, and by tomorrow evening we'll have another sub rendezvousing with *Roosevelt*."

"Good, let's muster the troops," Macklin said boldly as he rose from his chair. "We have a lot to do before I leave for Bangkok."

North Korea

Despite the United States's questionable decision to ease sanctions on North Korea, famine, starvation, corruption, sabotage, black-marketing, and exposure to the world of the country's irreversible problems had shaken the teetering system.

Unable to disguise the growing economic and political disasters, not to mention the 3 million people in a country of 22 million who had starved to death, the dictator of the rogue nation was rapidly losing control of his minor nuclear power.

Unstable and desperate, North Korea posed a serious threat to South Korea and the 40,000-plus U.S. troops stationed there. Along with the White House the South Korean political and military leaders were preparing for the worst.

With more than 1,065,000 military personnel, 3,600 tanks, 432 naval surface combatants, 82 bombers, 780 fighters, and 10,400 surface-to-air missiles, North Korea would be a formidable enemy.

The USS *Stennis* battle group was steaming at flank speed to the Yellow Sea, and the Pacific Air Forces, headquartered at Hickam Air Force Base, Hawaii, were sending additional bombers and fighter planes to Andersen Air Force Base, Guam; Yokota Air Base, Japan; Osan Air Base, South Korea,

Misawa Air Base, Japan; and Kadena Air Base, Japan (Okinawa). If the North Korean government collapsed and their military attacked South Korea, far more lives could be sacrificed than had been lost to starvation.

High above the Hungnam Seaport in the city and provincial capital of Hamhung, a Lockheed Martin U-2 reconnaissance plane was documenting the arrival of thirty-two MiG-21 fighters from Kazakhstan. The long-lived spy plane was observing the fifth shipment of warplanes from the former Soviet republic.

North Korea was rapidly adding more jets to the 140 MiG-21s it had previously purchased. The total force of jet fighter aircraft now totaled 803 and was growing. Sixteen Russian attack pilots were augmenting the training of North Korean fighter pilots. The Russian instructors were handpicked and very experienced veterans.

Southeast of North Korea's capital city of Pyongyang, a Central Intelligence Agency Gnat unmanned aerial vehicle was using an improved synthetic aperture radar to spot tanks and troops moving toward South Korea. A product of General Atomics and Sandia, the SAR was observing the lines of military equipment and personnel through clouds and light rain. The soldiers were going to one of three staging points that were increasing in size by the day.

Analysts at the CIA's Global Response Center were certain that North Korea was on the verge of invading their neighbor to the south.

The Oval Office

The president appeared to be relaxed and calm as he walked to his desk. It was framed on one side by the American flag and on the other by the presidential flag. He took his seat and adjusted his tie, while making eye contact with his staff and the camera technicians from major media outlets. The lights came on and he was given his cue.

"Good afternoon," he began without expression. "As many

of you know, early this morning U.S. forces went ashore i
Panama to liberate an American warship being held captiv
by Chinese military forces in the Panama Canal. This was a
intolerable act of blatant aggression by the Red Chinese mi
itary and the Communist Party leaders in Beijing."

Macklin's neck muscles began to tighten. "Furthermor
intelligence sources have confirmed that Chinese militar
forces were responsible for shooting down a U.S. reconnais
sance aircraft and damaging a Marine Harrier jet—both c
which were over the Panama Canal."

The network crews were riveted on the president. Thi
wasn't the friendly, jovial man they had come to know.

"I have spent my entire adult life dedicated to protectin
and preserving the freedom and security of our United State
of America. I will not tolerate this aggression against th
American people. Under the Panama Canal treaties of 197
we reserved the right to intervene militarily if the canal an
its operation were threatened. I invoked that clause this morn
ing."

Feeling tension creep into his shoulders and neck, Mack
lin forced himself to relax. "As president of the United States
I am assuming jurisdiction of the Panama Canal as of thi
date. I will ask Congress to render the treaties null and void.

Macklin's words deeply impacted those who were presen
Looks were exchanged in an effort to gauge reactions to wha
the president had said. There was no doubt President Mack
lin was showing the same fortitude and courage as presiden
that he'd shown in Congress and in fighter planes during Viet
nam. Who was going to tell the president of the United State
that he couldn't have the canal back?

"I am sorry to inform you that a number of American live
were lost today in the process of freeing our ship and re
claiming the canal. Our fine men and women in uniform per
formed their duties in an extraordinary manner. Ever
American should be proud of them."

Macklin had to slow his breathing. "No president eve
wants to put American military men and women in harm'
way, but we have been called upon to do so many times in th

istory of this great country. It is the price we must pay for
reedom."

The president's mouth quivered. "Our hearts and prayers
o out to the families and friends who lost loved ones in
'anama."

He tried not to show any emotion, but it was coming to the
urface. "Let me make it very clear to our allies, and most im-
ortantly to those who choose to be our enemies. While I am
resident of the United States of America, we will stand
houlder to shoulder with our allies and we will not tolerate
ny form of aggression."

Macklin stared at the camera for a long moment. "May
God bless America—our wonderful country built on freedom. Thank you."

Stone faced, Macklin waited until the lights went out and
quietly walked out of his office. No one dared ask him a single question.

23

The Halekulani

After the president's emotional address, Jackie punched the mute button on the television and turned to Scott. "What we have here is old-fashioned brinkmanship, and that doesn't bode well for the summit in Bangkok."

Scott walked to the window and took in the view of Waikiki and Diamond Head. "For the Chinese, this will be about saving face."

"After today's events, they'll have to tether Liu Fan-ding to the ground."

"Yeah, I'd hate to be one of his personal aides."

She sat her coffee cup on the table. "Do you think he'll cancel his trip to Bangkok?"

"Who, Liu Fan-ding?"

"No, President Macklin, our ride to Bangkok."

"He's the one who called for the summit—I expect he'll attend," Scott said, and glanced at the film footage from Panama. "This clash with China is even more reason for the president to solidify our position with the Southeast Asian nations."

Jackie stared at the television for a few seconds. "We'd better check with Hartwell and get an update on their plans."

"Good idea."

"We may not want to go to Bangkok."

"Having second thoughts?" Scott asked.

"Knowing Liu Fan-ding, he might bomb Bangkok after watching President Macklin take the canal back."

"I wouldn't put anything past him." Scott checked the time and reached for the phone. "I'll call Hartwell."

Jackie had just stepped out of the shower and wrapped a towel around herself when Scott finished his conversation with Prost.

"What's the current temperature?"

"Warm and getting warmer."

Scott gave her a quick brief about the two battle groups moving closer to the Taiwan Strait, then changed the subject to Bangkok. "The president's plane will be arriving here at one o'clock tomorrow morning."

"When do we leave?"

"As soon as the plane is refueled," he said. "He's using one of the command-post aircraft."

Jackie was surprised. "Wow, things must be getting serious."

"I didn't ask Hartwell why the plane change, but the president is certainly sending a message."

"Yeah, that'll flash around the world—maybe it's too provocative."

"Hey, he means business."

"Any idea yet about our role?" she asked.

"He didn't bring it up and I didn't ask."

"Well, we'll know soon enough."

"Oh, I almost forgot," he said. "The boys in Beijing are now missing *three* of their laser-weapons ships."

"What happened?"

"One of their ships—the *Deng Ju-shan*—took out an E-2C from *Kitty Hawk,* killing the entire crew. A short time later, the Chicoms' laser ship ran into a couple of torpedoes and went to the bottom."

"How coincidental."

"Yes, very unfortunate."

"What was the response from President Macklin?"

"The White House hasn't made a statement yet. For the time being, they're calling the loss of the Hawkeye an operational accident."

"Have the Chinese gone into full threat mode or do they know about their laser ship?"

"Beijing knows what happened to their ship, but they can't prove it. So, as it stands right now, it's a matter of who blinks first."

Jackie reached into the dresser for a pair of shorts and a colorful aloha shirt. "I have a very bad feeling about this brawl with China."

"Same here," he said, watching an update on the Panama Canal skirmish. "Another item of interest—Merrick Hamilton is back on active duty and has orders to an F/A-18 squadron."

"Great." She tucked the shirt into her shorts. "What about Zheng Yen-Tsung? Do they have any idea where he is?"

"The FBI thinks he went back to China. The feds are rounding up a large number of alleged Chinese spies who are singing their hearts out."

"I hope they're right about Zheng," she said. "But he could be anywhere—that's what frightens me."

"You're right," Scott said. "We'll have to keep our guard up, but I believe the FBI knows what's going on."

"There are plenty of ways he could track us. And you, of all people, know that's true."

"Okay, it's true. But their military and our military know about the lasers and the bogus holograms, so I don't see why Zheng Yen-Tsung would want to hunt us anymore."

"Well, the media hasn't picked up on it yet."

"After Bangkok I have a feeling it won't be long before the story is on the front page of papers all over the world."

"I hope so," she said.

"Hey, we're wasting the day. Let's hit the beach and get a Bloody Mary."

She pointed to the bathroom. "It's all yours. I'm going to check in with Mary Beth and see how everything is going at the office."

"Tell her hello for me."

Beijing, the People's Republic of China

The world-renowned Palace Hotel was rapidly filling with high-ranking military officers summoned to meet with President Liu Fan-ding before he departed for Bangkok. Located near major diplomatic and governmental offices, the stately hotel had been the gathering place for many pleasant military functions. This occasion would not be one of them.

Word of the meeting in Beijing had spread as rapidly as the news about the deadly military clash with the United States and the voided Panama Canal treaty. From personal observations by aides to the Chinese president, information about his ire had traveled across China like a lightning bolt. It was reported that President Liu Fan-ding was consumed with rage. Other accounts indicated that everyone around him was feeling his wrath.

Quoted in the military newspaper *People's Liberation Army Daily,* President Liu Fan-ding threatened to "use China's neutron bombs on America and Taiwan if the Panama Canal was not returned to Panamanian control immediately." He went on to say that "Americans are standing at a critical historical juncture and they should not act on impulse."

Liu Fan-ding also accused President Macklin of "using every possible means of treachery to undermine China." He went on to say, "Macklin is playing with fire, and he will die by fire if he doesn't return the canal to Panama."

Liu Fan-ding's closest aides admitted that his doctor was concerned he might have a stroke or a heart attack. One thing was certain: The highly agitated president couldn't wait to confront the American president in Bangkok.

Honolulu International Airport

Enjoying the tropical breeze, Scott and Jackie glanced at the golden moon and the star-studded sky while they waited for President Macklin and his entourage to arrive. Along with a large crowd, Jackie and Scott were standing on a wide parking ramp set aside for *Air Force One.*

Dressed in conservative gray business suits, white shirts, and black shoes, Scott and Jackie looked like the two special agents from the Secret Service office in Honolulu. All four had ear receivers and a wire running down their collar. They were also armed.

"I think they just turned final," Jackie said, watching the flurry of activity in the group of VIPs waiting to greet the president.

"You're right."

The portable lighting system bathed the ramp with enough brilliance to light a football field.

Four Hawaiian Air National Guard F-15 Eagles had just broken away from the president's plane and were preparing to land at Hickam Air Force Base. The quartet of fighters, along with two KC-135 aerial tankers, had rendezvoused with the airborne command post midway between California and Hawaii to provide additional security for the president.

Jackie and Scott quietly watched the giant E-4B Advanced Airborne Command Post "Night Watch" land and slow to a crawl before turning off the runway. Automatically designated *Air Force One* because the president of the United States was on board, the Air Combat Command E-4B was a modified Boeing 747-200 airliner.

Used by the National Command Authority as the National Airborne Operations Center for the president and the Joint Chiefs of Staff in all levels of conflict, including nuclear war, the aircraft could remain aloft for seventy-two hours with airborne refueling. At least one E-4B was always on alert at selected bases, including overseas military installations.

The four-airplane fleet also provided VIP transportation and supported the Federal Emergency Management Agency during times of natural disasters such as hurricanes and floods.

Scott and Jackie waited until the mobile stairway was in place and then joined the other Secret Service agents being escorted to the plane. Hartwell Prost met Dalton and Sullivan at the entrance to the big Boeing and directed them to a vacant conference/briefing room. The three of them would meet with the president after he spoke to the sizable crowd gathered to show their support for his actions.

The president's command presence during the confrontations with the Chinese had sparked a renewal of strength and support for President Macklin personally and for the office of the president. The headlines were calling the movement a tremendous rally, a common and just cause for the citizens of the last superpower.

When the E-4B was almost completely fueled, the president was discreetly prompted to return to the airplane. He made his closing remarks to the enthusiastic audience and listened to the spontaneous cheers and loud applause as he reboarded the aircraft.

Dressed casually in brown slacks and a cream-colored sport coat, Macklin entered the conference/briefing room. He gave Scott and Jackie a warm smile and firmly shook hands with them.

"Have a seat," the president said, motioning toward the conference table. He and Prost sat down across from Jackie and Scott.

"First, I want to extend my sincere thanks and deepest appreciation to both of you—what a job you did."

"Thank you, sir," Jackie and Scott said in unison.

"The two of you have demonstrated remarkable courage and ingenuity. I appreciate it, and someday a grateful nation will thank you."

"And," Hartwell said, "I want to add my thanks."

"Now I'll get down to current business," the president said. "I have another matter of urgency I want to discuss with you—a problem that is extremely important to our country and our future."

Under the table Jackie nervously squeezed Scott's hand.

"If the two of you find the risk factor greater than the reward, I will understand—it's up to you."

"We'll be honest, Mr. President," Scott said, and then couldn't stop a crooked smile from spreading across his face. "But, sir, we draw the line at bungee jumping."

Caught off guard, Macklin and Prost laughed while Jackie pinched Scott and wished she could kick him in the ankle.

"No bungee jumping." The president chuckled. "What I want you to do is rescue Dr. Richard Cheung from the Mianyang R and D production complex in China—deep in the heart of China."

"We're familiar with it," Jackie said.

"Good. We want Cheung back for more than one reason, but most importantly, we want to know with certitude what capacity the Chinese have to inflict damage on their enemies. It's imperative that we know exactly how far they've advanced with the development of the laser weapon, and what type of platforms they plan to use in deploying it."

"We want to offer Cheung a deal," Hartwell said. "If he'll work on a way to defeat the Chinese lasers, he can avoid the very *unpleasant* consequence of being tried for treason. Either way, we need to get him out of China. If he won't help us, we sure as hell don't want him helping the Chinese. That's what we hope the two of you can accomplish."

"And if he won't cooperate?" Scott asked.

"I'll leave the details up to your imagination," Prost said clearly, "but dragging him home to face charges of treason would be at the bottom of my list—the very bottom."

The president acknowledged his national security adviser's blunt remark with a slight nod.

There was a clumsy moment of silence as the lumbering command post began taxiing for takeoff.

Scott fastened his seat belt. "Let's go over the details of your plan and then we'll be able to make an informed decision."

"We can start on it right now," Prost suggested. "That is, if you're not too tired."

"Not at all," Jackie said.

"Please stay seated," the president said, rising from his chair. "Hartwell has all the details from our discussions with his friends from the Agency. I'm going to turn in and try to get some sleep on the way to Bangkok. Good night, and thanks again."

"Good night, sir," Scott said.

Macklin faltered in midstride and turned to face Dalton. "By the way, how did you get that Chinese sailor with the exaggerated smile to pose for the pictures?"

Not having known what was in the photos, Jackie was more than surprised by the revelation.

Scott searched for the right words. "We, ah, stumbled into each other and after the initial shock wore off, I told him I was a security inspector hired by Beijing and that he could lose his job if he didn't follow orders."

"And he believed you—a Caucasian standing there in a wet suit?"

"Yes, sir."

The president laughed. "That sailor is obviously depriving a village somewhere of an idiot."

Hartwell stared at Dalton for a long moment. "You must have an entire committee of guardian angels looking over your shoulder."

"I hope you don't mind"—the president smiled—"if I tell that story at my next cabinet meeting."

"Not at all, sir."

"I'll keep you anonymous, of course."

No one said a word until the president had disappeared.

"You didn't tell me about that," Jackie said.

"Actually, I was kind of embarrassed by being caught off guard."

Hartwell opened a leather case full of papers and maps and then spread them across the conference table.

"What we want to do is include you, with the proper papers attesting to your Canadian citizenship, on a legitimate tour of the Yangtze River."

"Canadian?" Scott asked. "Not Australian—'G'day, mate,' and all that?"

"Not this time. The Aussies are holding joint naval exercises with the *Roosevelt* battle group—near the Taiwan Strait."

"Ah, Canadian is an excellent choice."

Prost reached for two dossiers. "Corbin and Samantha

Hathaway, a married couple from Halifax, Nova Scotia. We've confirmed that none of the other couples are from Nova Scotia.

"The travel company has been in business for many years, since the seventies, and is well known and respected throughout the Orient. We have spent a great deal of time setting this up, so I'll start from the beginning."

He handed them two bound folders with the CIA logo on the covers. "As I said, if you agree to attempt this operation, we're going to insert the two of you into a legitimate tour group of Canadians. The group is arriving in Bangkok this afternoon. Few of them know each other, so it will be easier for you to fit in with them."

Scott opened his booklet and thumbed through it. "Do you have personal workups for us?"

"Sure do." Hartwell opened his notes. "Page seven, and as always, I suggest you memorize everything in the briefing book."

"If we decide to take this on, when do we shove off, and from where?" Scott asked.

"Day after tomorrow from Bangkok."

The E-4B began accelerating for takeoff.

"You're going to be replacements for a couple who had a family crisis and had to cancel their trip."

USS *Roosevelt* Battle Group

Seventy miles south-southeast of Taiwan the supercarrier and her escorts, the Aegis cruisers USS *Vella Gulf* and USS *Leyte Gulf,* the frigate USS *Kauffman*, and the destroyer USS *Hayler* were on station to monitor the anticipated Chinese missile exercises.

Positioned in the Bashi Channel near the Taiwan Air Defense Identification Zone, the battle group was only forty-five miles southeast of Lan Hsu Island. The officers and sailors on board *Roosevelt* and her escorts were preparing for any contingency.

The Royal Australian Navy guided missile destroyer *Brisbane,* the guided missile frigate *Melbourne,* and the newly commissioned *Collins*-class submarine *Dechaineux* were accompanying the U.S. warships. The recently refitted Royal New Zealand frigate *Canterbury* had joined the battle group a day earlier.

Over the sun-drenched Strait of Taiwan, F-14s and F/A-18s from *Kitty Hawk* and *Roosevelt* flew barrier combat air patrol while other fighters were on Alert Five status on the carriers. Two E-2C Hawkeyes were airborne, as well as two air force KC-10 tankers. Other tankers were manned and ready to launch from the carriers in a matter of minutes.

On board the carrier *Roosevelt,* RAdm. Mark Hannifin, commander of the battle group, had the responsibility of providing the tactical picture of the expected missile exercises to the president, the Pentagon, the Seventh Fleet flagship, and senior commanders throughout Southeast Asia.

The latest intelligence reports indicated that Beijing had ordered extensive live-fire exercises in and around the Strait of Taiwan, including a special ballistic missile closure area forty miles southeast of Taitung, Taiwan. A second missile closure area was designated at a point thirty-eight miles east of Hualien, while a third was targeted fifty-two miles southeast of Taipei, the capital of Taiwan.

If the ballistic missiles were launched from the same areas the Chinese had used in the 1996 crisis, the deadly weapons would have to fly directly over the island nation in order to hit their specific target areas.

The ominous ballistic missile exercise, according to Chinese president Liu Fan-ding, was to be a routine test of missile range and accuracy. In reality, the dangerous exercise was meant to send a thinly veiled threat to Taiwan, the White House, and the U.S. Congress.

After the Chinese military newspaper *People's Liberation Army Daily* printed a special "saber rattling" edition, in which it said, "America and her allies are sharpening their swords and bringing U.S. interventionism to China," commercial sea and air traffic rapidly began disappearing from the Taiwan Strait.

United Airlines canceled their popular San Francisco and Chicago flights to China, followed by cancellations of FedEx cargo runs and Northwest Airlines flights.

The *PLA Daily* followed the saber-rattling issue with one that stated in a bold front-page headline, "Taiwan Will Never Be Allowed to Be Independent." Another headline proclaimed, "China Will Spare No Effort in a Blood-Soaked Battle to Protect Territorial Integrity."

By the time the reckless ballistic-missile exercise was announced, civilian air and sea traffic had completely evaporated in the region. Now the strait was scattered with warships and fighter planes that had replaced the usual commercial airliners and international cargo flights.

The Aegis cruiser *Vella Gulf* was tasked by Admiral Hannifin with the primary responsibility of detecting and tracking any ballistic missiles fired from the Chinese mainland or from surface vessels or submarines.

All hands on *Vella Gulf,* the lone forward observer for the *Roosevelt* and *Kitty Hawk* battle groups, were acutely aware of the immediate danger they faced. Their orders were clear: They were to act as observers and conduct the operation in a passive mode.

The three missile closure areas were scheduled to become active at 1730 hours local time. With two minutes to go before the target areas would turn hot, the ship's crew was on a heightened state of alert. Closer than the other warships to the southernmost missile area, *Vella Gulf* was in a particularly hazardous area twenty miles north of Lan Hsu Island.

When the scheduled launch time passed without detection of any missile activity, Admiral Hannifin began to feel the first tentacles of anxiety creep into his mind. The anxiety was driven by a fear of the unknown. At 1742 hours the waiting was over.

Bong! Bong! Bong! "General quarters! General quarters!" an excited voice blared loudly and clearly over *Vella Gulf*'s 1MC, the ship's public-address system. "All hands man your battle stations! All hands man your battle stations! Ballistic missiles inbound!"

Throughout the battle group, young sailors and officers quickly settled into their GQ stations. Confident in their training and special skills, they had total faith in themselves and their shipmates.

Vella Gulf had detected two ballistic missiles rising over the Chinese mainland above the distant radar horizon. Both DF-21 missiles, fired from different locations hundreds of miles away, were tracking straight for the closure area adjacent to *Vella Gulf.*

In the ship's Aegis fire-control and combat-information center, the CIC watch standers were mesmerized as they tracked the ballistic missiles through the ascent phase of their trajectories, established tracks for the boosters, and generated reentry information.

The location of the missile launch sites in China had been carefully documented. Space-based assets and a Cobra Ball spy plane had provided the exact coordinates of the launch pads. The coordinates would soon be programmed into a number of U.S. weapons systems, including improved conventional air-launched cruise missiles aboard nine B-52 bombers sitting on the flight line at Andersen Air Force Base, Guam.

On the bridge of *Vella Gulf,* the captain gave the order to get under way as he maneuvered to get out of the immediate area.

Twenty seconds later, the CIC watch standers detected a third ballistic missile rise above the horizon and track straight for the target site southeast of Taipei. Seconds later, another missile, this time an M-9, rose from a different site and tracked toward *Vella Gulf.*

A mile south of the Aegis cruiser a LAMPS Mark III helicopter crew was waiting to observe the ballistic missile tests. As the helo crew monitored their radios, it became alarmingly clear that the M-9 missile was streaking toward their ship. The pilot began easing the SH-60B Seahawk closer to *Vella Gulf.*

The cruiser continued to track the missiles, while the CIC watch standers transmitted satellite voice and track reports to the battle-group commander on *Roosevelt,* commander, Seventh Fleet, and the task-force commander in Japan.

When the three missiles targeted at the area closest to the

cruiser began their descent, it became painfully obvious that one of the weapons was on a trajectory that coincided with the ship's exact position. This was now considered a deliberate and hostile attack.

After a frantic call from CIC, the captain ordered flank speed and a seventy-degree turn to starboard. A series of flash messages were quickly sent to the National Command Authority in Washington, detailing the attack, while the Aegis weapon system's battle diary recorded the launch and track for detailed evidence and reconstruction of the attack on *Vella Gulf*.

Ordering the LAMPS III helo away from his ship, the captain tried a tight high-speed turn at the same time the helicopter crew saw a bright flash and explosion in the designated target area. Seconds later, they saw another explosion in the same vicinity.

After confirming the Aegis information on the point of impact, the senior CIC officer didn't hesitate to transfer the primary Aegis responsibility to *Leyte Gulf*. The other cruiser immediately responded, since they were providing backup capability to place a protective missile umbrella over the entire fleet.

The senior CIC officer in *Vella Gulf* gave a frantic last-second warning over the 1MC. "Ballistic missile inbound! Brace for impact!"

The words were hardly out of his mouth before the supersonic missile slammed into the water eighty yards from *Vella Gulf*'s port bow.

The copilot of the SH-60B gasped as the warship, traveling at flank speed, disappeared inside a huge cloud of spray smoke, and flying debris. A shock wave violently rocked the helo as *Vella Gulf* emerged from the wall of water and rapidly slowed.

"That, my friend, was a close call," the pilot said as he added power and raced for the ship.

"If that had been a nuke," the copilot said, "the ship would be heading straight for Davy Jones's locker."

The pilot glanced at his shipmate. "If that had been a nuke Saint Peter would be taking your ticket stub about now."

24

Bangkok, Thailand

It was late afternoon in the capital and chief port of Thailand when the stand-in *Air Force One* approached the sprawling megacity. Four navy F/A-18 fighters from USS *Roosevelt* accompanied the flying command post. The Hornets, with the assistance of air force tankers, had relieved the Hawaiian Air National Guard F-15s near Guam. After the president's plane was safely on the ground, the navy fighters would aerial-refuel from the KC-10 tankers and return to their carrier.

Having been invited to the cockpit of the E-4B, Jackie and Scott had a commanding view of the famous Vietnam-era R and R destination for American servicemen. Located about twenty-five miles from the Gulf of Thailand, Bangkok was well known for its inner-city traffic congestion from taxis, private cars, motorcycles, buses, and various other forms of transportation.

"Look at this chaos," Scott said, scanning the wide array of crisscrossing streets and alleys.

"Yeah, Bangkok doesn't have a downtown. The streets and traffic veer off in every direction, then branch again and again."

Dalton studied the city. "It looks like it was designed by a committee that never collaborated with one another."

"Well, they obviously didn't form a planning or zoning committee."

"Definitely an ad hoc operation," Scott said, watching the copilot lower the landing gear. "We'd better get back to our seats and strap in."

They thanked the flight crew and left the cockpit.

"This place is enormous," Scott said.

"During the Vietnam War, Bangkok had a population of about one and a half million—today the population has sky-rocketed to more than eight million people."

"How do you know so much about Bangkok?"

"I visited here once."

"Oh, I see."

A minute later, *Air Force One* turned on final and gently touched down on runway twenty-one-left at Bangkok's famous Don Muang International Airport. The crowded airport is one of the busiest destinations in Southeast Asia. The E-4B command-post aircraft followed an airport security car to a designated position on the ramp and stopped.

Two presidential limousines and a fleet of Secret Service Chevy Suburbans awaited the president and his closest aides. Due to the growing hostility between China and the United States, security was extremely tight and the airport was dotted with special agents posing as pilots, flight attendants, mechanics, and passengers.

Scott and Jackie remained on board the airplane while President Macklin and his vast entourage were greeted warmly by members of the Association of Southeast Asian Nations (ASEAN). The tension over the strained China-U.S. relationship was evident from the grim faces on both sides.

After a brief ceremony with ASEAN leaders, the president would be going to his hotel, the Dusit Thani, site of the emergency meeting of ASEAN. Later he would attend a special Thai dinner performance.

Jackie looked out her window and saw China's new Air Force One, a specially configured Boeing 767-300ER. "Check Liu Fan-ding's new ride."

Scott leaned across her to take a look at the VIP jetliner. "How ironic that it's built in America."

Minutes after President Macklin and his aides departed *Air Force One,* Jackie and Scott were escorted to a Secret Service van and driven to the elegant high-rise hotel. A spe-ial agent greeted them in the lobby and then took them directly to their rooms at the Dusit Thani, long a favorite of Thailand's royalty and considered one of the best hotels in the Far East.

After they had refreshed themselves and changed clothes, Scott and Jackie went for a walk around the hotel's gardens and waterfall, then entered Lumpini Park and sat down on a bench.

"What do you think?" Jackie asked. "Can we pull it off?"

"With some luck. The Chinese make sure the same number of people who left for the Yangtze River cruise return to Shanghai. That could be a problem at the conclusion of the operation, presupposing we get Cheung out of Mianyang."

They fell silent, each pondering the risky plan.

"We'll come up with something," Scott said. "We always do when things get out of shape."

"That's what scares me. For once, I'd like to complete an assignment exactly as we planned it, no changes, no deviations, and no crashes."

Scott laughed. "Then it would be classified as a routine assignment, not a mission or operation."

"Thanks for enlightening me, Plato."

"Anytime." Scott stretched his arms across the back of the bench. "Let's table this for now and see the sites—how about it?"

"Sounds good to me."

"You've been here before, so I elect you as tour guide."

"I've been here exactly one time—for a total of one day."

"A veritable wealth of knowledge compared to mine." He leaned in front of her. "Time, she is a-wasting."

"Well, you have to see the Buddha first."

"Okay, whatever."

"I think it's some kind of Thai law for visitors."

"Hey, you're my tour guide."

After seeing the famous Wat Phra Keo, the Temple of the Emerald Buddha, they sailed by motor launch up the Chao Phya River to see the floating markets and homes, then

boarded a luxury-style river barge for the return trip. While
they enjoyed cocktails and sampled Mongolian barbecue,
Scott and Jackie took in the exotic river-life. They slowly
drifted along the crowded banks, waving at the children.

When the barge excursion came to an end, they had an au
thentic Thai dinner while a parade of beautifully costumed
dancers entertained them. After the relaxing dinner, they re
turned to the hotel and went up to the rooftop lounge to take
in the panoramic view of the city.

As they settled into comfortable chairs, Jackie quickly
spied one of Hartwell's personal aides walking into the ele
gant lounge. He looked around for a moment and then ap
proached their table.

"Here comes trouble."

"What?" Scott asked a moment before the man reached
the table.

"Mr. Prost wishes to see the two of you in his suite," the
man said impatiently. "He's waiting."

"Okay," Scott said. "We're on our way."

When they reached Hartwell's suite, Prost dismissed his
assistants and shut the door. The set of his jaw reflected bad
news.

"Sir, has the room been swept?" Scott asked.

"Yes." Hartwell motioned toward a couch. "No bugs or
video. Have a seat." He told them about the *Vella Gulf* en
counter and then brought them up to date.

"The ship is limping to Yokosuka and the injured, includ
ing the captain, have been flown to *Roosevelt* for treatment.
The president has just placed our forces in the Western Pa
cific and Southeast Asia in DEFCON Three status. He's tak
ing a very aggressive stand. He honestly believes that our
greatest exports are freedom and peace—and he wants to
make that clear to our Asian allies. The president wants to ex
pose the Chinese leaders for who they are. President Macklin
sees China as an enemy, and he's going to be straightforward
about his view."

Hartwell reached for a briefing folder. "Due to the vicissi
tudes of this dangerous situation with China, the tour com

any—all the tour companies, for that matter—have canceled all trips to Taiwan and China until things settle down."

Jackie and Scott had the same surprised reaction.

"Are we going to scrub the operation?" Dalton asked.

"No, but the insertion and extraction are going to be a bit more dicey."

"What's your plan?" Jackie asked.

"Well, let me explain the overall picture, then you and Scott may have some ideas to add to the script."

"Okay."

Hartwell eyed Jackie for a moment. "Have you flown Agusta helicopters, any of the models?"

"I'm afraid not."

"Okay, no problem." He opened the briefing folder. "We've had two new helicopters, Agusta A109Es, in China for the last five months or so."

"The one they call the 'Power'?" she asked.

"That's right. One of the helos is a corporate transport, while the other one has been configured as an EMS medevac. Ostensibly the helicopters are factory demonstrators, but we keep them in China for operations like the one we're planning. One of the helos, the medevac, is kept in Hong Kong while the other one operates from its base in Shanghai."

"Sir," Scott said, "I don't think a helicopter is going to have the range to get out of China without having to stop for fuel."

"Allow me to explain."

"Yes, sir."

Hartwell turned to Jackie. "After you're checked out in the Power, if you agree, we will transform you into a demonstration pilot and Scott into a vice president of international marketing for a holding company in Richmond, Virginia. We'll fly you and Scott to Hong Kong. As soon as you feel comfortable in the helicopter, the two of you will fly a Learjet to Chengdu."

"Can we get some manuals and training aids before we go to Hong Kong?" she asked.

Hartwell glanced at his watch. "They'll be here in about two hours."

Prost turned his attention to Scott. "We've leased a Lear 35A, so we won't have to waste any time training you in another jet. After you arrive at Shungliu Airport near Chengdu, Jackie will handle a helo demonstration for a prospective buyer—they're legitimate EMS executives."

"The helicopter?" Scott asked. "Who's going to preposition it?"

"One of our company people. He'll top it off with fuel and be long gone before you arrive. We can't have any Agency prints on this."

"Will the prospective buyers know when we're arriving?" Jackie asked.

"Yes. They'll be told that you had to do a demonstration in Hong Kong that morning, thus the need for a jet to take you to Chengdu."

"Okay," she said, fitting the pieces of the plan together in her mind. *Our timing is going to have to be very acute.*

"You'll have two rooms booked at a hotel close to the airport. You will appear to be staying overnight. This will give you the opportunity to reach Dr. Cheung under the cover of darkness and, hopefully, extract him."

Hartwell paused for a moment. "Once you have him in your guardianship, get out of Mianyang and return to Chengdu as quickly as possible. You'll leave the helicopter on the ramp and fly the Lear back to Hong Kong."

Prost turned a page in his folder. "From there you'll escort Cheung to Okinawa in a larger corporate jet—the Falcon jet that will take you from Bangkok to Hong Kong to begin the operation. The FBI will meet you at Kadena Air Base and take custody of Cheung."

Prost continued setting up the operation while Jackie and Scott were thinking many steps ahead.

"Sir," Scott said during a pause, "what if we have a problem getting back to Chengdu—to the Lear?"

"Arrangements are being made to have fuel prepositioned near Chongqing and Guilin—they're situated on a basic course from Chengdu to Hong Kong. That will allow for an ample fuel reserve to make it back to safety in the helicopter—if you have to."

Prost handed them enlarged sections of two satellite images and two grids on an operational navigation chart. "A small refueling truck will be parked in an isolated area near Chongqing—the same setup for Guilin. We can't risk landing at an airport after you have Dr. Cheung. The directions you have are very specific, so you shouldn't have a problem."

"If we get away clean," Jackie said.

Hartwell looked at her. "That's the key."

"Can you arrange some more firepower for us?" Scott asked.

"Sure, whatever you need."

"From what I make of this operation, we're going into an environment that would normally require at least one SEAL platoon with a lot of firepower."

"True."

"In light of the situation, I'd like to have some heavier bricks to throw—some SEAL weapons."

Hartwell reached for a note pad and his Namiki fountain pen. "What would you like?"

"Two complete sets of body armor with helmets, at least a dozen grenades, two H and K 9-millimeters, two Smith & Wesson .357s, and two H and K MP5 submachine guns—all with plenty of ammo."

"Anything else?"

"A Spooky gunship or a Super Cobra would be a nice addition."

"I'm sure they would," Prost said, and placed his notes down. "I know this may seem like mission impossible, but we really don't know how much resistance you'll encounter—if any. However, from past experience, I don't think you're going to be able to waltz in there and snatch him without some form of resistance."

Prost saw Jackie's concerned look.

"Anything else you can think of?" Hartwell asked her.

"Night vision goggles and binoculars—two of each."

"I'll have everything sent to Hong Kong."

Hartwell closed his folder and smiled. "Relax for the rest of the evening and enjoy Bangkok."

Taiwan Strait

The People's Liberation Army and Navy's six flotillas of submarines were preparing for imminent combat operations. Seventeen subs attached to three flotillas in the North Sea Fleet were joining the new Kilos from the East Sea Fleet opposite Taiwan. Two newly commissioned Mings from the South Sea Fleet were en route to the waters surrounding Taiwan. The attack submarines, both nuclear powered and diesel powered, provided the best chance of inflicting heavy damage on the U.S. carrier battle groups.

Compass Call

Three U.S. Air Force EC-130H information warfare aircraft were jamming Chinese military communications and vacuuming electronic data in the Taiwan Strait and along the coast of China from the South China Sea to the East China Sea. The aircraft's powerful computer let the crew jam enemy signals without affecting its own or other allied communications on nearby frequencies.

The Compass Call electronic warfare planes were causing bedlam with the Chinese missile firing exercises and live fire exercises in the strait. Although not required to fly directly over hostile territory, the closer the planes were to the enemy, the more jamming and collecting power they could generate. Because the jamming power decreases by the square of the distance between jammer and target, the aircraft were flying very close to the Chinese shoreline.

In fact, the three crews were inside the Asian Coastal Buffer Zone and had read the notices of danger or possible harm, including the following information on the aeronautical Operational Navigation Charts: WARNING—UNLISTED RADIO EMISSIONS FROM THIS AREA MAY CONSTITUTE A NAVIGATION HAZARD OR RESULT IN BORDER OVERFLIGHT UNLESS UNUSUAL PRECAUTION IS EXERCISED. CONSULT NOTAMS AND FLIGHT INFORMATION PUBLICATIONS FOR THE LATEST INFORMATION. The crews were also aware of the fact that they might be fired on without warning.

The highly valued Lockheed Hercules turboprops were considered so important to top military planners that the classified, closely guarded aircraft were always accompanied by fighter escorts when they were near hostile activity or inside a nonfree flying area.

If attacked by enemy interceptors, the EC-130H crew could jettison the large antennae mounted under the tail. Blowing the cheese cutter off the airplane would increase speed and maneuverability, but the big Hercules would still be easy pickings for an average fighter pilot.

Assigned to the 43rd Electronic Combat Squadron, the three Bats Compass Call aircraft were augmented by two Compass Call aircraft from the Scorpions of the 41st ECS. The 41st Hercs were covering the North Korean theater. Both squadrons operated as part of the Twelfth Air Force's 355th Wing at Davis-Monthan Air Force Base, Arizona.

The specialized aircraft also disrupted vital links between control facilities and antiaircraft weapons sites. Flying missions lasting as long as eighteen hours, which required aerial refueling, the aircraft could provide sustained jamming on a large number of frequencies simultaneously.

Compass Call exchanged information with other intelligence-gathering aircraft like the RC-135 Rivet Joint, which monitored the electromagnetic environment. Complementing the Compass Call aircraft, EC-130E Commando Solo psychological-warfare Hercules were used to capture enemy transmissions and insert false but believable data before retransmission. They could also monitor a wide variety of radio transmissions and television signals.

Major Chuck Burlingame, the Compass Call aircraft commander of Fresco 53, was flying a long racetrack pattern at twenty-five thousand feet extending from Hanjiang to Quanzhou when the Boeing E-3 AWACS radioed the first warning.

"Fresco Fifty-three, Big Eye has multiple targets closing from your five o'clock, ah . . . let's see—twenty-four miles, out of nineteen and climbing rapidly. They have to be fighters."

"Fresco Fifty-three," Burlingame said, then quickly checked with the flight leader of the four air force F-16s flying escort for the lumbering Hercules. "Razorback One, should we call for backup?"

"Stand by."

"Fifty-three," Burlingame radioed, and exchanged a cautious look with his copilot, Capt. Russ Spangler. "This doesn't sound good."

"Yeah, we need to get the fighters between us."

Twenty seconds of uncomfortable silence passed before Razorback One came up on the radio frequency being used for this mission.

"Fresco, we have two navy Hornets on the way," a voice said with an Arkansas drawl.

Burlingame keyed the radio. "Fifty-three."

"Razor Birds," the F-16 flight leader radioed, "let's arm 'em up."

"Two."

"Three."

"Four."

Some of the best fighter pilots in the world, the Viper wingmen were well prepared for any aerial engagement.

"Fresco Fifty-three, Big Eye with five more bandits from your two o'clock, nineteen miles, out of seventeen, climbing like a rocket."

"Great," Spangler said.

With the early morning sun to their left, Burlingame and Spangler anxiously searched for the targets to their right. They could see the runway at Luocheng, but the elusive jets were not visible at the moment.

The F-16s set up for an engagement and called for help from other air force and navy/Marine fighter planes in the immediate area.

The mission commander in the AWACS had seen enough. "Fresco Fifty-three, Big Eye recommends a heading of one-one-zero, now!"

Burlingame nodded to Spangler and smoothly banked the plane to the left. "I have the aircraft—you take the radios."

"Got 'em." The copilot adjusted his headset and microphone. *I have a bad feeling about this crap.*

"Fresco Fifty-three," Captain Spangler said with a suddenly dry mouth, "coming left to one-one-zero."

He looked at Burlingame and noticed the rising fear in the pilot's eyes, fear that Spangler had never seen before in the normally confident, quick-witted man.

"Fresco, Razorback One. Pick up the speed and head downhill as fast as you can pedal!"

"Fresco Fifty-three," Spangler said.

The aircraft commander added power and keyed the intercom. "This is Major Burlingame. Cease buzzer and secure all loose gear."

"Razorback One, Big Eye with more bandits at eight o'clock!"

"Razor copies."

Burlingame tensed and set maximum power on the engines. "Let's blow the cheese cutter."

Spangler keyed the radio. "Fresco Fifty-three is jettisoning the tail antenna in ten seconds."

"We're clear," Razorback lead replied, this time in a higher voice. "Let 'er go, Fresco."

The F-16 pilots saw the big rectangular antenna under the tail of the Hercules fly off and tumble out of sight. Seconds later, they turned to engage the Russian-built, Chinese-flown Sukhoi-27s.

The Chinese fighter planes were equipped with a 23mm gun, four air-to-air missiles, look-down/shoot-down radar with 130-nautical-mile search, and 100-nm track ranges. Capable of flying at speeds approaching Mach 2.3, the twin-tailed fighter has a combat radius of four hundred nautical miles. That was the upside for the Chinese air force.

The downside, according to the CIA director's annual report to the Senate Intelligence Committee, was the length and quality of training the Chinese fighter pilots received. Even the most skilled naturals generally flew only eighty to one hundred hours per year, some only fifty to sixty hours a year—not enough to be proficient in the deadly arena of aerial combat. If you finished second in a fighter plane, you'd have a high probability of being planted in the old boneyard.

Unlike most Western and European fighter pilots, who flew to the edge of the aircraft's performance envelope and their own flying ability, Chinese pilots stayed in the middle of their fighter's parameters. They were afraid of damaging or crashing their prized planes, an unforgivable act of recklessness in the eyes of their superiors.

Unfortunately for the PLA pilots, a typical Chinese Su-27 fighter jock was trained only in tail-chase intercepts against nonmaneuvering targets, a guaranteed way to waste his flying machine in a match with a U.S.-trained fighter pilot.

Therefore the Chinese pilots didn't have any idea what their Sukhoi-27s would really do, and they didn't know how far they could push themselves during a real dogfight. They would never entertain the idea of performing the cobra, a spectacular aerobatic/combat maneuver made famous by Russian test pilots.

From three directions, without even wavering, the eleven Sukhoi-27s merged on Fresco 53 and flew straight past the six U.S. fighters. The brief but violent clash initially cost the Chinese three aircraft and the air force an F-16 Viper, Razorback Two.

When an errant missile flew past his EC-130H, Burlingame banked the Hercules seventy degrees to the left and pulled two Gs. Seconds later, he unloaded the Gs and rolled the big plane to the right and lowered the nose to quickly build airspeed.

With such a concentrated attack on Fresco 53, it was only a matter of time before the giant turboprop would succumb to the assault. When bursts of 23mm rounds began ripping into the left wing, Burlingame rolled wings level at close to four hundred knots and then rolled the aircraft to the right and began pulling Gs. He unloaded the G-forces and violently leveled the wings, then abruptly pulled the nose up in a desperate attempt to save his crew.

A startled Chinese fighter pilot who was inverted and pulling into the Hercules reacted a half second too late. The Sukhoi-27 slammed into the top of Fresco-53's cockpit, causing a huge explosion that severed the nose from the rest of the fuselage. The wounded Hercules continued upward and over on its back, falling off the top of the perch into an inverted flat spin that sent it plunging into the Strait of Taiwan.

After the fur ball was over, China had lost five fighter planes and the United States was short three planes, including the EC-130H and her crew.

25

USS *Kitty Hawk* Battle Group

At 0905 hours the carrier's escorts, the cruiser USS *Cowpens* and the destroyer USS *Fife,* joined by the attack submarines SSN *Greeneville* and SSN *Seawolf,* began launching Tomahawk missiles at seven Chinese missile launch sites located deep in the Province of Jiangxi.

Escorts from the *Roosevelt* battle group followed with a second round of Tomahawks at 0914. Eight minutes later, the attack submarines SSN *Columbia* and SSN *Asheville* launched more Tomahawks at the Chinese missile sites and storage facilities between Shangrao and Ningdu.

In a matter of minutes, U.S. cruise missiles coming from various directions would be raining on China's missile infrastructure and selected satellite launch centers located in Jiuquan, Taiyuan, and Xichang.

At 0950, three B-52 bombers from Andersen Air Force Base, Guam, launched a total of six conventional cruise missiles from a position over the Bashi Channel between Taiwan and the Philippine island of Luzon. Seven minutes later, two other B-52 crews launched their cruise missiles at missile facilities at Tai-Hang and Wuzhai and then turned toward Guam.

Space-based assets immediately confirmed that the seven Chinese launch pads would not be used anytime in the near future, at least not for firing ballistic missiles over Taiwan. The destruction at the sites was complete and devastating.

F-14s and F/A-18s from *Kitty Hawk* and *Roosevelt* were

ying barrier combat air patrol over the Taiwan Strait while
veryone anxiously waited to see what would happen at the
mergency meeting of the ASEAN countries.

Bangkok, Thailand

1 an extraordinary reaction to security concerns, and to the
ertainty of violent anti-American demonstrations by groups
pposed to President Macklin's visit, the Thailand govern-
ıent strongly recommended changes in the president's
chedule and activities.

The senior Thai officials feared not only for Macklin but
is entire staff, his Secret Service agents, and the traveling
ress, who had no protection from the extremely militant
emonstrators. The government spokesman had made it
ighteningly clear to the Secret Service that the potential for
disaster was extremely high. The Thai authorities informed
enior U.S. officials about the thousands of e-mail threats
ıade against the president.

Responding to the warning, the Secret Service convinced
resident Macklin that the ASEAN meeting and the summit
ith Chinese president Liu Fan-ding should be restricted to
ıe hotel. With tensions rising by the minute between the
'nited States and China, the special agents didn't want the
resident to be exposed to rowdy crowds or possible traffic
ıms. The environment was just too unpredictable, the odds
f something happening in a motorcade too great, to leave
ıything to chance.

Before Macklin left Washington, a meeting room in the
'usit Thani that was capable of accommodating two thou-
ınd people was converted to a palatial conference room that
eflected traditional Thai influences.

An informal lunch hosted by the original ten countries that
ɔunded ASEAN was boycotted by the Chinese delegation
fter news of the U.S.-China military confrontation flashed
ıroughout the world. To the leaders of ASEAN nations, it
as another ominous sign of things to come.

The official gathering in the meeting room turned frosty when President Liu Fan-ding, wearing a bland dark-gray Mao-style suit, and his aides entered the large room. Gone was the Western-style suit and tie. Also missing was the constant rubbery smile and self-deprecating jokes that had been his persona during his first visit to Washington, D.C.

The always smiling, overanimated Liu Fan-ding at the White House state dinner was now the scowling, crimson faced communist dictator of Red China. This was the man who had recently stood on a stage in the Forbidden City and promised more than six hundred thousand Chinese that he would make China powerful beyond their dreams.

To solidify his own immortality and legacy, he vowed to reunify Taiwan with the motherland and blasted America's post-cold-war dominance of military power and money. After the rambling speech, Liu watched thousands of military men and female civil militia troops goose-step across Tiananmen Square.

Later the Chinese president beamed as four Dong Feng-31 solid-fuel ICBMs rolled past the hushed crowd, while helicopters and a formation of Su-27 fighters screamed low overhead. The Dong Feng (East Wind) ballistic missile had the range to reach American shores.

Within hours of the speech and the military parade, President Liu Fan-ding was quoted in the *People's Liberation Army Daily* as saying, "The Macklin Administration is trying to intimidate China and her people. I will teach the intimidators in Washington a tough lesson."

When he finished introducing the panel members, the gracious host of the Thailand delegation somberly introduced the American secretary of state. Throughout the huge room, there was the sense of an impending disaster that they knew would doom the summit.

Wearing one of his usual rumpled, oversized suits, Bret Shannon rose from his chair and walked to the elevated podium. Known to be a man who never minced words, the portly Shannon shoved his eyeglasses up and stared for a few seconds at the large audience. His job was to make a broad

tatement about the reason for the emergency summit and
en leave the howitzer shells to the president.

Secretary Shannon, a man who almost never laughed and
eldom smiled, gave Liu Fan-ding an icy look and then cast
is gaze over the anxious ASEAN members.

"We are gathered here today," Shannon began in a rich
aritone voice that cut through the damp air, "because China
s at a crossroad in her long and sometimes troubled history.
fter more than fifty years of Mao's revolution and more than
venty years of reform, it's time for the Chinese people to
ake a decision about their future. The path she elects to take
ill have a profound impact on all of us, including our
iends from Taiwan. As the younger generation clamors for
e downfall of communism, the dictators in Beijing must in-
reasingly play the role of politicians to the masses of Chi-
ese people."

The startled translator was trying to water down the rhet-
ric, but the message was clearly registering with the irate
hinese president.

"The other side of the coin is a treacherous journey of pla-
ating the communist hard-liners who are becoming di-
osaurs in the postideological era. At some point Beijing
ust become a welcome and responsible member of the
orld community—as Taiwan is—or China will return to the
ast."

The growing sense of uneasiness was pervasive.

"If China remains closed to the world, her economy will
lowly crumble and evaporate her aspirations of ever becom-
g a great power. It's the autocrats' choice, but time is run-
ing out on the decomposing remains of the communist
ystem. Communism is a failed experiment on our planet, a
ad relic of yesteryear."

Liu Fan-ding was livid when he rose to address the Amer-
an secretary of state. "I am warning you," the translator said
ith a startled look, "that any more harping on China or Tai-
an or how we run our country will lead to an armed con-
ict!"

The piercing vocal threat to the United States caused a

loud buzz throughout the meeting room. Before Shannon ha
a chance to respond, President Macklin rose and walked t
the podium.

"I'll take it from here," the president said as he gently pa
ted Shannon on the shoulder.

"President Fan-ding, we're already in an armed conflic
with your country. As for Taiwan, the United States stand
firm in our resolve to defend a valued ally. You and the othe
leaders in Communist China are on notice that any attempt t
take over Taiwan by force will be met with overwhelming re
sistance. You and your colleagues should come to your sense
before bombs and missiles take the place of diplomacy an
statesmanship."

The antagonistic Chinese leader bristled and said some
thing under his breath to an aide.

Macklin cast a glance at two staff members who were pre
pared to show the visual aids he had brought with him.

The American president looked unusually relaxed an
calm. "I'm going to show our friends in the Association o
Southeast Asian Nations why we're concerned about China
goals and ambitions. Let's have exhibit number one."

On a large easel, they placed a huge reproduction of a pho
tograph taken by a U.S. space-based asset.

"Ladies and gentlemen, you're looking at a laser bea
emitting from a *civilian* Chinese cargo ship, the *Chen Ziyan*,
which was retrofitted to carry the laser weapon. We also hav
video of the laser beam when it was fired at a U.S. plane fly
ing near the coast of California."

"This is American hoax," Liu said bluntly. "Nothing b
trick to make China look bad!"

Silence filled the cavernous room.

"Gentlemen, let's skip number two and three and move o
to number four," Macklin instructed in an even voice.

The enlarged photos were placed on the easel.

"Here we have a set of four photos taken on board th
Chen Ziyang, the *civilian* ship in question."

Liu Fan-ding turned ashen-faced. He started mumblin
something unintelligible to a staff member.

In a steady, calm voice, President Macklin continued. "We know from the Chinese writing on the laser weapon and in the control room, plus the Chinese sailor smiling in the pictures, that the photos are real."

Macklin paused and stared straight at the Chinese leader. "President Liu Fan-ding knows it too."

"Lies—all lies! American trickery and lies!" Liu said acidly. He rose and turned on his heel to leave. "These are all lies to diminish China's sovereignty in the eyes of world leaders!" he said to the American president as he left the room.

Stunned silent at first, many of the ASEAN members turned to each other. After the Chinese delegation stormed out of the conference room, the concerned ASEAN members began talking.

Macklin raised his arms to quiet the shocked leaders and their assorted entourages. "Ladies and gentlemen, please be calm. Those who are standing, please take your seats."

Hartwell Prost leaned close to Brett Shannon. "Well, that was certainly handled smoothly."

"Short and to the point was what the president wanted." Shannon calmly gathered his papers. "At least the world will get to see what Beijing has been up to."

"Yes, and we better go to a higher alert status."

"We're already there."

The President's Suite

Dark wood paneling, elegant silk upholstered furnishings, and authentic Thai art pieces and paintings by local artists decorated the plush suite. The lavish bar was fully stocked with top-of-the-line spirits, and fresh fruit and colorful flowers adorned the sitting room.

The ASEAN summit had been salvaged, for the most part, when President Macklin presented all the facts and information about China's secret laser weapons and what Beijing had been doing with them.

He had also explained to the delegation about the Panama

Canal and its current status under U.S. control. The Chinese military forces had been completely disarmed by elements of the U.S. Army and the U.S. Marine Corps while air force, navy, and Marine fighter planes orbited overhead. The Chinese officers and their troops were now incarcerated in seven holding pens awaiting transportation home.

The vast majority of leaders from the ASEAN countries agreed to join together in trying to diplomatically persuade President Liu Fan-ding to stand down from military operations in or near the Strait of Taiwan. They secretly prayed that President Macklin would temper his approach to China, but no one wanted to antagonize the most powerful nation in the world. No ASEAN leader openly wanted to voice the suggestion.

After a formal but subdued dinner and a short play by a Taiwanese touring company, Macklin and his closest confidants gathered in the president's suite.

Drinks were poured and cigars lighted when a senior military aide to Macklin was hurriedly ushered into the elegant room. The officer conferred with the president for about five minutes, answered a few questions from Macklin, and then quietly left the suite.

Continuing his conversation with his aides and advisers, the president patiently waited until nearly everyone had finished his or her drink to rise and suggest that it was time to call it an evening.

"Folks, we'll be leaving for Washington at a very early hour, so I'm going to have to retire. Thank you for your support and hard work. You've done a superb job under stressful circumstances, and I greatly appreciate it."

Macklin tossed back the rest of his Chivas and soda. "I'll see you folks in the morning."

Within a matter of thirty seconds, they had all finished the last of their drinks, placed the empty glasses on the bar, and said good-night to Macklin.

"Hartwell," the president said, "I'd like to have a word with you, if you don't mind."

"Yes, sir." Prost gently shut the door when the last person

left. "You need a fresh one?" Hartwell asked as he headed for the bar.

"Sure, thanks."

The president sat down on the sofa, removed his shoes, and wearily propped his feet on a stack of briefing folders. "The *Roosevelt* group just had another run-in with the Chinese."

"What's the situation?" Hartwell handed Macklin his Scotch and soda and sat down in a chair facing the president.

"Another round of missiles from three different locations in China heavily damaged our frigate *Kauffman* and the Australian guided missile destroyer *Brisbane*."

"What about our Aegis ships? How did the missiles get through?"

"The Aegis system worked well, but two missiles managed to evade the protective cover—don't know the technicalities of the situation."

"Casualties?"

"Six deaths confirmed on our ship and two on the *Brisbane*."

Saddened and feeling a growing sense of uneasiness, Hartwell looked at the president. "What condition are the ships in?"

"I don't know, but they're under way. The frigate is going to Yokosuka and the destroyer is returning to Australia."

"What kind of response do you want?"

"Since the attack, we've sunk four of their patrol boats and the *Haizhou*. It's one of the three *Sovremmennyy*-class guided-missile destroyers the Russians sold them. The destroyers were assigned to the East Sea Fleet to intimidate Taiwan."

"Are you going to target the new launch sites?"

"Oh, yes—they'll be history by sunrise."

Prost stared at his drink and mentally juggled all the possible things that could go wrong with the China-U.S. show-down.

"Hartwell, how far do we go before this mess becomes a declared war?"

"Sir, as you well know, during our struggle with Vietnam

we *never* officially declared war on the country—not formally or officially—but it's still called the Vietnam War."

"I know, but do we wait for another World Trade Center?"

"More like San Francisco or Los Angeles," Hartwell said, uneasy with the escalation of attacks and counterattacks. "As far as I can tell, Liu is totally unpredictable. We could be in serious trouble if we've miscalculated."

"How about if we remove him?" Macklin slowly sipped his Scotch. "Take him out?"

Prost studied the president for a long moment. "Sir, with all due respect, that is not a course of action I would recommend. Besides, the next dictator might make Liu Fan-ding look like Mother Theresa."

"Well, you do have a point."

"That's why it's so important to rescue Richard Cheung. Dalton and Sullivan must succeed in their mission. We have to know the capabilities of the Chinese lasers and how many they can field. We can't risk having our nukes shot down en route to their targets."

"As usual, you're right. But in the meantime, we're going to stand firm where Beijing is concerned."

"You have my vote."

The Pentagon

Air Force general Les Chalmers and his Joint Chiefs of Staff were concerned about Chinese early-warning radars around many of the missile launch sites. The radars helped to integrate the air defenses and needed to be alleviated. At 10:22 A.M. Washington time, a U.S. electronic intelligence-gathering satellite obtained an extremely accurate fix on the radar complexes.

Minutes later, Chalmers was handed a highly classified message by an aide. He quickly read it.

"We have them pinpointed," he said to the other four-star generals and admirals around the table. "Lets get a U-2 over them ASAP."

An air force brigadier general immediately contacted Beale Air Force Base, California, and instructed the pilot of a U-2 over the Strait of Taiwan to fly over Communist China and photograph the radar sites. Coordinates were transmitted to the pilot of the spy plane as he flew westbound toward the coast of China.

Once the U-2 was finished with the photo run, the data was transmitted straight to Beale AFB. After the information was confirmed and analyzed for precise coordinates of the radar sites, the target information was transferred to the Pentagon and then sent to the commander of the U.S. Pacific Fleet.

In Hawaii, the four-star admiral and his staff had been nervously waiting for the message from Washington. He immediately passed the orders to his type commanders.

Four minutes later General Chalmers and the joint chiefs received confirmation from the units that would execute the attack.

"The Tomahawks have been programmed," Chalmers said. "By the time we finish lunch, the radar sites and some of the missile sites will be a junkman's dream."

26

En Route to Hong Kong, China

Jackie and Scott were going over the final details of their upcoming operation when the chartered Dassault Falcon 50 jet began descending. The flight from Bangkok had been more than bumpy at times, but the Thai pilots had managed to work their way around most of the severe thunderstorms.

Scott glanced out the window as they flew through a heavy rain shower, and then turned to Jackie. "After the demo, we'll secure the helicopter for the night and make sure the jet and the helo are topped off with fuel, and then we'll check into our hotel. We'll wait there until after dark to make our way back to the airport and preflight the helicopter."

"Sounds good," she said, and looked at her briefing folder. "According to the map, it's just a short walk to the hotel."

"Looks like it." Scott thumbed through his aeronautical charts. "When we request permission to take off, we'd better fly southeast about ten to twelve miles before we turn the exterior lights off. Then we'll turn off the transponder and head north to Mianyang."

She rotated the round metal wheel of her small, pocket-size aviation computer. "Let's see, it's going to be about eighty-five to ninety miles from that point. We'll call it thirty-five, say, forty minutes to the grass field near the complex."

"That's about right." He studied the detailed aeronautical charts for the area around Chengdu and then turned his attention to the recently opened Mianyang Nanjiao Airport. The civilian airport was near Jiuzhaigou, one of the most popular tourist attractions in China.

"We're going to have to be careful around the new airport at Mianyang."

She nodded. "True, but we have to worry about getting there first. We need two ingress plans—one for good weather and another if we have to hug the ground."

Jackie looked at the charts. "Why don't we file IFR to Chongqing? When we clear the ridge, we'll cancel. That will put high terrain between us and Chengdu most of the way to Mianyang."

Chengdu was in a valley with an average elevation of 1,660 feet. Mountainous terrain to the northwest rapidly rose to a height of almost 21,000 feet. Fifteen miles to the southeast of Chengdu a narrow elevation of land nearly ninety miles long extended from fifty miles south to forty miles northeast of the city. The tops of the ridges ranged from 3,300 feet to nearly 3,700 feet.

Scott turned the chart and ran his finger along the ridge leading to Mianyang. "If the weather cooperates, that's a great idea. But if the weather turns sour, we'll have to stay on the west side of the ridge and follow the railroad to Mianyang."

Jackie pointed to the vast number of rice fields in the sparsely populated area. "The other side of the ridge gives us a better chance to arrive at Mianyang without being noticed by anyone, including the controllers at the new airport."

"That's a great plan if the weather's clear, but if we're in the clag and the GPS goes down, we're cooked—finished. We can't risk groping around in the dark trying to find Mianyang. We need to remain visual and follow the railroad up there."

She thought about it for a few moments. "Okay, let's be flexible and have two different flight plans to Mianyang—behind the ridge if the weather's good and following the railroad if the weather tanks."

"Sounds reasonable to me."

The landing gear dropped out of the Falcon's wheel wells and thumped into place. The pilot pulled the throttles to flight idle and rapidly increased his rate of descent.

"I just hope Hartwell's info on Cheung's location is correct," Scott said. He studied the map of the area surrounding the Mianyang complex. Next he turned his attention to the high-resolution commercial imagery provided by Space Imaging, Inc. The panchromatic satellite pictures of the secretive complex were extremely sharp and clear. "If it turns out to be heavily guarded, we're in trouble."

Jackie flipped through the pages of her folder. "It says the complex is guarded, but the housing area where Cheung is supposedly kept is totally enclosed by a high chain link fence. No mention of guards."

"What would keep Cheung, or any other detainee, from cutting through the fence and escaping?"

"A guard, or guards—maybe it's an electric fence."

"We'll know soon enough." Scott closed his folder and examined the various ships plying the waters of the South China Sea. "How's the Agusta cramming coming along?"

"No problem."

"Seriously?"

"I mean it. I have everything I need to know memorized. You've flown one, you've flown 'em all."

"*Need* to know," he said with a smile. "That would be category-one information, right?"

"That's correct. *Want* to know is category-two information, and who gives a rat's patootie is category-three info."

"Well put, my dear."

Jackie leaned close to him. "Something's bothering you—what is it?"

"I don't know. I just have an uneasy feeling."

"We don't have to do this, you know."

He rubbed his chin. "It's probably just anxiety from sitting around thinking about the unknowns."

"That'll do it every time."

"It'll go away as soon as we get started. It always does, at least for me, when I kick the tires and light the fires."

"Yeah, when you're scaring the hell out of yourself, you don't have time for self-doubt or introspection—just pure survival mode."

"You got it." Scott watched the container vessels and cargo ships rapidly grow larger as the tri-engine Falcon 50 approached Chek Lap Kok Hong Kong International Airport and marine terminal. Located on a 4.82-square-mile island outside the urban corridor, CLK is a key international freight hub for aircraft and cargo ships.

They remained quiet as the Falcon touched down, rolled out to a safe speed, turned off the runway, and taxied to the Hong Kong Business Aviation Centre on the south side of the airport. The pilot brought the sleek jet to a smooth stop in front of China's first business-aviation support center.

Jackie and Scott used their bogus credentials and passports to clear customs and immigration, and then they were approached by their contact from the Agency.

The tall American male was dressed in an airline pilot's uniform and introduced himself as Bob Smith. He had been briefed and was shown their photos only three hours before they arrived.

"Let's take a walk," Bob said. The trio headed back to the expansive aircraft parking area.

"This isn't my usual role," Bob admitted. "We've had some unusual . . . ah, circumstances that weren't factored in."

"Like what?" Jackie asked.

"Everything is okay, but your jet—the Learjet—is still at Shanghai's Hongqiao Airport."

"When is it going to be back?" Scott asked.

"We're not exactly sure. They had to change an engine part—I don't know what the hell it was. The replacement parts were shipped to Pudong International, Shanghai's newest airport. It's taken a while to get things sorted out, but the pilot said they should be here by early tomorrow afternoon."

Scott looked at Jackie. "I told you I had an uneasy feeling."

"I have the VIP lounge reserved for you. You can stay in there until your instructor arrives. He'll be back in about fifteen to twenty minutes."

"Sounds good," Jackie said, glancing at the low-lying mountains behind the Hong Kong Business Aviation Centre. "Is the helicopter here?"

"Ah, yes—it's in the hangar along with the, ah, supplies you requested. They're inside the helicopter and need to be camouflaged."

"Well, that's certainly good news," she replied. "Scott, let's check with Hartwell and see how this delay is going to affect the operation."

"You eyeball the flying machine and I'll work on camouflaging our *supplies*," Scott suggested. "I'll get in touch with Hartwell later."

"Whatever."

"Oh, a couple of other things," Bob said. "Since the Learjet and the helicopter are based here, and we have the fix in, you won't have to get landing permits—just the usual paperwork and flight plans."

"Great," Jackie said. "We appreciate it."

"No problem. You have reservations at the Grand Hyatt, and I'll be leaving you at this point. Whatever you're doing, good luck."

"Thanks," Jackie and Scott said, and then shook hands with Bob. The tall stranger walked to a waiting taxi and never looked back.

When Jackie and Scott entered the nearly spotless hangar, they were impressed with the gleaming orange-and-white Agusta A109E Power helicopter. The medevac interior included room for two patients, two medical technicians, and a pilot.

He picked two large canvas bags out of their luggage and loaded the weapons, grenades, body armor, helmets, extra ammo, night vision goggles, and the binoculars into them. Surveying the area for anyone or anything that looked suspicious, Scott locked the bags and concealed them in the back of the helicopter.

From the pages of the Agusta training manuals, Jackie had learned a lot about the powerful twin-engine helicopter with the innovative four-bladed main rotor system. Equipped with 640 shaft horsepower Pratt & Whitney Canada free-turbine engines, the EMS helicopter could hover on one engine, cruise at 150–155 knots, and had a range of more than five hundred statute miles, depending on the winds and fuel burn.

An optional SX-5 Starburst searchlight had been mounted on the helicopter. The installation limited the never-exceed speed to 140 knots.

While she was conducting an introductory preflight on the sleek helicopter, Jackie's instructor walked up and introduced himself to her. The retired former U.S. Coast Guard helicopter pilot would prove to be friendly and very skilled in the art of teaching.

Unable to reach Hartwell Prost, Scott joined Jackie and her instructor while the Agusta was being rolled out of the hangar. After introductions, Scott quietly took Jackie aside.

"Hartwell is in a meeting with the president. I'll try again after I check into the Hyatt, but I have to tell you that I have some reservations about this operation."

"So do I. Why don't you take the rest of our bags and check in to the hotel. When I get there, we'll discuss the overall picture and see if we're comfortable enough to continue."

"Yeah, we need to think through this." He glanced at the brightly painted helicopter. "Be careful."

"Always."

Beijing, China

President Liu Fan-ding, enraged over his humiliating experience in Bangkok, had called an urgent meeting of select Communist Party leaders. The men had gathered in secret within the confines of the Zhongnanhai, the sprawling estate that is considered China's contemporary Forbidden City and is located next to the original golden-roofed Forbidden City.

Following Liu Fan-ding's inflammatory remarks, top leaders met in private meetings of *xiao zu* (small groups) to discuss the dangerous standoff with the United States. The code of secrecy and loyalty among the men and their staffs was so intense that only a few individuals knew about the clandestine meetings.

To preserve the appearance of unity and harmony, the party leaders were accustomed to keeping their personal preferences and opinions well hidden. If there was dissension among them, the men kept it to themselves. They reached their decisions in private, with only cursory consideration of public opinion.

This occasion was no different. Even though China's immediate future was in jeopardy, the hostility between Beijing and Washington had become intractable. The bitterness was aggravated by China's intense lust for reunification with Taiwan and Washington's vow to intervene on behalf of Taipei.

After two hours of strenuous discussions and arguments, the decision was made, and it immediately disappeared behind the mysterious veil of official Beijing secrecy. Disregarding their personal concerns and grave reservations, the individual members of the Politburo reluctantly gave the flawed decision their seal of approval.

Liu Fan-ding had persuaded party leaders that it was time to call President Macklin's bluff—before the United States had time to complete the rebuilding of its downsized military and strengthen Taiwan's forces.

The People's Liberation Army was immediately granted permission to seize the renegade province of Taiwan before Taipei or Washington could implement a missile defense perimeter. The months of planning, stockpiling equipment and missiles, and staging warships, landing craft, airplanes, and soldiers was about to climax in the invasion of Taiwan.

Although China could seriously damage Taiwan, conventional wisdom concluded that Beijing didn't have the capability to make an opposed landing with amphibious forces. It would be even more difficult with American forces aiding Taipei.

Those logical conclusions were overlooked in Liu Fan-ding's fervor to rule Taiwan.

Grand Hyatt Hong Kong, China

Scott was admiring the magnificent view of Victoria Harbor just before sunset when Jackie gently knocked. He rose from his chair, then walked to the door and opened it.

"They wouldn't give me a—"

"Here, I have a key for each of us."

"Thanks."

"How'd it go?"

"It went very well," she said with a great deal of exuber-ance. "It's an easy ship to fly. I can't believe how much power has—it's like a rocket ship with rotor blades."

"Sounds like fun," Scott said, and motioned toward the sun-set. "Not a bad view, huh?

"It's beautiful, absolutely incredible."

"You want to change and go out for dinner?"

"Actually, I'd prefer to have a quiet dinner in the hotel and en take a long, hot bath—just relax."

"That sounds like a plan."

"Did you get in touch with Hartwell?"

"Not yet."

"Well, I'll change into something more comfortable," she id, turning toward the bedroom. "We'll try Hartwell later."

"Hurry—maybe we can catch the sunset."

"Ninety seconds."

The E-4B Advanced Airborne Command Post

he airplane was over Arizona when President Macklin walked to the conference/briefing room. Hartwell Prost and Brett hannon could see the anger in Macklin's eyes.

The latest intelligence reports painted a vivid picture of a angerous flashpoint developing in the Taiwan Strait. From all dications, China was about to launch an invasion to capture aiwan. U.S. forces and Taiwanese forces in the area were on gh alert. Many of the Southeast Asian allies were diverting eir warships to aid Taiwan.

SecDef Pete Adair and air force general Les Chalmers were n secure phones in the White House Situation Room.

Macklin sat down and punched the button for the remote peaker. "Pete, Les, can you hear me?"

"Yessir, Mr. President," they said at the same time.

"I've been over your plans and I completely agree with yo
As soon as Beijing fires the first volley, I want to put a lid o
this so fast they won't know what hit them—otherwise th
could escalate completely out of control in a matter of hours

"We have most of what we need in place," Pete Adair sai
looking at the current status board. "And we have more asse
en route."

"Excellent. Les?"

"Yes, sir."

"I don't want to leave us exposed anywhere else in the wor
but I'd sure like to have as many bombers as you can spare

"They're on the way, sir."

"Okay," Macklin said, glancing at the latest situation repo
from the Pentagon. "I'll see you in a couple of hours."

Hong Kong

After a sumptuous dinner of Peking duck, Jackie soaked in
hot bubble bath for twenty minutes and then joined Scott in t
living room.

"Feel better?"

"Like a new woman." She sat on the couch next to him. "I
cidentally, the helo is on its way to Chengdu. If the weath
holds, it will be there early in the morning."

"Good—at least something is going right."

"For a change."

"While you were soaking, I finally made contact wi
Hartwell—they were over New Mexico."

"What's the latest?"

"Well, he seemed a little detached, but he said everythi
was set for tomorrow night."

"He probably has jet lag."

"Or major problems with China."

"Let's discuss the Mianyang op," she said. "What do yo
really think our chances will be—the probability factor?"

"It's going to be a long shot—at best."

"What's your main concern?"

"All the unknowns," he said with a frown. "In this type of
[sit]uation, we're going to have to evaluate each step as we take
[it.] If it doesn't look right, we call it off—that's it."

"No argument here," she said. "If either one of us feels un-
[co]mfortable—at any time—we get out of Dodge. Agreed?"

"That's the way I see it. No heroics this time, just common
[se]nse."

She laughed. "That'll be the day."

The Situation Room

[Ge]neral Les Chalmers and Pete Adair were waiting when the
[pr]esident entered the room, followed by Hartwell Prost and
[Br]ett Shannon. As usual, Macklin's Secret Service agents qui-
[etl]y left the room when he sat down at the large conference
[tab]le.

"What do we know?" the president asked, looking at Adair.

"It's imminent—they've telegraphed everything but the
[lau]nch time."

"Brett, is there anything else diplomatically we can do—any
[wa]y to shock Beijing into reality?"

"Sir, I've tried everything I can think of. Our folks have
[ple]aded with everyone from Washington to Beijing."

Shannon took a deep breath and plunged on. "Mr. President,
[if] you would personally contact Liu Fan-ding, we might have
[a c]hance of stopping this madness."

"I'll give it a try." Without hesitation, Macklin initiated the
[cal]l and talked with three screeners before he was told the Chi-
[ne]se president was not available. Keeping his anger and dis-
[ap]pointment to himself, the president placed the phone down.

"Well, gentlemen, they're determined to risk it all, and I'm
[de]termined to stop them in their tracks. We will not use any
[am]biguous language, and we'll stand by the Taiwan Relations
[Ac]t of 1979. Any questions?"

The room remained silent.

27

Chek Lap Kok Airport

The engines on the white Learjet 35A were still war
when Scott began his preflight walk-around. Although it a
rived late from Shanghai, the freshly painted jet was in pri
tine condition.

Dressed in a stylish, conservative business suit, Scott mo
itored the refueling while Jackie checked the weather and fil
an instrument flight plan to the Shuangliu Airport ne
Chengdu, China. She was attired in black slacks and sho
white uniform shirt with four gold stripes on her shoulders, a
gold wings above the breast pocket of her shirt.

When Jackie joined Scott at the entrance to the Learjet, sl
handed him the latest weather update. "The forecast sa
rain—lots of rain—in the Chengdu area for the next twel
hours or more."

"Great, just what we need."

She made her way to the copilot's seat while Dalton enter
the jet and locked the cabin door.

"It looks like we're going to have to use the railroad plar
he said.

"I'm afraid so." She opened the large chart case and e
tracted the IFR en-route high-altitude charts and instrument a
proach plates for Shuangliu Airport. "There are four airpo
surrounding Chengdu, so we're going to have to be very car
ful—don't want to embarrass ourselves by landing at t
wrong airport."

"I just hope we can understand the controllers."

"Unfortunately," she said with a smile, "Chinese isn't one
f the languages I speak."

"Not to worry," Scott said, and handed her the checklist.
We'll make it up as we go—the old walk-in plan."

"Walk into the bank and then plan how you're going to rob
?"

"You have the gist of it."

A few minutes later, they taxied away from the Hong Kong
usiness Aviation Centre. Approaching the runway, Jackie
witched to the control-tower frequency and requested per-
ission to take off.

With the clearance granted, Scott lined up on the centerline
f the runway and advanced the throttles. At 1:02 P.M. local
me, the Learjet lifted off for the flight to Chengdu, the
ustling-bustling provincial capital of Sichuan. A nightlife city
nergized by tens of thousands of foreign and Chinese tourists,
hengdu is world famous for its cuisines featuring unique
lends of peppers and spices.

Located in the fertile Ch'eng-tu Plain, the busy city of mil-
ons has always been an important communication center.
oted for its historical remains and cultural activities, Chengdu
 adjacent to the Yangtze River (Changjiang) and its tributar-
s, the Min Chiang and T'o Chiang, which extend throughout
e Sichuan Basin and beyond.

The Chengdu Shuangliu Airport is a colossal, well-
anicured garden. It remains green year round, with thousands
f trees and sweet-scented flowers adding color to the beauti-
l scenery.

Considering the change in the time zone between Hong
ong and Chengdu, Scott expected to arrive at the Shuangliu
irport at 1:58 P.M. The only problems they had encountered
 far were a couple of controllers who didn't understand En-
lish very well.

As they began their approach to the Shuangliu Airport, the
eather rapidly began to deteriorate. They descended into
ark clouds and steady rain. Scott flew a smooth instrument
pproach to an uneventful landing. During the rollout, he saw
ree jet fighters parked at the far end of the terminal ramp. The

warplanes seemed incongruous with the lush grounds and th
beautiful flowers.

"What are MiG-21s doing here?" he asked.

She innocently smiled. "Actually, they happen to be Jian
F-7s."

Scott gave her a blank look. "I've never heard of them

"The Chengdu Aircraft Industrial Corporation—that's
mouthful—is licensed to build them."

"Okay, I'll bite." He turned onto the taxiway and shut dow
one engine. "How did you know that little tidbit of trivia?

She contacted ground control. "When I was checking th
weather and the airport particulars, out flowed all th
chamber-of-commerce info."

He chuckled. "Well, as far as I'm concerned, I would b
much happier if we weren't flying from an airfield with j
fighters sitting on it."

They parked close to the bright orange-and-white Agus
and shut down the other engine.

Scott grabbed two dark-green raincoats out of their equip
ment bag and handed one to Jackie. They slipped into them an
stepped out of the Learjet to greet the line service represent
tives. A large black car entered the ramp area and stopped ne
the helicopter.

Dalton ordered fuel for the plane and then followed Jacki
to the Russian-made Volga. The shiny, chauffeur-driven c
contained the two Medical Flight Service executives and the
interpreter, a young Chinese woman with short hair and h
morless eyes.

When the trio stepped out of the car and opened their un
brellas, Jackie and Scott detected an obvious aloofness in the
demeanor. The Chinese businessmen, both of whom we
short and trim, stopped about five feet from the Americans an
kept their hands in their pockets. Scott elected not to exten
his hand and place everyone in an awkward situation.

"We are pleased to meet you," Scott said. "I'm Barto
Rutherford, senior vice president of international sales, and th
is Lauren Isaacs, our chief pilot."

The two men merely nodded and spoke to their inter-
eter.

"Is it safe to fly today?" the woman with the dull eyes asked.

"I'll have to defer to our demonstration pilot, one of the very
st," Scott said, and glanced at Jackie.

"Yes, it's safe," she replied with a courteous smile. *This
ould be interesting.* "We have about a four-hundred-foot ceil-
g, so we can stay under the clouds."

The men conferred with their interpreter. She spoke slowly
d deliberately to Scott and Jackie. "Their time is extremely
mited. Fifteen minutes is all they can spare."

"That's fine," Jackie said. *We'll keep it to ten minutes.*

Holding an umbrella over the interpreter's head, Scott
lped everyone board the Agusta while Jackie gave the heli-
pter a thorough check before climbing aboard. The Chinese
ecutives sat in the two seats designed for the medical tech-
cians; Scott and the interpreter occupied the temporary seats
ljacent to the two litters.

The flight was a short, uncomfortable affair characterized by
total lack of enthusiasm on the part of the prospective buyers.
he Chinese didn't ask any questions and they didn't respond
Scott's sales pitch or to Jackie's friendly inputs.

After Jackie landed the Agusta, the reticent executives
ened their umbrellas and went straight to their Volga, while
eir interpreter turned to Scott.

"They will be in touch," she said to him, and turned to
ckie. "Thank you for your consideration and patience."

"You're very welcome."

The interpreter walked to the car and got in. Jackie and Scott
ood in the rain, smiling and waving. They talked without
oving their mouths.

"That went exceedingly well," she said.

"Oh, yeah." Scott watched the Volga drive off. "We're at-
mpting to sell these people a helicopter while both countries
e in each other's face—great timing for us."

"It does seem crazy."

"Yeah, I'm amazed that we haven't been taken into custody."

"Don't even think it," Jackie said. "We played our roles an
now it's over—move on to our other 'project.'"

"I'm just glad we're not real salespeople—we'd starve t
death."

"For sure." She looked at the hotel. "Let's get checked i
and get an update from Hartwell."

"Ah, first we have to top off the jet and the helicopter an
take care of the fuel bill."

"You do the fuel thing," she said with a smile. "I'll chec
us in to the hotel and contact Hartwell."

"Deal."

"See you in a few minutes." She headed toward the Learj
to get their bags and put on the engine covers.

During the short walk to the hotel, Jackie was surprised b
the throngs of bicycle riders and their wildly colored rain gea
The steady stream of bright colors was offset by the stone face
and unfriendly looks.

"This isn't good." Jackie pulled the hood of her rainco;
over her wet hair and cast her eyes down at the sidewalk. *Wh*
a time for a covert operation in China.

Taiwan Strait

By midafternoon the tension was manifest on both sides of th
strait. This was not going to be a sneak attack in the middle (
the night. From all indications, the Chinese were going t
mount an old-fashioned frontal assault on Taiwan—a head-
down, charge-the-line melee.

Taiwanese F-16s, Mirage 2000s, and F-5s patrolled th
strait while U.S. Navy and Marine Corps carrier-based fighte
planes provided backup. The F-14s and F/A-18s also supporte
the E-2C Hawkeye, and the S-3B Viking and SH-60 subma
rine hunter/killers. If needed, the air wing aboard the supe
carrier *Stennis* was prepared and ready for combat.

F-15 and F-16 fighters watched over four U.S. Air For
intelligence-gathering and information-warfare aircraft. Th

ring flight crews were making it very difficult, if not im-
ossible, for Chinese leaders to communicate with their mili-
ry commanders in the field and those who were at sea.

Joining the two U.S. carrier battle groups, the attack sub-
arines SSN *Louisville* and SSN *Helena* would provide addi-
onal firepower while they tracked two extremely lethal
hinese destroyers. The Russian-made warships carried su-
ersonic, nuclear-tipped antiship cruise missiles.

United States Air Force E-3 AWACS, KC-10s, KC-135s,
-52s, B-1Bs, and B-2s were in the air or standing by at vari-
us airbases, including Hickam Air Force Base, Hawaii; An-
ersen Air Force Base, Guam; and Kadena Air Base, Japan
Okinawa). Closer to the narrow strait, F-15s, F-16s, and F-
17s were ready to augment the carrier-based assets.

Over the coastline of China, from Songcheng to Fuzhou to
hinmen, a mixture of Su-27s, MiG-17s, MiG-19s, and MiG-
1s flew in thirteen different holding patterns. Inland, aerial
nkers and AWACS aircraft circled in oblong patterns. Far be-
w and out to sea, the entire length of the Taiwan Strait was
acked with Chinese destroyers, frigates, landing craft, and
upport vessels.

Without warning, China launched an opening salvo of
ort- and medium-range missiles from ships and shore in-
allations. The missiles were aimed at two main southern Tai-
anese ports and a dozen military facilities. Seconds later,
ores of Chinese missiles were launched at military airfields
d naval installations on Taiwan.

Two missiles went off course with disastrous results. One
t a parked China Airlines 747 at the Chiang Kai-shek Inter-
ational Airport, setting off a series of explosions that de-
royed three other jumbo jets. The other wayward missile
ammed into the famous Grand Hotel, one of Taipei's most
xurious, killing eleven people and injuring sixteen.

The missile barrage triggered a number of simultaneous re-
onses from both adversaries. Taiwanese fighter planes en-
aged the Chinese Sukhois and MiGs while the U.S. F-14s and
-18s attacked the various warships, including the patrol boats

and numerous landing craft. Other carrier attack aircraft wer
after shore-based mobile missile launchers and airfields sup
porting the military.

United States ships, submarines, and bombers launched
total of 136 Tomahawk missiles at preselected targets along th
coastline. The massive attack destroyed much of China's re
serve missiles, supplies, and airplanes, and damaged many ai
fields, port facilities, fuel caches, and other military installa
tions.

High above the Yellow Sea and the East China Sea, B-5
and B-1B bombers, escorted by air force fighters, dropped nor
lethal, air-launched weapons with very accurate inertial nav
gation systems. The bombs were programmed to descend o
Beijing and Shanghai power grids and transformer yard
where they would scatter reels of flexible wire in the air. Th
specially treated wire would unwind and drape like huge sp
derwebs over high-voltage lines, shorting them out and caus
ing large explosions of sparks and flash fires.

The resulting power surges would cause power-plant circu
breakers to pop, shutting off the distribution of electricity t
disrupt military communication systems and delay comman
decisions to air-defense centers and the entire command-and
control network. Without electricity, the military computer
would become worthless—masses of useless wires, meta
and plastic. The PLA commanders on the edge of the swor
would be left totally in the dark.

While the scenes over the strait and in Beijing and Shang
hai were very chaotic, the surface ships were in anothe
dimension. The officers and sailors monitoring informatio
systems in the combat direction center aboard *Theodore Roo
sevelt* were strained to the limit. Like shipmates on other com
batants, everyone in CDC was suffering from some degree o
information overload. Missiles were flying in every directio
as alarms sounded and people shouted orders.

Separated by the length of the Taiwan Strait, the survivin
pair of Russian-made *Sovremmennyy*-class guided-missile de
stroyers fired supersonic sea-skimming missiles at *Roosevel*
and *Kitty Hawk*. The Russian antiship cruise missiles, NATO

ode-named Sunburn, approached the mammoth carriers at wice the speed of sound.

Kitty Hawk's powerful CIWS defensive system opened ire, spewing 20mm shells made of depleted uranium at the SS-N-22 missiles. The Phalanx close-in weapons system com-ined a six-barrel Gatling gun with search-and-tracking radar o provide surface ships with terminal defense against weapons hat had penetrated other fleet defense systems.

With a range of 6,000 yards and a muzzle velocity of 3,650 eet per second, the CIWS put up a fence of steel between the arrier and the incoming targets. Howling at 4,500 rounds per ninute, the Gatling gun pulverized the two missiles, sending aarmless debris floating into the sea.

Roosevelt wasn't as fortunate. Her CIWS system destroyed ne of the Sunburns and then malfunctioned for a few seconds, allowing the second nuclear-tipped missile to breach the steel curtain.

The missile impacted the starboard bow thirty feet below he flight deck, shaking the mighty carrier like a rowboat. The norrendous, blinding explosion ripped through the forward end of the ship, destroying the bow catapults and leaving a gaping hole in the hull.

Quick reactions by the captain and crew saved the super-carrier from sinking, but she would be out of action for an ex-ended yard period in the United States. Between the ship's crew and the air wing personnel, 239 officers and sailors would not see another sunrise.

The attack submarine *Louisville* had been stalking one of he *Sovremmennyy*-class destroyers while *Helena* pursued the sister ship, the *Fu Zhou*. In a matter of seconds after the Chinese ships attacked the carriers, the submarines fired torpedoes at the destroyers. Both Chinese men-of-war were on the bottom of the strait eighteen minutes after *Roosevelt* was heavily damaged.

In all, after seventy-eight minutes of hard-fought battles and tumultuous confusion, the People's Liberation Army and Navy had lost nine warships, including five destroyers, *Xian, Luhu, Jinan, Zhuhai,* and *Kaifeng,* four of its *Jiangwei*-class frigates, six *Houku*-class missile boats, and three guided-missile patrol craft. The PLAN had also lost eight submarines, including two Mings and one Kilo, fourteen assorted patrol boats, and twenty-seven of their seventy-nine amphibious landing craft. Many other vessels were damaged to the point of being dead in the water.

Taiwanese losses included a *Kidd*-class guided-missile destroyer, the *Knox*-class frigates *Yi Yang* and *Ning Yang*, the *La Fayette*-class frigates *Cheung Ho* and *Cheung Ping*, three Kuang Hua–III patrol craft, the *Hsin Chiang, Tan Chiang,* and *Jing Chiang,* and four Kuang Hua–VI guided-missile patrol vessels. Various smaller boats were sunk or extensively damaged.

United States Navy losses included the frigate *Rodney M. Davis* and the destroyer *Hayler*. Besides *Roosevelt,* the cruiser *Cowpens* was severely damaged, as was the destroyer *Fife*. The American submarines came through the clash without any damage.

Not counting the *Roosevelt* tragedy, the loss of life had climbed to 93 with 176 injured, many seriously. The most serious cases were being flown to Okinawa for treatment or sent to Japan or Hawaii for specialized care and rehabilitation.

The heavy and sustained antiaircraft fire, surface-to-air missiles (SAMS), and air-to-air missiles took a big toll on both sides. Chinese losses were staggering, due primarily to the inability of the outdated MiGs to compete with the state-of-the-art fighters flown by the United States and Taiwan.

It was evident that the Chinese pilots didn't have the skill and/or training to hold their own in the myriad aerial engagements over the strait and mainland China. In another aerial clash near Quemoy Island, the PLA Air Force lost a tanker plane and a four-engine Shaanxi Y-8 surveillance aircraft.

The United States lost five F/A-18 Hornets and three F-14 Tomcats. All but two of the aviators and RIOs were rescued. Seven other planes, including three from *Roosevelt,* limped back to *Kitty Hawk* with varying degrees of damage. One Tomcat crash-landed on the carrier and was quickly shoved over the side after the crew exited the wreckage. The deckhands had to quickly make room for other damaged planes to land.

The U.S. Air Force lost two F-15s, one F-16, and one F-117. ne Taiwanese saw their aerial losses climb to a total of eleven -5s, six Mirage 2000s, and three F-16s. Captain Chang Dhao-ing, a gifted Mirage pilot from the 42nd Squadron, 499th Ving, at Hsinchu Air Base, shot down three Chinese aircraft.

By late afternoon, there were still sporadic clashes from one ad of the debris-strewn strait to the other. However, it was ainfully obvious to the Chinese leaders that the attempt to take aiwan by force had been ill conceived and foolhardy.

As the sun settled over the strait, the U.S. Navy was allow-ng the damaged Chinese warships to limp back to their ports ithout sinking them. Many ships had sunk, others were ei-ier dead in the water, still burning out of control, or listing adly as they made their way through the oil slicks and float-ig debris.

The carrier *Stennis* was providing air support so the crews f *Roosevelt* and *Kitty Hawk* could regroup and rest. Many of ie aviators from *Roosevelt* flew by helicopter to *Kitty Hawk* join the rotation of round-the-clock BARCAP pilots. After ansferring many assets, including two helicopters to the *awk,* the badly damaged *Teddy R* began the long voyage ome.

The Taiwanese people and their democratic island nation ad been badly bruised and bloodied during the short but fe-ocious battle, but their spirits were high. With the help of a usted friend and ally, Taipei had rebuffed a major assault on ieir freedom and sovereignty. What China might do next was nyone's guess, but the Taiwanese citizens, with the help of the Jnited States, had sent a strong message to Beijing—"Stay out f Taiwan!"

28

Shuangliu Airport, Chengdu, China

The rain was light but steady as Scott and Jackie trudge back toward the airport after dark. Although they were still reg istered at the nondescript hotel, they had all of their belong ings with them. In shock after finding out about the savage an deadly battle in the Taiwan Strait, they were on edge.

Hartwell Prost had given them the go-ahead by 6:00 P.M Chengdu time, but he had made it clear that it was up t them to proceed or cancel. The Chinese were not in a goo mood, and that meant an even higher risk if something wen wrong.

"Scott?"

"Yes."

"What do you think?"

"I'm not sure at the moment."

"Should we ditch this operation—before we get in over ou heads?"

He talked quietly as they approached the airport. "We'r here, so we might as well try to accomplish our objective."

"What if we *are* successful and we make it back here witl Dr. Cheung—and find the airport closed and our Lear im pounded?"

"I don't believe that's going to happen."

"You can't be sure."

Scott thought about the possibility. "The Lear isn't a war plane and we aren't soldiers—we're civilians."

"But we're going to be dressed like commandos."

"Let's just stick to our plan and see how things go."

"Okay," she said reluctantly. "But I don't have a good feel-g about this deal—especially now that we're in an unde-ared war with China."

"I know what you're saying, but the risk factor is the same, least the way I see it. Besides, now that we're in an all-out ooting war with China, there's even more reason why we ed to know what Cheung knows."

"Yeah, no kidding." She watched a commuter airliner take f and disappear in the rain and low clouds.

"Have you already filed?"

"Yeah, it's in the can."

She had used a handling agent specializing in interna-onal flight operations in order to obtain a weather report and le an instrument flight plan to Chongqing, China, the ouble-Blessed river port at the confluence of the Yangtze iver (long river) and the Chialing River. The intended desti-ation was in the opposite direction from Mianyang.

Washington, D.C.

artwell Prost was at the White House having a working break-st with the president, Secretary of State Brett Shannon, De-nse Secretary Pete Adair, and air force general Les Chalmers. hey were closely monitoring the provocative situation in China d waiting to see what Beijing would do next, if anything.

The president's press secretary was keeping the media in-rmed of the events taking place in the Taiwan Strait. Mack-n had instructed her to be completely open and honest about e explosive crisis, whether the news was good or bad.

While keeping an eye on the Chinese campaign the presi-ent and his team of advisers were anxiously awaiting news om the operatives who were about to embark on the precar-us mission to Mianyang. If the operation was a success, Dr. ichard Cheung could provide extremely vital information bout China's laser weapons, and he could furnish further roof about Beijing's deadly secret.

Chengdu, China

The parking ramp was dimly lighted and quiet when Jack
and Scott reached their helicopter. They quickly unlocked th
Agusta and climbed inside to get out of the rain. Working
the dark, they unloaded the two canvas bags and donned the
apparel.

Dressed in a black jumpsuit, body armor, helmet, and ju
gle boots, Jackie stepped outside and performed a thoroug
walk-around on the Agusta while Scott checked all of his ge
and weapons. She also removed the engine covers from th
Lear in order to save time when they returned to the airpor

Satisfied that everything was in order, he tested the pair
small, lightweight wireless headsets that would provic
hands-free two-way communication between them.

While Jackie brought the helicopter to life, received h
IFR clearance to Chongqing, and then strapped on her 9mm
Glock, the Smith & Wesson .357, and the H & K 9mm, Sco
liberally applied camouflage to his face, neck, and hands.

Dressed in specially made black-and-green fatigues, fu
body armor, helmet, and jungle boots, he carefully checke
his 9mm Sig Sauer, the S & W .357, the H & K 9mm, and h
extra clips of ammo.

Next, he placed the Sig Sauer in a holster on his right hi
the .357 on his left hip, and the H & K in a slot near his low
back. Finally, he filled two compartments in his fatigues wit
extra ammo and a waterproof flashlight, and then hung tw
grenades in straps on each side of the H & K. He capped o
his outfit by strapping on his K-Bar knife, a sturdy and deadl
weapon for those intimate moments in hand-to-hand comba

"Are you ready?" Jackie asked.

"All set." Scott secured the rest of the grenades and th
two H & K MP5 compact submachine guns.

After calling the tower and receiving permission to tak
off, Jackie eased the Agusta into the rainy sky, raised th
landing gear, and set a course toward the southeast. She co
tacted the departure controller and climbed slowly as the
rapidly distanced themselves from the airport.

Finally, after flying into conditions that were solid IFR, Jackie called the controller and said she was in visual flight conditions and canceled her instrument flight plan. The controller acknowledged the cancellation and gave her a different code to squawk in her transponder, the avionics device that emits a discrete signal from an airplane or helicopter and allows the controller to identify a particular aircraft. She turned the volume down on the radio, turned the transponder off, and then concentrated solely on flying.

The controller would lose their transponder return before the helicopter changed course and disappeared in ground clutter on the controller's radar screen. Without a primary return on the radar—and no information from the transponder—the Agusta became a stealth helicopter.

"We'll have to fly lower and slower because of the rain." Jackie began a shallow descent and turned off the exterior lights. Seconds later, she leveled the Agusta.

Even though Scott continued to have doubts about the mission, he remained quiet and concentrated on the instruments.

She turned the helicopter to fly parallel to the ridge on the west side of the long elevation of land and then squinted to see lights on the ground. She needed to fly lower and began a gradual descent. Off to her left, she could see the soft glow of the lights from Chengdu. As the altimeter slowly wound down, her pulse began to increase.

After trying to suppress her nagging doubts, Jackie breathed a sigh of relief when she began to see lights on the ground. "Ah, yes—we'll fly this heading until we cross the railroad tracks extending east from Chengdu. When we get there, I'll make a forty-five-degree cut to the left until we pick up the tracks leading to Mianyang."

Scott looked up from the enhanced satellite photographs of the Mianyang complex and studied the view through the windshield. "The forward visibility is zero point zilch, and it's raining harder."

"I know, but I can see the ground."

"What do you think?"

"Press on." She dimmed the interior lights to see the terrain better. "We'll just take it easy."

"Flying low at night in rainy conditions in unfamiliar territory *ain't* the smartest thing to do—not to mention that we're well below the tops of the ridge on our right."

"We're paralleling the ridge."

"We think we are."

"We'll be okay as long as we slow down," she said calmly. "Back me up on the gauges and I'll try to stay visual."

"You got it. Too bad we can't get a clearance, climb to a safe altitude, and go direct via the GPS."

"Yeah, then we drop off the radar at the restricted Mianyang complex," she said. "We might as well call them and let 'em know we're coming."

The rain intensified, causing Jackie to slow the Agusta even more. She concentrated on keeping the helicopter level.

Scott stared into the dark void and again had second thoughts. *This really isn't looking good, especially if there's a tower out here that isn't on the chart.*

She took a peek at the GPS and visualized where they were in relation to Mianyang. "The railroad should be coming up anytime."

A minute passed, then another, as they began to feel ill at ease.

Scott decided not to wait any longer. "You know, we may have flown past it and never saw the—"

"There it is," she interrupted. "I see the track."

Still concerned about their close proximity to the ridge, Dalton could barely make out the single-track railroad. "Yeah, that's it—let's come port forty-five degrees and get away from the ridge."

"Coming left to a heading of three forty-five." She began a smooth turn and a controlled descent.

"Not too low," Scott cautioned, feeling uneasy about trying to remain in visual flight conditions. *We're off to a bad start and making it worse.* "If the rain gets any heavier, we need to abort and try later tonight."

"If the rain gets worse, it'll mask the sound of our rotor blades better."

"How much rain does it take to mask the sound of a crash?" Scott asked.

They flew in silence, each contemplating the unknowns awaiting them. Without warning, two blinking strobe lights appeared in the dark. A second later, powerful landing lights flicked on. Moving very rapidly, the bright lights startled Jackie and Scott into action.

"Descend!" Scott said, fumbling for the exterior lights. "Hit the searchlight—they're almost on us!"

The unlighted Agusta appeared almost dead ahead to the pilots of the Air China International Boeing 737-300. At the same instant the powerful searchlight turned night into day, the Air China captain abruptly pulled the airliner's nose up and banked sharply to the right, abandoning his approach to the Shuangliu Airport.

Caught completely off guard, Jackie held the controls firmly as the Agusta was violently rocked in the turbulence generated by the Boeing's wingtip vortices.

"Sweet Jesus," Jackie said, extinguishing the searchlight and exterior lights. "That was close."

"Ah, Mother of mercy," Scott said, and took a deep breath. "We don't want to ever know how close."

"I'd better monitor the radio."

"That might be a damn good idea. We're going through an approach corridor and no one knows we're here."

They remained quiet while Jackie listened to an air traffic control supervisor at the Shuangliu Airport reassure the Air China International pilot that the controller didn't have any radar returns in that sector—except the 737 airliner.

Scott unrolled the high-resolution photographs of the Mianyang complex. He studied the landing spot behind a tall hill in the valley close to Mianyang's on-site living quarters. Next, he took a long look at the recent photograph of Dr. Richard Cheung. *I sure as hell hope he's there.*

A few minutes later, Jackie spotted the primary road from

Chengdu to Mianyang and then saw the rail line on the west side of the road. Cloaked in darkness, she banked the Agusta to the right to follow the tracks northeast to Guanghan and then to Deyang.

She switched radio frequencies to monitor approach control at the Mianyang Nanjiao Airport. "As long as we stay low, I don't think they'll get a primary target."

"Let's hope not."

The rain subsided as they neared Luojiang, allowing Jackie to increase the airspeed. Less than ten minutes later she lowered the landing gear and began her visual approach to Mianyang. The GPS was incredibly accurate. It placed the Agusta in the exact position Scott had circled on the satellite photographs.

"Any doubts?" she asked without taking her eyes off the scattered lights on the ground.

"Doubts, are you kidding? If I had any brains, we'd be doing something rational—like having a nice dinner at a fine restaurant where they don't allow firearms."

"Do you think we need some kind of counseling?"

"Counseling? No way—this is perfectly normal behavior," he said with a nervous laugh.

The rain increased, causing Jackie to lose sight of her ground reference points. She kept her instrument scan going as she eased the helicopter down. Finally, in near zero-zero conditions, she glimpsed the muddy field and began her approach.

Scott made a final check of his weapons and gear. "You keep the engines running, and we'll stay in touch by radio. If anyone comes near you, get the hell out of here and we'll work something out."

She nodded. "If you find him and he doesn't want to—"

"If he doesn't want to go, he won't be of any further use to the Chinese—end of story."

When Jackie began her flare for the landing, some of the lights in the Mianyang compound began to disappear behind the hill. As the Agusta touched down in the mud, all the lights had vanished from sight.

"Good luck," Jackie said, and squeezed his hand.

He reached for one pair of the night vision binoculars and a set of large bolt cutters. "Thanks—keep your eyes open."

"I will."

Scott stepped out into the cold, driving rain and hurried toward the isolated housing area. He stopped for a radio check after he had rounded the hill that obscured the helicopter.

"Eggbeater, how copy Nighthawk?" he asked while he panned across the area with the enhanced binoculars.

"Loud and clear."

"Same with you." Scott cautiously approached the complex. He dropped to the wet ground and began crawling toward the back side of the housing units. There were bright lights at each corner of the compound, one shining inside and two others casting beams of light into the darkness outside the compound.

He stopped and raised the binoculars to check on the poorly lighted areas on both sides of the housing complex. He didn't detect any movement and continued to crawl toward the living quarters.

About fifteen feet from the high chain link fence, Scott froze when he saw the glow of a cigarette. The sentry was sitting in an unlighted guard-shack near the rear entrance to the compound. The simple structure reminded Scott of a firecracker stand.

Approaching the wooden shelter, Dalton drew his K-Bar knife out of the sheath. When he was about three feet away from the guard, Scott started rising to his feet. After he was upright, he stepped on something that snapped. *"Shit!"*

The sentry spun around and Scott lunged at him, driving the knife deep into the chest of the Chinese guard. The soldier silently slumped to the ground. Dalton sheathed his K-Bar and then grabbed three keys off the wall and opened the gate with the second key he tried. He tossed the bolt cutters on the ground and wiped mud off his fatigues and body-armor vest.

"Eggbeater, Nighthawk," he whispered into the wireless radio.

"Nighthawk, go."

Scott reached for his Sig Sauer. "I'm about to enter the compound."

"Copy."

There were three buildings, each with a central hallway and four apartment-like living quarters. Scott quietly entered the closest building and heard Chinese music coming from the first apartment.

"I'm in the southernmost building."

"Copy—everything is okay here."

"Good."

He passed the closed door and crossed the hall to the next apartment, glancing through a partially opened door. Two men, both middle-aged Chinese, were playing a board game and watching television.

From the sounds coming from the next two apartments, one a very animated conversation, Scott could tell the occupants were Chinese.

He left the building with grave doubts about finding Dr. Cheung, let alone rescuing him. *What am I doing on this boondoggle?*

"No joy in the first unit." He moved slowly toward the next. "I'm entering the second building."

"Roger." Jackie searched for any movement near the helicopter and then glanced at the engine instruments.

Scott quietly entered the building and wondered how long his luck would hold out before someone spotted him.

He stopped and whispered into his radio. "I'm in the middle building."

"Copy."

Scott approached the first of the four living quarters. No discernible sound came from inside the apartment. He slowly opened the door and did a double take. Scott's heart caught in his throat as Dr. Richard Cheung, who was lying on a couch, looked up at him in slack-jawed silence.

The stupefied physicist turned pale and bolted upright to a sitting position, rigid with fear at the sight of the camouflaged, mud-covered warrior with the 9mm Sig Sauer. Stepping inside, Scott quickly closed the door and motioned for Cheung to keep quiet.

"I'm here to help you."

"What?"

"Don't say a word—just listen to me, understand?"

Overwhelmed with shock, Cheung swallowed hard and nodded his head. Jackie listened to Scott's conversation and maintained a careful watch for intruders.

"Do you want to get out of here?"

The plump man's face reflected raw fear and indecisiveness. "Yes," he answered in a faltering voice, "but I'm not sure if I should go back home—back to the United States— right now."

Monitoring the communication between the two men, Jackie spoke forcefully to Scott. "Tell him the truth—tell him what he's facing."

"Your laser project for the Red Chinese has been exposed. You've been found out and you're in deep shit, my man—up to your neck."

Stunned by the revelation, Cheung sagged against the couch, his eyes wide. "Oh, no, what have I done?" His voice was barely audible. "What have I gotten myself into?"

"You're facing a charge of treason—know what that means?"

"Yes—yes, I do." Cheung grimaced as he considered the enormity of his offense.

"On the other hand, if you cooperate with the U.S. authorities, they'll go easy on you—that's straight from the White House."

A blank look crossed Dr. Cheung's pasty face.

"Do you comprehend what I'm telling you?" Scott said, and grabbed the man by the collar of his shirt. "We don't have a lot of time to waste!"

Cheung had reservations, and it showed in his darting eyes. "I understand, but I'm not sure if that's what I should— if that's the right thing for me to do."

"Dammit, do you want to go back to your country or not— your decision, but make it quick!"

"Yes, I want to go home, but they'll kill me if I try to escape—they've made that clear."

"Listen to me. They're going to kill you anyway—when you're no longer useful to them."

Cheung's pleading eyes grew even larger as fear paralyzed his ability to think rationally. "No, they told me that I could go home when I completed the last of the tests and—"

Scott grabbed the man by the collar and twisted it. "Six of your colleagues—Mills-Morrison, Aycock, Owens, Douville, Fitzpatrick, and Kalenkov—have been murdered in the past three weeks. You and Dr. Nash will be next. It's just a matter of time—do you understand what I'm telling you?"

Like a guppy out of water, Cheung opened and closed his mouth without uttering a sound.

"Let's go," Scott said harshly.

Cheung began to tremble and his body went limp.

"Look, we don't have a smorgasbord of options here!" Scott snatched Cheung to his feet and shoved him toward a small closet. "If you have a raincoat, get it."

At the same moment, Jackie's concentration was broken when she saw beams from flashlights near the side of the hill. She immediately added power as a rifle round penetrated the clamshell door covering the right engine. Lifting free of the mud, Jackie raised the landing gear and pushed the Agusta to its performance limits as more rounds struck the helicopter.

"Scott, I'm taking fire and heading east! Do you copy?"

"Roger."

"We're going to have to use a different pickup point."

"I'll work on it—stay low."

"If I get any lower, I'll be plowing ground."

Dr. Cheung grabbed his weatherworn raincoat and shut the closet door. Frightened about having to face a charge of treason, he searched his mind for a bargaining chip. *I was kidnapped, held against my will, and I have the hard drives from the laser project they forced me to work on.*

Shaking from fear, Cheung looked straight at Dalton and spoke rapidly. "I can give you the hard drives—all the laser technology. I have access to the computer room."

Scott looked intensely at Cheung. "How many are there?"

"Four."

"The entire project is contained on four hard drives?"

"Yes," Cheung said in a whisper. "The Chinese were very suspicious of everyone. They kept the project very tightly controlled."

Scott paused, unsure if he should take the chance. "Where's the computer room?"

"It's in the building in front of these apartments."

"Is it guarded—anybody there at this time of night?"

"No." Cheung clutched his hands together to keep them from shaking. "An alarm sounds if the wrong access code is used."

"Okay, let's go."

They hurried outside and quickly walked to the building. Using his left hand to steady his shaking right hand, Cheung punched the code into the door lock and they went inside. The hallways were well lighted, but the computer room was dark. After they entered the room, Scott quietly shut the door. He used his flashlight to illuminate the computers while Dr. Cheung removed four hard drives and placed them in separate static sensitive bags. He bundled the hard drives together and put them in a large waterproof satchel.

A few seconds later the door flew open with a loud bang and two rounds from a 9mm Beretta blew holes in the wall next to Scott's head.

29

Manchuria, China

Fully integrated into the political structure of Beijing, Manchuria is the industrial heartland of China. On a secondary road in a heavily wooded area of the Mandarin Dongbei region, four road-mobile DF-31 ICBMs were being transported to a remote launch site. The ponderous vehicles had heavy-duty dual axles front and rear. They also had a powerful lift system to position the solid-fuel missiles for flight.

Capable of striking Hawaii, Alaska, and sites in western America, the East Wind ballistic missiles had single one-megaton warheads, an explosive force equivalent to that of a million tons of TNT. Showcased in the grand parade in Beijing marking the fiftieth anniversary of Communist rule, the three-stage ICBMs were central to China's military prestige.

The crack People's Liberation Army teams who maintained and fired the deadly missiles had been given orders, straight from Beijing, to prepare for a launch. Aware of the fierce battle in the Taiwan Strait, the men had heard many conflicting stories about the outcome of the conflict. Many of the soldiers believed that China was going to use short-range and medium-range missiles to attack U.S. military bases in Japan, South Korea, and Guam.

One thing was almost certain among the crews: The DF-31 East Wind ballistic missiles would be targeted at American soil.

Mianyang, China

"Drop your weapon," Zheng Yen-Tsung shouted, flipping on the light switch. "Drop it!"

Scott immediately recognized the man from his photograph.

"Drop your weapon!" Zheng said. "Drop it now!"

Silently cursing his bad luck, Dalton allowed the Sig Sauer to fall to the floor as he swept the tiny radio from his left ear.

Zheng glanced at the armed guards accompanying him, allowing Scott a second to surreptitiously drop the radio behind him.

Smiling with mischief in his eyes, Zheng searched Scott's face. "You're a very predictable man, Mr. Dalton."

Scott remained quiet and dropped his flashlight.

"Very predictable indeed," Zheng Yen-Tsung repeated with great satisfaction in his voice.

Scott was surprised that Zheng spoke English so fluently. He noticed the deep, reddish scar on the man's right hand. Part of his thumb and forefinger were missing. The wound was obviously the result of their close encounter in Pensacola.

"Put your hands on top of your head," Zheng ordered. "Now, before I blow your head off!"

Without any visible sign of emotion or fear, Scott complied while Dr. Cheung slowly backed away from the mud-caked American.

"I *knew* you would show up here," the ever-smiling Zheng said with a smug look. "You couldn't resist, could you?"

Scott kept his mouth shut.

"We've had you under surveillance—most of the time—from the moment you left the States. Now this building is being surrounded." He quietly laughed. "No place to go."

Scott glanced at the two uniformed guards standing in the doorway. The men were armed with AK-47s. Dalton had to get closer to Zheng. *I wonder if there are any more guards in the building.*

"That's why Dr. Cheung is still alive," Zheng crowed. "He's been our most potent bait."

The physicist blanched from mind-numbing panic, hi brain racing for a solution, a formula to solve the equation o escape and evasion—survival at its basic foundation.

"Now I can get rid of the bait *and* the fish."

Although Scott didn't appear to be coiling for a strike, hi adrenaline was flowing and his muscles were tense.

"There's just one other detail."

Scott looked him in the eye. "Catching the other fish."

"That's right." Zheng chuckled. "My people should hav her in custody as we speak."

"I think you're dead wrong," Scott said in an even voice "In fact, I know you're wrong."

There was a moment of doubt in Zheng's eyes—a flash o uncertainty on his face.

"Check with your men," Scott taunted.

Zheng's veneer was beginning to crack as his face twiste into a cautious half-smile. "She'll be here shortly and *you* ma not be alive to greet her before she dies."

Scott was waiting for the right moment to act, a flickerin moment of inattention from the man with the mangled righ hand. It had to be soon or the opportunities for escape woul rapidly dwindle in the seconds, or perhaps minutes, he had lef

Zheng's smile turned into a crooked smirk. "Although yo exposed our secret—our laser weapons program—you an Ms. Sullivan won't be causing us any more problems."

"She is about to cause you a *major* problem," Scott said i a confrontational tone of voice. It was just the right mix o bravado and smartass talk to provoke his quarry.

Switching his 9mm Beretta to his left hand, Zheng steppe toward Dalton and started to backhand him. Scott lunged for ward so hard that he slammed the Chinese gangster straigh through the door and knocked the guards down. Zheng stum bled backward and fell over the shocked men. Scott wrestle the Beretta from him and shot the three men in the legs, im mobilizing them. He grabbed an AK-47, kicked the othe weapon down the hallway, and then stuck the Beretta in th pocket of Cheung's raincoat. "Let's go!"

He scooped his Sig Sauer and the small radio off the floo

and then picked up the satchel containing the hard drives. He slid the radio into a pocket in his fatigues and stuffed the satchel inside his body armor.

"Is there a way to get on the roof?" Scott asked Dr. Cheung.

"Yes, follow me."

"Run!"

Cheung hurried up the stairs to the second floor and went into an office. "There's a fire escape next to this window," he said, yanking the sash open. "It's anchored on the roof."

"Start climbing," Dalton ordered. He retrieved the small radio from his fatigues and plugged it into his ear. He adjusted the short, thin microphone and tried to calm himself as he crawled out the window to follow Cheung.

"Eggbeater, Nighthawk."

"Nighthawk," came the instant reply. "Request a sitrep!"

"I have Cheung with me." Scott grabbed the rickety fire escape and looked up. "We're climbing onto the roof of the building adjacent to the apartments—know which one?"

"Yes—what the hell happened? I thought I heard gunfire."

"We had a surprise visitor."

A high-pitched alarm suddenly went off.

"This place is going to be crawling with—"

A burst of automatic gunfire ripped into the building and Dr. Cheung. Scott almost lost his grip on the AK-47 when Cheung plummeted into him and fell to the ground.

"Jackie," Scott said as he raced to the top of the roof in a hail of gunfire, "you gotta get here as fast as possible."

She turned toward Mianyang and accelerated. "I'm about seven miles northeast—use your flashlight to guide me in."

"I don't have it," Scott said, catching his breath. "I'll talk you down and give you covering fire."

"How many clips do you have?"

"Plenty, and I have an AK-47 with a hundred-shot magazine."

"I'm on my way."

"Copy."

She keyed her radio again. "Hang on."

"I'll do my best."

Soaked to the skin, Scott cringed when a staccato sound

broke the endless wailing of the alarm. Rounds from several AK-47s began impacting the side of the building. The guards were firing at him from the roof of another two-story structure about eighty meters away.

Dalton heard another loud sound and peeked over the lip of the roof. A hook-and-ladder fire truck was pulling up to the building. "Eggbeater, say your posit."

"I'm about two minutes away."

"Hurry every chance you get." Scott reached for a grenade and placed it next to him.

"From what direction should I make my approach?"

Scott paused and looked around the area. "I'd say come in from the northeast and stay low."

Jackie checked the GPS. "Is there enough room to land on top of the roof, or do I need to hover?"

"You can land and I'll dive in."

There was a slight pause. "You have Dr. Cheung with you right?"

"He's dead, but I have the info we need."

"I'll be there shortly."

"Keep your lights off."

"They're off."

Scott fired three clips from the Sig Sauer at the men on the other building and then retrieved the Heckler & Koch 9mm. He thought he heard the Agusta approaching at high speed.

"Come left a few degrees," Scott radioed.

The sky opened up and poured rain as if it were coming over a spillway.

"You're lookin' good—keep it coming."

"I've lost ground contact," Jackie said, feeling the first insidious effects of vertigo. Her instruments were telling her that she was flying straight and level while her senses were telling her she was in a slow turn.

"Scott, I'm going to have to use the searchlight."

"Okay, but keep moving forward."

The powerful SX-5 Starburst searchlight suddenly illuminated the top of the roof in a surreal scene of blinding white light.

"Is your gear down?" Scott asked, unable to see anything beyond the tremendous glare of light.

"Down and locked." She concentrated on edging forward. 'I can barely see the roof—I can't see forward."

"You're doing great." Scott saw the ladder slowly extending above the height of the building. He pulled the pin on the grenade and lobbed it at the fire truck. The explosion injured three people and sent everyone scurrying for cover except the heavily armored sniper climbing the ladder.

Jackie sensed the Agusta was beginning to drift to the left. *Fight the vertigo—don't let it get to you.*

"As soon as you touch down, kill the light!"

"Copy."

Using the AK-47, Scott opened fire at the people on the other building as Jackie eased the Agusta closer to the roof. She was about to touch down when a round penetrated the left cabin door and ripped one of the medical technician's seats to shreds. A second later, she felt the helicopter make solid contact with the roof. She instantly snapped the searchlight off and stared into the blinding rain.

Running toward the Agusta, Scott tossed his second grenade high in the air above the sniper. Dalton dived through the open door just as the grenade exploded eight feet above the soldier, blowing him off the ladder.

"Go," Scott shouted. A round penetrated the small window next to him, showering debris across his chest. "Go—go—go!"

Jackie reacted so aggressively that the Agusta lifted off as if it had been shot out of a cannon.

Scott grabbed one of the two compact submachine guns and began firing at the guards on the other roof.

She raised the landing gear and worked at flying the damaged helicopter as smoothly as possible.

Dalton continued to fire the submachine gun on full automatic at eight hundred rounds per minute. The Agusta quickly disappeared in the heavy rain and Scott secured his weapon. Forcing himself to breathe slowly, he removed his helmet and the body armor. He stuffed the hard drives into one of the oversized pockets on his fatigues and made his way to the

cockpit. Feeling the effects of the adrenaline rush, he c
lapsed on the floor.

"Are you okay?" he asked.

She never took her eyes off the dimly lighted instrume
panel. "So far. How about you?"

"I'm a helluva lot better now."

"You mentioned a surprise visitor?"

"None other than Zheng Yen-Tsung."

Shocked, she darted a look at Scott. "How did he know y
were there?"

"He said they had been tracking us since we left the Stat
but I think he was bluffing."

"Why?"

"He was trying to impress us with his supposed surve
lance capabilities. By the time we left California on the CO
with all the changes in locations we've made, there is no w
he could have tracked us. He figured we would probably ma
a play for Dr. Cheung if we found out where he was locat
All Zheng had to do was wait."

"I'm not so sure about that."

"If he'd known where we were—Hong Kong a
Chengdu—he would never have allowed us to get close to M
anyang."

"What if you're wrong, and they're waiting for us
Chengdu?"

"Well, we'll soon find out."

"Did he kill Dr. Cheung?"

"No." He filled her in on the details of what had happer
to Dr. Cheung.

"You said you had the info we need?"

"We have the hard drives—the whole ball of wax on th
laser weapons program."

"You *have* to be kidding."

"Nope—Cheung had access to the entire program. He w
the mastermind behind the project, and the hard drives are
my pocket."

"I'll be damned," Jackie said, leveling off at four hund
feet in turbulence and rain. "What a gold mine."

"The bad news is the Chinese are going to find out the hard drives are missing, if they haven't already. They're going to come after us with everything they have."

She tuned the radio to the primary frequency for Shuangliu approach control and heard a multitude of voices.

Scott sensed they had a very small window to transfer to the Learjet and get airborne. "We're going to have to maintain radio silence and go into the airport without lights."

"And we don't have much time," Jackie said, monitoring Shuangliu approach and tower frequencies. "We've stirred up a hornet's nest. Everyone is trying to sort out the situation—but one thing is clear."

"I'll bet."

"From what I'm hearing—some of it in English—all hands are looking for a helicopter with American spies from Mi-anyang."

"Great—that's exactly what we need."

He momentarily thought about diverting to Chongqing, refueling the Agusta, and then heading for Hong Kong. *Better stick with the jet and get out of the country as quickly as possible.*

He looked at Jackie. "We're going to have to land next to the Lear, get the engines fired up, and take off on the nearest runway or taxiway we can get to—we can't afford to be caught on the ground."

The rain was subsiding and Jackie could see lights below. She began a gradual descent to three hundred feet above the ground. "We could continue in the helicopter, not even take the chance of landing."

"I think we're better off with the Lear—we'll be in Hong Kong before they get organized in Chengdu."

"Hope you're right."

Scott noticed how the visibility was improving. It was still raining hard but he could see a multitude of anticollision and strobe lights flashing in the dark sky. "It looks like we have several other helicopters up here."

"And most of them are probably looking for us," Jackie said in a tight voice. She altered course to fly along the ridge and approach the Shuangliu Airport from the south.

"I'm going to get our gear together," Scott said. He gath
ered their weapons and equipment while Jackie began a low
sweeping approach to the airport. The rain was still comin
down in sheets, but the visibility was reasonable.

As she neared the parking ramp there was a large knot o
fear in her heart. She began bleeding off airspeed and aime
for a spot on the left side of the Learjet. As she began her flare
Jackie noticed a fuel truck approaching their plane.

"Scott, we may have a problem."

Dalton hurried to the cockpit in time to see the truck par
directly in front of the Lear. "What the hell is he doing?"

"I don't know, but I don't see any cops or soldiers wit
him."

Scott saw the driver get out. "Go ahead and land."

"Are you sure?"

"Yeah, I'll have him move the truck." He placed hi
weapons on a passenger seat.

Jackie made a smooth transition to a hover. "I don't lik
this."

"We don't have much choice."

They touched down behind and to the left of the Learje
Still covered with camouflage and mostly-dried mud, Sco
immediately jumped out and looked at the driver.

Manchuria, China

The DF-31 transporters pulled into the remote launching sit
and the soldiers began making preparations to plunge into ac
tion. The missile crews worked rapidly to stabilize their bi
rigs and then raised the ICBMs into the launch position.

Within minutes, targeting coordinates were received i
code and verified by the commanding officer of the missi
detachment. The information was carefully programmed int
the East Wind ballistic missiles, and the crews anxiousl
waited for the launch order.

30

Shuangliu Airport

Dalton approached the fuel truck driver. "Hey, we need to move your truck out of the way."

The short driver with the hooded rain jacket slowly looked up and tossed the hood back.

Scott was in total denial for a few seconds when he saw the 9mm handgun pointed at him. His heart skipped a beat and he stopped dead in his tracks. *I have to move fast—do something.*

"I have been ordered to block the jet until the police arrive." The Chinese man spoke English very well.

"Who are you?" Dalton asked.

"I'm the airport manager."

"Why are you blocking our plane?"

"Apparently there is some doubt about your reason for being in Chengdu."

"We've been here on business."

The manager eyed Dalton from head to toe. "Dressed like that?"

"Yes, of course."

"What kind of business are you in?"

"Research and restoration." *That was lame.*

"And you do this on rainy nights?"

Scott heard the sounds of sirens approaching. In the distance, he could see flashing lights on the street leading toward the airport. "Well, let me shut down the helicopter before we talk to the authorities."

"Go ahead, but don't try anything—I won't hesitate to u[
this."

Jackie wondered why the fuel truck driver was followir
Scott, and then she saw the weapon. *No, this can't be happenin*

She drew her 9mm Glock at the same time Scott reache
the helicopter. In one swift movement, he swept his H &
9mm off the seat, spun around, and shot the airport manag
twice in the chest. "Cut the engines—let's go!"

They carried their gear to the jet and flung it into the pa
senger compartment. Scott glanced at the left engine. "Is t
other engine cover off?"

"Yes."

While Jackie moved the fuel truck, Scott piled into the le
seat and initiated the engine start procedure.

She ran to the plane, jumped in, and quickly locked t
door. "Chocks are clear—let's hit it."

With their lights and transponder turned off, Scott starte
taxiing to the nearest runway. Lights along each side of t
taxiway and runway made it simple to stay on the pavemen

He was fastening his seat belt and shoulder straps whe
more than a dozen police cars and military vehicles co
verged on the airport parking ramp.

"We have company," Scott said as he added power to ta
faster. Jackie strapped in and tuned the radio to the tower fr
quency.

Some of the police cars raced down the taxiway after t
Lear, while the other cars and military vehicles headed for t
midpoint of the runway.

Scott made a wide sweeping turn onto the runway ar
shoved the throttles forward.

Jackie could not believe what he was doing. "Scott, there
an airliner on short final—cleared to land!"

"I know."

"They can't see us!"

"Jackie," Scott said in a calm, even voice, "the police wo[
block the runway with an airliner about to touch down."

She shook her head. "It'll be academic if they land on t
of us."

The China Airlines Boeing 737 was just touching down
when the captain saw the Lear in his landing lights. He
started to go around and instantly rejected the idea. The risk
of having a midair collision was too high. He went into full
reverse on the engines and commenced heavy braking.

The police and military personnel were astounded when
the Learjet appeared out of the glaring lights of the airliner.
The Boeing's engines were howling in reverse and the tires
were screeching as the plane almost overran the small jet. The
Lear rotated at the same moment the 737 blew a smoking tire
and veered slightly to the right. The authorities stared in frustration as the darkened corporate jet hugged the ground and
disappeared into the rainy night.

Scott adjusted the power and began a shallow climb. "We'll
have to expose ourselves to radar to get over the ridge."

"I don't think it'll make much difference—too much clutter if we hug the ridge like a crop duster."

"We better stay low and head straight for Hong Kong."

The Chinese authorities had a visual identification on the
Learjet that had taken flight. They had associated it with the
helicopter that had recently landed at the secretive Mianyang
complex. In the eyes of the senior officers in the military, the
people in the jet were spies and they had to be stopped at all
costs. The powers that be already knew the Americans in the
corporate jet had the hard drives to one of China's most sensitive weapons systems.

President Liu Fan-ding, who understood what was at risk,
had ordered the military to use whatever resources they needed
to find and destroy the Learjet and its occupants. The plan was
to put an aerial net out in every direction for a thousand miles
and slowly pull it in. The jet wasn't going to disappear.

"On second thought," Scott said dryly, "there are a couple of problems with going straight to Hong Kong. Every
asset the Chicoms can get airborne is going to be looking
for this jet, plus the airports are going to be saturated with
police and military personnel—including Hong Kong."

"Oh, yeah—they have the color and the tail number."

"Absolutely." Scott concentrated on flying as low as dared at night. "It isn't like we kidnapped the night mana; of some fast-food restaurant. We have the blueprint to Chin highly sophisticated laser weapons system."

"I still can't believe it."

"They know the Lear came from Hong Kong, so that ro is probably going to be swarming with search planes a fighters."

"What do you suggest?" she asked.

Scott checked their fuel. They were burning it rapidly low altitude. "We don't have the fuel to reach any sovere: U.S. territory, and we can't take a chance on landing ai where in China or any neighboring countries."

"Where we could be arrested?"

"Right." Scott altered his course to a more easterly he: ing. "Jackie, we need to get offshore in the East China and ditch the Lear next to a carrier battle group."

"At night?"

"Well, we don't have enough fuel to stay airborne unti gets light outside—plus the longer we're up here, the be: chance the Chinese will find us."

"True."

"The other option would be a night approach to a bai cade arrestment on a carrier."

"Ditching sounds like a better deal." Jackie reached for satellite phone. "We might even get a fighter escort."

"Let's hope so."

She tried to contact Hartwell Prost, but the signal k breaking off.

The weather continued to improve as they flew east o the expansive rice fields and the small rural communities a villages. Minutes later, they were flying under a moonlit s splashed with stars.

Jackie studied the city of Changsha as it flashed past their left. "The moon is so bright it's like daylight."

"That's what worries me."

Manchuria, China

When the launch orders were received, the East Wind crews quickly but thoroughly went through their checklists. This was not a rehearsal, and their spirits were high. There was no room for mistakes. Unlike all the practice sessions and redundant game playing, the teams were about to deliver a major blow to their primary adversary.

At three-minute intervals the powerful DF-31 ICBMs ignited and lifted off on their history-making flights. The plumes of flame and smoke were mesmerizing to the launch crews. The missiles accelerated out of sight in a thunderous roar. Rocketing toward their targets in the gravity-free near vacuum of space, the lethal weapons were precisely tracking their programmed courses.

Moscow, Russia

Staffed around the clock seven days a week by Russian and American personnel, the Joint Data Exchange Center (JDEC) was humming with activity. The multilateral warning center for information on missiles and space launches was fully manned. The senior American and Russian officers were trying to deal with the ambiguous situations arising from the launch of the Chinese ICBMs.

Although the United States and Russia provided each other launch information that was near real time, the Chinese ballistic-missile strike had caused a glitch in the computers. Instead of data relating to the time of the Chinese launch, the launch azimuth, the generic missile class, the geographic area, and estimated time of impact, the information indicated missile launches from the Great Plains of the United States and the interior of Russia.

JDEC vice commander Brig. Gen. William W. Burgess, USAF, was livid. He was using a backup communications channel to assure his Russian counterpart that the 90th Space Wing at F. E. Warren Air Force Base was not launching ICBMs from Nebraska, Colorado, and Wyoming.

The reassurances had to be cross-pollinated between the North American Aerospace Defense Command, Moscow, and the U.S. Air Force Space Command located at Peterson AFB, Colorado.

Once things stabilized to the point that no one was shouting, General Burgess turned to his director of operations, Capt. Clay McMasters, U.S. Navy.

Burgess spoke in a quiet voice. "This whole thing goes back to insufficient attention to four major policy concerns."

"A big one was Taiwan," McMasters said.

"And the others were American missile defense, our nuclear diplomacy with Russia, and the Chinese nuclear modernization."

"Yes—exactly," McMasters said. "All of them are tied together, and we took a laissez-faire approach that has backed us into a corner."

"Any bets on where the missiles will land?"

"No, sir—I've blocked it out of my mind."

Burgess studied the data displayed on his computer-generated screen. Both sides were supposed to be able to monitor each other's information, but things were scrambled to the point of being useless.

McMasters looked at his boss. "Thank God we have our Russian counterparts at NORAD and Space Command."

Burgess sighed. "True, but we have some major work to do on this program. It's a piece of junk—garbage."

North American Aerospace Defense Command

Located deep inside the hundred-million-year-old Cheyenne Mountain near Colorado Springs, Colorado, NORAD is charged with the missions of aerospace warning and aerospace control for North America. Aerospace warning includes validating an attack against North America by aircraft, missiles, or space vehicles.

Canadian general Derek Bancroft, the commander in chief of NORAD, was responsible to both the president of the United States and the prime minister of Canada. As CINC-NORAD his duties included providing integrated tactical warning and assessment of an aerospace attack on North America to the governments of Canada and the United States.

This would be a day General Bancroft and his deputy commander, U.S. Air Force lieutenant general Kurtis Wentworth, would not forget.

Because of the deadly clash with China, NORAD, like many other military commands, was on high alert. The first indications of a missile launch from inside Manchuria, China, were quickly verified by reconnaissance aircraft and space-based assets.

However, the information had been sabotaged before it could be displayed in Moscow. Someone had hacked into the Joint Data Exchange Center and displayed erroneous information. The Russian officers inside NORAD had calmed down and were busy monitoring every aspect of the operation.

Although Bancroft and Wentworth had anticipated a possible retaliatory strike on the United States, the actual authentication of the missile attack was still a shock for both of them.

"It's validated," the barrel-chested Wentworth said to his boss while the first missile was still accelerating.

General Bancroft impatiently waited to receive the first indication of a probable impact point and then picked up the phone to contact President Macklin.

Bancroft tried to steady his nerves while the seconds passed, but he couldn't take his eyes off the status displays.

When the president came on the line, CINCNORAD spoke with sadness in his voice. "Mr. President, General Bancroft at NORAD. We have an authenticated missile launch from a location in Manchuria."

He saw Wentworth hold up two fingers. "Our information indicates the first missile is targeted at Hawaii."

The serious-minded Canadian officer glanced at the status

displays. "No, sir, we can't verify whether it's a convention
warhead or a nuke—we have a second launch and it appea
to be targeted at Alaska."

The Situation Room

The president drummed his fingers on the conference tab
while General Bancroft updated him on the inbound ballist
missiles. When CINCNORAD paused to talk to his depu
commander, Cord Macklin looked at his advisers.

"Four in all, two headed for Alaska and two trackin
toward Hawaii."

"What about the time?" Hartwell Prost asked.

The president glanced at his wristwatch. "As of now, a
proximately twenty-nine minutes to Hawaii—less to Alask
Warnings have gone out to all military commands in the ta
geted areas and to the appropriate civilian authorities."

General Chalmers was on another phone talking to th
senior officer at the secret experimental missile defense si
in Alaska, and to his colleague on Kwajalein Atoll in th
Marshall Islands. Chalmers cupped the phone in his hand a
turned toward Macklin. "They're ready—going to do the be
they can with what they have."

The president looked at Pete Adair and Les Chalmer
"Our response needs to be equal but measured—even if the
are nukes."

Aleutian Islands, Alaska

The scientist and engineers, both military and civilian, we
working at a feverish pace at the national missile defense te
site. They had two exoatmospheric kill vehicles ready
launch, but they wouldn't have time to ready a third interce
tor.

On Kwajalein Atoll they had only one EKV ready for in

nediate launch. It would be aimed at the first East Wind en
oute to Hawaii.

The kill vehicles were quickly launched and the nerve-
acking waiting games began. As the technicians proclaimed,
he challenge was akin to hitting a bullet with a bullet.

Guided by experimental radar units and space-based sen-
ors, the EKVs zeroed in on their prey. Once free of its
ooster rocket, the ungainly-looking 120-pound assortment
f thrusters, star-sighting telescopes, mirrors, antennae, liq-
id propellant tanks, and batteries closed on the enemy
CBMs at incredible speeds.

The men and women at the test sites prayed as they watched
he clock and monitored the EKVs. The control rooms were to-
ally silent. The gravity of the situation had sunk in.

The scene was the same at NORAD and at the White
Iouse. The waiting was painful and the results weren't guar-
nteed. With only a limited missile defense system in place,
hey all knew at least one ICBM would penetrate the barrier
nd reach the Hawaiian Islands.

Hawaii

The residents of the island chain were extremely fortunate.
The EKV interceptor launched from the Kwajalein test site
hattered the first ICBM into a million fragments. The second
East Wind missile, which developed a minor malfunction in
he inertial guidance system, flew directly over Honolulu and
xploded in the Kaiwi Channel between the islands of Oahu
nd Molokai.

The tremendous explosion created an intense light flash, a
udden wave of superheated air, and an earsplitting roar. The
hock wave echoed across the water and slammed into the
outheastern side of Oahu and the western side of Molokai. A
all of fire rose rapidly, followed by a huge mushroom cloud
hat billowed to more than sixty thousand feet. The trade
vinds carried most of the fallout away from the islands.

The horrendous explosion boiled the ocean water for a r
dius of nine hundred yards, created a ten-foot tidal wave, a
vaporized or heavily damaged several private boats, killi
sixty-three people and injuring more than two hundred oth
in the area. Although the aftereffects were minimal compar
to what could have happened had the nuclear missile land
in the middle of Honolulu, the message was clear; Hawaii h
dodged a major disaster.

Anchorage, Alaska

The leading DF-31 survived a close encounter with the fi
kill vehicle, but the second EKV destroyed the trailing E
Wind ICBM. Aimed at Elmendorf Air Force Base, the hor
for the Eleventh Air Force, 3rd Wing, and other comman
the first missile impacted ninety miles north of Elmend
near the Talkeetna Ranger Station.

Miraculously, due to faulty engineering, the nuclear w
head did not detonate, but the powerful blast killed tv
rangers and seventeen tourists who were on a nature-hi
camping trip. It also destroyed the ranger station and start
a fire that would take two days to extinguish.

31

The Situation Room

President Macklin placed the phone receiver down and propped his head in the palms of his hands. Everyone in the room was aware of the two kills and the two payload impacts. Even though the missiles weren't as accurate as the experts had thought they would be, and one of the warheads had not detonated, the threat was real. China had nukes that could easily reach Hawaii and Alaska. It was time for a decision.

The president raised his head. "When you consider the potential for disaster, we were *damn* lucky this time. I'm reconsidering our response."

He looked at Adair. "What's the smart thing to do?"

"Mr. President, if we don't respond forcefully to Beijing, they'll use us as a punching bag. We'll be their new test range. Worse yet, North Korea may decide to attack South Korea if we don't show our resolve."

"Hartwell, what's your thinking about our next move?"

Prost shrugged his shoulders. "If we don't do something to stun them into submission, we could soon have nuclear-tipped DF-5s raining down across the mainland."

"The DF-5 is an old, liquid-fueled missile," Adair said. "How reliable could it be?"

Hartwell was trying to be patient. "Accuracy is apparently not China's forte—range is. The East Wind has an approximate range of five thousand miles, but the DF-5 can travel more than seven thousand five hundred miles. How accurate do you have to be when you're terrorizing your opponent in his own backyard?"

"We *have* to try diplomacy first," Macklin said. "If we don't have any success, I'll warn them that Beijing will go next—if they launch another attack—then Shanghai, et cetera."

The president frowned. "Sometimes, as history sadly reminds us, you have to get people's attention the hard way."

Silence filled the room as everyone contemplated the enormous havoc and destruction the atomic bombs had caused at Hiroshima and Nagasaki in August of 1945.

Prost turned to the president. "In the meantime, we had better get every Aegis-equipped ship we have along the West Coast, Alaska, and Hawaii."

Chalmers nodded in agreement. "And we had better have as many kill vehicles as we can muster standing by in Alaska and Kwajalein."

NORAD

With Lieutenant General Wentworth minding the store, General Bancroft had managed to slip away for some food, shower, and a nap. Both men were determined to remain at their posts until the crisis was over. They were privy to the White House plan to retaliate if China fired another intercontinental ballistic missile at the United States.

Feeling refreshed, the Canadian general returned to relieve his deputy commander. "Any news?"

"Not yet. You know, if this situation gets out of control, we could set off a global free-for-all that could kill hundreds of millions of people."

"Or worse," Bancroft added. "With nukes flying in every direction, the planet might not be habitable when it's over."

"We may have to flatten Beijing to get their attention," Wentworth said. "Trouble is, Russia might jump in and do something stupid—then we're all cooked."

"That's the risk . . . and it's real."

The Oval Office

It was early morning, and President Macklin was so angry he could barely contain his rage. After all the hard work by the State Department and scores of people on both sides of the issue, China and the United States were again locked in a standoff.

Liu Fan-ding had unexpectedly issued an ultimatum to the president of the United States. The Panama Canal had to be returned to Panamanian control in the next three hours or China would launch more nuclear missiles at American cities.

"That son of a *bitch*," Macklin said through clenched teeth. He turned to his secretary of state. "Brett, I want it made graphically clear to everyone in the Chinese loop—especially Liu. The canal will *not* be returned to Chinese control, *and,* if they launch nukes at us, they will rue the day."

"Yes, sir," Brett Shannon said, fatigued from lack of sleep.

Macklin's hand shook as he picked up his coffee cup. "We may take some damage, but their cities—their country—will be flattened like a pancake. Make damn sure they understand that."

"I will, Mr. President."

Macklin turned to General Chalmers. "Les, are you confident if we have to use our Triad?"

"Yes, sir, very much so."

The chairman of the joint chiefs looked directly into the eyes of his longtime friend. "This clash we had over the Taiwan Strait, and the situation that prevails right now, has caused North Korea to go back into their bunkers."

"Good. They better damn well stay there—or they'll be next."

The Pentagon

The Joint Chiefs of Staff had gathered and more people were pouring into the building. The official word was quickly spreading. The news of the Chinese president's demands—

some called it a case of blackmail—had been leaked to th
mainstream media, and the big-name news anchors wer
rushing to their studios.

At the White House, President Macklin was preparing t
leave on *Marine One* to travel to Andrews Air Force Base an
board the E-4B National Airborne Operations Center.

The State Department had sent North Korea a stern warn
ing not to become involved in the situation or they would suf
fer dire consequences.

NORAD was briefed for the worst, and America's nuclea
deterrent Triad, including land-, sea-, and air-based system:
was primed. The most powerful strike force on the eart
awaited the president's order.

The Learjet

Scott carefully adjusted the power to climb over some moun
tains that rose to more than eight thousand feet. "Jackie, yo
may want to try Hartwell again."

"For sure—we're getting closer to the coast." She tried an
still could not maintain a signal. "I'm going to try the one i
back."

"Yeah, we have to get something going."

She stepped into the cabin, picked up the Honeywell mul
tichannel satcom terminal, and placed a phone call to Prost :
his office. Hartwell was greatly relieved to hear from Jacki
and he was very excited about the hard drives. He didn't hav
any comment about the tragic fate of Dr. Richard Cheung.

Hartwell then gave her a quick overview of the situatio
with China. Three minutes into the lively conversation, Jacki
put the satellite phone down and went to the cockpit to chec
their position on the GPS. "I caught him just before he wa
headed to Andrews."

"Good."

She wrote the coordinates on a piece of paper and wen
back to the phone. Jackie quickly copied the information an
gave Hartwell their aircraft satcom identity.

Passing south of Shangtang, Scott began a gradual climb weave through the mountains in the distance.

When Jackie returned to the cockpit, she sat down and oked at the rising terrain. "The clash with the Chinese has ken on a new twist."

"What now?"

She filled him in on the ICBMs.

"That's crazy."

"I agree, and things aren't looking very promising." She osed her eyes and leaned her head back. "But it looks like e have an option—if we have enough fuel to get there."

"Well, out with it."

Jackie opened her eyes. "He's *extremely* happy that we're ive and that we have the hard drives—he couldn't believe "

"What did he say about Dr. Cheung?"

"Nothing—not a word."

"What about a carrier?"

"The *Kitty Hawk,* after the crew finishes recovering air-aft, will be on its way to a rendezvous with us. I have their rrent position and they have ours. It looks like we should : overhead the carrier when they're approximately seventy iles north-northeast of Taipei."

Scott reached for a chart. "We're going to be cutting it ighty close. Is there anything closer—another carrier or a ip we could ditch beside?"

"No, the *Kitty Hawk* is our only option in the next couple 'hours—if we can stretch the fuel that far."

"Well," Scott said, calculating the fuel burn, "we still have make our way to the coast without being shot down."

"They're sending fighters to escort us from Songcheng."

"Songcheng?"

"It's on the coast just north of our route." Jackie checked e fuel. "We'll be in contact with a Hawkeye—call sign Lib-ty Bell—in about forty-five minutes."

"That's good news."

"Yeah, but they don't want me to use the radio—a female ice could set off alarms."

"Makes sense. What's our call sign?"

"Kilo Hotel Zero One."

"Kitty Hawk?"

She nodded. "We're the number-one priority at the m‍ment—actually, the hard drives are number one."

The satcom in the back chimed. Jackie stepped into t‍ cabin and sat down. After a brief conversation with Hartwe‍ she entered the cockpit. "Not good news."

"What?"

"The seas are very heavy and they—the skipper of the ca‍ rier and the admiral—recommend that you *not* ditch t‍ plane. They know you're a tailhooker and they want to 'ba‍ ricade' you."

Scott allowed himself a brief glance at Jackie. "If the se‍ are rough, the last thing you want to do is ditch a plane‍ those conditions. You're taking a much bigger risk than lan‍ ing in the barricade—plus you don't get wet."

"What's the reason for a barricade?"

"If you have a battle-damaged plane or can't get the lan‍ ing gear or tailhook down—and you can't make it to a div‍ field, and airborne refueling isn't an option—then the bar‍ cade is better than jumping out or dumping your ride in t‍ water."

"Ah, yes," she said with a smile. "There's just one min‍ difference in our situation—this airplane *wasn't designed*‍ fly from carriers."

He deselected the autopilot and made a heading chang‍ "That's why it's so much more interesting."

Jackie shook her head and began computing time and fu‍ to reach the carrier. Scott hand-flew the airplane low over t‍ mountains, skimming through shallow passes and huggi‍ the high ground.

"What do your numbers say?" he finally asked. "Are ‍ going to make it to the boat?"

She looked at her calculations for a few moments. "‍ can probably make it about a hundred twenty, maybe a hu‍ dred thirty, miles offshore, but that still leaves us short of t‍ carrier by fifteen to twenty miles."

Scott's curiosity was piqued. "You figured from where the arrier was—the coordinates that Hartwell gave you?"

"Yes." She rechecked her numbers. "I figured the carrier's)eed at twenty knots—if the seas are rough."

Scott made another minor heading change to fly directly ward Songcheng and the waiting navy fighter planes. The me dragged on as the fuel steadily declined. Trying to ease r anxiety, Jackie recomputed their relative position to the arrier every few minutes. It was clear that the situation asn't getting any better.

The Learjet was passing close to a mountain peak when ne of the Hawkeye's mission-systems operators finally con- cted Jackie and Scott.

"Kilo Hotel Zero One, Liberty Bell—how copy?"

Scott turned the volume up on the cockpit speakers and eyed his radio. "Liberty Bell, Kilo Hotel Zero One reads)u loud and clear."

"Roger that, squawk three-seven-five-two and ident."

"Thirty-seven, fifty-two, and ident, Kilo Hotel," Scott id. Jackie assigned the code to the transponder, energized , and hit the identification button.

"There you go," Scott said.

A few seconds passed before the E-2C systems operator ade contact with the Lear again. "Kilo Hotel, we have a ck—stop squawk."

"Copy stop squawk, Kilo Hotel."

"Keep truckin'," the Hawkeye operator said. "Your course Mother looks good for right now."

"Kilo Hotel."

Thirty Miles South of Songcheng, China

Chinese AWACS, a modified version of the four-engine ussian Ilyushin Il-76, orbited high above the sea near the)astline. Assigned to the 13th Air Division in Hubei rovince in south-central China, the aircraft was monitoring e Taiwan Strait and the activities of the *Kitty Hawk* battle

group. The AWACS was also waiting for a flight of four Chinese navy fighter planes to check in.

Equipped with an Israeli-designed Phalcon early warning
and airborne control system, the Chinese AWACS had detected the evasive Learjet when the E-2C Hawkeye identified
the plane.

Fifteen miles west of the AWACS, four of the Chinese
navy's new F-8-II fighters finished refueling from an airborne
tanker. The flight leader checked in with the AWACS for a
vector to the airplane carrying the American spies.

Based on Hainan Island between the Gulf of Tonkin and
the South China Sea, the highly touted planes had been sent
to Fuzhou to patrol the Taiwan Strait during the ongoing conflict with the United States.

The message for the Chinese squadron commander and
his three talented and experienced pilots was very clear.
Whatever it takes, shoot the Learjet down—or ram it—before
it reaches safety.

The Learjet

"Kilo Hotel, Liberty Bell." The voice was very tense.

"Kilo Hotel," Scott said.

"Ah . . . you have—I'm seeing multiple bandits at your one
o'clock, seventy-five miles and rapidly closing."

Scott and Jackie had a sinking feeling.

"Well, that's just dandy," Scott said to Jackie, and keyed
the radio. "What about our fighters—can they engage them?"

"Stand by."

Dalton's frustration suddenly flared. "Hey, we're gonna be
confetti if we don't have some help—like immediately."

Another voice, calmer and steadier, came over the radio.
"Your original escorts are refueling. Two of the BARCAP
Hornets are on their way and the *Hawk* is launching the Alert
Five birds as we speak."

"Tell 'em to buster every chance they get!" Scott said, eaing the Learjet closer to the terrain. He checked to make sure their exterior lights were off.

"They're in burner," the mission systems operator said, and talked to someone else on another radio. "We suggest that you get down in the grass and try to make yourselves invisible."

"We're workin' on it," Scott said, and looked at Jackie. "The barricade idea looks better all the time."

"Say hallelujah!"

"Kilo Hotel, bandits still at one o'clock," the Hawkeye operator said, checking his scope. "Now sixty miles."

"Where are my heroes?" Scott asked.

"Twelve o'clock, seventy miles—goin' at the speed of heat."

Scott keyed the radio. "I just hope the cavalry gets here before we're turned into chop suey."

"Kilo Hotel, our Hornets—your original escorts—have just this moment engaged the Chinese fighters, but two of the Gomers have slipped away to hunt for you."

"What about the other fighters—ours?"

"We have two more Hornets headed toward you and a tanker to support them—just hang in."

"We're running out of time."

"Kilo Hotel, Liberty Bell," a new voice said. "Our fighters should be getting close to you—should be with you in a matter of seconds."

"I hope so."

Andrews Air Force Base, Maryland

While the E-4B National Airborne Operations Center taxied for takeoff, President Macklin, Hartwell Prost, Brett Shannon, and Pete Adair conferred with various people from NORAD, the State Department, the Pentagon, the Joint Data Exchange Center in Moscow, and various civilian and military authorities. General Chalmers was at the Pentagon with the other joint chiefs.

The media outlets were offering a menu of breaking news stories every few minutes. The deadline from Beijing was rapidly approaching. Panicked by the impending disaster, and knowing what had happened in Hawaii and Alaska, millions of Americans were trying to get out of major cities and vacation centers like Honolulu.

Gridlock, worse than any seen before, had set in at U.S. airports, and the crowds were growing at a rate that was alarming. The scene was the same in cities in China. Millions of people were vacating their homes, businesses, and hotels to escape the looming nuclear exchange.

The hotels in Beijing, Shanghai, and many other cities were rapidly emptying. After all the years of the Cold War Era, and then the horrors of nuclear proliferation, the genie was finally out of the bottle and all bets were off.

When the E-4B lifted off from Andrews AFB and climbed into the blue sky, Cord Macklin looked out the window at the unbroken chains of automobiles and then turned to Prost. "The freeways are packed—worse than any rush hour I've ever seen."

"They'll be at a standstill before too long."

The secretary of state placed his phone receiver down and looked at the president. Brett Shannon's puffy eyes were red and sad. "Still no change, Mr. President."

"Keep trying."

32

The Learjet

Kilo Hotel," the Hawkeye systems operator said in a frantic voice, "break left—break left!"

Scott immediately snapped the jet into a port turn and pulled as many Gs as he felt the well-built airplane could stand.

The moonlight was so bright the Chinese pilots would be able to see the white Lear from quite a distance.

Straining to see behind him, Scott keyed the radio. "Who's on me?"

"You have two bandits on your tail—the Hornets are jumping them!"

"Tell 'em not to take any coffee breaks."

"Copy."

In knife-edge flight and bleeding off airspeed, Dalton unloaded the airplane in the same profile and went negative G for a few seconds, then again pulled hard into the turn. He was hoping the Chinese pilots might see the Learjet drift out of their sight and snap their fighters over when the corporate jet was going the opposite direction.

With his head twisted around, Scott finally saw the camouflaged bandits closing from his eight o'clock. The brilliant moonlight had become Scott's worst enemy. An air-to-air missile flashed close over the top of the Lear and corkscrewed toward the ground.

"The MiGs are on us!" Scott radioed as he looked out the window. He saw the twinkling flashes coming from a MiG-19's 23mm cannons.

Scott sharply pulled the nose up and did a displacement roll, then lowered the nose and proceeded to sideslip the airplane in a near ninety-degree bank. One of the MiG-19s slashed past the Learjet so close that Scott and Jackie felt the fighter's wake turbulence.

Dalton neutralized the flight controls and then rolled into a steep, face-sagging 360-degree turn. "What do you have out your side?"

"We have a shooter coming in high from our five o'clock," she said, tightening her seat belt and shoulder straps. "Break right—break hard right!"

Suddenly, 23mm cannon fire ripped through the leading edge of the right wing. Seconds later, another missile shot past the nose of the Lear.

"That was close!" Scott snapped the airplane into knife-edge flight and pulled hard into the attacker. He could clearly see the pilot's helmet when he flashed overhead.

"Reverse!" Jackie said, seeing the MiG pull up in a steep climb. "Reverse and go for energy!"

"Who's flying this airplane?"

Using negative G-forces, he abruptly unloaded the plane, then snapped the Learjet over to the left and pulled into a steep, tight descending turn. Leveling off close to the ground, he began skidding, slipping, and yawing the jet right and left while constantly changing altitude and direction.

"One down and one to go," the Hornet flight leader radioed.

The Chinese wingman fired his last missile at the Learjet. It flew straight into the right engine and exploded with devastating results. Scott and Jackie felt the powerful impact and immediately reacted to the warnings in the cockpit. Jackie was going through the engine-out checklist when Scott caught sight of the F/A-18 Hornets. He saw the telltale wisp of smoke from the air-to-air missile the Hornet flight leader had fired.

"Come on, guys," Scott said, watching the missile track toward the closing F-8-II. The seconds seemed to last forever before the second Chinese fighter exploded in a spectacular fireball and plummeted into a valley, cartwheeling across a narrow dirt road.

"He nailed him—fantastic!" Dalton told the Hawkeye operator, and glanced at Jackie. Drained from visceral emotion and high G-forces, she was temporarily speechless.

"Kilo Hotel," the systems operator said in a calmer voice, "Hornet lead confirms your six is clear—turn on your lights."

"We're eternally grateful," Scott said as the jet's exterior lights highlighted the plane. "Would you be kind enough to ask the Hornet drivers for their drink orders?"

"Will do."

The Hornets coasted up on each side of the Learjet.

"Kilo Hotel, Dambuster One and his sidekick are dedicated tequila drinkers—José Cuervo."

"Tell them they can each expect a case," Scott said, giving the flight leader a circled-thumb salute.

The Hornet pilot gave Scott a hearty thumbs-up and broke away with his wingman to fall in behind and above the Learjet. They would escort the damaged civilian plane to the carrier.

"Kilo Hotel," the Hawkeye systems operator said, "our team downed one of the other Gomers, but one got away."

"Good shooting. Thanks for everything."

"We do our best."

Jackie went back to the cabin to check the right engine and returned to the cockpit. "The engine is gone."

"Yeah, I know it."

"No, I mean it's gone—not on the airplane—blown completely off."

Scott shook his head in disbelief. "Bombardier Learjet, you folks definitely build a fine airplane."

They remained quiet, watching for the first sign of the East China Sea while their pulse rates slowly returned to normal. After they went feet-wet south of Songcheng, Scott was surprised at how rough the open water was. From his vantage point, the endless troughs and towering waves stretched as far as the eye could see in the moonlight. He studied the angry whitecaps. The foaming crests blew horizontally from the tops of the waves. Trying his best not to show his concern about the sea conditions, he turned to Jackie. "You've been awfully quiet."

"Yeah," she said, and raised an eyebrow. "I'll be a lot more talkative when we're on board the carrier—if we get there."

"Don't give up yet."

"I'm not giving up, you know that, but I *am* concerned about landing on the ship in these conditions."

"Boat."

"Okay, *boat*—whatever."

"Jackie," he said with the aplomb of a seasoned carrier pilot, "they've been conducting air operations tonight—it's an aircraft carrier."

She gave him one of her "serious" looks. "How many years has it been since *you* landed on a carrier—in a conventional aircraft, not in a Harrier."

"Hey, it's like riding a bicycle, like flying a plane."

"You're talking to another pilot—don't try to snow me."

"Relax," Scott said, looking at the churning ocean. "The worst is over."

"Sure it is." She concentrated on ranking the ten best restaurants she had experienced, followed by the ten best movies she had seen. It was a mind game she played when she wanted to distract her thoughts from what was sure to be a less than pleasant experience, but it wasn't working this time. Finally, the carrier seemed to levitate from the illusory, moonlit background. "I see it—straight ahead!"

"What a sight," Scott said as his fears began to dissipate. "All we have to do is get aboard."

"No comment."

Jiangxi Province, China

At one of the remote control centers for ICBMs, Lt. Gen. Chen Bodong had given the launching sites for the DF-5 long-range nuclear missiles the signal to launch on his command. Final fueling was under way and the countdown would soon begin.

After receiving confirmation from the DF-5 site commanders, the general notified the officer in charge of the detachment in Manchuria to prepare the DF-31s for launch.

33

USS *Kitty Hawk*

Because of the rough sea conditions, the flight deck was moving up and down plus or minus twelve feet with a dangerous Dutch roll, a combination directional-lateral oscillation. Due to the unpredictable gyrations, the pitching deck had caused an unusually high number of wave-offs and bolters all evening.

The deck crew couldn't rig the barricade until a Hornet with a hydraulic malfunction had trapped. The pilot had to make two attempts to get aboard the carrier, but the second try was flawless. After the F/A-18 was safely on deck, the crew quickly removed the four arresting wires and moved Tilly into position.

The 130,000-pound crash crane is placed in the rollout area abeam the carrier's island. If a plane goes through the highly reinforced barricade, Tilly is there to stop the aircraft before it can do any damage to other planes parked on the bow.

The deck crew raised the jet-blast deflectors for the port and starboard bow catapults as a final measure of protection for the many aircraft spotted on the bow.

Off to the right side of the ship's island, an SH-60 Seahawk helicopter on plane-guard duty was keeping pace with the ship. The helo carried a rescue swimmer who would be available to assist the occupants of the civilian plane if it went into the water.

The commander of the air wing, known by the time-honored acronym CAG (commander of the air group), was on the bridge conferring with the captain. Having been personally briefed by the commander in chief, U.S. Pacific Fleet, they knew why it was so important to safely recover this civilian plane.

Along the starboard foul-deck line, more than a hundred deck crewman and air-wing personnel waited for the signal to go into action.

"Rig the barricade!" a booming voice said over the flight-deck 5MC. "This is not a drill!"

The crew locked the deck plates and hooked a tractor up to pull the barricade from the storeroom. They quickly began hauling the barricade across the landing area.

"We have a plane at ten miles," the loud voice said over the 5MC. "Let's hustle—let's move out!"

After a couple of snags that consumed precious time, the crew finally managed to stretch the barricade across the landing area.

The air boss in PRI-FLY, the carrier's control tower, patiently searched for the Learjet's external lights. He turned to his assistant, nicknamed the "miniboss." "This should be *very* interesting—considering the sea conditions."

"At least he's a tailhooker."

"Yeah, he wouldn't have a prayer otherwise."

NORAD

General Bancroft and his deputy commander watched the clock, counting the minutes until the deadline was up.

Kurtis Wentworth was tired and irritable. "This may turn into World War Three, but if it sets China back fifty years they'll know why."

"That's for sure," Bancroft said glumly. "He made a demand in front of thousands of people, including the media—that's what we're seeing over and over. He may be unable to back away from this terrible decision."

The Learjet

Descending through two thousand feet, Jackie and Scott began stowing loose objects.

She looked down at the rough seas and whitecaps. "What are you going to use for a pattern altitude?"

"Eight hundred feet."

They descended through fourteen hundred feet and began to experience some light-to-moderate turbulence.

"What's a good approach speed?" she asked.

"Let's see—engine out, landing on a carrier, rough seas, gusty winds, night approach, I'd say a hundred forty knots should do it."

"Seat of the pants."

"It hasn't failed me yet."

At six miles from the ship, the mission systems operator in the Hawkeye called and gave them a VHF frequency to contact *Kitty Hawk*. The carrier's air traffic controllers had been informed that the Learjet was single engine and critical on fuel. After Scott checked in with the ship, he was handed off to the carrier-air-group landing signal officer.

Having been briefed about Dalton's background as a tail-hooker, the senior LSO had a question for the former Marine aviator. "Have you ever made a barricade arrestment?"

"Negative," Scott said, trying to recall everything he had been taught during carrier qualifications in the training command.

"I understand you've lost an engine?"

"That's correct—literally."

CAG Paddles, the controlling LSO, gave Scott a quick brief on flying the ball for a barricade engagement. In the background Jackie and Scott could hear the muffled shouts coming from the flight deck. It sounded like a zany Three Stooges scene.

"One more thing," the LSO said. "How much is your gross weight, including fuel?"

"About eleven thousand five hundred pounds, including approximately four hundred pounds of fuel."

"Did you say four hundred pounds of fuel?"

"Affirmative."

"Okay," Paddles said, watching the ship's fantail dance back and forth. "We're going to keep this approach in close."

Scott took a peek at the fuel. "The tighter, the better."

"You got it, Sport."

The ship's 5MC could be heard over the radio. "Emergency aircraft at three miles. Let's get into battery."

Surrounded by two fellow LSOs, Paddles talked into the radio more forcefully to overcome the gusty wind and chaos on the dark flight deck. "I'm going to have you start your approach amidships."

"Copy." Scott looked at Jackie. "Since we don't have headsets, and we're using microphones, I suggest you talk on the radio."

"Yeah, you'll be busy." She stared at the carrier as it plowed through the huge waves. "I'll take care of communicating—you get us on deck in one piece."

"Sounds like a winner." He made a slight power adjustment to the left engine, lowered the flaps, and extended the landing gear.

She rechecked the gear down. "Landing lights?"

"No, it might blind the LSO—we don't want that." He gave her a brief smile. "Try not to worry."

"Absolutely—hadn't even thought about it," she said, and shook her head. "This would be crazy in perfect conditions."

"I can understand your concern," he said as he began to slow the plane to the approach speed of 140 KIAS. "Except for riding in the COD, you've never flown from the deck of a carrier."

She looked at him and rolled her eyes heavenward. "You think that might have something to do with it?"

The rig master, a grizzled flight-deck veteran, was guiding the deck-crew and air-wing personnel in erecting the barricade. They connected the upper and lower port terminals and pulled the barricade to the other side to connect the load straps. Next the crew began taking tension until the barricade was in place.

The rig master saw the Learjet's lights when the plane was approximately one mile away. He turned around to watch his crew. The barricade cross-deck pendant was finally placed into battery. With a quick glance at the Learjet the rig master knew he was in trouble.

He yelled for the crew to start raising the barricade. Unbeknownst to him there was a problem with the barricade cross-deck pendant. It was damaged and had to be replaced.

34

The Learjet

Feeling a heightened sense of anxiety, Scott leveled the plane at eight hundred feet and adjusted the power to maintain a speed of 140 knots. Passing the bow of the carrier off to the left, the Learjet felt comfortable. Dalton was prepared to commence his approach.

"Here we go," he said, beginning a shallow, descending left turn abreast of the ship's island. "This looks good."

Because of the gust factor, Scott had to keep varying his bank angle while in the descent.

"You're lookin' good," CAG Paddles said when the Learjet was halfway through the 180-degree turn to final. "Slightly high, ease it down, ease it down a little—take your time."

Scott barely inched the power back to make the correction.

"Kilo Hotel," Jackie acknowledged, glancing at the stormy seas. She shifted her gaze to the pitching deck of the carrier. "This does *not* give me a warm, comfortable feeling."

"Yeah, there are other things I'd rather be doing," Scott said, keeping his focus aimed at the carrier deck. "But you have to admit it's exciting."

"So is jumping into an alligator pit."

Rolling wings level on short final, Scott picked up the bright yellow-orange meatball in the middle of the Fresnel optical landing system. The ball provided a visual glide-slope to the pilot on final approach.

"Okay," Scott said, "Learjet, ball, state three hundred pounds."

"Learjet, ball, three hundred pounds," Jackie radioed to
e LSO while Scott was maintaining 140 knots.

"Roger ball," CAG Paddles said, shooting a look at the
ght deck and deck-status light. It was red, indicating the
arricade wasn't ready. He waited until the last second, hop-
g that he could bring the Learjet aboard on this pass.

"Kilo Hotel," the LSO said with clear irritation in his
ice, "do a three-sixty to port—the barricade isn't rigged
t."

Scott swore to himself, added power, and rolled into a 360-
gree turn to the left. "Great—just perfect."

Jackie acknowledged the instructions and saw the airspeed
dicator fall slightly below 140. "Watch your speed."

"Got it," Scott said, easing the left throttle forward.

Her heart was clutched by a grip of ice and her blood
illed. "I don't like this—we're running out of fuel."

Very gently, Scott juggled the power and tried to be pa-
nt. "Come on, people, get it together."

The rig master was personally changing the barricade pen-
nt when he caught a glimpse of the civilian plane turning
ward the carrier. He worked feverishly, but time was against
m.

Rolling out on final, Scott maintained his altitude until he
as in close and had a centered ball.

"Learjet, ball, two hundred fifty pounds," Jackie reported.

Scott began a descent to keep the ball centered.

"Roger ball—you're right on," Paddles said in a soothing
ice. "It looks like you do this every day."

Scott knew the LSO was nursing him, but it helped him
ncentrate on his flying technique. Nearing the flight deck
 his second pass, Dalton was trying to keep the ball in the
nter and maintain lineup in the gusty winds. They were
ly a few seconds from being on the flight deck.

"Wave off, foul deck," CAG Paddles grumbled, initiating
e bright red wave-off lights. "We're going to make this hap-
n, I promise."

"Damn," Scott said to himself. "Do you believe this?"

Jackie was silent, her heart pounding against her chest.

Dalton slowly added power, lowered the left wing a fe
degrees, and fed in rudder to counter the airplane's tendenc
to yaw. The struggling Learjet barely cleared the barricade a
it was being raised.

"Turn downwind," Paddles said, watching the deck-cre
and air-wing personnel clear the landing area. The men ra
toward the safety area behind the starboard foul-deck line.

"Kilo Hotel, you have a clear deck and the barricade is
position—bring it aboard."

Jackie acknowledged the transmission while Scott smooth
banked the Learjet into a tight left turn. He focused on wh
he knew would be their last pass. "Well, Jackie, think abo
the bright side of this situation."

She gave him a suspicious look. "And what would th
be?"

"If we go into the drink, at least we won't hit any orpha:
ages or retirement homes."

Jackie was suffering from a severe case of dry mout
"Graveyard humor, that's exactly what I need right now."

Scott rolled into the groove near the back of the pitchi:
and rolling ship and immediately tried to spot the deck—ey
ing the flight deck instead of flying the ball—something a
LSO doesn't like to see.

"A little power," CAG Paddles coached. The deck bc
tomed out of a trough and began moving upward. "Power .
power."

Dalton was making the adjustment when the left engir
began spinning down. "Uh-oh, brace yourself!"

"Power!" the LSO radioed in an effort to salvage the lan
ing. "Power, power, POWER!"

Total silence followed. Scott lowered the Learjet's nose
a desperate attempt to maintain airspeed. The plane-cur
glider was now descending like a manhole cover. Scott kne
he would soon be out of airspeed, altitude, and ideas—but l
was on centerline and had plenty of forward motion. "This
gonna be ugly!"

Just before he crossed the round down, Dalton heard tl
famous words that were now meaningless.

"Cut, cut, cut," CAG Paddles yelled over the radio. The ?ck heaved upward to meet the Learjet.

Reflexively, Scott pulled the useless power lever to idle ?d planted the Learjet in a bone-jarring arrival. The crash ?nding snapped the nose gear off and drove both main land-?g gears up through the wings.

The airplane sailed up the flight deck and viciously ?ammed into the barricade, which brought the heavily dam-?ed Learjet to a quick and safe halt.

Jackie and Scott had been hanging in their shoulder straps ?om the tremendous G-forces during the rapid deceleration.

The crash crew raced toward the airplane, but there was no ?re—the fuel tanks were almost bone dry. The crew could not ?lieve the right engine was missing.

Thankful that they were on deck safely, Scott heaved a ?gh of relief. "Well, folks, that was one of my better land-?gs, and we look forward to serving you in the future."

"At least we're in one piece," Jackie said, unbuckling her ?at belt and shoulder straps. "Under the circumstances, I ?ve you an A-plus."

35

The E-4B

The flying command post was on the first leg of a round robin course when the five-minute warning arrived.

President Macklin was on a conference hookup with General Bancroft at NORAD and General Chalmers at the Pentagon. Everyone at the top of the chain of command, both civilian and military, was in agreement. United States forces would counterattack with overwhelming nuclear force NORAD detected and authenticated a missile launch from China.

Gathered around a long conference table, the president and his men watched the minutes tick away as General Bancroft gave them updates and silently prayed.

With one minute to go, the president rose from his chair. "Well, gentlemen, this is the time when we have to believe in—"

The secretary of state's phone rang, shattering the silence. Brett Shannon snatched it off the cradle, listened intently, and looked at Macklin. "Liu Fan-ding has had a stroke."

"Who's in charge?" the president asked. "What are their intentions—has the deadline been called off?"

Shannon repeated the questions to the caller while the last few seconds to deadline were ticking away.

"Say again," Shannon said in frustration. "Has the deadline been canceled—where do we stand on the deadline?"

"Mr. President," General Chalmers said, "we're about out of time."

Macklin tightly gripped the handset. "Hold on, Les—let's sort through this new information."

"What?" Shannon asked. "Slow down and speak clearly." He listened to the fast-talking spokesman and asked him to repeat his statement.

"What do we have?" the president asked. "I have to make a decision."

Shannon's tense features suddenly relaxed and a smile spread across his ashen face. "The crisis is over—it's over!"

Macklin looked at Shannon. "Give me the details—I need confirmation and details."

The passengers in the cabin were erupting in wild celebration. Backslapping and bear hugs were the order of the day.

Shannon listened for a few more seconds. "That's the party line—the stroke story is smoke and spin. Our sources closest to Liu have confirmed that he was physically removed from power and is currently under house arrest. The new leadership—a triumvirate of senior Communist Party leaders—have issued a request for a summit with President Macklin at his earliest convenience."

The president sighed and then gave Chalmers and General Bancroft the order to stand down. "Cigars for everyone."

"Mr. President," Hartwell said, "this would be a good time to call the new leadership in Beijing—a very good time."

Epilogue

After a restless night on *Kitty Hawk,* Scott and Jackie wer
flown to Kadena Air Base at Okinawa, Japan. Along with se
nior officials from the Central Intelligence Agency and rank
ing members of the U.S. State Department, the commander o
U.S. Naval Forces, Japan, greeted them when they arrivec
Jackie and Scott turned the Chinese hard drives over to th
CIA and then went to one of Scott's favorite restaurants t
enjoy Kobe beef and hot sake.

The next morning they were transported, as requested, t
the U.S. Virgin Islands on a C-32A VIP jet from the 89th Ai
lift Wing. En route to their enchanting destination, Scott mad
arrangements to charter a thirty-six-foot sailing yacht—san
crew.

For the next eleven days, they investigated pristin
beaches, sheltered bays, coves, coral reefs, and enjoyed th
friendly people they met on each island they visited.

Finally, they returned to the calm bays of Norman Islanc
their favorite anchorage near the Sir Francis Drake Channel.

Refreshed from a leisurely snorkeling session, Jacki
emerged from the cabin and accepted her rum surprise. Nicel
tanned, she was attired in baggy shorts and one of Scott's col
orful, oversized aloha shirts.

Dalton was about to propose a toast when his satellit
phone rang. He answered it and smiled when he hear
Hartwell's voice. After a pleasant but brief conversation, Sco
signed off.

Jackie had instantly known it was Prost. "What's up?"

"Well, the president is going to Beijing next week, and th

hinese have recalled their ships containing the laser
eapons, so relations are thawing nicely. The Chinese troops
Panama are on their way home and Beijing has agreed to
smantle their laser production facilities under our observa-
on."

She raised her glass in a toast. "That's some progress."

"And," Scott said with a faint grin, "you won't believe
is."

"I'm listening."

"Merrick Hamilton has been selected by the Blue Angels."

"You're kidding."

"Nope—she's slated for jet number three in the left wing
ot."

"That's great, really great." Jackie eyed Scott. "Did
artwell have anything to do with her selection?"

"No way." He sipped his rum drink and smiled. "The team
lects their own replacements, and Merrick is certainly qual-
ed."

"She really is, and I'm happy for her."

"Speaking of Hartwell, he said we can start looking for a
ving machine whenever we're ready."

"Well," Jackie said with a radiant smile, "I think it's time to
lebrate."

"We're certainly in the right place."

"*And* the night is young."

The White House

n a cool, crisp morning, President Cord Macklin walked to
e Rose Garden to greet his distinguished guests. Among the
ests were the wife and family of Dr. Richard Cheung.

While Macklin secretly detested Cheung's traitorous acts
;ainst the United States, he knew it was in everyone's best in-
rest to let the story rest as the American media had portrayed
—Cheung had been taken against his will, forced to assist
e Chinese with their laser weapon development, and ulti-
ately gave his life for his country. To do so made Dr. Cheung

a hero while the Chinese received unfavorable press for their aggressive acts.

Understanding the impact on world opinion, President Macklin had decided to overlook his disdain for the traitor. After several minutes of praise for Dr. Richard Cheung's heroic service to his country, the president presented the Medal of Freedom to Cheung's widow.